A Heart for Milton

by
Trudy Brasure

Cover design by Heathradesigns.com

This book is dedicated to those who believe that love *can* conquer all.

CONTENTS

Introduction
and Acknowledgments   vii

Chapter 1   1
Chapter 2   9
Chapter 3   17
Chapter 4   23
Chapter 5   33
Chapter 6   45
Chapter 7   67
Chapter 8   87
Chapter 9   101
Chapter 10   119
Chapter 11   141
Chapter 12   161
Chapter 13   177
Chapter 14   191
Chapter 15   211
Chapter 16   231
Chapter 17   253
Chapter 18   271
Chapter 19   293
Chapter 20   307
Chapter 21   329
Chapter 22   343
Chapter 23   361
Epilogue   371

Introduction and Acknowledgments

The true test of a great love story is whether it speaks to the ages. *North and South* is such a story. Written over a century and a half ago, Elizabeth Gaskell's novel tells of a love that emerges amid the confusion and commotion of England's Industrial Revolution. Her characters are vibrant with emotion and suffer the trials of change and circumstance.

In 2004, the BBC's brilliant adaptation of this novel created legions of swooning fans and introduced this timeless story to a new generation. No doubt, the success of this production was largely due to an amazing cast, headed by Daniela Denby-Ashe and Richard Armitage as Margaret Hale and John Thornton.

A Heart for Milton shines with the borrowed light of all these great artists. I have taken the characters from the book and endeavored to make them come alive with equal inspiration from the actors of the film production.

My tale weaves a change in the original plot to create a wholly original sequence of events that extends beyond Gaskell's written conclusion.

My aim has always remained the same – to depict more of the bliss of new love, which was so achingly brief in Gaskell's work.

I am forever thankful to Nancy Klein, who encouraged me from the beginning, offering her expertise as an editor and challenging me to produce my best.

I am also grateful to Lori Sheppard, who joined my writing journey early on and helped to ensure that my characters reflected Gaskell's own.

Thanks to Jane Dallimore for being a wonderful resource concerning all things English and for offering a wealth of knowledge about domestic life, the countryside, and the sights of England.

I could not have asked for a better team of editors, each of whom has left their own indelible mark in this work. They not only helped enhance my story, but have enriched my life as well. Thank you.

Trudy Brasure
July 2011

Chapter One

Margaret sat staring blankly at her father's books, unable yet to comprehend the fact that she would no longer see him, or hear his voice. He had been her last anchor to the carefree childhood she remembered. Since coming to Milton, life had seemed an endless struggle. She had tried so hard to keep her parents happy, to be cheerful in the face of the hardship and pain. It was all too much. She felt adrift, lost in a merciless sea, the waves of which were relentlessly dragging her down until she felt she would finally sink.

Now she was alone. Both her parents were gone. Aunt Shaw had come to take her away. She had lost her family and now she would lose her home, to become a permanent guest in her aunt's home. She would be swallowed up in the daily routine of her cousin Edith's comfortable and pretty life.

"The suffering you have endured, my dear!" Aunt Shaw emphatically declared. "We must leave this place as soon as possible. Dixon will stay and arrange an auction for everything," she announced with an air of great decision.

Margaret stirred from her reverie to amend her aunt's command. "These books I wish to keep," she pleaded. It was all she had left of her father, books he had spent so much of his life reading and thinking about. They had shaped his very life. Indeed, she felt they had, in turn, led him to leave Helstone for Milton.

Milton. She would be leaving Milton now that she had come to appreciate it. She had grown to admire the industrious pace of the city and the practical, hard-working people who lived there. She was comfortable with their simpler, unpretentious ways. She would miss seeing her friends Nicholas and Mary and the Boucher children.

"You must not stay here another day," Aunt Shaw continued, increasingly convinced that Margaret's recovery depended upon it. She stood with her handkerchief at the ready, gazing agitatedly at the cramped and cluttered room in the Hale's house. How Margaret had borne living here she could not imagine! This dirty, smoky town was offensive and utterly unsuitable for a proper family. And to think her poor sister had been forced to move to this wretched place - no wonder she had died here!

"Why your father ever left his country parish I shall never know. And to bring you to such a horrid city!" she castigated, feeling quite justified in disparaging the man her sister never should have married.

Too weary to respond, Margaret thought of how her father had also suffered, bearing the burden of guilt for bringing his family to such an unfamiliar place. He had watched his wife descend into despondency and become slowly weaker with disease.

Her mother had hated coming to Milton, and her father had been well aware of it. Margaret had tried to mend her mother's spirit and had outwardly kept a light heart for her parents' sake. There was no helping her mother, though. She succumbed to resentment and bitterness.

Oh, Father, I do not resent you. I will not regret the time I lived here, where you brought us. It had opened up whole new worlds for her. Everything had been so different from Helstone, she had been overwhelmed by the stark change. But father had embraced the change, had seemed to thirst for it. He had been so hopeful to begin a new life as a tutor and scholar. And she knew he had thrived on his discussions with Mr. Thornton.

She would no longer see Mr. Thornton. The realization of it cast a shadow of desolation over her. She told herself it would be proper to visit the Thorntons before leaving. They had been her parents' only friends. She must let Mr. Thornton know how much his friendship had meant to her father.

"I must bid goodbye to our friends," she requested plaintively, a faint glimmer of her usual self-determination coming to life.

"I wonder at what kind of friends you could have here!" Aunt Shaw exclaimed with disdain. "If you must make these calls, I will accompany you. However, we must leave at once," she decided with authority.

Margaret stood up unsteadily, glancing around the room. It came to her then what she should do. She furtively perused the titles of the books piled on the furniture surrounding her. Grabbing the object she sought, she slowly headed for the door, somberly casting her eyes over the Crampton home for the last time.

Margaret looked dazedly out the window as the carriage clattered through the streets to Marlborough Mills. She did not want to think of Mr. Thornton, but found herself inevitably drawn to his image time and again. In her mind, he was unsmiling, his stern brow creased in displeasure. It grieved her to think she was the cause of it. Oh, everything had gone so horribly wrong! If only she had not been tempted to lie, he

2

might have still held her in some esteem. She dared not ruminate upon what he must think of her now.

She hated to leave Milton before she had a chance to redeem herself in his eyes. Why did she care so much for his good opinion? She felt the awful irony of her plight. She who had held him in contempt now desperately wishing for his kind judgment. How ignorant she had been! And how harshly she had treated him!

More than anything, she wanted him to know that she had changed her estimation of him. She wished that he could know how much she had come to appreciate the strength and goodness of his character. She was filled with remorse to remember the times her callous words had hurt him. She hoped now to speak so kindly to him that her gentle words would linger in his mind and come to replace those unpleasant memories she had instilled.

As their coach approached the familiar gates of Marlborough Mills, Margaret felt a knot begin to form in her stomach. The sight of the place brought to mind her actions on the day of the riot and the unfathomable chain of events that had ensued.

He had spoken of his love for her the morning after the riot. She had not known it then, but she had since learned that he had spoken truly, as he always did.

There was no use in thinking of it. It was in the past and nothing could be done. She had cast aside his love and he had since renounced his passion for her. But the thought of his honest affections had never left her. The words he had spoken still echoed in her consciousness, although she might try to ignore them.

After her mother had died, it seemed that everything had spun out of her control. She felt like a helpless observer, watching with trepidation as the Fates wove the myriad threads of her life into an intricate tapestry which could not be unraveled or altered by mere mortals.

The jerk of the carriage as it came to a halt reawakened her to the task ahead. She closed her eyes and took a deep breath before she emerged into the cold.

◦≫◦

The funeral at Oxford was attended by a scattering of people, enough to dignify the passing of the former vicar - certainly more than the dismal showing Mrs. Hale's funeral had brought in Milton.

Mr. Thornton was glad he had come to pay his final respects to his friend. His affections for Mr. Hale had only grown stronger in the past few months, while he had tried to help his friend during his struggle with grief. He felt his loss keenly, as he would the loss of a kind father. In truth, had his dearest wishes been fulfilled, Mr. Hale would have been his father-in-law.

"Thornton!" Mr. Bell called to the tall, brooding man as he descended the granite stairs of the ancient church to meet him. "How good of you to come. Richard would have been pleased, I'm sure. He held you in very high regard, I believe."

"And I, him," Thornton acknowledged. "He was like a father to me," he added honestly.

"Yes, indeed," Mr. Bell contemplated, the corners of his mouth edged upwards as he regarded Mr. Thornton studiously.

"Margaret was quite devastated, I fear. Poor girl. I'd hoped you might be able to lend a hand, Thornton, in settling Hale's affairs in Milton. Margaret will be leaving shortly for London. I rather thought you might step in to assist her in the manner of a kindly brother or uncle." Mr. Bell faced Mr. Thornton directly, watching for his response.

Mr. Thornton stiffened involuntarily, but his face remained impassive, as he endeavored to mask the distinct discomfort he felt under such scrutiny by the sprightly Oxford scholar. "I will be happy to assist in any way I am able," he replied in a constrained voice.

Mr. Bell couldn't suppress a knowing smile. "I knew I could count on you, Thornton!" he enthused.

Mr. Thornton cocked his head slightly. "When does Miss Hale leave for London?" he could not resist asking, even though he hated to do it.

"Today or perhaps tomorrow. Her aunt was insistent on their leaving as soon as possible," Mr. Bell answered, immediately sensing the dismay the news had inflicted.

Mr. Thornton could only nod his head in response.

"Good day to you then, Thornton. I shan't keep you any longer. You'll be wanting to get back to Milton, I presume," Mr. Bell guessed correctly.

"Yes. Good day, sir," Thornton returned, tipping his hat politely before turning to leave.

He walked briskly through the streets of the city, a steady wind chilling his nose and ears until they turned pink. Oblivious to the cold, his thoughts descended into a maelstrom of anguish and despair.

Margaret! He longed to comfort her now, to hold her close against him to assuage the pain of her loss, but she would not seek refuge in his arms. It tore his heart to think that someone else might receive her affectionate attention. The vision of her in the fond embrace of that other man continually tormented him. If only she would come to care for him! No one could ever love her as he did.

Although she would not love him, he had built his world around her.

Just the hope of seeing her and hearing her voice had given him something to live for. Without her, he feared his whole world would collapse.

He had spent most of his life working to improve his lot and that of his family, and he had been eminently successful. He had been content enough.

How insipid his life seemed now that he had caught a glimpse of what life could be! She was all that was good and beautiful in this world, and he knew he wanted her in his life. He had envisioned a life of tenderness and peace, of joy and affection. Even if she would not have him, he knew he would never be the same.

She did not love him, so he would love her from afar. He would never regret loving her, though it brought him to his knees with its sweet torture. She was all he ever dreamed of, all that he ever wanted.

The sky darkened with threatening clouds as he reached the station. He hoped he was not too late already. He wanted desperately to see her one last time.

Mr. Thornton saw the carriage outside and knew he had arrived in time to see her, if only to say good-bye. He hurried into the house, brushing the snow off his arms and shoulders, before removing his hat and gloves. As he silently came into the room, he overheard the sweet, low tones of Margaret's voice. She was speaking to his mother, who warily glanced in his direction. Alerted to his presence behind her, Margaret turned to face him.

How beautiful she was, even in her distress, he thought. Her hair was loosely pinned at the back, allowing auburn waves to frame the porcelain skin of her face. He noticed immediately how tired she looked, how pale and weakened. His heart contracted in silent longing. He wanted to reach out and hold her close against him to comfort her.

His eyes followed her as she glided towards him, her large sorrowful eyes mesmerizing him, pulling him deeper under her power. He was overcome by the intensity of feeling that swept over him. How he loved her! The thought of losing her forever sent a tremor of terror through him.

"You are going then," he heard himself say.

She bowed her head slightly to avoid the intensity of his gaze. "It would seem I've no choice," she whispered.

Mr. Thornton's eyes narrowed, his mind racing to grasp the meaning of what she had said. She did not want to leave? His breath quickened as a thrill of hope began to take hold of him.

"You would stay?" he asked incredulously.

She lifted her face to meet his steady gaze. "I...have grown fond of Milton," she faltered, her eyes pleading for him to understand.

"Have you?" he hoarsely whispered, his eyebrows arching slightly in wonderment. His body was frozen in absolute astonishment at what he thought she was trying to say. Had she changed her mind? Did she care for him at last? But how could he know? He could not speak freely to her in this place. Panic gripped him. He must know her heart, before he could let her go.

He watched as she moved her arms to hold out a book to him. "I've brought you father's *Plato*. I thought you might like it," she offered warmly.

Touched that she should think to give him something of her father's, he blinked and a soft smile lifted his serious expression. "I shall treasure it. Along with your father's memory. He was a good friend to me," he assured her.

It came to him suddenly what he should do. "If you will excuse me a moment, there is something I should like you to have," he stated with inscrutable hospitality. Margaret nodded her assent.

Mr. Thornton strode from the room and hastily made his way to his study. He grabbed the quill from the mammoth oak desk and scrawled a quick note, not bothering to sit. Then he scanned the books standing on the corner of his desk and pulled out *The Economy of Cotton*. He picked up the note, folded it once, and placed it within the pages of the book as he returned to the drawing room.

"Something to remember Milton by," he explained as he held the book out to her, searching her face with unhidden adoration.

"It is not necessary," she politely protested.

"Please," he begged, a sense of urgency escaping from him.

"Thank you." She took the book, a hint of confusion crossing her face.

"We must catch the next train to London. I'm afraid we cannot stay a moment longer," Aunt Shaw's voice pierced the room with her abrupt announcement.

"Yes," Hannah Thornton agreed wryly. "Not a moment longer," she repeated as she cast an exasperated glance at her son.

Mr. Thornton escorted the visitors to their carriage. The mill yard was covered in a blanket of white snow. The stillness was broken only by the sound of the muffled stamping of the horses, eager to be on their way.

Margaret stopped at the carriage door and turned to Mr. Thornton, her head bent demurely. They shook hands without a word. The exquisite pleasure of holding her gloved hand in his sent a surge of tender longing and desperation through him. He stared for a moment at their clasped hands. No one would know how much strength of will it took for him to release her hand and let her go.

Their eyes met briefly and he saw the pain and loneliness in her expression before she turned to go. His heart cried out in protest. He yearned to call out to her, to beg her not to leave him; he wanted to know if she could care for him at last. But he remained silent, clinging desperately to a tenuous, fevered hope that she would come back to him.

He remained motionless, standing in the falling snow, and watched the carriage disappear from view.

❧

Margaret did not look back, although she wondered if he was still there, watching her depart. At the last moment, before she had left him, she had felt a fleeting urge to faint in pretense, so that she he could feel his strong arms around her. How unlike her to even think of such a thing! She must truly be exhausted from the strain of her grief.

She hoped she had relayed to him something of her regard for him. She thought that he had reacted positively to her admissions. He had seemed surprised to hear that she had come to like Milton. She felt certain that he had wanted to say something more to her, but was deterred by the company surrounding them.

She had been aware, too, of something strange about the manner in which he had left the room to retrieve her gift. It was quite unusual for a gentleman to give a young lady such a book. She glanced down at the book in her lap and began to open it to peruse its pages. As she did so, a piece of paper fell out and slid down the folds of her skirt. She quickly caught it in her gloved hand and opened it to discover its contents. It was a note written in a vaguely familiar handwriting:

If you have had a change of heart, give me but a sign.
My heart remains forever yours.
    John Thornton

She was stunned to realize that he had written her a note. Her body froze; her hand was utterly still. Then she read it again and the realization of its import began to dawn upon her. He still loved her! He had not given her up after all!

"What is it, Margaret?" Aunt Shaw asked, noticing the curious reaction the note had caused her niece.

Margaret jerked her head up to stare at her aunt. "It…it's a note in my father's writing," she stammered, wanting to dissuade her aunt's interest.

Aunt Shaw nodded in sympathetic comprehension.

Margaret folded the note and stuck it back in the book, the words of it already burned into her heart. She turned to look out the window to avoid her aunt's attention. Her heart was racing. 'Give me but a sign,' he had said. What sign? What could she do? What had he wanted to know? "If you have had a change of heart." He wanted to know if she cared for him!

She hardly knew what she felt. Overwhelmed by a deluge of emotions, she tried to comprehend what it all meant. And suddenly, as she recalled the glimmer of longing in his eyes at their parting, she knew. She knew it as if it had always been true, but was long hidden, like the sun bursting forth amid a clouded sky. She loved him!

A flood of joy overtook her as she basked in the light of this simple revelation. She loved him! And how amazing that he should still love her!

But how would she let him know? She could not ask to go back. A feeling of desperation and panic began to creep through her veins.

"Nicholas!" she said out loud at the sight of him and his daughter Mary hurrying along the street. "Stop!" she demanded the driver, and leapt from the compartment.

"Margaret!" Nicholas exclaimed in joyous relief at finding her. "We thought you had already gone."

"I couldn't leave without saying goodbye to my friends," she comforted, giving both Nicholas and Mary an affectionate hug and kiss.

Before she knew what she was doing, she addressed Nicholas again. "Nicholas, would you do me a favor?" she asked him, her eyes filled with wistful hope.

"Aye, you know I'd do anything for you," he replied sincerely.

"Would you relay a message to Mr. Thornton for me?" she pleaded. Nicholas noted the serious tone of her voice and contained the smile he felt pulling on his face. "Would you tell him that..." she hesitated, searching for the right words. "Would you tell him that my heart belongs in Milton?" she asked anxiously, her pulse quickening.

Nicholas gave her a reassuring smile. "Aye, I'll tell Thornton," he promised.

Margaret returned his smile and gave him one last hug before returning to the coach.

"What have I done?" she asked herself as she was hurried away to the train station.

Chapter Two

Mr. Thornton sat in the quiet of his office in the mill, his eyes drifting over the room to finally rest on the clock, whose faint ticking had drawn his dazed attention. He felt strangely calm at the moment. He had offered his heart once again, and now he could only wait for her response.

When would she find the note? What would she do? He had acted so impulsively, he had not had time to consider all the consequences of his deed.

What if he was mistaken? Perhaps he had been too eager to see what was not really there. Whisperings of doubt began to grow louder in his unsettled mind. Her demeanor towards him had softened. He knew this much, but did it mean that she cared for him? It was possible that she was just being kind to her father's friend.

But she had not wanted to leave Milton. No, more than that, she had said she had grown fond of it. He wanted to believe that he was the reason, and she had looked at him in such a way that he had felt his hope soar. Had she affection for him after all? What of the man at the Outwood Station? Had she given him up?

He thought he had seen longing in her eyes, but was it just the despair and loneliness of her grief? Her father had just died; it would be natural that she should feel uncertain and alone. He had wanted so desperately to believe that she might care for him that perhaps he had imagined he had seen it in her eyes. *What a fool I have been!* he thought, as the onslaught of his doubts battered against his wounded heart.

A loud rapping on the door interrupted the train of his tumultuous thoughts.

"Who is it?" Mr. Thornton barked, annoyed to be disturbed in his private enclave.

"It's me, Higgins," Nicholas clipped. "I've a message from Miss Margaret," he announced through the door.

Mr. Thornton was at the door in an instant, flinging it open. Higgins

9

wore a slight grin, as he surveyed the bewildered expression of the hopeful lover.

Mr. Thornton stood staring, his body frozen in anticipation. Had she found the note already? "What is it?" he croaked, finally finding the presence of mind to speak.

"She asked me to tell you that her heart belongs in Milton," he relayed carefully, watching the Master closely.

Mr. Thornton was thunderstruck. She had answered him! His heart clattered in his chest, and his breath quickened as he attempted to comprehend the meaning of her words. *Her heart belongs in Milton.* To him? He'd asked for a sign if her feelings had changed. She had sent a message to him as a sign! She did care for him! She was telling him that her heart belonged to him!

"You'll want to be quick about it, if you mean to catch her," Higgins prodded, his smile widening as he watched the myriad emotions play over the Master's face.

Mr. Thornton's head jerked up to meet Higgins' stare, surprised to discover someone speaking to him. His brow furrowed slightly and his eyes were distant, as he faintly nodded in acknowledgement of Higgins' words. He bolted out of the door, as Higgins quickly stepped out of his way.

"You'll be wanting a horse, she's well on her way to the station by now!" Higgins called out after Mr. Thornton's retreating figure, hoping his words would penetrate the befuddled brains of the Master of Marlborough Mills.

Thinking only that he must reach her in time, Mr. Thornton's hands trembled as he helped the flustered stable boy ready the chestnut-brown stallion. A moment later, he mounted the horse in one sweeping motion and galloped away from the mill.

The steady clopping of the horse's hooves matched the drumbeat of his heart. As he rode on, he began to realize the enormity of what was happening. If she truly loved him, she would become his wife! He must ask her again. The expectation of her acceptance seized him with a joy so profound that his body ached. How long he had dreamed of receiving her tender affections!

The freezing air whipped through the thin cotton of his sleeves, and numbed his hands, but he gave little heed to the cold, vaguely aware that he had neither coat nor gloves. Instead, he fought to concentrate on what he should say. He only knew that he must try her again, and that he must hurry.

As he arrived at the station, he recalled the last time he'd seen Margaret there and the fleeting image of her in the embrace of the other man came unbidden to his thoughts. He pushed the vision aside as he jumped off the horse, swiftly hitched it, and ran in search of her, looking franticly across and down the length of the station platform. He glimpsed her a short distance away, standing apart near the open train.

"Miss Hale!" he called, striding toward her with his heart pounding in his chest.

Margaret gasped to hear his familiar voice, and turned to see Mr. Thornton making his way toward her. She was arrested by the sight of his tall, commanding frame without the traditional black covering of his coat. Her eyes were drawn to the shape of his firm arms visible through the snow-dampened cotton sleeves. She lifted her gaze to admire the strong, angular lines of his face and noticed his dark hair was glistening with melted snow. His blue eyes seemed to pierce through her with a heated urgency, and she quivered within to think that such a man should love her.

"I have received word from Nicholas," he began, catching his breath. There was no time to waste. "Margaret, I have never stopped loving you," he declared fervently, his eyes searching hers. "Will you marry me?" he asked, his voice cracking with the intensity of his emotion.

"Margaret!" Aunt Shaw broke in, arriving at Margaret's side in a breathless flurry, confusion spreading over her full face. "Mr. Thornton!" she exclaimed with considerable shock, as she realized he was not properly attired. "Whatever is the matter? Is something wrong?" she asked with increasing alarm, looking quickly back and forth between the two of them.

Mr. Thornton opened his mouth, but no words came out. Margaret hastily intervened. "Mr. Thornton had something of significance to relate," she offered.

Aunt Shaw cast her attention to Mr. Thornton, her expression growing dour in dubious consternation. Noticing the stunned reaction of Mr. Thornton to her quick reply, Margaret continued on. "You see, Mr. Thornton and I have recently become engaged," she announced with some authority, not daring to look at Mr. Thornton.

Mr. Thornton's heart leapt in his chest in exaltation. She had accepted him! He was dumbfounded to hear those words from her mouth. Her very boldness thrilled him, yet caused a shadow of doubt to cross his mind. Had she another reason to accept his offer? Had he won her heart after all? It seemed too much like a dream.

Aunt Shaw was speechless as she looked from one to the other in an attempt to verify such an incredulous statement. "What? Is this true?" she sputtered. "Why have we not been told?" she demanded irritably.

"We have not had the chance to tell anyone," Margaret replied honestly. She bowed her head to avoid the gaze of her aunt. "Everything has happened so suddenly since father died," she said quietly, remembering the sorrow of the past few days.

"I see," Aunt Shaw mused, her agitation mollified a little by the mention of Mr. Hale's death.

A smile crept over Mr. Thornton's face as the full realization of what was happening came over him. She had announced her intention to be his wife! He had won her at last!

Margaret looked cautiously to Mr. Thornton to see how he had reacted to her brave deception, and was rewarded with a glorious smile. She smiled in return to think of how she had pleased him.

"Really! This is most irregular!" Aunt Shaw exclaimed in some confusion, not quite knowing how to continue. "This is hardly the time to conduct such a conversation," she chastised. She turned to face Mr. Thornton. "You are welcome to visit us in London, Mr. Thornton. However, Margaret must be given proper time to grieve for her father. You must understand."

His radiant smile evaporated, and his expression darkened. Careful to sound composed, he was able to formulate the appropriate response. "Of course, I understand," he managed to say, while his entire being screamed in silent agony at the thought of being torn from her now. He wanted only the chance to hold her in his arms and hear her tell him that she loved him. He swallowed hard, forcing himself to exude a tempered manner he was far from feeling.

He slowly turned his gaze to Margaret, and his breath stilled in rapturous wonder to find her soulful eyes regarding him with tender yearning.

They remained locked in a breathless stare for a moment until the final call for the London train was announced and Mr. Thornton reluctantly moved forward to help them board. Aunt Shaw was safely inside as Margaret stood in the doorway, facing him. He reached out to her and taking her hand, placed a lingering kiss on the back of it. He wanted nothing more than to pull her to him and enfold her in his arms.

He watched in amazement as she brought the hand he had kissed up to her face and pressed it to her own lips. The gesture was at once so innocent and yet so sensual that he felt his heart melt at her beauty while a kindling of heat rose from deep within him.

She lifted her luminous eyes to meet his mesmerized stare. She smiled wistfully at him and quickly whispered, "Write to me." Then she turned to go.

He took several paces back to keep her within his sight, his eyes riveted to the object of his adoration. She seated herself in the window to discreetly look out, with her aunt seated across from her. They gazed longingly at each other while the train hissed and creaked as it pulled slowly away.

He didn't move for several minutes. It was the second time he had watched her leave him today. He felt trapped in some Greek tragedy, with the gods laughing in derision at his plight. But then the heady recollection of what had occurred dawned on him. She had accepted him! She would be his wife! He, a cotton manufacturer of Milton, was to marry the lovely Miss Hale of Helstone! He sighed and closed his eyes to allow the reality to settle within.

⬸❦⬸

Hannah Thornton sat sewing, her fingers deftly moving over her needlework as she contemplated the unfamiliar atmosphere of the room. She lifted her eyes from her work to study her son. Mr. Thornton sat across the room from her, reading a newspaper in the light of the lamp on the table next to him. The light created a gentle glow over his angular profile. He was not smiling, yet she sensed in him a light-heartedness, as if some burden had been lifted from him. She had noticed it at supper as well, but had said nothing.

He put the paper down and went to the sideboard, picked up the decanter to pour a drink, quickly set it down again and walked to the fireplace to stand staring into the glowing embers of the dying fire. After a few moments, he returned to his chair and picked up the paper again.

He was fairly bursting with some kind of hopeful energy and Mrs. Thornton felt her stomach tighten in unknown dread. Miss Hale would be safely in London by now. She had expected that the girl's departure would cast him into a dark, impenetrable mood, as had happened when she had so callously rejected him some time ago.

How audacious that girl had been to refuse him! She would never meet a man more worthy than her John. It was the girl's rejection of him that continued to gall her.

Mrs. Thornton could not blame John for being attracted to Miss Hale. She was lovely to look at and bore herself with an uncommon grace. John had innocently fallen in love with her. Mrs. Thornton had been surprised at first, since he had never given much thought to such things before. But she told herself that it was quite natural that a man would be susceptible to a pretty face sooner or later.

She thought that time and circumstances would cure him of his attachment to her. Although they never spoke of her, Mrs. Thornton knew that John had not given her up. She still hoped that he might, but she admired his devotion nonetheless. It only proved what she had always known: that her son had a tender heart that was strong and true.

As she continued to surreptitiously study his expression, she thought she detected a faint smile on his lips. She grew increasingly discomforted.

He was not reading, she knew, but was deep in thought. Something had happened. But what? She had been in the room with them when they had exchanged their goodbyes. She had tried not to listen to their lowered voices, but despite that, had heard portions of their conversation and had noted nothing that would have given him hope to win her.

Mrs. Thornton looked down to continue her stitching, recalling how irritated she had been this afternoon when John had abruptly left the room to get a gift for the girl. How impetuous he could be when Miss Hale was present! Mrs. Thornton had seen the look on her son's face when he had placed the book in her hands. She sighed. He would love her still, after all that the girl had done.

She glanced up at him again. She must know why he seemed so pleased.

"Is there any good news at the mill, John?" she queried, hoping there might be another reason for his good mood.

"Hmm?" he mumbled, his thoughts reluctantly coming back down to earth at the sound of his mother's voice. He had to think quickly to recall what she had asked. "Nothing new," he replied casually, "all is well for now. Why do you ask?" *Was he so readable?* he wondered. Could she tell how differently he felt? How amazingly alive and hopeful he was?

Mrs. Thornton did not want to mention the girl's name. No, she would not bring it up. "You seem rather content this evening, John. I thought you may have heard some good news," she offered as an explanation.

She had noticed, John thought, smiling. He put the paper down and got up slowly from his chair.

Mrs. Thornton watched him warily as he made his way towards her and gently crouched down at her knees. Her body tensed in foreboding and her hands stilled. His face was glowing with joy, and in spite of her worry, Mrs. Thornton proudly recognized how handsome he looked.

"I am engaged to be married, Mother," he told her with an uncontrollable smile, tempering his voice from any excitement for his mother's sake.

She gasped to finally hear it, feeling her strength deflate in defeat. She stared at him transfixed for a moment, trying to regain her composure.

"How did this come about?" she sputtered, her brow furrowed in bewilderment.

His smile faded as he raised himself and turned to walk to the window. "I went to speak with her at the train station," he stated simply.

"Why?" she asked with exasperation.

He did not look at her, but instead blankly gazed out the darkened window. "I had reason to believe she had changed her mind," he said softly.

Hannah kept quiet. She would not pry. Whatever his reasons, he had evidently been correct. But why had the girl changed her mind? Hannah was quick to calculate against her, seeking to defend her son from Margaret's fickle behavior.

"And what of this other lover?" she shot at him, forcing him to confront the issue he would so easily dismiss.

He snapped his head in her direction and gave her a piercing glare. He had known that she would try to dissuade him. He remained silent.

"Has she not yet explained her behavior? You must be certain of her motives, John. If there are complications…."

"I trust her, Mother. That is enough!" he snapped. He turned to look out the window again for some solace, but his mother's questions began to seep into his mind, reawakening the doubts he had consciously swept aside for hours.

The memory of seeing her in that man's arms still haunted him. It bothered him immensely to not know who he was.

"What of her aunt? Does she know of this?" Hannah asked pointedly, trying to imagine how events had transpired at the station. "Surely she does not approve of such a hasty arrangement!"

John turned to answer her. "She is under the impression that we have been engaged for a short while," he revealed cautiously.

Hannah raised her eyebrows in astonishment. *What had happened?* she wondered, her curiosity piqued.

"I will go to London in a few weeks to settle things," John told her in an attempt to allay any further inquiry on the circumstances of the day's events.

"A few weeks?" she echoed, surprised her son would wait that long to go to the girl.

"Her aunt insisted that Margaret be given time to grieve for her father," he answered, looking at his mother steadily, hoping to finalize the conversation.

But Hannah persisted. "Have you considered that her relatives may not approve?" she asked more softly, knowing she was treading on dangerous ground. She wanted him to be aware of obstacles he may have to face should he insist on pursuing this engagement.

He looked at her sharply, his eyes flaring. He could count on his mother to bring up every one of his own lingering doubts!

"What are you implying, Mother?" he asked coolly, daring her to explain.

Hannah bent her head in an uncomfortable shame. She had spent years instilling pride and confidence in her son, despite the difficult circumstances he had endured. It was she who had always told him that a man who was true to his own principles was more than equal to any gentleman.

"They may think you are not a suitable match," she offered weakly, still unable to meet his gaze.

John closed his eyes. "I have thought of it, Mother. You have no need to remind me of my position," he said calmly, letting the words themselves cut her.

She winced inwardly to have made him feel unworthy, and glanced at him to gauge the damage she had caused.

He was solemn and pensive, standing in the middle of the room. She had succeeded in stealing his joy, and was sorry for it. But she could not bring herself to apologize in any way.

"Let us speak no more of it tonight, Mother," he pleaded in resignation.

She nodded her assent.

He walked over to her, and bent down to kiss her cheek. "I will bid you good night then." He tried to smile, but failed.

She glanced up to see his somber face and felt a pang of regret for causing him sorrow. "Good night, John," she said in gentle contrition and watched as his figure retreated into the darkness.

Chapter Three

Margaret's eyes opened to see the white canopy and wooden crossbeam of the four-poster bed. She was not at home. *I'm in London,* she recalled lazily. The reason why she was there returned to her, and forced her to acknowledge again the difficult fact that her father was indeed gone. Allowing herself to languish in bed, she rolled over onto her side and slid her hands under her cheek. She would not be expected to be punctual today.

I'm engaged to Mr. Thornton! she remembered, her mind speedily reviewing the course of yesterday's events to reassure herself of its verity. She felt ashamed now to recall the way she had spoken so boldly. She hoped Mr. Thornton would not think badly of her for being so forward; she had acted impulsively when Aunt Shaw had interrupted them. It would have been disastrous for her aunt to know that he had come to propose marriage, so she had instinctively spoken up to protect their secret. Would he forgive her for her deceptive statements? She thought he would, and smiled as she remembered how stunned he had looked.

She longed to write and tell him of her feelings, to explain why she had acted so hastily in accepting his proposal; however, propriety dictated that she wait until he wrote first. She did not wish to appear so shamelessly forthcoming, so she would give him the proper deference that was his due as a man and as her future husband. Besides, Margaret thought with a pang of amusement, Aunt Shaw would certainly not approve of her dashing off love letters right away.

She felt a twinge of guilt to be thinking of Mr. Thornton when she was supposed to be grieving for her father. She imagined her father would have been surprised at her acceptance of Mr. Thornton, but she believed he would have approved. He had esteemed Mr. Thornton very highly. How pleased he would have been to see his daughter marry his good friend! She sighed aloud for what might have been.

Aunt Shaw would be an altogether different case. Margaret knew that she held to very traditional views of social standing, and that she would consider a manufacturer an unsuitable match for her niece. It disturbed Margaret to think that Mr. Thornton should be judged by anything other than his sterling character. Her aunt had started to speak to her in the train yesterday, but Margaret had truly been exhausted and had requested to defer the conversation. Aunt Shaw had complied, but Margaret knew she would not remain silent for long.

Rousing herself at last, Margaret decided she would not mention her relationship to Mr. Thornton today. It was still so new to her, and she wanted time to quietly cherish it; to think of what it meant to her. She wanted to contemplate the direction her life was taking without the intruding opinions of others, however well-meaning they might be.

Edith was the first to greet her later that morning, as Margaret took her breakfast in the bright and airy dining room. "Good morning, Margaret. I had begun to think you might keep to your bed all day," she gently chided as she seated herself at the table to keep her cousin company. "You look well rested. I am glad for it," she commented. "I'm certain it will be good for you to be here with us, and away from…Milton," she finished, hesitant to mention any unpleasant particulars.

Margaret smiled warmly at her cousin, grateful for her sincere affection. "I am glad to be here, Edith. I think I shall enjoy the peace and quiet for now. I feel I've much to ponder. I hope you won't feel I'm being neglectful if I sometimes keep to myself a little," she said in earnest.

"I think I'll understand," Edith replied honestly, although she was obviously disappointed.

"I look forward to being with Sholto," Margaret added to appease her.

Edith's face instantly brightened. "Oh, Sholto loves to play with you! You are so very good with children, Margaret," she praised.

Margaret smiled in response. *Sometime soon I may have children of my own,* she thought with a thrill of wonder at the possibilities her future might hold. And then a sudden flush of anxious alarm came over her to imagine sharing a bed with Mr. Thornton. She felt herself blush as she chastised herself for being so foolish for not having yet considered all the aspects of marriage. She knew, of course, there were certain intimacies required between a man and wife, but she felt apprehensive to admit that she was not exactly certain she knew what these intimacies entailed.

"Margaret!" Edith worriedly exclaimed. "Are you all right? You look distraught," she asked with concern.

"I am all right, Edith," Margaret assured, quickly recovering. "I suppose I am still feeling rather unsettled," she reasoned, giving her cousin a weak smile.

Margaret determined to dwell on more comfortable thoughts. She was sure her anxieties were normal and most likely superfluous. Right now she was enjoying the sweet, newfound pleasure of loving and having that love returned. She was content to know that she would not be alone. She would very much enjoy spending her days getting to know her betrothed better, and she smiled as her thoughts drifted happily to the man she had left behind in Milton.

⚬⚬⚬

Mr. Thornton woke face down with his hand hanging over the edge of his broad, oak framed bed. He stirred himself immediately and got up to shave and dress. It was his longstanding habit to rise early and go to work, and this day would be no different.

But today, his smile could not be contained. He would no longer live in a prison of solitude. Margaret Hale would be his wife, and this beautiful and spirited woman would fill his world with her presence. His days would never be ordinary again.

Although he hadn't slept well at first, the doubts his mother had voiced echoing in his head, he had finally found peace in writing a letter to Margaret. He had remembered her whispered entreaty to write to her, and had climbed out of bed in the early hours of the morning to sit at his desk and write. At first he had been anxious that he would not know the right words to use, but he had found it to be very natural and satisfying to express himself to her, as if it were something he had always done. He had slept well thereafter.

As he looked in the mirror to tie his cravat, he studied himself a moment and wondered again how he had become so fortunate. He did not think himself handsome, and he did not have the refined manners of a proper gentleman. He had worked when others were schooled and he had known scarcity and shame. And yet, he had won the hand of an accomplished lady.

He shook his head in disbelief and headed toward the door. He did not understand it, but he thanked God for such a tremendous gift.

Mrs. Thornton was already at the breakfast table when she heard the quick steps of her son coming down the stairs. Much to her surprise, he smiled and greeted her warmly. She regarded him thoughtfully as he sat and ate his eggs and toast, his eyes on the folded newspaper beside him. It seemed nothing would dampen his spirits this morning. She felt a pang of jealousy to see him so happy, even as she reasoned that he justly deserved it. He had worked hard all these years. She would be content, Mrs. Thornton told herself, if she could only trust the girl who held her son's heart in her hands.

"Have you finished the Richards order?" she asked, resorting to their normal topics of conversation, as she finished sipping her tea.

"Not yet, but it should be done by week's end," he answered. "Let's hope he will pay for his order on time," he sighed, being forced to descend for the moment into the financial worries that he tried to keep at bay. Mr. Thornton gulped his tea, and then rose from the table to go.

Mrs. Thornton eyed her son with pride. She was glad to see he would still concentrate on his work today, despite the lively turn of events of the day before.

But Mr. Thornton did not go directly to work as his mother expected. Before he set foot in his office, Mr. Thornton took a brisk circuitous walk to post a letter to London.

Late in the afternoon, Mr. Thornton followed the familiar trail to Crampton, evoking all the bittersweet memories of the hope and heartache he had felt while traversing this same path. A shrill wind blew at the crest of the hill of the old graveyard, threatening to remove his hat.

He had promised Mr. Bell he would help with the Hales' property, and he now had a compelling personal interest in the matter as Miss Hale's fiancé.

He did not look forward to working with the supercilious Dixon, but he wanted to take in the atmosphere of the Hales' home again. He wanted to feel close to Margaret.

Dixon was greatly relieved to find help in any form, and welcomed Mr. Thornton more congenially than he had expected. "There's plenty of work to be done around here. It's more than one poor person can do, I tell you. I've spent all day here just packing up Miss Margaret's things to be sent to London. I've not touched another thing," she complained, as she led him further into the house.

Mr. Thornton was busy contemplating how Miss Margaret's things would be making only a temporary detour to London. They would eventually find their final home here in Milton, when she came back to be his wife.

"I would like to gather all the items that might be of particular value to Miss Hale," he requested, catching the suspicious glance of the servant. "Miss Hale and I are engaged to be married. I would like for her to have anything from her family home that would make her happy," he informed her in a straightforward manner.

"Married! I beg your pardon, but I've not heard of any such thing and I am sure I would have heard of it. I just saw Miss Margaret yesterday before she left and she told me of no engagement!" she huffed, crossing her arms defiantly.

Mr. Thornton turned his head away a moment in an attempt to ignore the slight and keep his temper. "I believe it should be granted that I know of what I speak!" he retorted, speaking through his teeth. "I also saw Miss Hale yesterday, before she left," he hinted as a way of explanation.

Dixon's mouth hung open as she realized that her mistress had betrothed herself in haste to the Master of Marlborough Mills. She had not seen it coming.

"Now, if you would assist in selecting some of the things that she might like to keep," he continued, satisfied that he had made himself clear. "I should like to look around to see what items might be sold," he informed her, hiding his real interest in surveying the household.

Dixon grumbled something under her breath and went off to continue her task, leaving Mr. Thornton at liberty to enter the drawing room alone. He enjoyed the warmth and comfort that surrounded him in this place. It seemed the soft chairs and casually placed books welcomed one to relax and read or to enjoy the company of family. He hoped his home would become such a haven when he married the girl who had lived here.

He spotted the china tea set on the tray table in the corner of the room, and at once recalled the first kindling of desire he had felt as he watched her pour tea for him. How soft and lovely she had looked in the glowing candlelight! He sighed and blinked his eyes to return to the present. He was determined to save the tea set.

Eventually, Mr. Thornton climbed the stairs to survey the family's private living space, assured that Dixon was busily tending to her supper preparations. He had often been to Mr. Hale's study, but this time he made his way down the hall to peer briefly at the furnishings found in the bedchambers. When he found Miss Hale's bedroom, he stopped at the threshold, afraid to violate with his ungainly presence what seemed to him a sanctuary of maidenly purity and refinement.

He studied in reverent fascination every object within that had held communion with her: the rose-colored curtains, the elegant marble-topped vanity, the glass-framed pressed flowers hanging on the wall, and the simple chest of drawers with a lace overlay. The trunks Dixon had packed lay opened on the floor, bulging with all the delicate finery of a lady's wardrobe.

His eyes narrowed with interest as his gaze rested upon the garment that lay at the top of the pile. It was the elegant gown she had worn at the dinner party those many months ago. He stepped forward and crouched down to examine it. Touching the silk fabric gingerly, he recalled how stunningly beautiful she had appeared that evening. Amazement washed over him once more at the realization that she had accepted him. He had not thought such a lady of refinement could ever be his.

It remained a wonder to him that he had somehow won her regard. Of old, she had always spoken to him with harsh disdain, never more so than when he had first told her of his love.

Crouched there, in the middle of her room, he become aware of the faint fragrance of jasmine. He closed his eyes to better concentrate on the scent, which instantly brought to mind the tremulous moment when he had nearly brushed against her as he had secured the door behind her on that fateful morning. She had seemed so fragile and beautiful. He had yearned to feel the smooth skin of her face; to draw her to him and claim her as his own in some presumptuous way.

He brushed his fingers reverently along the folded silk for a lingering moment before slowly straightening himself to stand.

The fading daylight warned him it was time to leave. He glanced around the bedroom one more time before stepping out into the hallway. Dixon passed by him when he had reached the foyer, and he politely told her he would return again at some later day. "Good evening then, sir," she replied with a curt nod and continued on her way to the stairs.

Mr. Thornton stepped outside and closed the door behind him. The open sky above reawakened him to his isolation. She was miles away. He breathed a sigh of aching loneliness, and reluctantly headed for the vacant house where his supper awaited him.

Chapter Four

Aunt Shaw regarded Edith and Margaret affectionately as the cousins chatted amicably in the front parlor. It had been the better part of a week since Margaret had arrived at Harley Street, and she seemed to be doing very well. She was quiet and subdued, but that was to be expected after the horrible ordeals she had endured this past year. Aunt Shaw was determined to protect her niece from anything that would disturb her peace. She wanted to allow her the space and time to leave the memories of that horrid town behind her.

She had been greatly distressed when Margaret had announced herself engaged to the stern-looking Milton manufacturer, but she had kept silent at Margaret's request, perceiving the girl's exhaustion. She felt certain that Margaret's good judgment had been clouded by the unseemly environment that had surrounded her in that city. Aunt Shaw conjectured that Mr. Thornton might be considered a good match for a Milton girl; however, Margaret was not of their ilk. She did not belong in such a place. Aunt Shaw hoped that the allure of London's charms and fine society would restore her niece's good sense and instill in her a desire for a more suitable husband.

She was encouraged by the fact that Margaret had not mentioned her engagement since she had arrived, and she was resolved to keep her own silence on the subject as long as possible. Unless Margaret showed an interest in this matter, she would not bring it to her attention. There was no need at present to stir up any unsettling emotions in the girl.

Aunt Shaw had been dismayed, in course, to find a letter addressed to Margaret from Mr. Thornton shortly after her arrival. She had hesitated to hand the letter over to the girl at that time, worrying that his letter would solidify the girl's decision before she had had time to consider other possibilities. Aunt Shaw convinced herself that there could be no harm in setting aside the letter for just a day or two. After all, she felt it was now her duty to protect and guide her sister's daughter with all the motherly wisdom accorded her. She had not intended, though, to forget the letter after the said two days had passed.

Margaret was content enough to live among them, but she dwelled in a world apart. Her mind wandered between the mists of memory and the sunshine of hope and wonder. She remembered the playful days of her childhood and the bitter trials of moving to Milton. She recalled her every encounter with Mr. Thornton and wondered what it would be like to be kissed by him.

Most of all, she remembered the fleeting moments at the station with Mr. Thornton – the words he had spoken and the way he had looked at her. She blushed to remember the feel of his lips on her hand.

Margaret treasured the private moments spent in her room or the nursery. She lingered in bed in the mornings and tried to imagine what Mr. Thornton might be doing at that very moment. And as she let her mind drift to the past, her thoughts fluctuated between memories of Milton and of her childhood in Helstone. She fondly recalled the days in her childhood when she had held her father's hand, skipping along the meadow paths as he made his frequent visits about the village. Yesterday, while Sholto fell asleep in her arms, she was suddenly overcome by sorrow to realize that the children she might have would never know their grandparents.

She had begun to worry why Mr. Thornton had not yet written to her, and had lain awake for some time the previous evening thinking on it. She had tried to convince herself that a delay in the post or the overwhelming demands on him at the mill would easily explain the lack of correspondence, but she had not been able to keep from wondering if he might be having second thoughts about marrying her. Perhaps she had been entirely too audacious at the station, for she had barely let him say a word. Or maybe he had thought more seriously about her tarnished character. She had not yet explained to him about her lie and the circumstances of Fred's departure. Why, it was even possible he still thought she had been involved with another man! It troubled her greatly to imagine that he might think such a thing. If only they had had time to speak with each other!

Margaret also worried that Mrs. Thornton would strongly oppose their match and sow seeds of doubt in Mr. Thornton's mind. Although she did not like to think of it, she was aware that Mrs. Thornton had disliked her from their first meeting. It hurt her to be judged so unfavorably, and she despaired of ever winning her approval. Margaret smiled sadly as she supposed that Mrs. Thornton would not think anyone was good enough for her son. She hoped Mr. Thornton would not be unduly influenced by his mother's opinions of her.

Margaret tried to rally her spirits in the morning, but could not shrug off the lingering fears that had stolen her restful sleep. She would have kept to her room for a while, but knew that Edith would be expecting her.

Edith greatly enjoyed the company Margaret provided and found numerous occasions to allow Margaret to spend time with Sholto. She noticed that Margaret was a little more sullen this morning, but she attributed it to the ebb and flow of her grief. Indeed, Edith recalled that just yesterday she had entered the nursery to find tears coursing down Margaret's cheeks while she had held the sleeping boy in her arms. Edith duly recognized her own pleasant circumstances, and felt sympathy for her cousin, who was unmarried and now recently orphaned.

"I do hope you will come visit the Powells with me next Wednesday, Margaret," Edith entreated, her hands busy sorting fabric she had chosen for some of her summer gowns. "Do you like this one?" she asked Margaret, holding up a swath of creamy yellow linen with a delicate pattern of tiny periwinkle flowers.

"It looks to your taste, Edith," Margaret commented with a courteous smile. "It will be perfect on you."

Edith smiled happily. "I would like to help you choose some new clothes, especially since winter is now over. You must retire all your drab dresses, Margaret. They really won't do now that you are in London," she emphatically instructed. "Whenever you are done with your mourning attire, that is," she added with a hint of impatience.

"I'm sure you could help me choose some lovely things, Edith. I would very much like to go shopping with you, if you will promise to let me have a say," she teased her cousin good-naturedly.

"Of course I shall!" Edith protested. "I only want you to look your best," she continued defensively. "After all, you might soon find yourself thinking of marrying," she suggested, glancing slyly at Margaret.

Margaret bowed her head to hide her broad smile, then brought it up again to speak. "I'm afraid I have been rather secretive, Edith. I believe I shall be married before the year is through," she admitted.

Edith looked confused at first but then brightened with enthusiasm. "I am glad you are open to the idea, Margaret. I know of a particular gentleman…."

"No, you don't understand," Margaret interrupted, "I am already engaged to be married," she explained as gently as she could.

"What?" Edith cried out in consternation. "But you have not spoken of anyone in your letters," she objected. "Oh, Margaret, who is it? Surely you would not marry some cotton mill hand in Milton?" she pleaded with disdain, recalling Margaret's sympathy for the factory workers.

Margaret retained her poise, but was inwardly hurt by her cousin's condescending tone. "Of course not, Edith. But you may remember my fiancé, Mr. Thornton, is a cotton manufacturer. He is Master of Marlborough Mills in Milton," she announced proudly, noting the look of distress Edith had exchanged with Aunt Shaw, who was sitting across the room listening intently to the unfolding discussion.

"But Margaret, you can't possibly marry Mr. Thornton! You don't even like him! You said so yourself in your letters! And you have been so miserable in Milton, how could you go back?" Edith exclaimed, unwilling to believe Margaret's recent revelation.

Margaret winced to recall her earlier letters. "It's true, I did not see much to admire in Milton at first. I was too harsh in my criticism, I fear. You will probably not understand, but I have become quite fond of Milton… and of certain people there," she added as the color rose faintly to her cheeks.

Aunt Shaw rose from the sofa and came to stand near them. "Perhaps now would be a good time to discuss your situation," she announced, directing herself to Margaret.

Margaret stiffened to hear the authoritative tone of her voice and choice of words, but nodded in assent.

"Would you allow us to speak privately a few moments, Edith?" Aunt Shaw asked her daughter.

"I will visit the nursery," Edith replied, and obediently left the room.

Aunt Shaw sat across from Margaret, steeling herself for the unpleasant task ahead. "My dear Margaret," she began gently, "I had hoped we would not need to have this little talk," she sighed.

Margaret gave her a puzzled look.

"I hoped once you were here you would eventually come to see what a mistake it would be to continue this…this arrangement," she explained.

"You do not approve," Margaret said succinctly, lowering her eyes dejectedly. She had harbored a fragment of hope that her aunt would let her engagement stand uncontested, but now resigned herself to the fact that she would counsel strongly against it.

"Margaret, I'm certain you feel that your father would have approved of Mr. Thornton; however, I don't believe your father was aware of how much more suitable it is to marry someone of one's own society. You must know, my dear, how difficult it was for your mother to be married to your father.

Margaret bristled to hear her father discreetly but distinctly maligned. "I believe father would have judged Mr. Thornton on his character and not his lineage or position in society, and I have learned to judge others in a similar manner," she honestly admitted.

"Margaret!" Aunt Shaw declared with considerable shock at Margaret's blunt retort.

"I have not met a finer man than Mr. Thornton, Aunt. Truly, I have not," she reaffirmed in response to the dismayed look on her aunt's face. "I do not believe I could find a finer man in London. That he happens to be a manufacturer in Milton is decidedly beside the point," she concluded.

"It is of the utmost importance that he be able to provide the means to maintain the lifestyle of a lady of your station!" Aunt Shaw declared.

"And what if I do not wish to be a lady of leisure?" Margaret countered.

"Whatever do you mean by that?" Aunt Shaw demanded, her face turning a blotchy pink.

Margaret softened her tone to calm her obviously flustered aunt. "I mean no offense, Aunt, and I do not wish to displease you, but I should like to decide for myself what my station in life should be. I have no desire to spend my time in idle amusement. I should like to assist in some way the lives of others. It cannot be helped. I suppose I am like my father in that respect," she explained.

"It seems you are more like him than I imagined," Aunt Shaw noted with displeasure. "And I see you have developed quite a revolutionary attitude during your time in Milton among all the working folk. I am greatly distressed that you should disparage the Beresford heritage with such theories of commonness. I only wish to see you comfortably situated in a marriage that befits your standing. Is it any wonder I worry for your future, Margaret, when you would choose to be a tradesman's wife?" she asked earnestly, searching Margaret's face for sympathetic understanding.

Margaret looked down at her folded hands for a moment to contemplate how she should respond. "It is not my intention to dishonor the Beresford name. Mr. Thornton has attained a highly regarded position in Milton society as a successful manufacturer and magistrate. He has the means to provide a comfortable life for his family. I shall not want for anything, Aunt Shaw. I do not wish for anything more. You needn't worry for me," she assured her.

"And what if his business should falter or fail? How would you manage, Margaret?" Aunt Shaw asked.

"I am not afraid to cast my lot with Mr. Thornton. Should circumstances arise to bring him to ruin, I do not doubt but that he would rise as the Phoenix. There is no one else in whom I would entrust my happiness and welfare. I have every confidence in Mr. Thornton's ability to succeed at whatever he does, and I shall be honored to be his wife," Margaret proudly asserted.

"You believe yourself in love with him," Aunt Shaw candidly reasoned.

"Yes," Margaret acknowledged without hesitation, as the words her aunt had spoken reverberated within her, astonishing her anew with their truth – she was in love with him!

"Margaret, there are many reasons to marry," Aunt Shaw began.

"Yes, but I wish to be permitted to marry for love as Edith has done," Margaret interjected, pleading for her aunt to understand.

Aunt Shaw sighed. "You have always been a determined young girl," she recalled pointedly. "Are you certain you wish to proceed with this engagement, Margaret?" she asked in defeat.

"Yes," Margaret answered in eager anticipation of her aunt's concession.

"Then I feel I have no choice but to accede to your wishes," she allowed with gravity, knowing it would be fruitless to continue arguing with her niece.

"Oh, thank you, Aunt Shaw!" Margaret excitedly exclaimed as she rushed to give her aunt a quick hug and a peck on her cheek. Aunt Shaw gave a restrained smile and then grew stern again.

"I will give you my blessing on one condition," she announced as she held Margaret squarely by the shoulders.

"Yes, what is it?" Margaret enthusiastically agreed.

"That you will come to me if you have any reservations or doubts about this. An engagement can be broken without much trouble. Marriage cannot," she counseled sagely.

"I know," Margaret acknowledged solemnly and averted her eyes from her aunt's gaze.

"What's wrong, Margaret?" Aunt Shaw asked as she noticed the sudden change in the girl's demeanor.

"I fear Mr. Thornton may be having second thoughts," she confessed in dismay.

"Whatever would make you think that?" Aunt Shaw asked, her brows furrowed in confusion.

"He has not yet written to me," Margaret replied, unable to hide her anxiety.

Aunt Shaw's expression relaxed and she took a deep breath before speaking.

"Margaret, you must forgive me, I felt I was acting in your best interests," she confessed apologetically.

"He has written to me!" she breathed aloud as she grasped the meaning of her aunt's admission. "I have been waiting to hear from him. Did you not think I should care?" Margaret questioned her with a look of hurt confusion.

"I am sorry, Margaret. I did not know you had formed such a strong attachment," her aunt endeavored to explain. "Come with me, and I will give the letter to you," she directed.

As they passed by the nursery, Edith rushed out to discover what had transpired. "Is everything all right?" she asked Margaret hesitantly as she held her arm to detain her.

"Everything is settled. I shall marry Mr. Thornton," Margaret gladly shared. "Please be happy for me," she pleaded upon noting the glimmer of disappointment Edith showed to hear her news. Edith nodded slowly and let Margaret continue on.

Aunt Shaw returned to the hallway from her room to hand over the letter. Margaret took it reverently and studied the handwriting on the envelope as her face began to glow with joyous expectation. "Thank you!" she whispered and hastened to her room to read it in private.

Mr. Thornton rubbed his forehead as he tried to make sense of the figures in front of him. He had been at work for hours, but had accomplished very little. As the days wore on, he found it increasingly difficult to concentrate as he began to worry why Margaret had not yet written to him. It pained him to think that her pleasant surroundings in London might give her pause in accepting him. Would she renounce her regard for Milton now that she was removed from the grime and smoke of it?

He stood up from his desk and walked to the window overlooking the mill yard. He tried to imagine how Margaret might feel living next to the noise and bustle of the place. It was all he could offer her, and he prayed it would be enough.

Did she truly love him? The question burned in his heart. He longed to know what her feelings were and what had urged her to respond to him so quickly the day she had left. If only she would write to him!

He reasoned hopefully that she might have waited to receive his letter first. If so, tomorrow's post would surely bring him word from her. He felt he must find a way to stop fretting and attend to his business, so he snatched his coat and ventured out.

Higgins stepped outside the workers' dining hall to make a sweeping glance in each direction for the Master. He hadn't spoken with Mr. Thornton since the day he had run off to catch Margaret, but Higgins had watched his employer like a hawk whenever he came out of his office to make his rounds of the mill. On more that one occasion, Higgins had triumphantly detected a curious half-smile on the Master's face that he had never seen before.

Higgins glimpsed Thornton at the end of the yard and waited in the doorway for him to pass by. "Master, come in. Eat with us," Higgins earnestly invited, as he drew near.

Mr. Thornton stopped and looked at Higgins appreciatively. "I've not eaten," he considered aloud as he raised his eyebrows.

Higgins smiled and led him to a gray wooden table to sit between the other workers. Mary quickly served them their food, as she always did when the Master came to dine.

"Did you catch her then?" Higgins asked as they began eating. He looked askance at Thornton, allowing the din of the hall to shield their privacy.

The corners of Mr. Thornton's mouth curled upward in response but he did not look at Higgins. "Yes," he answered steadily, wary of the direction the conversation would be taking.

"Will we be seeing her back in Milton before long?" Higgins continued to probe his reticent colleague.

Mr. Thornton's smile grew broader at Higgins' insistent questioning. He relished the opportunity to share his news with someone who would be happy to hear it. "Yes, I believe we will," he replied in an even tone that belied the joy he felt.

Higgins slapped the table, rattling his spoon and mug, and drawing a few startled glances in his direction. "I knew it!" he declared loudly, unable to restrain his delight.

"Congratulations, Thornton! You'll not find a finer lass," he continued more quietly. "Of course, I'd say she's found a decent catch herself!" he appraised, with a twinkle in his eye.

"Thank you," Mr. Thornton replied, touched by Higgins' enthusiastic approval.

"If you don't mind me saying, I've had you two pegged for some time," Higgins revealed. "I'm glad to see you both come to your senses!" he added good-humoredly.

"What do you mean?" Mr. Thornton asked curiously, furrowing his brow in confusion.

"I mean she's had her eye on you," Higgins explained as he watched to see how much the Master understood.

Mr. Thornton shook his head in disbelief, his expression still one of incomprehension. "But she did not like me..." he stammered absently.

"Aye, she wouldn't let her heart talk to her head, I'd say. But it looks like she's finally come around," Higgins elaborated with a sly grin.

Mr. Thornton returned the smile stiffly, lost in thought. Had she resisted her true feelings? How long had she felt something for him?

He mulled over Higgins' words the remainder of the day, and well into the night.

⚬⚬⚬

Margaret set a candle on her bedside table and climbed into bed, bringing Mr. Thornton's letter with her. She had read it countless times this afternoon, treasuring his every word to her, and she had immediately sat down at her desk to make her reply. How glorious it felt to finally tell him of her feelings for him! She rejoiced that he would soon know why she had acted so boldly that day at the station.

She unfolded the paper to read it once more.

My dearest Margaret,

Forgive me if I do not use the elegant words of a poet to describe my feelings for you. Although my prose may be plain, I hope you will understand that I write from the depths of my heart.

There are no words to describe the joy I felt when you declared our engagement in front of your aunt! Your courageous spirit and quick mind will never cease to amaze me. That you have agreed to be my wife seems to me a dream, as I have loved you for so long.

Do you know the power you have to bewitch me? I am captivated by your beauty and goodness. Will you think me too forward if I tell you that I long to hold you close? In truth, I feel I must keep myself from gathering you in my arms whenever you are near me.

Will you tell me something of what is in your heart? Margaret, if you will truly be mine, I will live in constant wonder of the blessing that has befallen me. Will you not write to me some words of affection, until I can hear them from your own lips?

I think of you every waking moment, and wish the miles between us would vanish so that you were here with me.

I am, and forever will be, your own

  John Thornton

She brushed her fingertips over his signature in tender affection before refolding the letter and slipping it under her pillow. She leaned over to blow out the candle, and then settled down to sleep with a smile on her lips. She knew the letter would bring her sweet dreams.

Chapter Five

A warm spring breeze blew through the open windows at the Crampton house, stirring the chintz-curtains in the drawing room and chasing the winter's dust in circles on the hardwood floors. Dixon was busily arranging folded linens into a pile on the sofa. The room was cluttered with crates of household goods and sundry light furnishings from around the house.

Dixon stood up to survey the space around her. It was a sad reminder of all that had passed here in Milton, to see all of the Hales' belongings stacked and packed about the room and spilling into the hallway. By nightfall, she hoped to be finished here, but this morning she must clean the floors and the kitchen. Mr. Thornton would deal with the arrangements for selling and moving the heavy furniture that remained upstairs. The things she had set aside for Margaret were in the dining room.

She shook her head to think of Miss Margaret moving to the Thorntons' residence. What would her late mistress have thought of this match? Surely it would further weaken the lofty Beresford heritage to be linked to a tradesman in such a dismal city. But even so, Dixon was forced to admit her respect for the man Margaret had accepted. Mr. Thornton had always acted the part of a gentleman, and had been especially considerate to her late mistress during the months of her failing health.

Dixon was looking forward to going to London -- at least until Miss Margaret would wed. She did not relish the thought of living in the same house as Mrs. Thornton. She and her son were a pair - dressed all in black and looking so stern! She was certain she'd never seen a more serious-looking set, Dixon clucked to herself. It would do them good to have Margaret in their home. She was a cheerful girl for the most part, and would bring a good deal of lightheartedness to the stuffy atmosphere that Dixon thought must pervade the place.

She was well on her way to the kitchen when she heard a loud knock at the door. She tried to imagine why Mr. Thornton would come at this time of day, as she grudgingly retraced her steps towards the main hall.

Swinging the door open with impatience, she was stunned to find herself face to face with a young man dressed in the impeccable uniform of Her Majesty's Navy. Her face blanched in terror for a brief moment before quickly recovering herself in an attempt to appear unconcerned.

"Lieutenant Bexley of Her Majesty's Navy," the officer introduced himself bluntly. "Is this the Hale residence?" he began with authority, casting his eyes beyond her large form to look for any movement from within.

"Yes, it is," Dixon answered firmly, desperately trying to keep her voice from betraying the tremulous swell of fear coming over her.

"The Navy is seeking the whereabouts of a Mr. Frederick Hale," Bexley announced with great formality. "May I speak with a... Mr. Richard Hale?" he asked, having pulled out a card with the pertinent information scribbled upon it from his breast pocket.

"Mr. Hale has passed away very recently, and his wife has also passed away," she informed him smugly.

"I'm sorry," the lieutenant stated with solemn courtesy. "Then perhaps I may speak with his daughter, Miss Margaret Hale," he persisted, having glanced again at the card in his hand.

"Miss Hale is away in London. She won't be back for some time," Dixon offered elusively, hoping to prevent any further inquiry about her young mistress.

"In London? With relatives, perhaps?" he cleverly surmised with a slight grin.

"With family from her mother's side," she emphasized defiantly, noting irritably that the young whippersnapper could hardly be older than Master Frederick himself.

"And when do you expect her to return to Milton?" he continued. "You did say she would be back, didn't you?" he asked, effectively cornering her into giving him a reply.

Dixon had no idea when Margaret was planning to return, and for once she was glad to be so uninformed. "I don't know when she's to return," she replied honestly, with some triumph. "She's to marry Mr. Thornton of Marlborough Mills, but that's all I've been told. I'm just a servant here," she smartly reminded him.

"Mr. Thornton, did you say?" he asked, his brow contracting in vague recognition of the name. Scanning his written information yet again, the young man's face suddenly lit with comprehension. "Ah, yes...he's a local magistrate here in Milton, is he not?" he asked, looking to Dixon for confirmation.

"That's him," she affirmed with slight trepidation.

"Very interesting," he mused, his chin jutting upward as he appraised this convenient coincidence. "Just the man I should like to see," he decided aloud. "Thank you very much for your assistance," he added wryly to Dixon. "Good day, ma'am," he said with a quick nod, and abruptly turned to descend the stairs.

Dixon gave a curt nod and shut the door before she lost all composure and began to wring her hands in despair. "Oh, Master Frederick!" she wailed in a fit of fearful distress. Although she felt some relief in having deflected the officer from pursuing Margaret for inquiry, she worried to think of throwing Mr. Thornton into the middle of such private family business. But it could not be helped. He would soon be family after all.

She grunted in smug satisfaction to imagine that the brash young officer would more than meet his match in Mr. Thornton. She was certain no one could intimidate the likes of him.

Lieutenant Bexley stood in the mill yard watching the workers unload a mountain of cotton bales that had recently arrived. He was already impressed with the scale of the enterprise, and curious to meet the man who managed it. Finding the man was a different story. He had been told at the main residence that Mr. Thornton could be found at the mill, and now he was waiting for a mill hand to fetch him. He was growing increasingly impatient as the minutes wore on.

He straightened himself when an older man emerged from the mill and headed in his direction. The man had a mustache, and was dressed in an undistinguished brown coat and cap – hardly the leader of industry that the lieutenant had expected.

"Mr. Thornton?" Bexley cautiously greeted him.

"No. No. The name's Williams. I'm the overseer here," he explained apologetically, whisking off his cap in respect. "If you'll kindly follow me, sir, I'll find the Master," he offered with a short bow of the head and an outstretched arm pointed towards the mill.

Once inside, Williams addressed the lieutenant again. "If you would wait here in his office, sir…"

"If you will allow me, I would prefer to accompany you on your search," Bexley requested, more out of interest in seeing the inner workings of the mill than in efficiency of duty.

Williams nodded, and led the lieutenant through the mule room to the sliding doors of the weaving shed. When the doors opened, Bexley stood transfixed a moment as he took in the scene before him. The noise was deafening, but the vision of the cotton snow floating blithely in the air gave the place an ethereal sense of tranquility.

Bexley followed Williams down one row of machines, and around the corner of another. He halted as the overseer bent over to speak to a man who was crouched down in front of a loom that was obviously not functioning, its attendant standing helplessly by.

Mr. Thornton turned and stretched himself up to his full height, and fastidiously rolled down the sleeves of his cotton shirt. The man shrugged into his black overcoat unhurriedly and raised his chin in acknowledgment of the uniformed man in front of him.

Lieutenant Bexley knew without a doubt that he had found the Master.

"Mr. Thornton, sir. May I speak with you?" he shouted awkwardly in an attempt to make himself heard.

"Come with me," Mr. Thornton responded in a strong voice that was adjusted perfectly to pierce the din of the clacking looms.

Unconcerned by the passing stares of the workers, Bexley quickened his pace to keep up with the long strides of the Master as he led him back through the long rows of machinery.

Inside the privacy of the office, Bexley began to speak. "Lieutenant Bexley of Her Majesty the Queen's Navy, sir," he announced formally.

Mr. Thornton sat down at his desk and offered the lieutenant a seat with a motion of his hand.

"How may I help you?" he asked, intrigued as to the purpose of this visit.

"The Navy requests your assistance in revealing any information you may have concerning a midshipman who has been charged with mutiny. We have received notice of late that he was in this vicinity this October past," he explained.

"His name?" Mr. Thornton prodded, doubtful he could be of any help in the matter.

"Frederick Hale." He annunciated the name clearly, and watched for any reaction the name might invoke.

"Hale?" Mr. Thornton repeated hollowly, his brow knit in confusion. His body tensed as his intuition warned him of impending danger, and he listened intently for the next words to be spoken.

"Yes, the son of Richard Hale of Crampton," he elaborated, regarding the cotton master curiously.

Mr. Thornton staggered inwardly at the revelation. *Mr. Hale had a son!*

He was stunned to realize that Margaret had a brother. They had kept it a secret. Immediately, a deluge of images and remembered instances flooded his consciousness. His mind swam to make sense of it all. Amidst the flotsam of scattered reminiscence emerged the memory of Margaret as she stood before him at her father's house, saying in a soft voice, -- *The secret is another person's. I cannot explain it without doing him harm.* He flailed frantically to place this occurrence in the correct time frame, and quickly recalled that it had been October, shortly after her mother's death.

It suddenly dawned on him, the beacon of truth brilliantly illuminating the vision of her in the embrace of the other man - *It was her brother!*

"Mr. Thornton," Bexley called out, attempting to gain Mr. Thornton's attention.

A wave of relief and ecstatic joy washed over him, causing the corners of his mouth to edge upwards in a small, irrepressible smile. He had seen her in the arms of her brother. There had been no lover!

"Mr. Thornton!" the lieutenant called more sternly.

Mr. Thornton turned to look at his visitor, steeling himself to discuss the issue at hand. "I have no knowledge of the man," he stated honestly.

"Do you mean to tell me you have no knowledge of your fiancé's brother?" he asked skeptically, attempting to reveal any deception on Mr. Thornton's part.

Mr. Thornton's eyes narrowed. "My relationship to Miss Hale is not common knowledge," he stated in a constrained voice, his anger rising at being spoken to in such a manner.

"I was told by the servant at the Hale's home," Bexley offered as explanation.

"I was not aware Miss Hale had a brother," Mr. Thornton reiterated, wishing to finish this meeting as soon as possible.

"I find it hard to believe that a man such as yourself, a magistrate and a leader of industry, would be connected to such a family," the lieutenant commented haughtily. "Your fiancé seems less than truthful," he added disdainfully.

Mr. Thornton stood up forcefully, sending his chair rolling backward to crash against the wall. He made his way briskly around the desk to confront the lieutenant, who had quickly gotten to his feet in nervous surprise.

"I do not believe it is your business to cast judgment on persons whom you have never met," he hissed, his face dark with barely controlled rage. "It has been my experience that one cannot always be held responsible for the actions of a family member," he continued, glaring at the man who vainly attempted to appear unafraid. "It has also been my experience to find that there are few families that do not carry a closely guarded secret," he finished, releasing the man from his piercing stare.

"As to his whereabouts," he continued, "I am certain that I do not know. It seems logical to assume he has left the country. What notice have you received to suggest he was here in Milton this past October?" Mr. Thornton asked, curious to know the reason the search had been initiated.

"We received a letter from a woman who claimed her fiancé was killed trying to bring Hale to justice. Evidently, the man knew there would be a reward. It's a pity she did not write sooner. It seems she only wrote to inquire if her letter might help in securing a reward for herself," Bexley explained.

Mr. Thornton instantly realized that it had been Jane who had sent the letter, but he pushed his thoughts aside to concentrate on what he should say next. "If indeed Hale were here at that time, I am certain he has returned to his place of exile. I assure you that I have neither met the man nor have heard anything about his location," he stated sincerely, hoping to finalize the whole matter.

"You are certain he has left England?" Bexley queried.

"As I said, I know nothing about him. I can only presume that he has fled the country. I do not expect I shall ever meet him," Mr. Thornton said to appease the lieutenant.

"I hope you will remember that you have sworn your loyalty to the Crown, if future events should lead you to find Mr. Hale," Bexley cautioned him, his chin held high.

Mr. Thornton gritted his teeth. "I am well aware of where my loyalties lie, Lieutenant," he managed to say in a civil tone.

"Good day, sir," Lieutenant Bexley replied, giving a brusque nod of the head before he turned to leave.

Mr. Thornton remained standing after the door rattled shut, allowing his body to relax. *Margaret!* If only she had confided in him! Had he been so unapproachable that she could not tell him of her brother? A sharp stab of self-loathing tore through him to recall how he had lashed out at her with his cruel words, his foolish jealousy provoking him to seek retribution for his bitter anguish.

She had borne his anger bravely at a time when she had most needed his kindly compassion. She had lost her mother, and had to endure the frightening prospect of losing her brother as well. Mr. Thornton was grateful to remember that he had been able to help her in stopping the inquest concerning Leonards' death. But he felt a sting of remorse for his blind fury and his wavering faith in her character. How he wished he could have helped her!

He was ruminating over all that had passed when a knock sounded at his door. "Come in," he called wearily.

Higgins opened the door and poked his head in to look around before letting himself in. "Is Master Hale safe?" he asked with great concern.

Mr. Thornton gave him a puzzled look. "You knew?" he questioned in bewilderment.

"My Mary worked for the Hales those days the missus were ill. She doesn't talk much, but she tells me things," he explained. "So, is he safe?" he repeated, looking earnestly at the Master.

"They know he was here, when his mother died. They don't know where he is now," he related. "Do you?" he added, suddenly thinking to ask Higgins.

Higgins nodded. "In Cadiz, Spain," he told him.

"Spain?" the Master echoed, thoughtfully considering the news. "He had best stay there," he added grimly.

Margaret was enjoying an especially quiet day at the Harley Street residence. Edith and Maxwell had gone to a grand luncheon and Aunt Shaw was in her room napping. Margaret sat comfortably on a powder blue sofa, her legs tucked under her, and a pile of books splayed out next to the sofa. She was happy to read whatever suited her mood, sometimes picking up poetry or, more often than not, reading some favorite book she remembered reading as a girl.

Margaret was engrossed in *Ivanhoe*, when the footman announced that she had a caller. She stood up to allow the black folds of her dress to fall to the floor and brushed her hand down the length of her skirt to chase away the broader wrinkles. When she looked up, she was pleasantly surprised to discover who her visitor was.

"Mr. Bell!" Margaret cried out, smiling brightly as she rushed forward to clasp his hands. "I am so glad to see you!" she enthused.

"I thought I would come to see how you are doing. Cheer you up a bit, that sort of thing," he said light-heartedly.

As Mr. Bell surveyed his goddaughter closely, his brow creased in puzzlement. "My, but you look well!" he noted with curiosity.

Margaret blushed and dropped her head coyly before she looked up again, her face pink and glowing with happiness. "I am well. I am engaged to be married!" she informed him gladly.

"My word!" Mr. Bell exclaimed with surprise. "I must confess that I am exceedingly jealous. I see that my offer to entertain you is not required. You are positively beaming, my dear!" he teased. "Who is the fortunate gentleman? Anyone I know?" Mr. Bell inquired with a knowing grin.

"I believe you may have already guessed," she challenged him, with a twinkle in her eye.

"Mr. Thornton," he conceded, with a wry smile.

Margaret nodded.

"I wish you every happiness, my dear. You will make an extraordinary match. He is a good man. Your father would be pleased," Mr. Bell told her.

"Do you think so, Mr. Bell?" she asked him, pleased to hear his opinion.

"Yes, but he was quite certain you did not like the poor fellow," Mr. Bell confided.

Margaret cast her eyes downward as she remembered her former attitude towards her betrothed. "I was very unkind to him at first. I judged him wrongly, I'm afraid," she confessed.

"Indeed. He is a very private man. It's difficult to get to know him," Mr. Bell acknowledged. "I believe you will do him a world of good. At least, I expect he won't be scowling about in the future," he remarked, a gleam in his eye. "As for his mother, I think it is a nigh impossible case," he said as he winked at her.

"Mr. Bell!" she laughingly protested.

"Now, then," Mr. Bell began more seriously, "I thought you might like to escape your present confines for awhile to enjoy a bit of culture. I'm told that the Sacred Harmonic Society is quite magnificent," he informed her. "Would you care to join an old codger for an evening at the Strand?" he asked.

"Really? I have not been to a concert in such a long time. I should love to go," Margaret responded enthusiastically.

"Good. Then it is settled," he replied as he gave her an appreciative smile.

Mr. Thornton closed the office door behind him and made his way into the dusty courtyard, headed for home. There would be no more postal deliveries today, and he had still had no word from Margaret. A dull ache began to form in the pit of his stomach. He was certain she should have received his letter by now. *Why had she not answered?* he wondered, painfully recalling his written plea that she reveal her feelings.

He wanted to believe that her aunt had prevented her from writing, that somehow she had been thwarted in her attempts to communicate with him. Although it filled him with dread to think that Margaret's relatives did not approve of him, it was comforting to believe that her intentions were unchanged. Certainly, he thought, Margaret must be of age, and was able to make her own decisions.

He did not wish to dwell upon any other reason for her silence. The possibility that she had changed her feelings for him threatened to paralyze him with fear. What if she preferred to live in London? Perhaps she had been persuaded that a better match could be found there, or she had recovered from the shock of her father's death and had come to realize that her affections for him were casual and fleeting. The contemplation of such ideas seized him with a pain so great that he felt he could not breathe. How would he survive if she were to refuse him again? He felt his heart had not yet healed from the blow of her rejection that fateful day when he had first told her of his love.

Mr. Thornton forced himself to consider instead the news of Margaret's brother. It gave him great hope to know that she had not loved another, as he had so foolishly believed. The shock of discovering that she had a brother had increased his desire to speak with her, and he had decided that he should go to London to ensure that her brother safely abided in Spain and to warn her of the impending inquiry.

He knew, though, the real reason why he was going. He could no longer abide the torture of living in this state of limbo, caught between eager hope and utter despair. He needed to know that his future was secure, that she would come back to live in his house and sleep in his bed. He needed to know that she loved him.

As he stepped into his dining room, he untied his cravat. It had been a strenuous day, and he longed to be released from all of his anxieties.

His mother entered the room across the way, having just come from the kitchen where she had given additional instructions to the cook. "You are home early," she noted, giving him a cursory glance.

"It has been a long day," he replied wearily, heading for a comfortable chair in the drawing room.

"Is everything all right?" she asked, studying him closely as he sat. "What did the man from the Navy want?" she asked, remembering the stranger who visited earlier that day.

Mr. Thornton gave her a puzzled look.

"He came to the house and asked for you," Mrs. Thornton said, answering his unspoken question.

Mr. Thornton gave a low sigh. "He was looking for a man charged with mutiny," he began slowly.

"Here? In Milton? Were you able to assist in the case?" she asked with great interest.

Mr. Thornton looked at his mother and took a deep breath. "The man he was looking for is Margaret's brother," he revealed.

Mrs. Thornton lowered herself onto a chair and stared at her son in bewilderment. "Her brother?" she repeated with disbelief.

"He is in Spain now, but he came to Milton to see his mother before she died," Mr. Thornton continued, allowing his mother the chance to consider what he had said.

Mrs. Thornton stared blankly at the carpet, her brow wrinkled in concentrated thought. After a moment, she lifted her head to meet her son's searching gaze, her expression one of sudden realization. "The man at the station…" she reasoned aloud, "it was her brother."

Mr. Thornton gave her a small smile of acknowledgement.

Mrs. Thornton was quiet for a moment, recalling with remorse the tongue-lashing she had given Margaret for her perceived indiscretion. She felt a modicum of sympathy for the girl. Mrs. Thornton recognized now that Margaret had withstood undue censure for her brother's sake. She was impelled to grant the girl credit for her strength and grace under such difficult circumstances, and discerned that Margaret had the capacity to be faithful and true. "I misjudged her, John," she offered as an apology to her son, unable to look him in the eye as she spoke.

Mr. Thornton was grateful for her admission, but remained silent.

"I have decided to go to London," he announced quietly, hoping his mother would understand.

She looked up at him. "When?" she asked.

"Tomorrow," he answered, "I do not wish to wait to settle things," he vaguely explained.

"You are uncertain?" Mrs. Thornton assessed, discerning the uneasiness in his voice. She felt compassion for her son. He had suffered much heartache in his quest for Margaret's hand, and now that he had received her consent, unfavorable circumstances threatened to undermine his confidence in securing it.

Mrs. Thornton wished to reassure him, but still held reservations about the wisdom of choosing such a wife. Mrs. Thornton had never met a more impetuous or strong-headed young woman than Margaret Hale, nor a more proud and independent one. It annoyed her that John would dismiss the girl's faults as inconsequential. In fact, he rather seemed to admire the girl for them. Did he not foresee how unmanageable she would be as his wife? It would be far better for him to find a girl who would respect his authority and possess more docile manners and feminine proclivities to help maintain the respectability he deserved as Master of Marlborough Mills.

But John would not change his mind. He would have Margaret as his wife, and it would behoove her to accept her son's decision in this regard. It had been her duty and privilege these many years to support such a fine son as he in all his endeavors for success. She did not wish to stand in his way now.

Was it possible that Margaret had truly changed in her regard for her son? Did she love him? Mrs. Thornton would not know for certain until she had seen with her own eyes how the girl treated him. But the elder woman reasoned that since it was now clear that Margaret had not had another lover, her motive for marrying John seemed genuine. That she should choose to return to Milton when she could remain in London gave Mrs. Thornton cause to believe that Margaret may indeed have fallen in love with her son.

"It is well you should go to London," she said firmly. "It will allow Margaret to explain everything to you. You have not had time to speak to one another," she asserted him, eliciting a surprised but grateful look from her son.

"Do you have a ring for her?" she queried, remembering something that she had been considering.

Mr. Thornton hung his head in discouragement. "No. I thought I would have more time…" he began.

"Stay here. I may be able to help you," she informed him, and left to go upstairs.

When Mrs. Thornton returned she held out a small piece of jewelry to him. "It was your grandmother's engagement ring. It belonged to your father's mother, Sophie Thornton," she told him, as he gently took the ring from her, examining it closely with reverence. The ring held a blue oval sapphire surrounded on either side by a cluster of small diamonds. The edging and band were delicate gold filigree.

"Your grandmother had blue eyes, like your father," she remembered aloud. "And, as I recall, she was a bit of a fiery spirit herself," she said, giving her son a candid smile.

Mr. Thornton was speechless for a moment. "Thank you," he managed to say at last. "Will she like it?" he asked with a boyish yearning for assurance.

A wave of tender affection washed over her as she saw his deep need to be loved. She fervently prayed that he would find his happiness, even as she felt a tug of jealousy to know he would not look to her for it. She hoped the girl would love him as he so deserved to be loved. "It is beautiful, John," she stated as a matter of fact. "If she truly loves you, she will be honored to wear it," she promised him.

Mr. Thornton glanced at his mother to ascertain her sincerity, and then looked down again to stare at the object in his hand with wonder.

Margaret was enraptured. The somber, floating tones of the tenor's solo spoke to her of the trials and losses that beset mankind. An occasional tear slid down her cheek as she was beckoned to recall her own sorrows. And when the choir and orchestra swelled to the full, glorious heights of praise to the Creator, she felt her soul fill with wonder at the goodness of God and man. She had never been so moved by music before.

Mr. Bell enjoyed the concert immensely, but found even greater enjoyment watching the music's effect on Margaret. He had noticed her moist eyes and the subtle movements of her lips, and he had been fascinated to see her face glow with joy at the mighty strains of the full chorus.

As the last majestic chord broke into silence, they both joined in the hearty applause. Margaret turned to give Mr. Bell a radiant smile in appreciation.

Mr. Bell was deeply impressed -- Margaret was truly the most extraordinary woman he had ever encountered. Mr. Thornton was a very fortunate man indeed. Mr. Bell was utterly convinced that winning Margaret's heart was Mr. Thornton's crowning achievement.

Chapter Six

The rhythmic sound and steady movement of the train slowly coaxed Mr. Thornton into a restful sleep. It was sorely needed; he had spent hours lying in bed the previous evening imagining countless scenarios of his impending reunion with Margaret, and he had woken very early to board the first train to London.

He awoke from his nap to find himself being studied by a young lad across the way. Mr. Thornton gave the boy a kind smile, which the child returned before turning his attention back to the window.

Mr. Thornton pulled out his father's pocket watch to determine the time. It was after ten o'clock. He would be in London within the hour. His nerves pricked as he thought that soon he would discover his fate. Would she welcome him with eager joy, or would he find her manner chilled with a practiced civility?

If only he knew why she had not written! He worried that her family might persuade her to release him of his obligations. Now that Margaret was bereft of father and brother, and had no other male family to care for her, Mr. Thornton knew that custom would have her safely married, and that she had tacitly designated him as her protector when she had announced their engagement. How he longed to fulfill that role, and marry her as soon as possible! If she held any affection for him at all, he hoped she would not be convinced to cast him aside for some London gentleman. He would do anything to secure her promise; he would not allow others' opinions to stand in their way. He refused to lose her again.

The train rolled through the countryside. Flowers spotted the lush grass that covered the ground, and the fresh smell of spring permeated the air. There was nothing in Milton to compare with it. This thought cut him with its undeniable truth. How natural it seemed to envision Margaret growing up in such open verdure. Was he so selfish that he would keep such a beautiful flower in Milton to brighten his own colorless world?

Would that he were gentry, and could offer her a country manor where he imagined she belonged. But his life's work was in industry, and could not escape the confines of the city. Could Margaret find happiness in such a place?

He recalled with a kindling of hope that she had declared that her heart belonged in Milton. Mr. Thornton remembered the thrill that had shot through him when he had first heard those words. That she would want to be with him was his greatest hope.

He was still astounded that she had announced their engagement in front of her aunt. He shivered to recall the way she had looked at him at the station that day, and prayed he would soon receive such a look again. Could she truly be in love with him?

Mr. Thornton remembered kissing her hand and the surprising way in which she had received his kiss! His hopes soared to dangerous heights to imagine that she might gladly receive his more ardent ministrations. He had long dreamed of how it would feel to kiss her, and felt a rush of exhilaration to think of finally bestowing a kiss upon her lips.

She was so beautiful! He could not stop thinking of her day or night. For months, she had haunted his dreams with elusive images of loving entreaty. But now that she had promised to be his wife, the vision of her was even more vivid, more alive.

Mr. Thornton's thoughts eventually drifted to the events of the day before. The shock of discovering that she had a brother had diminished, and he was now able to consider more deeply how the consequences of that secret had affected Margaret.

He felt tremendous compassion when he contemplated how faithfully she had kept her brother's secret at the time of her mother's death. How lonely she must have felt, and how frightened she must have been for her brother's safety during the scuffle with Leonards at the station. Mr. Thornton regretted that had not been there at the right time. If he had, perhaps he could have helped in some way. Instead, he was disgusted to recall how he had left the station in a self-consumed huff of jealousy and wounded pride.

How much time he had wasted agonizing over that whole scene! He had wrestled mightily with her perceived impropriety, and had been endlessly tormented by the notion of her loving another. Was he so blinded by his foolish jealousy that he could not have discerned the truth?

It pained him to think how his angry words must have added to the burden of isolation and forbearance Margaret had carried. How he wished he could have been a companion to her in her hardship, and that she had felt she might come to him as a safe harbor from storm-tossed seas.

He vowed she would never again have to face life's trials alone. He would do everything in his power to protect and comfort her. No wife would be more cherished or loved than she, he fervently promised. He only yearned to know if she would accept his love.

Margaret breakfasted late, cheerfully recalling the grand concert of the night before. She had been quite weary upon retiring late the previous night, but was feeling wonderfully refreshed today.

The warm sunshine poured through the windows of the dining room, creating a glowing pattern of elongated rectangles on the Oriental carpet. The morning sky was solid blue, promising a beautiful day and beckoning Margaret to enjoy the outdoors.

Eventually, Margaret joined Aunt Shaw, Edith, and Maxwell in the parlor. "Good morning," she greeted them brightly.

"How was your evening at the Strand, Margaret?" Edith asked, curiously. "I have not been there in some time myself," she noted aloud, giving her husband a demure glance as a subtle hint.

"It was absolutely wonderful," Margaret enthused, her face expressing her delight.

"I'm glad you enjoyed going out, Margaret," Aunt Show commented. "It was kind of Mr. Bell to visit you at such a time," she allowed.

Margaret gave a small smile in agreement, and sat down in the heavy upholstered chair opposite Edith and Maxwell, to chat and read. But as the morning wore on, Margaret became increasingly restless and was unable to concentrate on her book. "It looks to be quite lovely out today. I think I should like to take a short walk," she finally announced, rising from her chair.

"Alone?" Edith asked with a look of surprised concern.

"I will not go far, I would just like to enjoy the fresh air and see the open sky," she told them.

"Maxwell, could you not accompany her?" Edith asked her husband hopefully. Captain Lennox had just stood in acquiescence to his wife's entreaty when his brother entered the room.

"Henry," Margaret greeted him kindly, a trace of uneasiness in her voice.

"Margaret, I was very sorry to hear about your father. My sincere condolences," he said with proper solemnity.

"Thank you," Margaret replied in kind.

"Perhaps Henry would care to accompany you on your walk, Margaret," Edith readily suggested. "Margaret was just going out for a walk," she explained to Henry.

Henry smiled at the prospect. "It would be my pleasure," he gallantly offered.

"Very well," Margaret replied with a polite smile, and they headed for the door.

"Henry doesn't know about Margaret, does he, Mother?" Edith asked with concern, when the couple departed. Edith had hoped Margaret would take an interest in Henry while she was in London, and was still disappointed that her cousin had other plans.

"No, he doesn't," Aunt Shaw answered plainly. "Perhaps Margaret will tell him herself," she suggested doubtfully, her face unsmiling.

Outside, Henry and Margaret began to stroll silently side-by-side down the avenue, maintaining a slight distance between them. Margaret was happy to be in the sunshine, and relaxed a bit as she looked about.

"You've been away," she commented with a lilt in her voice, filling the silence between them.

'Yes, I had business in Edinburgh," Henry replied. "I returned just yesterday," he added.

"You had a very long journey. Did you enjoy the scenery? I have heard how lovely it is there," Margaret asked.

"I suppose, although I fear I am not one to appreciate nature the way you do," Henry complimented her, watching for her response.

Margaret avoided his gaze, feeling a little flustered by his warm tone. "I used to think that everyone appreciated the outdoors as I do. Or at least that they would, if they were given the opportunity," she admitted.

"You must be glad, then, to no longer live in Milton. There is no beauty there to commend it," he remarked.

"It is true that there is not much in the way of fields or forests there, but I found that there were other things to appreciate," Margaret told him, wondering how she might tell him her news.

"Oh!" she suddenly cried out, losing her balance and teetering precariously.

Henry lurched forward to steady her, grasping her forearm firmly. "What is it?" he asked in alarm.

"I believe my heel is stuck between the cobblestones," Margaret explained as she attempted to release her foot from its trap. "Oh, dear," she exclaimed with exasperation. "I've broken it," she announced, stepping forward to reveal the piece of her heel that remained lodged between the stones.

Henry stooped down to retrieve the remnant, wiggling it loose and putting it in his coat pocket. "Are you all right?" he inquired with concern. "Shall I call a cab?"

"No. I'm quite all right, just a little surprised. We have not gone far, I'm sure I can manage to return home," she assured him with a faint smile.

"Allow me to assist you," he replied, proffering his arm with a satisfied smile.

"Thank you," she answered politely, taking his arm.

Margaret endeavored to carry herself with a measure of grace as they began their return to the Harley Street house.

❦

Mr. Thornton was glad to escape the tedious confines of the train compartment. It was invigorating to utilize his long legs to bring him closer to his purpose. He made his way briskly through the streets of the city, valise in hand, towards Harley Street.

The promise of her sweet affections, expressed in tender glances and soft-spoken words, quickened his steps and buoyed his hopes. The thought of touching her, of finally claiming her with his arms and lips, ignited his passion. As he came ever closer to his destination, the corners of his mouth began to crawl upwards in an uncontrollable smile.

As he rounded the last corner, his eyes focused on a couple a short distance ahead. The lady was leaning against her companion in a considerably conspicuous manner. He froze as he recognized the lady – it was Margaret. As the pair turned to enter the short walkway to the house, he caught a glimpse of the man accompanying her. He was young and handsomely dressed. Mr. Thornton watched helplessly; he heard the low voice of the gentleman, followed by a delightful burst of laughter from Margaret.

Mr. Thornton staggered from the unexpected blow of this vision, grasping the wrought-iron gate to steady himself. A slow, sickening feeling rose from his stomach as he thought of how comfortably she nestled against her escort. His heart constricted in pain as he recalled the sound of her laughter. How he had dreamed of being the recipient of such a beguiling gift!

Had he been so easily replaced, he wondered? He felt as if his world were crashing down around him as his dreams shattered.

Mr. Thornton's breathing became quick and uneven as he strained to think of what he should do. He was tempted to leave, to return where he belonged so that he might never have to see her again. But he knew that he must face his fate squarely. He had come to determine if she was true to her word, and he would not leave until he had heard from her own lips what she would make of him.

Gathering his resolve, Mr. Thornton released his hold on the gate, straightened himself, and determinedly walked to the door and knocked. The footman bade him enter the main hall, upon hearing Mr. Thornton's introduction.

Overhearing the low voice, Henry Lennox was intrigued by the appearance of the Milton manufacturer. "Mr. Thornton, what brings you to London?" he asked. "Henry Lennox," he added as a way of formal introduction, extending his hand.

"Mr. Lennox," Mr. Thornton acknowledged with guarded civility, unable to bring himself to smile beyond a slight twitch of his face as he reluctantly but firmly shook the London man's hand.

"What brings you to London?" Henry inquired again curiously, leading Mr. Thornton to the back drawing room, where he could speak privately with him.

"I have some personal business to discuss with Miss Hale regarding matters of her father's estate" he replied, unwilling to disclose anything of his true purpose.

"I see," Henry drawled, regarding Mr. Thornton suspiciously as he beckoned him to be seated. "Tell me, Mr. Thornton, how is business faring in Milton?" he requested with a wily smile.

Margaret had just changed her shoes and was descending the stairway to rejoin her family when she caught her breath to hear the familiar velvet tones of a Darkshire accent coming from the drawing room. *He was here!* Her stomach fluttered, and she thrilled to hear his voice. A warm smile spread over her face as she walked through the doorway.

Both men rose from their chairs. "Margaret," Henry greeted her fondly. Mr. Thornton thrust his chin upwards, his eyes coolly regarding her. He did not smile.

Margaret's heart sank and her smile vanished to see his stern face. He was not pleased to see her. She began to tremble inwardly to think that he had changed his mind after all. She stared vacantly at the floor, trying to maintain her composure.

"Mr. Thornton has been telling me that the Milton economy has not quite recovered from an unfortunate strike last summer," Mr. Lennox commented glibly, aware of something odd in Margaret's behavior.

"If you would please pardon us, Mr. Lennox, I have some private matters to discuss with Miss Hale," Mr. Thornton requested politely in a constrained voice that barely veiled his impatience. His eyes remained transfixed on Margaret.

Henry looked to Margaret for her assent.

"It's all right, Henry," she assured him, giving him a weak smile.

Mr. Lennox glanced warily at Mr. Thornton before he exited the room.

Mr. Thornton brushed closely by Margaret as he crossed the room to close the drawing room door. "You have known Mr. Lennox a long time?" he asked flatly.

Margaret did not move, but held her breath as he moved past her again. "I have known him for a few years. We met shortly before Edith's wedding to Captain Lennox," she answered dutifully.

"You enjoy his company?" Mr. Thornton continued, his fists clenching involuntarily at his sides.

"Yes, I suppose. Why do you ask such a question?" she queried in bewilderment, looking up at last to search his face.

"I saw you out walking just now. You seemed very....close," he said, his voice tight with seething jealously.

Margaret was stunned to find herself accused, and felt a flare of righteous anger ignite within. Incredulous, she stared at him, noting how severe and formidable he appeared as he stood glaring at her. Upon closer reflection, however, she saw the hurt in his eyes that he tried to hide, and a sadness that revealed his yearning to be saved from this torturous speculation. He was jealous of Henry! Her heart went out to him as she realized how little he must know of her true feelings. She felt a tender compassion well up inside of her for all that he had endured in his love for her, both in the past and at present. Her foremost wish was to wash away his pain.

"I can explain," she began gently. "You see, while we were out walking, the heel of my boot came off, which made walking more difficult for me. I found it helpful to lean on Henry for support," she explained. "I am sorry if I have appeared indiscreet. I do not wish to dishonor you," she added meekly, her eyes cast downward.

Mr. Thornton was amazed by her conciliatory manner, which rekindled his hope. He felt a stab of self-loathing to see her express remorse for what now appeared to be an innocent occurrence. She did not deserve his jealous accusations!

He took a step closer to her, willing her to look up at him. "Margaret, forgive me. I have done nothing but think of you since you left. We did not have the chance to speak to each other. I wished to hear from you, and when you did not write..."

"I did write to you!" she exclaimed, as she took a step towards him. "I did not receive your letter until two days ago, but I did write you," she earnestly promised him.

A flood of joyous relief washed over him to realize she had not forgotten him, and he thrilled at her eager reassurance. "What did it say?" he asked, his voice wavering just above a whisper as he waited breathlessly for her response.

Margaret smiled sweetly at him and took another step closer. "I told you how much I enjoyed your letter," she said gently, watching for his response.

"Margaret!" he hoarsely whispered, marveling at her simple revelation.

"And I asked if you would forgive me for my rash behavior at the station," she continued. "But I didn't want to lose you. I was foolish enough to let you go once. I couldn't let you go again without letting you know the depth of my feelings," she confided, searching his face to see if he understood.

"Margaret!" he exclaimed with a tremor of emotion. "You once said that you did not like me," he reminded her, his eyes searching hers for the truth.

Margaret bowed her head, ashamed to recall her harsh words. "I did not like what I thought you to be," she confessed, unable to look at him. "I did not know you then," she said quietly, and slowly raised her soulful eyes back to his.

"And now?" he asked, moving closer still as he reached out to touch her cheek. His thumb gently stroked her silken skin in heightened desire as his eyes drank in her feminine beauty.

"I have come to think very highly of you," Margaret quavered as she turned her cheek into his hand.

Mr. Thornton grasped her arms, his eyes scanning her face intently. "Do you love me, Margaret?" he demanded urgently, desperate to hear her avowal.

"Yes," she answered immediately, instinctively averting her eyes. The next instant, she determined she would not hide from him and returned his gaze. "I love you, John," she admitted freely, drowning in the depth of his blue eyes.

Mr. Thornton swiftly enfolded her in his arms, binding her to him. "Margaret!" he rasped, nestling his face into her sweet-smelling hair. The joy of hearing those words from her lips and the feeling of her soft form against him at last threatened to bring him to tears.

Margaret rested her head upon his chest, her arms gently encircling his waist. She marveled to feel so at home in his strong embrace, the sound of his rapid heartbeat comforting her. She breathed in deeply, smelling the closeness of him in the faint scent of sandalwood.

After a few moments of sublime stillness, Mr. Thornton rubbed his cheek against her hair, and gently moved his hands up the length of her back. He began to caress the back of her neck with his fingers, reveling in the soft feel of her.

Gently lifting her head from his chest, he placed delicate kisses on her temple. His lips brushed softly against her skin, descending down her cheek in agonizing slowness. Margaret felt weak with the breathless anticipation of his final kiss. When at last he reached her mouth, he pressed his lips gently against hers.

She was not prepared for, could never have imagined, the warm, melting sensation that coursed through her body at that first intimate touch. She was stunned to find herself completely overwhelmed by the simple union of their lips. Slowly, she began to move her lips in concert with his, reveling in the softness of his touch. As his kisses became more insistent, she eagerly responded.

When at last he pulled away, he gazed at her in tender adoration. "You will be my wife?" he asked, still not believing that she would truly choose to be his.

"Yes," Margaret answered, giving him a blissful smile. She still felt wobbly from his amorous attentions.

"I have something for you," he told her as he reached into his waistcoat pocket to pull out a small object. He held out a ring to her, watching her face for her reaction.

"Oh," she exclaimed, gently taking the ring from his fingers and studying it with reverent fascination. "It's beautiful," she uttered, unable to take her eyes off the gift.

"It was my grandmother's. Her name was Sophie Thornton," he informed her, gratified to see her obvious appreciation for the family treasure.

"I shall be honored to wear it," Margaret promised him, finally looking up at him, overjoyed to receive such an exquisite token of his love.

"May I?" Mr. Thornton asked. Gently taking the ring from her grasp, he fit it upon her third finger. Kissing her newly adorned hand, he took both of her hands and placed them around his neck with a satisfied smile.

"I can vaguely recall how it felt to have your arms about me," he murmured. "Yet it was so long ago, I'm afraid my memory needs refreshing," he teased.

She blushed to recall her impulsive act the day of the riot, but obediently slid her hands around his neck as he requested. "Like this?" she asked, her eyes dancing in playful delight.

"Yes, just so," he said with a glorious smile. "But this time I shall request that you keep them there," he told her, his arms tightening around her.

"And this time I shall willingly obey," she promised, looking lovingly into his beaming face.

Mr. Thornton thrilled to experience her soft submission, since she had spent most of their history together defying him!

A rap on the door drew them abruptly apart. The maid opened the door and said, "Mrs. Shaw asks if you will join them in the parlor."

"Thank you, Ellen. We shall be there momentarily," Margaret replied to the relieved girl.

"Your aunt…" Mr. Thornton had forgotten to ask about her. His eyes questioned Margaret with cautious hope.

Margaret understood his concern. "She did not look favorably on our engagement at first," she began.

Mr. Thornton's brow furrowed in indignation, his pride quickly touched. "She would prefer you to marry a London gentleman," he surmised, his anger rising.

"Yes," Margaret answered honestly. "But I do not wish to marry anyone but you," she quickly reassured him, reaching out to gently grasp his arms.

"She has tried to convince you that you could marry better," he continued, unable to let the subject rest, so galled was he by the thought of it.

"She could never convince me. I have told her that there is no finer man than you, John," she declared, seeking to soothe him. "She knows that I will not be persuaded against you," she assured him.

Mr. Thornton confirmed the truth in her eyes, his expression softening as he saw the unwavering affection in her gaze. He smiled in amusement to imagine Margaret's fiery defense of him against the onslaught of her aunt's adamant opinions. "You are indomitable!" he declared, studying her with a sense of admiration and pride, as he wrapped his arms around her waist and drew her against him.

"Perhaps," she reluctantly admitted, not wishing to appear to him so truculent. "But I shall be very amenable to my husband," she sweetly promised with an adoring smile.

Her husband! The word conjured up images of the close relationship he would soon share with her, and a lump formed in his throat. He swallowed hard. "Your aunt will be waiting," he croaked unevenly, and reluctantly moved to release her from his embrace to guide her to the door.

Margaret gracefully linked her arm through Mr. Thornton's as they entered the front parlor together, softening her fiancé's entire demeanor with her possessive gesture.

Maxwell was the first to greet the new visitor. "Mr. Thornton, how good to meet you! Maxwell Lennox," he introduced himself as he stood up to shake Mr. Thornton's hand heartily. "I must congratulate you on your engagement. I confess I have been quite interested to meet the man who has persuaded a Helstone girl to live in Milton," he said in good humor.

"Thank you. I cannot speak for Miss Hale, but I assure you that I am well aware of my great fortune," Mr. Thornton replied with candor, feeling his heart swell with pride to acknowledge aloud their betrothal.

"Indeed," Henry intoned, "I am surprised to find that Margaret will settle in a place so unlike her Paradise," he commented with a stilted smile, throwing Margaret a stinging glance. He had been told of Margaret's intentions only minutes ago and was still burning with deep disappointment and indignation to find his plans of courting her instantly abolished. "Congratulations, Mr. Thornton, on winning such a fine prize," he praised with a hint of sarcasm, conceding his loss with a slight bow of the head. Mr. Thornton bristled, but retained his faultless poise.

"May I wish you every happiness for the future," Henry formally addressed Margaret, narrowing his eyes in feigned indifference, his practiced smile fading.

"Thank you, Henry," she warily accepted his felicitations as she tightened her hold on Mr. Thornton's arm.

"Mr. Thornton," Aunt Shaw called out, seated on the sofa next to Edith.

"You must forgive me for my hasty manner of last week. I am sure you understand that the circumstances were very disagreeable," she said.

"I am sorry to have appeared importunate and am grateful for your forbearance of my sudden intrusion that afternoon. Miss Hale and I had not discussed our situation," he replied as he gave Margaret's arm a slight squeeze.

Aunt Shaw was tempted to be impressed. Mr. Thornton seemed to be well-spoken and carried himself like a gentleman. She was relieved, too, to discover that he did not speak in the colloquial tongue in which she had feared he might.

She had inquired about Mr. Thornton's reputation at every turn this past week to learn what type of man he was. In every instance, he had been touted as a trustworthy and intelligent businessman. These evaluations had reassured her that Margaret's judgment of character was sound.

Mr. Thornton was properly introduced to Edith, who was also impelled to assess him favorably for his gracious manners and fine bearing. She smiled charmingly, but held lingering doubts about the man her cousin had chosen.

Henry excused himself abruptly from the party, claiming to have several matters needing his attention due to his recent absence.

Luncheon was announced shortly thereafter. During the course of polite conversation at the table, Maxwell discovered that Mr. Thornton would only be in London one evening and had not yet secured a room for the night.

"You must stay here, then," Maxwell magnanimously offered without a second thought. "We will keep company with you and Margaret this evening," he added, noting the look of alarm on his mother-in-law's face. "You are soon to become family, after all," he reasoned openly, giving Margaret a warm smile. She exchanged a brief glance with Mr. Thornton, who was seated across from her.

Aunt Shaw was taken aback a moment, but hastily approved her son-in-law's friendly invitation so as not to appear ungracious. "Yes, of course. I will have Ellen ready a room," she offered. She had reservations about such an arrangement, but decided that his visit would not be long enough to merit undue anxiety.

So it was that Mr. Thornton became a welcome guest at the house in Harley Street, much to the delight of the newly engaged couple.

Not long after returning to the parlor, Mr. Thornton suggested that Margaret join him for a walk. Her previous attempt to enjoy the outdoors had been thwarted, and she was eager to be alone again with her betrothed.

"You are well cared for here?" Mr. Thornton asked with a twinge of trepidation as they started down the street. He had carefully observed the grand and beautiful home in which Margaret had been ensconced, and noted how rested and content she appeared now. He hoped she would not grow so fond of her quiet life in London, that she would hesitate to return to Milton.

"Yes, everyone has been very kind," she replied wistfully with a forced smile.

"You miss your father," he said quietly, discerning a lingering sadness in her manner. He had not forgotten the reason they had been parted this past week.

"Yes," Margaret confided, "I was not prepared…I wish that he could have…," she stopped, struggling to find the words to convey her feelings.

Mr. Thornton halted and turned to face her, his eyes regarding her with tender compassion as she avoided his gaze. "You have suffered much. I wish to be of comfort to you, if you will allow me," he offered earnestly. "I will miss your father as well. Truly, he was a good friend to me," he reminded her gently, willing her to look at him.

Margaret lifted her head to see his face glow with such tenderness that her eyes misted over. How good he was to her! She felt the burden of loneliness lift from her, unaware that she had long been wearing its mantle. The sweet promise of his tender solicitude filled her with aching gratitude. But as the memories of her father's fond relationship with Mr. Thornton began to flood her consciousness, she felt the tears well up until they begin to fall unbidden from her eyes. How she wished her father had lived to see their happiness!

Her tears surprised him, moving him to gently gather her in his arms, heedless of their surroundings. He held her in silence, content to patiently wait until she would release him of his service.

Mr. Thornton handed a handkerchief to her when she stepped back to recover herself. "How silly of me," she began to apologize as she dabbed at her eyes.

"It is not wrong to have deeply loved," he told her softly, loving her all the while for her tender heart.

Margaret regarded him with loving appreciation, and threaded her arm once more through his as they continued their walk to the park. "I wished that father could have shared in our happiness," she confided as they walked. "He was very fond of you. I think he would have been very glad to see our match," she told him with a measure of sorrow in her voice.

"I am not certain he was aware of my interest in his daughter," Mr. Thornton mused with a wry smile. Indeed, the Hales had not seemed to notice his attraction to Margaret.

"No, I don't believe he was. But he did begin to wonder when you stopped coming so often to your lessons," Margaret hesitated to tell him, uneasily recalling how she had refused his initial offer of marriage.

Mr. Thornton hung his head, remembering the terrible emptiness he had felt when he discovered she would not have him. "I could not bear to see you at times," he admitted, "I wanted so much to have you in my life, and you would not have me," he confessed, wincing at the memory of it.

They arrived at a bench in the park and sat down under the shade of a large oak tree. "I am sorry for it, John. You do not know how much I regret my words," she ardently declared, her eyes pricking with tears to imagine how deeply she had hurt him. Why had she been so vehement? She had stunned herself that day with her impulsive and harsh defense. Why had she felt so threatened?

"Why did you...?" he began, his pain still evident in his questing eyes.

Margaret looked down at her hands, not knowing how she could explain the conflicting emotions that had consumed her that morning. "I...I don't know. I was confused and a little frightened, I suppose. I did not expect that you should truly care for me," she started to tell him. "I was embarrassed that others' should misconstrue my motives in...in protecting you. I did not want you to feel it was your duty to rescue my honor," she continued haltingly. She looked up to find he was patiently listening, his eyes studying her.

"Why did you protect me, Margaret?" he asked. "You braved the danger of an angry crowd for my sake."

"I was the one who put you in danger," she asserted with regret. "I could not bear to see any harm come to you, John," she remembered.

"When I saw you lying lifeless at my feet, I knew I could not live without you," he told her. "I asked you to marry me because I love you, Margaret. Did you not believe me?" he asked, yearning to plunge to the depths of her hidden, nascent feelings for him and bring them to the surface.

Margaret stared at her hands again, endeavoring to make sense of all she had experienced. "I don't know. I was not prepared to hear it, I suppose. I did not understand...I was afraid to think I might have feelings for you," she admitted, bringing her eyes up to meet his adoring gaze.

Mr. Thornton's face illuminated to imagine that she had even then felt a stirring of affection for him, although she had fought mightily to repress it. Perhaps Higgins had been correct - she had tried to deny her feelings.

"When did you know that you might care for me?" he gently demanded, eager to know how long he had suffered in vain, thinking that his love was unrequited.

She hesitated, taking a few breaths before returning his searching gaze to guiltily confess. "When you left the room," she answered quietly, with slight trepidation at how he might respond.

Mr. Thornton stared at her in disbelief. He was astounded at her answer. He had spent months writhing in the agony of her rejection of him, when all the while she had been harboring a secret affection for him! Why had he not discerned it?

"Margaret, if I had only known!" he exclaimed with poignant yearning to reclaim the time they had spent estranged from each other. He took her hands in his, bringing them up to his lips to kiss her fingers. "I thought you were lost to me!" he said fervently, remembering that he had thought her to be in love with another man.

His words brought to Margaret's mind the recollection that he had seen her with Fred at the train station, and that she had not yet told him about her brother.

"I have something I must tell you," she said seriously, wishing now to dissolve any secrets between them. He looked at her expectantly, uncertain of her intention.

"I have a brother who came to visit when mother was dying. He was the one you saw with me at the station," she blurted out, finally looking to see his reaction. She was surprised to find him calmly regarding her with a faint smile of admiration. "You know..." she stopped herself.

"I only discovered it yesterday," he told her candidly, bracing himself for the task of telling her of the Navy's inquiry. "Margaret, you have been brave to keep your brother's secret amidst so much adversity. But you will no longer need to face difficulty or sorrow alone," he promised earnestly, holding her hands in his and staring intently into her luminous eyes. "I wish to be a comfort and protection for you. You do not know how much I wish it," he solemnly avowed, his love for her overwhelming him.

A strong breeze blew the loose tendrils of Margaret's hair and rustled the young leaves of the tree above. She felt suspended in an enchanted dream. His love permeated the very air she breathed, filling her soul with a peacefulness she had never known before. She could only stare at him in wonder of his very existence.

"The Navy came to inquire after your brother," Mr. Thornton told her calmly, not wanting to alarm her.

"What? Did they come to you?" she exclaimed in surprise, fear quickly taking hold of her.

"Yes, but they could find nothing, my love. All is well. If he is safely in Cadiz, no harm should come to him," he assured her.

"Oh, John, you did not know!" Margaret declared worriedly, releasing her hand from his to grasp his wrist. How shaken he must have been to discover the truth in that manner. "What happened? Why did they come? Will they come to find me?" she wondered aloud in agitation.

"They went first to your home, and Dixon sent them to me. It was a surprise, but I was not able to help them since I honestly knew nothing about him. Higgins told me afterward that he is in Spain," he told her. "I do not believe they will come to you. There is nothing they can do," he reassured her again, taking her hand to place a kiss upon her palm.

She was quiet for a few moments in contemplation of what had occurred. "Why could you not tell me?" Mr. Thornton ventured to ask, wanting to know why she had not trusted him before. "Was I so unapproachable, my love?" he queried cautiously.

"I wished to tell you, John. You don't know how much I wished to tell you, but I was afraid," she admitted with feeling. "Father wished to tell no one of it, and you are a magistrate. I did not want you to compromise your position," she told him honestly, hoping he would understand.

"I did not make it easy for you. I spoke harshly to you. I am sorry for it," he apologized, sadly recalling the words he had spoken to her.

"You said you had given me up," Margaret remembered tentatively, not wishing to hurt him, but curious to know why he had said so.

Mr. Thornton met her gaze honestly. "I wanted you to love me, and I thought you loved another," he smiled ruefully to think how foolish it now seemed.

"There has never been another," she declared lovingly, longing to release him from any memory of the painful misunderstanding. "I have not loved before. You are the only one," she confided, watching him as his eyes began to blaze with intensity into hers.

"And I have not loved before. You are the first, and the only one I shall ever love," he promised, studying the beauty of her face. He longed to taste her lips again and show her his ardent affection, but restrained his desire for propriety's sake. He lifted her hand to his lips once more and bestowed upon it a rain of deliberate kisses that revealed the fervor of his passion for her.

When they returned to the house later and settled down once more in the parlor, they had been there only a short time when Edith entered the room in obvious distress. "Oh, Margaret, you are back!" she called in relief to find her cousin and Mr. Thornton seated together on the divan. "Sholto has been quite uncontrollable and refuses to take his nap without seeing you!" she wailed.

"I will go to him for a few moments," Margaret assured her cousin. "I shall not be gone long," she promised her fiancé with a sweet smile.

A few minutes later, Mr. Thornton was surprised to see Margaret come into the room comfortably carrying a young child on her hip. Edith followed behind her in some dismay, looking to her mother in apology for Margaret's unconventional behavior. Aunt Shaw was shocked to watch her niece bring the child straight to Mr. Thornton's side. The girl was quite unpredictable!

Mr. Thornton was stunned. It was not the breech of custom or the sight of the boy that caused him to stare transfixed as Margaret settled herself next to him. It was the vision of Margaret holding the child that entranced him. It seemed to him the most natural thing in the world to see her thus occupied. He had never given much thought to having a family before, but now he felt a burning desire to see her hold his child – their child – in her arms.

"I should like you to meet Sholto. He has been a good companion to me this week, have you not, Sholto?" she asked the boy, who had become shy next to the stranger, and buried his head into Margaret's shoulder. Mr. Thornton smiled and pulled out his pocket watch to show the boy how the cover opened and closed.

Margaret directed Sholto's attention to it. "Look, Sholto," she coaxed him. Once the boy looked, he was intrigued by the shiny gold toy and slowly climbed into Mr. Thornton's lap to examine it further. Edith and Aunt Shaw exchanged surprised glances.

Mr. Thornton was amused by the boy's innocent curiosity and charmed by his willingness to sit on a stranger's lap. He was pleasantly surprised to discover his own inherent ease with the child. Mr. Thornton had never held a little one before, but found it strangely relaxing to enjoy the guileless qualities of the child and reached up to tousle the boy's hair.

He ventured to imagine how it might feel to hold his own child and turned his gaze to Margaret, who was fondly watching them. She caught her fiancé's gaze and returned his smile with renewed admiration.

The remainder of the day was spent pleasantly. Maxwell and Mr. Thornton were amicable companions, and spent a short time discussing the cotton industry together after dinner as the women retired to the drawing room.

"I believe that Maxwell has taken a liking to your Mr. Thornton, Margaret," Edith noted kindly, growing more accustomed to the idea of Margaret's engagement to the Northern manufacturer.

"Yes, Maxwell is a dear man," Margaret complimented her cousin in kind, grateful that Edith's husband was so affable and genuinely welcoming to his guest.

"It looks like Mr. Thornton is quite fond of children," Edith commented.

Margaret blushed at the implication of her cousin's comment. "I was not really aware of it, although I knew him to have a kind heart," she replied thoughtfully.

"He seems very fond of you, Margaret. I don't think he is quite able to let you out of his sight. How did you become acquainted with him?" she asked, curious to know how the couple had developed such a strong attachment.

"Mr. Thornton came often to discuss literature with father," Margaret explained. "He was father's favorite student," she added.

"And yours, it seems," Edith teased with a smile, causing Margaret to blush profusely in acknowledgement.

The men rejoined them a short time later, and Mr. Thornton's eyes immediately sought out his betrothed from across the room. Margaret smiled demurely to catch his affectionate glance. His short absence had seemed entirely too long to her, and she wondered how she had become so enamored of him in one day's visit.

The evening passed without event. Maxwell continued to converse with Mr. Thornton while Edith played the piano in the far corner. Margaret was obliged to turn pages for Edith, and stood by her cousin at the piano to perform her task. Several times she caught the heated glance of her fiancé as he looked at her from his seat in the dimly-lit parlor. Her stomach fluttered in response as she recognized his yearning to be free from the restraints of the company surrounding them. They had spent precious few moments alone together and were anxious to be reunited in private.

When Edith announced that she would retire for the evening, the party broke up, sending everyone to their rooms for the night with good wishes for pleasant sleep. Tomorrow, they would go to church, have luncheon, and spend a little more time together before he had to return to Milton.

As Margaret undressed and brushed her hair, she pined for her beloved. She wished fervently for the night to pass quickly so that she could wake to see him in the morning. Regarding herself in the mirror as she laid her brush down, she was fascinated to observe in her own likeness a woman in love. How much she had changed, it seemed, from the last time she had lived in London. She settled down in bed and tried to sleep.

Mr. Thornton was given the grandest guest room, but he did not notice the fine linens and elegant furnishings. His mind was too much beholden to the woman he loved. Today had been the culmination of his fondest dreams. He had claimed Margaret Hale as his future wife and taken his first taste of promised pleasures in her tender kiss.

Although the day had been replete with the joy of being with her, he was mystified to find his desire to be in her presence growing ever more insatiable. He reasoned that he should be satisfied with such a momentous day, but could not repress his aching need to see her again. To know that she was under the same roof seemed a type of delicious torture. He had no fear of losing his steeled self-control this evening, but he would not wish to test his endurance in this manner for any length of days.

He knew sleep might prove to be elusive tonight, but he resolved to at least lay still and rest.

Margaret rolled over and then sat up. She had dozed a little, but had woken for no apparent reason. She got up to get a drink of water, but discovered there was no glass in her room. She decided to go downstairs to fetch a fresh glass of water, hoping the small journey would aid in curing her restlessness. She donned her thin summer dressing gown and stepped into a pair of slippers. She lit the candle by her bedside and curled her finger through the brass holder to carry it with her out into the hall.

She was puzzled to see a faint light coming from the study at the end of the hallway, and conjectured that someone had inadvertently left a light burning in there. She headed down the hallway to snuff it out. Pushing the door open from its half-closed position, she was startled to find Mr. Thornton standing across from her on the other side of the room. His back was to her as he perused the volumes of books that filled the length of the wall. He swiveled to see who had discovered him, and was equally astounded to find Margaret standing just outside the doorway.

"Margaret!" he whispered aloud in wonder as he deftly maneuvered around the furniture between them to come to her, afraid she might vanish as a dream if he did not hasten to her side. He stopped at the doorway, taking hold of the doorframe with his hand as if to steady himself.

Margaret watched entranced as he crossed the room to her. She saw that his throat was exposed by the open collar of his shirt, and that his waistcoat was left unbuttoned, showing more of the thin cotton shirt that loosely covered his strong frame. She felt a warm flush as she recognized how handsome he was.

She instinctively clutched her dressing gown to her chest to be found in such a state of undress. She knew she should remove herself at once to fetch her glass of water, but found she could not move.

"What are you doing here?" he asked, finding his voice first. His pulse hammered as he took in the sight of her in her thin nightclothes. She looked like a goddess in her flowing white dressing gown, her auburn hair spilling down her back, laying in long tendrils around her shoulders.

"I…I was going to get some water, but saw a light here," she managed to say as a way of explaining herself, feeling a little out of breath to be standing so close to him. "What are you doing here?" she asked him in turn, casting her eyes downward to stare at the fabric of his waistcoat.

"I could not sleep and thought I might read," he explained in a soft, low voice that stupefied her. His eyes raptly travelled the length of her. Margaret stood in the dim shadow of his towering form; the candle flickering in her hand cast a warm glow on her face and illuminated the draping cloth that covered her body, revealing a tantalizing outline of her waist and hips.

"Do you often have trouble sleeping?" Margaret inquired curiously, her speech wavering as she cautiously lifted her face to meet his heated gaze.

"Lately, yes - when I cannot stop thinking of you," Mr. Thornton intoned breathlessly, his blue eyes blazing with ardor. He felt himself perilously close to certain danger. He knew he should disengage himself from her, allow her to recover her modesty and flee from his presumptuous gaze. But he could not tear his eyes from her for fear that she would indeed escape from him.

"Oh," Margaret uttered, transfixed by the intensity of his stare and the play of candlelight dancing across the chiseled features of his face. He was so close to her that she could smell the clean scent of sandalwood emanating from his body.

Wordlessly, Mr. Thornton reached out a trembling hand to grasp a long lock of her hair, watching in fascination as the silken tress passed languidly through his fingers. Margaret felt her knees weaken in response to this intimate gesture, and her heart pounded in her ears.

"I should go," she breathed, weakly attempting to recover her sensibility; however, she lifted her eyes to his and was drawn to him like a moth to the flame.

"Yes…you should," he whispered, bringing his face closer to hers, unable to resist the beguiling sight of her parted lips.

She did not move, but closed her eyes in anticipation of his touch. He brought his face to hers and gently sought her lips, allowing himself the luxury of a few stolen kisses before stepping away from her. Every fiber of his being ached in furious protest of his reasoned determination to act with honor.

Margaret's eyes flew open to find his head turned away from her.

"Good night, Margaret," he said with solemn finality, not daring to look at her as he bid her good night.

She felt a tug of shame and a broad measure of admiration for his strong resolve to end their clandestine encounter. She bowed her head and continued on her way down the hall and to the floor below to accomplish her original task.

Mr. Thornton watched in silent anguish as she swiftly retreated down the hall, her dressing gown floating delicately around her. "I love you," he heard her whisper before her lighted figure turned and disappeared down the stairs.

Overwhelmed by her honest admission, he stood with his mouth ajar, unable to breathe. He longed to chase after her and show her the depth of his affection, but he could not move. The contemplation of her guileless love for him made his heart ache with profound joy.

Rousing himself from his trance, Mr. Thornton extinguished the lamp in the study and reluctantly returned to his room. Closing the door behind him, he leaned heavily against it for support and shut his eyes. He felt drained of all energy; it had taken every ounce of will-power he possessed to let her go -- to not detain her a little longer and continue to partake of her delectable kisses. Slowly, the relentless pounding of his pulse subsided and he moved towards his bed.

When Margaret returned upstairs, she felt a pang of disappointment to see the darkened room at the end of the hallway. He had returned to his room. She chastised herself for being so immodest as to linger in his presence, and felt a twinge of shame to admit that she had not wanted to leave. In fact, she had wanted him to continue his affectionate ministrations. The strong feelings that he stirred in her were new and startling, overturning all her trained conduct and composure and awakening in her something entirely unknown and yet strangely natural.

She felt alive in his presence, as she had never felt before, and she wanted to experience more of it.

Climbing into bed once more, she remembered with sorrow that he would be leaving London tomorrow. She did not wish to be parted from him, now that she knew the wonderful feeling of his comforting arms and potent kisses. How would she endure the coming days and weeks without him?

She resolved to only think of the morrow, when she would be with him once more. She closed her eyes, hoping sleep would hasten the morning's arrival.

Chapter Seven

Margaret awoke early to find sunlight filtering through the translucent curtains of the Eastern windows, filling the room with a soft glow. She smiled to consider, as she usually did, what Mr. Thornton might be doing, since *this* morning it might easily be discovered. The contemplation of his proximity increased her excitement to see him.

Margaret threw off her coverlet to begin her toilette. She calculated that his many years of diligent work must have established in him a habit of early rising. She hoped that she might find him breakfasting alone, knowing that her family would not appear for their morning tea until later.

She was amused to find herself rushing about in her haste to see the man whom she would see every morning for many years hence. How was it that she could not stop thinking about him? She had scarcely been able to fall asleep, dreaming of the tender kisses he had bestowed on her last night in the shadowed doorway of the study. She had been unable to move, completely mesmerized by the nearness of him. In fact, she recognized that she could not concentrate on anything else when he was near. Was this how one acted when one was thoroughly in love? She felt the impulse to be with him with every breath she took, until it quite alarmed her with its intensity.

She set about brushing her hair and winding it into a coil on her head. How was it that only a week ago they had not known of each other's affections? It amazed her to think how markedly everything had changed since they had made their avowals. She considered herself almost a new person, and yet she felt much the same as she had as a young girl in her hope and expectation of good.

It was the renewal of joy in her life that she felt most acutely. The months of trial she had spent since moving to Milton were now seen in an entirely different light. All the events that she had so grievously endured had, in truth, only engendered the unique circumstances of their acquaintance and, consequently, their abiding love for one another.

Everything that had happened there now seemed to bind her inextricably to him. She did not believe she could be any happier, or love him any more, than she did at this moment.

Buoyed with anticipation, she quickly descended the stairs to the main floor, restraining herself from the inclination to run down them like a young schoolgirl.

As she stepped into the dining room, a cursory glance at the round breakfast table brought a pang of disappointment to find it unoccupied. In the next instant, her eye detected movement from the far side of the room. He had been standing at the window and now bounded toward her with a smile that warmed brilliantly as he approached her.

Margaret slowly drew her breath in as her eyes roamed over his tall figure. It struck her forcefully how handsome he was. He was especially well dressed, wearing the silver-gray waistcoat and matching cravat that Margaret recognized as the same he had worn at Fanny's wedding. She remembered how dashing he had looked that day, and remembered equally the sharp feeling of regret that had come over her when she had thought him lost to her. She recalled how unhappy he had appeared, and realized in an instant's insight that he had loved her even then.

They reached out simultaneously to clasp hands. "Do you always rise so early?" Mr. Thornton asked her curiously, looking at her with a measure of wonder that she should be there with him.

"Not always, no," she replied. "I thought I might find you here...before the others arrived," she admitted shyly.

Mr. Thornton marveled to discover her eagerness to see him. Could she be as drawn to him as he was to her? How irresistible she was to him! He could not refrain from touching her when they found themselves alone. "Did you sleep well?" he inquired, languidly moving his thumbs across the back of her hands.

"Yes, eventually. Did you sleep well?" she asked politely, recalling with some embarrassment what had happened late last evening.

"Eventually, yes," he replied with a mischievous smile as he released her hands to take hold of her waist and gently pull her to him. Margaret rested her arms softly against his chest.

"I had a dream that an angel in white robes came to me in the night," he began to tell her, staring with fascination at the features of her face that were so near to him now.

Margaret listened attentively until a gleam in his eye exposed his jest. "It was not a dream!" she protested, pushing away from him slightly, taking mock offense at his insinuation.

His eyes shone with mirth to see her response, but became gradually heated as he held her with the longing that had consumed him the previous evening. "Will you remind me of its reality?" he implored huskily.

She bashfully averted her eyes from him for a moment, but gradually moved her face closer, lifted her chin, and closed her eyes in compliance.

The memory of their midnight encounter had never left his mind. He gloried in the remembrance of her seductive beauty and the feel of her soft lips. Now that she stood submissively before him once more, his passion quickly rose. He fought to restrain himself from regaling her with the full force of his desire, reminding himself to treat her gently.

His touch came swiftly, causing Margaret to give a slight gasp in surprise. He gently plied her lips with his own, searching for the soft underside of her lips that made her tremble at his touch. Her heart beat rapidly, sensing his nascent urgency to know more of her. She wished to follow where he would lead, to experience more of his exhilarating kisses. She slid her arms around his neck to ensure his continued attentions.

Mr. Thornton groaned at the feel of her soft arms around him and instinctively pulled her closer. He brought one hand up to curl his fingers behind her neck, holding her fast to him while his pulse hammered furiously. How softly and willingly she melded to him!

Emboldened by her response, his kisses became more insistent as his mouth slowly coaxed hers to open to him, their tongues touching tentatively at first and then entangling blissfully in growing hunger. Lost in the heady sensation of his deep kisses, Margaret felt her whole body shudder in response.

Finally tearing his mouth from hers, he pulled away. They stared at each other in rapt wonder at their newfound intimacy, the sound of their ragged breathing filling the silence around them.

"Margaret, I don't know how I can leave you today," he said despairingly, his eyes frantically drinking her in. His body still pulsed from the powerful urges that racked him.

"Please, don't speak of it," Margaret begged him, unwilling to think of his departure later in the day.

Mr. Thornton gently held her face in his hands and studied it as if to memorize every nuance of her beauty. "Margaret, when will you marry me?" he asked desperately, needing to know when she would come home to him.

"I...I thought perhaps in June," she told him haltingly, hoping he would be pleased with the date she suggested.

"June?" he repeated vaguely, attempting to calculate how long he would have to wait. It was nearly May now. He gathered her hands in his and held them fast.

"Yes," she responded hesitantly, still uncertain if he was happy with her answer. "Is it too soon?" she asked anxiously.

"No!" he countered immediately, his blue eyes blazing with alarm that she might think so. "I would marry you and take you home with me today if it were possible," he declared in earnest, scorching her with his penetrating gaze.

Fear and elation stirred within her breast to recognize how profound was his passion for her and how zealously he would carry out his intent. "The reading of the banns takes three weeks," she gently reminded him.

"A special license can be obtained…" he began in earnest, haunted by the thought of how lonely his life in Milton would be without her.

Smiling endearingly at him, Margaret reached up to stroke the strong line of his jaw. "John, I shall marry you soon, I promise," she assured him. "But I think our families would not understand our haste. I think it is best we have a little time to prepare," she reasoned, taking his hand again.

He bowed his head in concession, not willing to appear unreasonable. The dread of isolation and emptiness began to settle over him. He hated to be parted from her, now that he knew the tremendous joy of her close company. How long he had wished for her sweet presence to fill his days!

"Let us marry three weeks from the morrow," Margaret proposed, moving the date back to accommodate his wishes. "It will not be long, John," she promised him.

Speechless, Mr. Thornton regarded her with elated hope and boundless love. She would be his wife in three weeks! He bent to kiss her again, his lips gently finding hers for a brief moment, until the sound of approaching footsteps interrupted them, drawing them apart.

"Your tea, sir," the maid announced as she placed it on the table. They stood a moment while the servant departed and quickly returned to place a second teacup on the table for Margaret.

They sat down to breakfast. "I have not yet asked how your mother received our news. I fear she does not have a very good opinion of me," Margaret said despairingly before taking a sip of tea.

"Her opinion has already improved," Mr. Thornton told her. "She will come to know you well. It is inevitable," he stated confidently as he gave her hand, which rested on the table, a reassuring squeeze.

He did not relinquish his grasp, nor did Margaret withdraw her hand. Gradually, their fingers began to mingle as if by their own impulsion, until they began to interlace and unlace with gentle fervor. Their teacups sat untouched as they both stared transfixed at the amorous dance evolving between them, amazed to discover the pleasure of such an unassuming gesture.

The spell was broken by the approach of Edith and Maxwell.

Withdrawing their hands reluctantly, they took up their neglected tea with affected normalcy. Margaret momentarily avoided Mr. Thornton's gaze to guard her poise.

"Good morning. I see that one must wake early to dine with Mr. Thornton," Edith commented brightly as Maxwell helped seat her at the table. "I suppose that your work requires you to be punctual," she said, addressing her cousin's fiancé.

"Indeed, I am predisposed to waking early, even when I am at my leisure," he answered her with a warm smile.

"And have you much time for leisure, Mr. Thornton?" Maxwell asked interestedly, having seated himself nearby.

"Not at present," he answered ruefully. "Unfortunately, my business requires strict attention."

"Oh, dear," Edith exclaimed with a look of sympathy towards her cousin. "I fear you may not see much of your husband, Margaret, once you are married," she surmised.

Margaret glanced quickly at her intended, who was observing her to see how she would respond. "I know that he often works long hours, but I shall not feel neglected. I hope he knows that I will anxiously await his homecoming, whenever that might be," she told Edith. Stealing a glance at John, she was happy to find that her answer pleased him.

Mr. Thornton's heart warmed to think of coming home to Margaret's loving attentions. For many years, he had worked with little reward but to advance his family out of debt. How pleasant it would be to have such a sweet reward awaiting him at the end of the day! A warm smile grew upon his face as he gazed at her with loving admiration.

"It seems a shame to be always so busy," Edith noted honestly. "Perhaps he might be persuaded to spend less time at the mill," she suggested.

Margaret smiled at Edith's remark, and glanced again at her fiancé. Although Nicholas had told her that Mr. Thornton sometimes worked late into the night, she hoped she might be able to lessen his burden somehow, and she couldn't help but hope that he would find more time to be at home.

"Perhaps I may," Mr. Thornton answered, looking directly at Margaret with a sly smile.

Margaret stared straight ahead at the dark paneled pulpit, her hands properly folded in her lap. The ornate beauty of the chancel and solemn atmosphere of the church reminded her that she would soon stand before God and man to recite the sacred vows of matrimony. She vainly attempted to listen to the vicar's sermon, but found her mind too full of other things.

She felt the dichotomy of being seated between her Aunt Shaw and Mr. Thornton. On one side, she was compelled to follow the dictates of society and righteous decorum; on the other, her senses were keenly attuned to the presence of the man who set her soul afire.

Without any movement of her staid countenance, Margaret could see the black length of his thigh touching the folds of her skirt, and was aware of how close his elbow must be to hers as he sat placidly beside her. She longed to touch him, to hold his hand as they had done this morning. Chastising herself for being so distracted, she repeatedly endeavored to concentrate on the echoing words of the vicar.

Mr. Thornton was having similar difficulties in paying attention to the religious proceedings. Seated next to Margaret, he found his mind incessantly occupied in remembering the feel of her body pressed to his, the soft pressure of her arms about his neck, and the rapturous warmth of her kiss. Acutely aware that such musings were inappropriate in church, he brought his wandering thoughts to the present only to find himself conscious of how near she was to him. He yearned to be free of the strictures of these surroundings, wanting to be alone with her so that he could hold her in his arms again.

When they both reached for the same hymnbook, their hands collided, sending a tremor of sensation through their arms and sparking their latent desires. Glancing briefly at each other in embarrassed confusion, they recognized their mutual attraction.

Looking on to the open book in John's hand, Margaret was enthralled by the rich sound of his baritone voice as the congregation joined together in song. Mr. Thornton was, in turn, enchanted with the melodious voice of his betrothed as she sang the familiar strains of a beloved hymn.

When at last the organ trumpeted the triumphal notes of the postlude, the couple stood gratefully and acknowledged each other with a shared smile. As soon as they escaped into the aisle, Margaret gently took his arm, reveling in the simple pleasure of this conventional contact.

The corners of Mr. Thornton's mouth edged upwards as he felt the gentle pressure of Margaret's arm wound within his. It pleased him immensely to think that henceforth she would thus appear with him in public. Captivated by her unparalleled beauty and grace, he watched as she conversed charmingly with a few of Edith's acquaintances. Margaret retracted her hand a moment as she obligingly showed her engagement ring to the small gathering of women. Mr. Thornton marveled to see her glow with happiness as the ring was dutifully fawned over with lavish praise and cheerful felicitations. The fact that she seemed proud to be linked with him, a plain uneducated man amidst the throng of gentleman and ladies dressed in their Sunday finery, filled him with amazed gratitude. How he had won her was still a mystery to him, but he knew he would hold her fast to him the remainder of his days.

As they emerged into the brilliant sunlight, the family parted ways as Mr. Thornton and Margaret deferred the carriage ride for a leisurely stroll, giving themselves the coveted time alone they both zealously desired.

Walking in comfortable silence for a few moments, they enjoyed the steady movements of their synchronized gait as they contemplated the converging paths of their future. The sounds of passing carriages and chirping birds; the sight of the gilded doorways and gates of the street were all lost to them as they ambled down the walkway in perfect contentment at being together.

"Do you wish to marry in London?" Mr. Thornton quietly asked at length, seeking to gain a clearer image of his wedding day and solidly secure the event in the definable facts of place and time.

"No," Margaret answered. "It should be a quiet affair," she said softly, a trace of sadness in her voice.

Mr. Thornton knew at once her meaning. Her recent loss was never far from his mind, casting a shadow of lingering sorrow over the joyous events of the past week. He gave her hand a gentle squeeze with his own free hand. He was aware that the wedding would need to be simple and private – even Milton might be too busy for such an occasion.

"I thought perhaps we could marry in Helstone. I should like to show you the village," she confided, hoping he would be interested in seeing her childhood home.

"I would very much like to see it," he answered readily. Margaret glanced at him, and was pleased to see his approval confirmed by a warm smile.

"Perhaps we could stay a few days," she was emboldened to propose, knowing that she was impinging on the prerogative of the groom to plan the wedding trip. "If you can take the time away from the mill, of course," she hastened to add.

"For our wedding holiday?" Mr. Thornton inquired casually, although the subject attracted his rapt attention.

"Yes," she faltered, feeling her cheeks burn as she continued. "I believe I may be able to secure very pleasant lodgings in the countryside. There are a great many lovely walks we could take," she suggested anxiously.

Amused by her daring initiative on the matter, Mr. Thornton complied willingly with her plans. "If you will relieve me of the duty of making such preparations, perhaps I will find more time to prepare the mill for my absence. I believe that I can manage to be away for a week without precipitous damage to the business," he remarked with a mischievous smile.

Surprised by his easy manner, Margaret looked askance at him to determine his intent. "You wish me to make the plans for our stay?" she asked, still a little uncertain.

"If you will let me know of your plans once you have arranged them, I am perfectly happy to allow you to chose our lodging. I am confident you know the area quite well," he calmly elaborated. "In fact, I will only concern myself with the reading of the banns and contracting the services of the vicar. You are at liberty to make all other arrangements according to your fancy, my love," he told her with an affectionate glance.

In truth, Mr. Thornton was very grateful to have a small wedding which would not require his attention. He had grown extremely weary of Fanny's endless chatter concerning the details of her extravagant wedding some weeks ago. He trusted that Margaret would have good sense as well as excellent taste, and would accomplish everything with aplomb.

Margaret returned his loving gaze and hugged his arm a little closer with a contented smile.

When they returned to the house, Mr. Thornton and Margaret found the family comfortably seated in the front parlor, awaiting the dinner hour. Margaret's arm remained linked around her fiancé's as the couple stood in the middle of the room. Having recently settled the date and location for their nuptials, the couple had decided to announce their plans to the family.

"Did you enjoy your walk?" Edith asked politely.

"Yes, very much," Margaret answered candidly, before looking at Mr. Thornton with some anxiety.

"Mrs. Shaw," Mr. Thornton formally addressed Margaret's aunt. "I am very much obliged to you for your generous care of my fiancé since her father's death," he kindly thanked her. "Margaret and I have settled on an arrangement for our marriage that will allow me to assume proper responsibility for her without extensive delay. We will have a quiet wedding in Helstone in three weeks' time," he announced with calm authority.

"So soon?" Edith blurted, disappointed that she would lose her cousin's company within a month.

Aunt Shaw raised her eyebrows slightly, but acknowledged Mr. Thornton's right to claim her niece with a gracious bow of the head. She was surprised to note her growing admiration for the man - his manners were faultless, and his bearing was at once thoughtful and commanding. It was obvious that he was quite infatuated with Margaret, and she sensed that he would be a devoted husband.

She noted that Margaret seemed pleased with the announcement. Aunt Shaw sighed inwardly, however, as she contemplated Margaret living in that dismal, dirty city amongst the working classes. She dearly hoped her niece would be happy with the life she had chosen. "Margaret, my dear, are you pleased with this arrangement?" she inquired, wishing to make certain the girl was prepared to take this momentous step in a few short weeks.

"I am," Margaret answered happily, "I never wanted a grand wedding," she confessed, smiling contentedly. "I shall very much enjoy having a small wedding in father's old church."

"Wonderful!" Maxwell exclaimed, "I have not had the opportunity to see this idyllic Helstone," he cheerfully remarked. Edith gave a forced smile in a meager attempt to match her husband's enthusiasm.

The afternoon passed all too quickly for the lovers, who spent most of their time seated next to each other, holding hands and conversing with each other or with the others. Margaret and Mr. Thornton were thoroughly relaxed and happy. They endeavored to banish from their minds the bane of his impending departure from London until the hour of the afternoon tea approached.

The arrival of Dixon punctuated the lazy atmosphere of the house. Margaret swiftly rose to fondly greet her mother's dearest servant in the doorway of the drawing room and inquire if she had received her letter explaining her recent news. Dixon had not expected to find Mr. Thornton in London, but was surprised to note how normal it seemed to see him here with her mistress. He looked quite resplendent in his dapper clothes and easy manner. Although he could never be a proper gentleman, Dixon was pleased for her mistress' sake to see that he could be easily mistaken for one.

Dixon quietly asked Margaret if the Master could spare a moment of his time to speak with her. Margaret hesitated, but went to fetch her betrothed.

"Have you told Miss Margaret about the inquiry?" Dixon whispered worriedly when Mr. Thornton arrived at her side.

"Yes, she knows of it. I told her that it is unlikely they will pursue the matter further. Mr. Hale should be safe if he remains abroad," he calmly assured Dixon.

"I didn't mean to send that horrid man to you, but I didn't know what to do," she began to apologize.

"It was right to send him to me. The matter should be at an end now," he told her. She nodded and took her leave to settle herself in the servants' quarters.

Dixon's appearance reminded Margaret of Milton and the home that would soon be hers. She had recently made up her mind to write Mrs. Thornton a letter of conciliation, but had not done so yet. She explained her purpose to her fiancé and moved to settle herself at a writing desk across the way, while Mr. Thornton picked up the newspaper, a poor substitute for her company.

Shortly thereafter, Edith excused herself and went to the nursery. Her husband followed suit a few minutes later, leaving the engaged couple alone in the drawing room, Aunt Shaw having departed for her usual rest some time before.

Mr. Thornton's hands were dutifully employed in holding the paper, but his mind was otherwise occupied. His gaze turned often to Margaret, who sat positioned at the desk in a way that allowed him to see some of her profile.

Aware that she was being watched, Margaret smiled to herself before speaking aloud. "I fear I must ask you to find another diversion, Mr. Thornton," she said with mock solemnity, not taking her eyes from her task.

Taken aback by her implied allegation, he opened his mouth to speak, but then closed it as a wicked smile formed on his lips. Laying down *The Times* with decision, he stood and crossed the room to her. With one hand on the back of her chair, he leaned over to speak close to her ear. "I find you to be the most diverting thing in the room," he told her in a sultry voice that sent shivers down her spine.

Her quill stilled, but she attempted to appear unaffected. "How can I finish this letter to your mother if you insist upon distracting me?" she asked pointedly, her body tensing in anticipation of his response.

"If you will bestow upon me a few moments of your undivided attention, I will allow you to finish your task in peace," he suggested in the same low voice, more determined than ever to tempt her to leave her work. He straightened, obviously expecting her to rise from her chair.

"I fear that my attention, once given, will be required of you longer than you imply," Margaret replied haughtily, keeping him at bay a little longer.

"It is entirely possible," he admitted with a mischievous smile, her feigned resistance to his request increasing his desire to see her.

"And you promise to let me go?" she taunted him, still seated at the desk.

"Only this once," he answered. "I make no such promises of the future," he added, a tinge of warning in his voice.

She quietly put her quill back in its holder. "I am glad of it," she replied as she finally rose to face him with a playful smile.

His smile broadened and his eyes sparkled with amusement for a moment before becoming heated with ardent affection. He was amazed that she should be standing there waiting for his fond attentions.

He reached out to hold her waist and she stepped forward to drape her arms about his shoulders. They gazed into each other's eyes a moment before closing them as their lips met in a kiss. Tenderly, their lips converged, gently grazing and exploring the sensation of this simple but intimate union, restraining with effort the ferocity of their growing desires until at last their mouths opened tentatively to each other for the deeper kisses they had tasted once before.

Their hearts pounded as they felt the quickening flames of ardent passion rise about them. Mr. Thornton was the first to retreat, fulfilling his promise. "I told you I would let you go," he panted, his body protesting its stifled pleasure.

"Mmmm," she mumbled in faint agreement with his words, all the while resisting his message. She made no movement to withdraw from him.

"The drawing room door is open. I must not take such liberties..." he rasped unevenly, grasping for a reason to stop and allow her the opportunity to escape from him.

"There is no one nigh at present," she whispered in reply, her face still flushed with longing.

His resolve melted at her words and he renewed his ministrations with vehemence. He pulled her flush against him, causing her to emit an indiscriminate noise in surprised response.

Margaret struggled to keep pace with his fervent kisses, quivering in frightened delight at his ardent passion. Pressed against his firm body and aroused by his masterful kisses, she felt herself melt under his blissful possession.

Mr. Thornton burned with desire, falling further into unquenchable flames as he allowed himself to briefly satiate his longing to be one with her - to bodily claim her as his own with his unyielding kisses. He knew he must stop, and calling forth the full force of his reasoned self-control, he tore his mouth from hers and loosened his tight grip.

Astonished by his own potent reaction to her willing submissions, he cautiously sought her gaze to determine how she had fared under such treatment, his chest still heaving with barely bridled passion.

Margaret slowly raised her eyes to his, taken aback by her own abandoned behavior under the spell of his amorous demands, while her pulse gradually lessened its rampant beating.

Detecting the slight trepidation in her eyes, he hastened to apologize for his rash behavior. "Margaret, I...you do not know how it makes me feel when you allow me to love you like that," he endeavored to explain, his hands still caressing her waist.

"I think I may know something of what you describe…" she openly admitted, bravely holding his gaze so that he might understand her meaning.

"Margaret!" he breathed, marveling at the revelation that she might feel something of the same impulses that coursed through him so readily. Mr. Thornton drew her close and gently kissed her forehead. Taking her face into his hands, he searched it intently, amazed to find only her unabashed love for him. "Margaret, I dared not dream that you should care for my touch! I fear I will not be able to survive long without your kisses!" he ardently declared.

Margaret gently covered his hands with her own. "I do not wish for you to leave me," she confessed, but then smiled to remember his earlier promise. "It seems you have detained me a little longer than you intended," she remarked ruefully.

"I fulfilled my rightful obligation," he insisted defensively. "I gave you the opportunity to take your leave of me, which you promptly ignored," he accused her with a devious smile.

"Did I?" she inquired innocently, feigning a forgetfulness of her own culpability.

"Yes, you did," he emphasized slowly, straining to keep himself from pulling her to him once more.

"Then I suppose I must confess that I find you equally distracting, Mr. Thornton," she teased him with a coquettish smile.

His smile broadened as he comprehended her meaning and he threw aside his restraint to draw her to him once more. "Then perhaps you will consent to being distracted a moment more," he suggested, his eyes revealing the ardor that quickly replaced his playfulness.

She smiled at his request and lifted her chin in consent. Their mouths met with a gentle firmness, and they kissed slowly and deliberately for a lingering moment until both gradually withdrew from the pleasurable contact.

"I will allow you to return to your letter," he told her, at length, unable to take his eyes off her as he marveled at their familiar intimacy. "I will ready my things for my departure, and return to you soon," he promised in a soothing voice. With those words, he kissed her forehead once more and departed from the room.

Margaret stood motionless for a few moments, deep in thought, before returning to the desk to finish her task.

Mr. Thornton's London visit drew to a close when afternoon tea was cleared away. After fond farewells and gracious thanks were exchanged in the parlor, Margaret escorted her fiancé to the grand hall to say their good-byes.

He turned to her upon reaching the door and wordlessly held out his arms. She rushed to fall into them, wrapping her arms around him in fierce possession, her cheek pressed against his chest. His long, dark overcoat shielded her embrace, enveloping them in a moment suspended in time and space – hidden in a world all their own. Mr. Thornton breathed a slow, shivering sigh of rapture to feel her clinging tightly to him. Allowing a hand to travel up the length of her back, he reached the soft column of her neck and nestled his fingers in her hair to hold her close against him.

He could not move or speak, wanting only to remain forever in this embrace, feeling as if his heart would burst with love for her. Everything he wanted was firmly in his grasp at this moment. How he hated to leave! The insidious sinking feeling of loneliness began to creep over him as he thought of returning to Milton without her. "Margaret, I need you with me!" he cried out hoarsely, as the months of longing for her came to the fore, crashing over him with sudden force. "We could marry in Milton…" he began desperately, before being silenced by Margaret's fingertips gently touching his lips. He grasped them in his hand and kissed them fervently.

Margaret regarded him with tender compassion, her heart also leaden at the thought that he must leave her behind. "It is settled, John," she said softly, gently reasoning with him. "We will marry soon, it will be well enough," she reassured him, her eyes imploring him to understand. "I also wish never to be parted from you," she confided. "Soon it will be so, John. We will never be parted again," she promised earnestly.

Her words soothed him, and he mutely nodded his accord. He bowed his head, ashamed of his unguarded outburst.

Margaret moved to pull a small cloth from the folds of her skirt. "I wish to give you something of mine – a very meager token of my love, I'm afraid," she told him as she held out to him a delicate handkerchief, edged in fine lace.

He took it eagerly, cherishing anything that would remind him of her. He examined the embroidery carefully to see a tiny yellow rose and her initials inscribed in colored thread.

"I have always loved the yellow roses growing around our home in Helstone," she explained with a sheepish smile. "I will have to change my initials. I will no longer be Margaret Hale, but Margaret Thornton," she added thoughtfully.

The sound of her name attached to his tugged at his heart, winding around it a tight band of excruciating joy. She would be his!

With utmost resolve and infinite tenderness, he placed a lingering kiss on her lips. "I will see you in Helstone, my love," he said as he caressed the loose tendrils of her hair with his fingers. Releasing his hold on her, he gave her one last penetrating glance before opening the door and walking through it.

The sound of the door as it clicked shut echoed in the hall, unexpectedly harsh in its finality. Margaret stood still; the empty walls of the room seemed to loom larger, unsympathetic to her sorrowing heart. She felt the separation from him keenly. The one person who knew her and loved her best was gone. She felt panic slowly rise in her, as she realized that she would not see his face or hear his voice in many days.

Caring nothing for appearances, she hurried past the parlor entrance to the back drawing room, rushing to the window to find one last glimpse of him.

She caught sight of him and watched for a brief moment until his dark-clad figure disappeared around the corner. She put her hand to the window and moved her lips in a silent adieu.

Mr. Thornton forced himself to continue walking, straining to overcome the frantic urge to turn back at each step. How he longed to cast aside the barriers of custom and propriety and return to her aunt's home, to lift her into his arms and carry her to the train station so that she was forced to come home with him to Milton! He clung to the remaining fragments of his inherent reason, mastering the motions of his body with steadfast resolve as he placed one foot in front of the other to continue to the train station. He always thought of himself as having an iron will, but the trials of this day proved it beyond a doubt. How else could he leave his heart behind in London?

He arrived at the station, and boarded the train to Milton with resignation. The weight of responsibility began to settle over him - the shackles of obligation and duty slowly displacing the sublime freedom he had known during his short stay with Margaret. He must return to the mill and renew the interminable schedule of his work. He would come home to his mother and sleep in an empty bed, as he had done for years.

The meaningless chatter of the strangers around him seemed only to amplify his solitude. Unclenching his fist, he was comforted to find the sole remnant of his visit. *Margaret would be his wife. Soon, he would no longer live alone.* The thought of it made his chest ache with its profound promise of happiness. Grasping her handkerchief in his fist once more, he pressed it against his face for a moment to breathe in the faint fragrance of jasmine. He brought his hand to rest on his lap, keeping tight hold of the small piece of fabric as the train slowly started its long journey north.

Margaret was relieved when dusk came and she could remove to the privacy of her room. She had attempted to remain cheerfully cordial with her family since Mr. Thornton's departure, but felt the dull ache of his absence with every passing hour.

Alone in her room, she was content to sit and dream of him, remembering wistfully the bliss of his strong embrace. How much she missed him already! She had felt so at home in his arms that she could no longer imagine living without him. She smiled to think how akin her sentiments were to his now – that she would marry him tomorrow, if only she had dared to agree!

But there would be much to do in the coming days to prepare for the wedding. Three weeks would pass quickly enough, she told herself. If she kept herself busy, she would not feel his absence so sorely.

A knock on the door jolted her from her reverie. Dixon let herself in at Margaret's beckon.

"I am glad you are back," Margaret commented as her mother's dear confidant began to help her undress. "It seems so much has happened since I left you in Crampton," she continued.

"Indeed it has," she exclaimed as her eyes widened in agreement. "It was quite a shock, I can tell you, to find you had engaged yourself to the Master," she told her. "It was your father that held such a high opinion of him. I didn't think you paid him any attention," she remarked. "Other than that time he came to tea…," she added as she loosened the lacings of Margaret's corset.

"I had noticed him, Dixon. I was not sure how to view him, I suppose. Things were so different in Milton," she told her.

"Huh!" she retorted gruffly. "About as different as could be! I never saw such a filthy, crowded place. It was enough to frighten your poor mother, I'll tell you," she continued disdainfully.

"Dixon," Margaret called her attention firmly, but kindly. "Milton will be my home, I do not wish you to disparage it," she reminded her. "Do you wish to stay here in London?" she tentatively asked the family's faithful servant, uncertain if Dixon would wish to return to the city she disliked.

"Of course, not, Miss Margaret!" she exclaimed in consternation as she helped her mistress slip into her nightgown. "My place is with you. Your mother would have wanted it," she affirmed. "Besides, I would hate to see you have to do battle with that woman all on your own!" she added decisively.

Margaret stifled a giggle to realize how pervasive Mrs. Thornton's stern reputation was in Milton. "I don't think she will be difficult to deal with, once we understand her ways of doing things," Margaret tried to convince herself.

"Humph!" Dixon huffed doubtfully as she began to brush out Margaret's hair. "Just the same, I don't want you to have to learn your way around that house all alone," she firmly stated.

"Thank you, Dixon," she replied. "But I won't be alone. I'm getting married - Mr. Thornton will be there," she reminded her with a lighthearted smile.

"Hmm," Dixon responded knowingly, doubting the Master would know ought of the household domain to which Margaret would be relegated.

"Dixon," Margaret began cautiously, "I have not told you – we are to marry three weeks from the morrow," she informed her, watching for the servant's reaction in the mirror.

The brush stilled a second before resuming its brisk course. "So soon, Miss Margaret?" she asked in slight dismay, wondering what her late mistress would have thought of such an arrangement. "And here I've come rushing to London for such a short stay," she shook her head, despairingly.

"I'm sorry, Dixon. Everything has happened so quickly, I'm afraid. But we wish to be together as soon as possible," she explained honestly.

Dixon raised her eyebrows in response, curious to know if such a feeling was indeed mutual, or if her mistress had been pressed to give up her maidenhood at the earliest date. She had not had time to truly observe the couple and could only surmise from Mr. Thornton's behavior in Milton that he was eager to marry. Whether Miss Margaret was as thoroughly in love, she had not yet determined.

Studying Margaret's face a moment longer in the mirror, Dixon began to see for herself. A dreamy-eyed stare and lingering smile told her all that she needed to know - the girl was besotted. Dixon heaved a sigh and finished braiding Margaret's long auburn hair.

Smiling at last, Dixon relished the thought of seeing her mistress happily married. "You will make a beautiful bride, miss," she told her mistress in a congratulatory tone.

Margaret beamed. 'Thank you, Dixon," she replied as she gave her a peck on the cheek and bid her good night.

Snuffing out the lamp, Margaret was drawn to the beauty of the moonlight pouring in the window and lighting the crimson carpet with the sun's borrowed brilliance. She stepped to the window to gaze at the shining white orb. Silently spreading its glorious glow over all the earth, the moon seemed to stand watch over the mortal scenes below. Staring out at the calming sight, she thought of her beloved – far away, under the same moon.

Slowly climbing into bed at last, Margaret was mystified to feel paper under her shoulder. She knew her letter from Mr. Thornton was safely tucked away in a drawer. She sat up and picked up the new envelope. Angling the paper to the moonlight, her heart began to beat rapidly as she recognized her name scrawled in John's handwriting.

Hastily, she climbed out of bed to relight the lamp on the nearby dresser. Tearing open the envelope, she pulled out the folded paper to read her lover's message.

My darling Margaret,

I love you, and will always love you.

For months I have been enslaved to you, seeking a word or a look from you that would give me hope of gaining your affections. Did you suspect how your voice and your slightest touch affected me?

I dared to dream of making you my own, longing to fill my days with your enthralling presence. Even when it seemed you would not love me, I continued to love you with my whole heart, unreservedly.

Can you imagine the joy that was mine to hear from your own lips that you love me and will be mine? – how I feel when you look at me with tenderness and wrap your loving arms around me?

When I hold you in my embrace I feel such astounding happiness that I never want to let you go. Is it any wonder I wish to marry you instantly so that my bliss will not end, so that I will not perchance awake to find it all a dream?

Margaret, I love you. I do not know of any other way to adorn this sentiment with words, but wish you to know the depth of my affection and how much I long to be with you, to spend every moment with you. You have captivated my heart and my soul, and I resign myself most contentedly to this sweet captivity forever.

I am entirely yours,

John

Margaret read it twice more with rapt attention. Finishing the last lines again, she drew a deep breath, unaware that she had been holding it for some time. She moved to stare out the window and contemplate the emotions stirring in her breast. The moonbeams bathed everything in a soft glow, mirroring the ineffable love she felt radiating her life. She held the letter to her breast as a gentle smile of pure happiness spread across her face.

The evening air was cool, and the moonlight cast deep shadows across the landscape of the city. Mr. Thornton walked unhurriedly towards his home, taking in the full brilliance of the heaven's display over the manmade structures surrounding him. The rows of plain homes, the brick facades of the factories, and the painted storefronts all shone with a white light that seemed to transform the mundane into illumined magnificence.

No longer fated to toil endlessly with little hope of experiencing life's higher joys, he found his future glowing bright with a love that outshone everything he had known before. It seemed that Providence would restore to him the years that the locust had eaten, and that he would find sweet recompense for all the struggles and sufferings of his past.

He felt his hope soar even as it mixed with the solemn thought of her long absence. He was eager to bring her home to Milton, so that they could begin their life together. He did not believe he could feel completely at peace until she was his - irrevocably and entirely his.

As Mr. Thornton approached his home, he was relieved to find the house darkened. He would have time enough tomorrow to tell his mother his happy news. He relished the present opportunity to cherish all that happened in the secret chambers of his mind without the prying comments of others.

He made his way to his room without candles or lamplight, walking through the dim shadows and patterns of light gliding in from the windows.

Setting his valise down inside his room, he untied his cravat and shrugged off his coat, removing from the breast pocket the letter Margaret had written for his mother. Laying his coat over a chair, he moved to deposit his cravat and the letter upon his dresser, noting curiously another envelope clearly set out upon its surface. Picking it up with interest, he began to breathe more rapidly as he quickly realized it could be the letter from Margaret he had long awaited.

He hastened to light the lamp on his desk along the far wall, and studied for a moment the look of his name written in her elegant handwriting. He carefully opened the envelope, urgently desiring to read the words she had carefully written for him alone.

My dear John,

Your endearing letter has given me much pleasure. I should not wish to read flowery words of professed love that are shallow vanities of truth, but I shall never tire to know of the sentiments which move you to write to me with such stirring honesty.

Until I discovered your heartfelt message within the pages of the book you gave to me, I thought you had foresworn your love for me. The knowledge that you still cared for me opened the door to my hope for happiness and revealed to my own suffering heart how much I had come to love you in return. I had not dared to dream of regaining your affections after all that had passed between us.

It was with newfound hope that I sent Nicholas to you with my response. God bless him for his prompt dispatch! I had no thought of what you might do in return; I only wished you to know that I would welcome your affections – that they would no longer meet with cold indifference or harsh disdain.

I cannot tell you how I felt when I heard you call my name, as I waited to board the train for London. I knew instantly, when I turned to see you, how deeply you must feel for me – you, who pursued me in the bitter cold without thought of donning coat or gloves! I could scarcely breathe as I waited to hear what you would say, and when you asked me to marry you, my heart leapt at the chance to answer aright what I had so foolishly declined before.

John, I hoped you would forgive me for my bold assertion that day! I could not let you leave without an answer – without telling you somehow the joy that would be mine to claim a place by your side as your wife. Aunt Shaw would not have understood our impetuous meeting! I felt I had no choice but to announce ourselves engaged as if it had already been established between us. I don't think I have ever seen you look so surprised, but I am certain now that you did not dislike my decision to speak so impulsively.

I will be your wife, John. It will not be a dream. I know I have hurt you most unconscionably in the past, but all that is done away. I know now who you truly are, and I cannot help but love you for all the kindness, strength, and selfless endeavor that I see in you. It shall be my privilege to be your wife and to bring you every happiness which is in my power to bestow.

I wake each morning thinking of you, and find my wandering mind constantly drawn to the thought of you. Will you believe me now if I tell you that I love you? I have never had such feelings before – you, alone, have the power to affect me so.

I long to come home to Milton, where I belong, so that we will no longer be apart. Until then, I eagerly await for you to visit me in London so that you may fulfill your wish and that I may feel your strong arms around me.

With all my love and affection,

Your very own Margaret

Mr. Thornton closed his eyes to remember the unparalleled bliss of holding her tight against him, his longing so intense that his arms veritably ached to hold her. He let out a low sigh and opened his eyes to the present.

Still clutching the letter in his hand, he moved to the window, looking out at the moonlit scene of the mill yard below. Margaret was far away now - the distance between them was great. *But she would come*, he thought, laying aside the anxious yearning for her immediate presence that threatened to invade his peace. *She would come and transform his life into something entirely new – something indescribably beautiful.* A smile of deep contentment slowly illumined his face.

Chapter Eight

The pink light of early dawn cast its first rays on the mill yard as Hannah Thornton sat waiting at the breakfast table. She had been restless during John's absence, torn between the hope of his happiness and the niggling worry of being displaced in her own home. She prayed that John would return from London with the knowledge that Margaret would accept his hand. It was unthinkable to imagine otherwise.

In spite of her hopes for John's happiness, Mrs. Thornton could not help but dread the girl's coming to live with them. She imagined that as mistress of Marlborough Mills, Margaret would bring a host of changes to their daily routine and customs. She would bring her Southern ways and graces to bear on the household in some manner; Mrs. Thornton was convinced of it. And John would no doubt delight in and indulge her every whim and fancy, oblivious to whatever consequences such indulgence may have.

Reflecting more deeply upon her anxious judgments, Mrs. Thornton was inclined to admit that Margaret did not seem the type of girl to spend an inordinate amount of attention to matters of décor or domestic detail, unlike Fanny who seemed to constantly fill her thoughts with the latest fashions and ostentatious display.

Perhaps Margaret would not deign to redecorate or make dramatic alterations in the established running of the house per se, but would instead suggest to John how he might run his mill, conjuring up some additional scheme meant to improve the lives of the workers at the mill's expense. Mrs. Thornton was certain the workers' kitchen that John had established could be attributed to Margaret's influence, and worried that the girl would attempt to meddle with John's authority and decisions in business.

A sigh escaped her lips as she thought of how vulnerable her son might be to his wife's manipulations. Mrs. Thornton had never seen John so unguarded as when it concerned Margaret Hale. He practically worshipped the girl, and would not hear a word against her. This was what most worried her, she decided: that John would unwittingly abandon his long-practiced reason to follow the dictates of this young woman, who knew next to nothing of the hard work and trials that had enabled him to attain his present position in business and society.

Mrs. Thornton was certain that John would not have told Margaret of the mill's present financial troubles, not when he wished to secure her hand in marriage. But she would need to know soon enough that her life here would not necessarily be one of ease and carefree habit as she may imagine it to be. She would need to appreciate the wealth that John had already carefully secured, as well as maintain a healthy respect for the caution and insight needed to ride the stormy cycles of the industry in which he worked.

The sound of her son's quick footsteps descending the stairs broke the train of her troubled thoughts. She was relieved to see his easy smile, even as her stomach churned to think of its meaning.

"Good morning, Mother," he greeted her cheerfully as he took his seat.

"Good morning, John," she replied in her usual moderate tone. "Your trip went well, I presume?" she inquired casually, permitting him to bring up the pertinent details of all that had transpired since he had departed.

"Yes, all is settled," he told her as a warm smile spread across his face, the memory of Margaret's sweet affections filling him with effusive joy.

Mrs. Thornton noted his relaxed and happy manner. How changed he looked to be at ease with the world! She had never seen him so content, and was almost alarmed at the dramatic contrast to the agitated, hopeful lover that had departed for London two days ago. She was forced to admit how much power Margaret wielded over her son's temperament, and was saddened to recognize how much further her influence on her son would be diminished when he brought his wife home.

"We will marry in three weeks," he informed her cautiously but with great satisfaction as his breakfast was set before him.

Mrs. Thornton was taken aback. "Three weeks? Certainly there is no reason to rush," she blurted, having waited until the servant had closed the door before speaking her mind. She had not expected such an early date, and rebelled against losing him so quickly.

"She has lost her father, and her brother is not able to assist in her care," he reminded her, hoping to appeal to his mother's regard for convention.

"But surely her aunt has the means to care for her for some time," his mother countered, realizing once the words were spoken how indelicate her response would appear to her son. She would keep silent on the subject now; this was not her affair but John's. He would not understand how fiercely she wished to cling to the present - to keep things just as they were between them. He would not know how much she feared losing the first place in his heart which she had held and cherished so long.

"It is what we wish," he stated candidly, disappointed that his mother should question his decision.

Mrs. Thornton raised her eyebrows at his answer, not doubting that it was what her son wished, but dubious as to whether Margaret had truly been inclined to marry in such haste. Her expression was lost on John, for he had already turned his attention to his eggs and toast.

"Do you marry in London?" she asked in an attempt to regain their familiar rapport.

"In Helstone," Mr. Thornton answered simply, watching his mother for her reaction.

Mrs. Thornton said nothing but her countenance once again revealed her surprise.

"It must be a quiet affair, of course," he explained. "And I believe it will mean much to Margaret to marry there," he added thoughtfully.

"Of course," his mother agreed, guarding her tone from any indication of disappointment or censure.

"You will not be required to concern yourself with endless details, Mother," he assured her with a knowing smile, hinting at the tedious planning that Fanny's recent wedding had involved. "You need only come to the wedding," he warmly encouraged her, his eyes shining with open enthusiasm.

Mrs. Thornton's heart melted to see him thus. She recalled his boyhood days of happy innocence and easy confidence. How dearly she held to every memory of his fond affection and trust! Such tender looks from him had been her daily sustenance for years, when her lot in life had seemed too hard to bear. He could not know how much she feared to lose that familiar bond, to have it fade into the forgotten shadows of his life.

He would never know, too, how long she had imagined an elegant wedding for her beloved son. She had looked forward to proudly watching John elicit the envy of the city's best society in the splendor of a grand wedding that would befit his standing and success in Milton.

She did not relish the thought of his marrying in Helstone. She was afraid that the superior beauty and peacefulness of the setting would disparage the city that represented all that he had accomplished. She had not wished to travel elsewhere for many years, proudly convinced that Milton could offer everything that was required to live properly and happily.

She smiled pleasantly for her son's sake, and he responded in kind.

"I almost forgot," he declared, as he took one last gulp of his tea and rose from his chair. Pulling out an envelope from the breast pocket of his coat, he handed it to his mother. "Margaret wished to write to you," he explained, pleased to offer proof of his fiancé's thoughtful consideration. He smiled at the startled look on his mother's face. "I have not read its contents," he added, deferring any questions she might pose.

She stared bewilderedly at the envelope as Mr. Thornton moved to leave. "John!" she suddenly called out to him, before he quit the room. He turned back attentively. "Fanny takes tea with us this afternoon," she informed him. "She wishes you to be present," she emphasized.

"Then I will endeavor to be on time," he promised in deference to his sister's request.

"You will tell her your news?" Mrs. Thornton questioned him, knowing his penchant for privacy.

"I suppose I must," he agreed with a reluctant sigh. "Although I do not relish having my personal affairs discussed as idle amusement for Milton society," he said, voicing his concern aloud.

"John!" Mrs. Thornton exclaimed. "Fanny is your sister!" she reprimanded him.

He grinned in response and approached his mother to give her a quick kiss on the cheek. "I will see you at tea," he said fondly and left the room.

Mrs. Thornton smiled to herself as she thought of her son's affectionate gesture. She sighed to think of the stark contrast between her two children. It would be difficult to conceive of any pair so opposite in character and constitution as John and Fanny. She had often wondered if she had somehow erred in Fanny's upbringing to raise such a flighty, self-absorbed girl, but consoled herself with the remembrance that she had thought it best to protect her daughter from the struggles that John had been forced to face.

Her thoughts returned to the present as her eyes fell on the letter in her hand. She was genuinely surprised, but gratified, that Margaret had thought to write her a note. If nothing else, Mrs. Thornton expected that living with Margaret would never be dull. She was a high-spirited girl and entirely unpredictable.

Curious to know what Margaret would write, Mrs. Thornton wasted no more time and opened the letter.

Dear Mrs. Thornton,

I thank you for your great kindness to my family and myself, especially to my mother who found comfort in your gracious attention.

I hope you will understand that I am quite anxious to write to you in the hope of gaining your good favor. I mean no disrespect by my frankness, but feel that you would prefer me to be forthright on this occasion.

Perhaps you were surprised that I accepted John's hand, knowing that I dismissed his previous offer of marriage. I can only tell you that I was under great stress at that time, and shamefully ignorant and presumptuous in my view of Milton, and John in particular. I did not know him, as you told me yourself, but I believe I do know him now. I esteem him above all other men, and am honored to become his wife.

I have no illusions that we will immediately understand one another, but I fervently hope that we can learn to live together quite peaceably. I wish it not only for myself, but also for John's sake, so that all will be harmonious and pleasant when he is home. I would not wish to add to his burden, which is already quite great as Master of Marlborough Mills.

It may very well be that you remain doubtful as to my intentions and feelings towards your son. If so, then I only wish for the opportunity to prove myself a most devoted and loving wife.

Please give Fanny my regards. I will be very happy to see both of you in Helstone for the wedding.

Sincerely,

Margaret Hale

Mrs. Thornton was pleased to discern humility in the girl's letter, remembering in a flash the conciliatory words that Margaret had spoken to her before leaving Milton. She was glad to catch a glimpse of the softer side of her character, and hoped it indicated a permanent change in her demeanor.

She was also satisfied to note that Margaret was obviously impressed with her son: that was as it should be. However, whether or not her professed admiration of her son and her intentions to be a selfless wife would endure the test of time and circumstance remained to be seen. Whether she truly loved John could not be discerned in a mere letter.

Although she inherently admired the girl's strength of conviction and forthright nature, she worried that these generally admirable qualities could become upsetting when coupled with Margaret's implacable determination. Mrs. Thornton could foresee how turbulent a relationship between two such strong-willed persons as John and Margaret might be.

Taking a deep breath in resignation, she determined that there was nothing she could do but hope for the best.

❧

The early afternoon was quiet at the Harley Street house as Margaret happily visited with Edith in the drawing room. The bride-to-be had spent considerable time that morning writing letters. After such dismal news of father's death, she hoped that it would cheer Fred considerably to hear that she was to be married. She had also written to Mr. Bell, as well as to the Lennard Arms Inn and Mrs. Thompson of Helstone to inquire about lodgings.

Pleased to have accomplished this much toward her wedding preparations, she was able to relax in the pleasant company of her cousin. She was determined to cherish her remaining time in her aunt's home, for she knew such days of close, feminine companionship would soon be at an end when she moved to Milton.

Edith was animatedly enumerating the shops which they would visit to acquire Margaret's trousseau when Henry Lennox quietly entered the room.

"Henry, I didn't hear you come in!" Edith exclaimed with some surprise, a welcoming smile crossing her face to see her husband's brother.

"I gather you were busy discussing matters of vast importance," he teased his sister-in-law with a slight grin.

Edith tilted her head and dismissed his quip with a twist of her lips.

"Margaret," Henry formally addressed her with a slight nod, his smile now strained.

"Henry," she acknowledged rather uneasily in return, only briefly meeting his eyes.

"You did not stay long on Saturday," Edith noted. "I will go fetch Maxwell, he will be glad to see you," she offered enthusiastically, rising to go.

Margaret's body tensed in apprehension as her cousin left the room. She had no desire to be left alone in Henry's company.

The room fell into silence.

"When do you move to Milton?" Henry asked in a tempered voice, stealthily seeking to know if a wedding date had been set. Sitting down across from her in a velvet-upholstered chair, he awaited her response.

Margaret agitatedly shifted her position. "I will be in Milton four weeks hence," she answered dutifully, forcing herself to glance at him for civility's sake.

"Ah," he acknowledged, raising his eyebrows in slight surprise that she would remove from London and marry so soon. He was pensive a moment before speaking again. "Forgive me if I sound impertinent, but I was under the impression that you were not ready to marry anyone," he said abruptly, using her past words as a subtle rebuke.

Henry was curious to know - to be absolutely certain of - the reason she had decided to marry the Milton manufacturer. He held a tenuous hope that perhaps she had accepted the offer of marriage due to her father's unexpected demise, and might be persuaded to reconsider her options.

"Much has happened since I moved from Helstone," she stammered, taken aback by his remark.

"Indeed," he readily agreed in a sarcastic tone. He felt it was an ill-fated circumstance that had brought Margaret into the realm of that man. Had she never been displaced to that foul city, such a match would never have happened. In truth, beyond his blatant disgust for Milton's drab and polluted environment, Henry had deemed Margaret above the society there. He had thought that she was destined for pleasant elegance among the higher society that one could easily find in London.

"I must admit it is difficult for me to believe that you would choose to return to Milton. I did not think that city suited you," he continued to pry, pressing her to explain herself more clearly.

"I have come to appreciate Milton, although I admit it is very different from London," she stated honestly.

"Different?" he scoffed, "there is a league of difference between the bucolic fields of Helstone and the grimy streets of Milton," he said, vainly attempting to hide his disdain.

Margaret was discomfited by his caustic remark, and her ire was sparked by his condescending tone.

"Margaret," he began again apologetically, "you must understand my concern for your welfare. From what Mr. Thornton has told me, the cotton industry can be a volatile business. At present, he finds himself in a precarious position of stability," he explained earnestly, hoping to impress upon her the seriousness of her choice.

Irritated at his insinuation, Margaret was quick to defend her decision. "I am aware that there are risks involved in business. And I am confident that if anyone can capably manage them, it is Mr. Thornton," she boldly asserted, holding her chin aloft.

Henry was taken aback by her ardent defense, his face hardening in a deep frown.

Softening her manner, she looked down at her hands before confessing her heart. "I do not marry for money," she said simply, feeling warmth rise to her cheeks.

He instantly perceived her meaning, and sat motionless while he felt his last remaining hope of winning her drain away. "I see," Henry said solemnly, leaning back in his chair. He felt a stab of wounded pride that she had not chosen him, but loved another.

Henry quickly convinced himself that although she was graceful and beautiful, she was perhaps far too intelligent and independent to make a perfect wife. It would be far more fitting for him to find a docile girl. He smiled to think of the difficulty Mr. Thornton might encounter with Margaret's strong inclination to forge her own path, and felt his bitterness subside as he released the vision of the match he had stubbornly held for so long.

"I hope you will be happy," he said at last with quiet sincerity, breaking the awkward silence that had filled the room.

"Thank you," she intoned with some surprise, grateful for his friendly wishes.

"Sorry to be so late in coming," Edith called out as she burst into the room with her husband. "I quite believe that Maxwell is becoming sentimental. I found him in the nursery of all places!" she related in gleeful wonder as she grasped her husband's arm affectionately.

Henry and Margaret looked at each other and smiled in shared amusement at Edith's dramatic entry.

Fanny arrived on schedule. She was annoyed to be kept waiting for John in the drawing room with her mother. "Work, work, work. That's all he ever does, Mother!" she complained. "No wonder he is not married. I should like to know when he will ever take the time to find a wife!" she smugly remarked.

Mrs. Thornton remained silent. They both heard the door open and close, and recognized John's approaching footsteps.

"Good afternoon, Fanny, Mother," he greeted them warmly. "I am sorry to be late. Are you well, Fanny?" he made a point to inquire as he sat down in a chair across from her.

"I am, thank you," she replied, softening her demeanor to receive his attention. "You seem well, John," she noted curiously as Mrs. Thornton began to pour tea.

"I am, thank you," he responded evenly with a contented smile.

Fanny turned to her mother, remembering the reason for her visit. "I have exciting news, Mother," she announced auspiciously.

"What is it, Fanny?" Mrs. Thornton asked with more enthusiasm than she felt as she handed her daughter her tea.

"I am a member of the Milton Ladies Society!" she proclaimed proudly, holding her head high, her tea precariously positioned on her knees.

"I'm certain that it must be a distinguished group. Congratulations," her mother praised her.

"Thank you," she smiled happily. "But that is not all!" she began. "We have decided to host a ball in Milton!" she declared, barely able to contain her excitement. "And I have been elected to the Planning Committee!" she concluded with great aplomb.

"That suits you perfectly, Fanny. How wonderful for you," her mother congratulated her with her brightest voice.

Fanny beamed with self-contented pride. "Yes, it will be a grand ball, and it's high time for one, too!" she enthused, taking a sip of her tea with an affected flourish.

Disappointed that John had not said a word, she directed her attention to him. "I should hope you would attend, John. I'm certain that Miss Dallimore will be there," she mentioned slyly, a lilt in her voice. Fanny knew that the fair Eva Dallimore, whose father was a wealthy railroad investor, had every intention of putting an end to Mr. Thornton's bachelorhood.

Mrs. Thornton threw a glance at her son as he shifted uncomfortably in his chair and set his tea down on the low table in front of him.

Sensing his resistance, Fanny began to chastise him. "Really, John, how do you expect to find a wife if you do not get away from the mill on occasion!"

Goaded by her ignorant comments, John reveled in the thought of how shocked his sister would be at his next statement. "You should not be so concerned for me, Fanny," he replied calmly with a wry smile. "I am to marry Miss Hale," he stated in dead seriousness as a broad smile spread over his face.

"Miss Hale?" she practically shouted, looking back and forth between John and her mother in momentary speechlessness, her mouth ajar. "But she's in London!" she sputtered in confusion. "Why would she want to come back to Milton? And she is not rich, John," she thought to remind him, beginning to question her brother's motives as well.

Mr. Thornton exhaled in exasperation. "There are many reasons for marrying, Fanny. Is it so difficult to imagine that I may have a heart?" he asked in disgust.

She opened her mouth then closed it before opening it again. "You love her?" she asked in surprise as the truth dawned on her.

John averted his gaze to hide his bitter annoyance with his sister's tactless behavior and shallow consideration of his feelings.

"Well!" she exclaimed with a flourish. "I didn't see it; that much is certain. You are so secretive, John!" she accused him, shifting in her seat with discomfiture. "Why did you not tell me?" she pouted, realizing that she had been excluded from this fascinating development. "How long have you known?" she directed her question to her mother.

John glanced at his mother, then back at Fanny. "We came to an understanding shortly before she left for London," he explained. "I wished to keep it a secret until we had settled on a date," he added to mollify her.

"Oh," she said, as she attempted to make sense of what he had relayed, slightly baffled as to when such an understanding could have come about, and still reeling from the thought that her brother had fallen in love with Miss Hale. She had known of Miss Hale's attraction to him, of course, from her brazen behavior the day of the riot. But she had not considered that John might have had feelings for her.

"When is the wedding?" Fanny inquired with great interest. She took another sip of tea as she awaited his answer.

"We will marry in Helstone, three weeks from today," John gladly informed her, delighting in the thought of the day's eminent approach.

"Three weeks?" Fanny exclaimed with dismay. "There will hardly be time to make all the arrangements...." she began in flustered shock.

"You will remember that it must be a quiet affair, Fanny," John calmly reminded her with a pointed look that conveyed his meaning.

"Oh, you are right. I had quite forgotten," she confessed, her excitement deflating in solemn respect for Margaret's loss.

"When is the ball to be held, Fanny?" Mrs. Thornton asked, centering the conversation around Fanny once more.

"In just one month, perhaps a little more. But in any case, there is very little time to prepare. I shall be very busy with all the arrangements," she answered her mother with renewed enthusiasm and self-importance.

"You must invite Miss Hale to the ball, John," she decided aloud. "Although I suppose you will be married by then, will you not?" she asked no one in particular. "It would be the perfect way to introduce her to Milton society as your new wife! You will not need a grand wedding at all. How lucky you are we have arranged this at the perfect time!" she rattled on excitedly.

John looked doubtful, opening his mouth to speak but uncertain as to the proper reply.

"Fanny is right, John," his mother admonished him. "It will be a fine opportunity to officially introduce Margaret to Milton as your wife," she encouraged him. "No doubt she has attended such elegant occasions in London. She should be shown Milton at its finest," she said, hoping to appeal to his sense of pride.

"Oh, yes, John!" Fanny agreed enthusiastically. "She will need occasions to wear her best gowns," she wisely counseled him, forgetting the manner of plain dress that Miss Hale had habitually worn when she lived in Milton.

"I do not believe Miss Hale will need to be impressed by any such affair. She is quite happy to be moving back to Milton," John insisted, irritated that they should suggest otherwise.

His mother looked at him with a doubtful expression. "Regardless of her opinion, John, you must agree it would be a fine affair to attend," she emphasized once more. "For business relations, if nothing else," she added pointedly.

Still hesitant, John divulged the latent reason for his aversion. "I'm afraid I may have forgotten how to dance," he confided uncomfortably.

Discerning his embarrassment, his mother ventured to allay his fear. "I can show you again, John," she offered, remembering the long ago days when he had been instructed in the social graces. "Do not worry. I am sure you will do fine," she reassured him.

"You are going, then?" Fanny asked anxiously, turning her attention to her brother.

"I suppose I must acquiesce," he sighed. "You are both quite compelling," he reluctantly admitted, giving his mother a knowing smile.

Mrs. Thornton smiled back at him, grateful he had acceded to their reasoned entreaties.

"It will be a lovely time, you will see," Fanny promised him with her most winsome smile.

Margaret held Sholto in her lap, her chin barely touching his soft blond hair. As she read nursery rhymes to him, she loved to indulge her inclination to kiss the top of his head, taking in that sweet, clean fragrance that seemed to emanate from all infants. The gentle weight of his body and the feel of his soft little arms against hers always seemed to comfort her.

She remembered how easily John had gained Sholto's trust. Thinking of his tenderness, she imagined with a flutter of warm anticipation what a wonderful father he would be.

Edith stood smiling outside the nursery, surreptitiously listening to her cousin's melodious voice as she read to her son. She was happy to give Margaret the opportunity to practice her motherly skills as long as she was here - she certainly seemed to have a natural connection with children. It was easy to imagine her with children of her own.

Gliding into the room at last, Edith relieved Margaret from her evening sitting to put the boy to bed.

Margaret excused herself for the remainder of the evening, telling her cousin she would retire a little early. Closing the door to her room, she headed for the drawer that contained her fiancé's letters. She never tired of reading them; they were tangible evidence of his love that she would always cherish.

After Dixon had come and gone to help her prepare for bed, she happily climbed into bed to think awhile. Was it only yesterday that John had been here? She had tried to fill her day with busy activity and conversation, but the thought of him had drifted into her consciousness at every turn, and the day had dragged on without him. She clung to every recurring memory of his visit, vividly recalling the powerful feeling of being wrapped in his tight embrace.

Lying in bed and staring for the thousandth time at the ring on her finger, she wondered with a flush of heated exhilaration what it would be like to share his bed. She felt her cheeks burn and her heart race to contemplate his more intimate advances. The thought frightened and thrilled her at the same time, as she remembered how his intoxicating kisses left her wanting more.

She closed her eyes and attempted to think of other things.

Mr. Thornton removed the embroidered handkerchief from his waistcoat pocket and placed it reverently on the side table. As he undressed for bed, he ruefully acknowledged his success in surviving the day without her.

He had found his mind constantly returning to the memory of how gloriously beautiful her face had looked when it was flushed with longing, and the feel of her soft form pressed against him. The thought of how willingly she had submitted to his ardent attentions never ceased to fill him with awe.

He wondered if he would always find it so difficult to concentrate, now that such pleasing memories wandered unbidden through his consciousness, interrupting his train of thought at inopportune moments. He worried for his success in accomplishing his pressing work, but could not regret such pleasurable interruptions.

He read her letter once more before extinguishing the light and getting under the bed covers. Her words never failed to fill him with the wondrous joy that she should love him. The constant longing to hold her in his arms and taste her delicious kisses sometimes overwhelmed him.

Sleep was often elusive until the midnight hours, as the luxury of allowing his thoughts to wander inevitably led him to think of her - to imagine her next to him, in the very bed he now occupied. The thought of it was almost painful in its intensity, as he imagined the feel of her soft skin against his.

Abashed at his more vivid imaginings, he got up to pace the floor of his room, attempting to employ his practiced self-control and direct his thoughts to other things.

He decided to read awhile, and slowly became involved in the epic journeys of Odysseus.

At long last, his eyes grew weary and he closed the book to return to bed. Slipping into a deep slumber, his consciousness began to weave together the teeming images of his mind into a fantastical dream:

He was alone on a raft, adrift at sea with dark clouds hovering close by. Scanning the horizon for harbor he saw only the endless gray of sky and sea. Confused and fearful, he desperately sought guidance so that he might find his way home. They would miss him at the mill... and he must get home to Margaret!

Casting about for any useful tool, he tore a plank off the raft to use as a paddle. Dipping it in the water, he suddenly heard the wafting strains of music, pierced by clear, beguiling, feminine voices. Looking towards the sound, he watched transfixed as shadowy forms emerged from the mist. Upon a great rock, he saw three beautiful maidens whose nakedness was covered only by their long tresses — one of golden hair, one of raven locks and one of auburn curls.

He stared at the girl with auburn hair, amazed to recognize his own love beckoning to him. As he did so, the other two maidens vanished, leaving Margaret seated alone. Spellbound, he remained motionless as the mists once again enshrouded her from his view.

Frantically, he began to row towards his lover's voice as the sea swiftly became boisterous. Rising and falling with the growing waves, he caught frightening glimpses of a swirling whirlpool drawing him perilously closer to its dark funnel.

He jumped from the raft to evade his fate and attempted to swim but was dragged down by the weight of his clothes and the merciless waves. Struggling to keep his head above water, he grieved that his great love should die without a lifetime to bestow it. "Margaret!" he cried out before succumbing to the sea.

No longer flailing, he felt his head being lifted above the lapping waves...Slowly, he realized that he was lying in the surf of a sandy shore. A soft voice was calling his name...she was cradling his head on her lap, gently caressing his face with her hands as she comforted him with her words. "You are safe, John. I am here."

The maiden's voice was calling him to life...Opening his eyes he found she was leaning over him, her long hair cascading around him like a curtain. She smiled and spoke again. "John, I am here!" she soothed.

"Margaret!" he rasped, overwhelmed with tremendous joy and relief to be safe in her arms.

She brought her face closer to kiss him....

His eyes opened to stare at the ceiling. He let out a tired groan, realizing that he was awake.

The early morning light gradually replaced the darkness, uncovering the shades of night to reveal the objects of his everyday life.

He closed his eyes again to avoid reality. He wanted to recapture the bliss of being tenderly held and to feel the kiss that had almost been his. He languished in bed dreamily for a few more moments.

But he was awake now. He sighed.

My God, did she know how torturous this separation was? She invaded his dreams and his every waking thought. It was only the second day without her. How could he keep going?

Patience, he reminded himself. He almost laughed out loud. He had prided himself on his patience, but ever since he had met the girl from Helstone, his patience had all but failed him.

Soberly, he recalled the darkest days and weeks – when she had rejected him and he had loved her still. How long would it have continued - the pain of thinking that she did not love him?

No, he should be grateful that fate had brought them together before she had left for London. He was not suffering the cruel pains of unrequited love, but only the constant, aching desire to fulfill all his dreams of love and happiness. He would wait a lifetime for the privilege of marrying her. What was a few weeks more?

He threw back the covers to begin his day.

Chapter Nine

Mr. Thornton walked briskly down the long row of working looms, the cacophony of the clattering machines drowning out the sound of his footsteps. Stopping near the far end, he folded his arms and waited patiently as he observed Higgins instruct a new hand how to check the quality of the weave.

A small smile formed on his lips as he realized how much he had grown to admire the man that Margaret had befriended. He had been wary of hiring the former union leader at first, but had quickly found he was reliable and trustworthy. After further acquaintance, he discovered that Higgins had a keen mind and a genuine concern for others. Mr. Thornton had been surprised to find that he enjoyed working with him to create the workers' dining hall.

The Master had realized some time ago that he felt comfortable speaking to Higgins as an ally and confidant – much more than he did with the other Milton masters. He was naturally drawn to this affable fellow, and had become fond of his forthright manner and clever wit.

He recalled with warm affection that it was Higgins who had offered him the heartiest congratulations on his impending marriage – and he would never forget how efficiently he had relayed Margaret's message to him.

Higgins finished his demonstration and turned to see Thornton.

"May I have a word with you in my office?" Mr. Thornton asked respectfully, as he unfolded his arms and led the way.

Arriving at the office, Mr. Thornton took a seat behind his desk, and motioned for Higgins to sit. "I will be leaving for a short time in a few weeks," Mr. Thornton began, "and I would like for you to assist Williams while I am gone," he announced, watching Higgins to ascertain his reaction.

Noticing a flicker of surprise in his colleague's eyes, Mr. Thornton continued. "I would like you to help manage the hands so that Williams may pay more attention to matters of orders and inventory. Of course, with additional responsibilities, your wages will be increased," he explained. "Is this agreeable to you?" he asked with a slight grin.

Higgins shook his head slowly in disbelief. "It is more than agreeable," he answered humbly. "Thank you for your trust in me," he said with sober respect for his employer.

Feeling uncomfortably like a benefactor, Mr. Thornton swiftly justified his decision. "I do not bestow favors. I have seen your work, and you are good with the men," he rationalized. "You have proven to be one of my best workers," he openly admitted upon a moment's further reflection. "How remarkably insightful I was to have taken you on," Mr. Thornton added sarcastically, the corners of his mouth edging upwards as he gazed directly at his fiancé's friend – and, he realized belatedly, his own.

Higgins face broke into a hearty grin. "She'll do you good at every turn," he wisely predicted with an upward jerk of his chin.

Looking down at his desk, Mr. Thornton nodded his head in agreement as a broad smile spread over his face.

"When do you leave?" Higgins asked, bringing the subject back to work. "Or, should I ask, when is the wedding?" he prodded his colleague with a twinkle in his eye.

"We wed in Helstone in three weeks," his employer answered in an even voice, attempting to appear dispassionate about an event that threatened to consume his every waking thought.

"I see you don't waste any time," Higgins ribbed him affably, eliciting a bashful twitch of the Master's lips. "Mary an' me will be glad to see her come back. She's a right good favorite with the children, too. She brings them treats when she comes to visit," he remarked with open affection.

"I am certain she will continue to enjoy visiting your family when she returns," Mr. Thornton assured him.

Higgins regarded the Master with admiration.

"I will review with you your new duties tomorrow," Mr. Thornton stated, drawing their discussion of business to a close.

Higgins nodded and rose to leave.

"Higgins!" the Master called out impulsively, before the man had reached the door. The former union leader stopped and looked expectantly at his employer.

Mr. Thornton was on the verge of forging a new path. He could no longer in good conscience hold to rigid distinctions instigated by pride and enforced by unthinking custom. He wished to eschew the binding chains of prejudice that plagued society and make his own judgments of persons based on intelligence, kindness, honesty, and right endeavor.

Mr. Thornton paused briefly. "Will you stand with me at my wedding?" he asked quietly with import, steadily meeting Higgins' startled gaze.

Higgins hesitated, unsure how to respond to such an unexpected question, and uncertain for a moment how aware Thornton was of the implications involved in such a request. Seeing only sincerity and expectancy in his friend's demeanor, Higgins decided to accept. "Aye, it will be an honor," he answered reverently.

A smile of pleasure came over Thornton's face as he acknowledged his friend's acceptance. "Thank you," he said simply. "There was no one else I preferred to ask," he admitted honestly. "Besides," he continued, "I believe we have not yet compensated you for your messenger's service," he added with a mischievous gleam in his eye.

Higgins smiled with an equally mischievous gleam in his eye. "It were a favor to Margaret. I'll not ask for your first born," he quipped with a wink and slipped out the door.

Mr. Thornton smiled in genuine amusement at his quick wit.

◣

The next afternoon, Mr. Thornton received an unexpected visitor to Marlborough Mills. Looking up from his ledger at the sound of his name, he stood up to greet his landlord. "Mr. Bell, how good to see you. What brings you north?" he asked politely, cocking his head in wary curiosity, immediately apprehensive as to the older man's purpose.

"I've heard from a very reliable source that you are to marry my goddaughter," Mr. Bell announced ominously, taking a seat across from the desk.

Mr. Thornton's nerves pricked, aggravated by the habitually evasive tactics of the Oxford scholar. "Yes," he confirmed tentatively as he sat down once more. "However, I was not aware that Miss Hale was your goddaughter," he reluctantly admitted, not wishing to begin the conversation at a disadvantage.

"Yes, yes. Mr. Hale was my oldest friend," Mr. Bell explained soberly. "Anyway, I promised Hale that I would take care of her in the event of his passing," he continued. "I must confess that I have taken Margaret to heart. I have not met anyone quite like her. Her intelligence and spirit, as well as her great compassion, are extraordinary," he remarked with admiration. "She is a singular beauty, Thornton," he appraised, studying the Master's face as he voiced his evaluation.

Mr. Thornton's countenance glowed as the exalting words resounded within him, swelling his heart with pride to be reminded of his great fortune. "She has no equal," he agreed with a sense of awe, his voice low and reverent, like a spellbound traveler before a vista of incredible grandeur.

Mr. Bell smiled; the look on Mr. Thornton's face verified his assumptions. "I always suspected you were a man of uncommon perception and judgment. You have surpassed your peers, Thornton, with your choice of a wife," he remarked. "I believe it is a fair match, and I offer you my heartiest congratulations. You are a lucky man," he praised as he rose to offer his hand.

Mr. Thornton stood to shake hands warmly with his landlord. "Thank you," he replied, gratified and relieved to receive his favorable approval.

Mr. Bell sat back down, having yet to disclose his real purpose. "I know Richard held you in high esteem. I am certain he would have been very pleased to place his daughter in your care," Mr. Bell kindly remarked, regarding his tenant carefully.

"I would like to believe so," Mr. Thornton replied solemnly, seated once again behind his desk.

"Now then," Mr. Bell began auspiciously, "I have come to offer you a dowry in lieu of her father," he stated with decision.

Mr. Thornton was taken aback at the suggestion.

"Come, come, Thornton, there is no need to equivocate upon the matter. Margaret is a gentleman's daughter. I should like to offer a substantial dowry for such a precious pearl," Mr. Bell reasoned, persuading the proud self-made man to acquiesce to social custom.

"I was not expecting financial gain from my marriage," Mr. Thornton answered somewhat stiffly, feeling uneasy with the proposition of money from a third party such as Mr. Bell.

"Of course, I did not expect you should. However, I feel it is my responsibility to offer you a fair sum," Mr. Bell insisted. "I am aware that business is not as it should be at present. I am certain you would wish Margaret to have every security," he carefully remarked.

Mr. Thornton bristled at the insinuation that Margaret might not be safely provided for in his care. "I have everything in control at present," he politely assured him with an air of confidence.

"Yes, yes, of course you do, and I am certain you will ride out the storm," Mr. Bell affirmed with a lingering twinge of doubt. "May I offer £500?" he inquired, looking the younger man squarely in the eye.

Mr. Thornton blinked at such a sum. "I believe that half as much will suffice, and I thank you for your generous offer of more," he responded graciously.

"Very well, then, it is settled," Mr. Bell declared with finality as he stood up to leave. "I will not take up any more of your precious time. I must return to Oxford immediately," he abruptly announced.

Mr. Thornton stood. "You will not dine with us this evening?" he politely invited. "You are welcome to stay at Marlborough Mills and take your journey on the morrow," he offered sincerely.

"No, I thank you for your kind invitation, but I must not stay long," he answered as he turned to leave, but then stopped and turned once more to address the groom-to-be. "Forgive me if I intrude, but have you set a wedding date yet?" he asked curiously.

Mr. Thornton could not suppress the small smile that accompanied his answer. "Yes, we marry in Helstone in three weeks," he announced, feeling the import of the words every time he repeated them.

"Helstone!" Mr. Bell exclaimed. "What a clever girl!" he declared in a jocular tone. "Then I hope I shall see you on your happy day, Thornton," he concluded with a parting nod and was gone.

Mr. Thornton arrived home well before dinner. Seeking the quiet of his room, he climbed the stairs to find much hustle about the hallway and in the adjacent room. Perplexed and intuitively uneasy, he heard his mother giving orders from within as Jane came out to add a small end table to the various items already lining the hall.

Increasingly anxious to know what his mother planned, he strode into the room. "What are you doing?" he asked calmly in spite of his bewilderment, finding his mother and another servant clearing a space along the back wall of the room.

Mrs. Thornton stopped momentarily, turning her attention to her flustered son. "We have not much time to prepare Margaret's room. Everything needs a thorough cleaning before she arrives, and things must be rearranged properly," she informed him with a tinge of impatience that he should question her endeavor to properly welcome Margaret into her new home.

Mr. Thornton felt his heart sink as he listened to his mother's explanation. He had not realized until that very moment how central to his dreams of happiness was the thought of falling asleep with his wife securely nestled against him. He felt a sense of panic slowly rise within him.

Sensing his resistance, Mrs. Thornton quickly justified her purpose. "A woman of means should have her own room. A wife needs her privacy, John," she explained, searching her son's face to gauge his reaction.

Mr. Thornton absently gave a slight nod of his head, although he had no comprehension of what his mother meant. *Her privacy* - the words cut to his heart, opening afresh the painful wound of loneliness that Margaret had so recently healed. It had never occurred to him that she might have – or want - her own room – that she might not wish share his bed every night. He struggled to accept such a possibility, willing to deny his happiness for that of his wife.

Mrs. Thornton was taken aback at his obvious distress. She saw before her not the steely, commanding Master of Marlborough Mills nor her patient, self-sacrificing son, but simply a man whose love burned to express itself in the more intimate and tangible bonds which marriage allowed. She was strangely amused to be reminded of how all-consuming this physical desire could be for the opposite gender, and she recognized, with a tug of compassion, that her son was not immune from this strong proclivity that seemed so prevalent among men.

"Her room adjoins yours, John," she brusquely reminded him, attempting to break his vapid stupor with this encouraging fact. "You will remember that there is a door behind the bureau in your dressing room that marks the passageway between your rooms," she told him as she watched a flicker of hope enliven his countenance.

"I had forgotten it," he acknowledged and gave her a meager smile before turning to go to his own room.

Closing the door behind him, he let out a sigh of despair. Would he ever be rid of the imprisoning barriers of social custom? Was nothing sacred? His frustration give way to anger as he felt his comforting dream of warm intimacy dissipate under the penetrating glare of society's austere injunctions. Could he not even enjoy the privacy of his marriage without the intrusive opinions of others thrusting their judgments of propriety upon him? Could he and Margaret not decide for themselves their own living arrangement, he fumed?

Suddenly, like a cooling balm, the thought that they *could* choose for themselves soothed his irritated unrest. They might be given separate rooms, but no one could dictate how they chose to use them. He felt a flutter of exhilaration as his resurrected hopes of sharing their nights together awakened the memory of their passionate encounters. He blissfully remembered how willingly she had welcomed his touch; how fiercely she had clung to him as he was about to leave.

Perhaps his mother was too set in the ways of the past, in which marriage had often been a convenient arrangement between persons who were not always compatible. She was not aware of how much he and Margaret longed to be together, of how finely attuned to one another they were. She did not know how in love they were – so much so, that he could not imagine spending a night away from her.

Certainly, he thought – no, he prayed -- Margaret would not wish to be parted from him. Had she not said so before he departed? But would she want to share a bed with him every evening? Perhaps he had envisioned too much, without considering her needs or wishes. What did he know of women's concerns? He would never wish to impose upon her.

But as he recalled her reluctance to part from him and her willing submissions to his ardent demands, he felt impelled to believe that she would want to stay with him throughout the night. He fervently wished it to be so – that her room might be a refuge for her during the daylight hours, but vacant come nightfall. He refused to relinquish this most pleasant dream of being close to her.

It was the usual, serene master of the house that joined his mother for dinner that evening at the candlelit table.

Mr. Thornton had been relieved to find dinner a mercifully tranquil event immediately following Fanny's wedding. But over the course of several weeks, he had found it unutterably quiet with only his mother and himself. Now that he knew it would only be a matter of time before Margaret would join them, he was eager for the day when she would enliven their tepid conversations with her effervescent spirit and keen insight, and grace the table with her elegance and beauty.

He was grateful this evening that he had something of import to say that had not been heretofore discussed. "There are some furnishings and other sundries in Crampton that I wish to be incorporated into our home," he announced calmly as he dabbed the corner of his mouth with a crisp, white napkin. "Most of these items, I believe, will be for her private bedchamber," he clarified.

Mrs. Thornton stiffened at the mention of this first tangible intrusion of her home by Margaret's impending succession. Her face froze only for an instant before exuding an exterior of calm submission, which her shifting eyes betrayed. "There are already sufficient furnishings for her," she gently suggested, as she took a bite of her food.

"These are things of sentimental value from her parents' home. I wish that she should feel at home here," he explained, desiring to elicit a semblance of compassion from his mother. She nodded her accord.

Home, here – the words reverberated, sending a tremor of exquisite joy through him. That she would make her home here seemed almost unfathomable, and yet he could no longer imagine his life without her. He yearned for it to begin and thought of it constantly: how it would feel to wake up with her next to him, how she might greet him when he came home, how her things might adorn his bedroom, and how it would feel to retire for the night and not be alone.

"I will have them brought to the house tomorrow," he told her. "Will you see to it that her room is arranged with them?" he asked politely but with firm intent. "I will be happy to assist in any way," he added sincerely.

"I'm certain it can all be worked out, John. You need not concern yourself with such matters. If I have any questions, I will come to you," she promised, giving him a pleasing look with a trace of a smile.

John smiled blandly in agreement and quietly returned his attention to his dinner.

Monday morning at Harley Street found Margaret and Edith meeting with the dressmaker in Margaret's room. Miss Bouvier (Edith had insisted that even one's dressmaker should be French) had brought the bride's wedding gown and other garments for fitting.

Margaret had just been helped into the voluminous swaths of silk, tulle, and lace of her wedding gown when there was a knock at her bedroom door. Edith opened it carefully to find Ellen with an armful of yellow roses. "For Miss Margaret," she announced and handed the flowers and an accompanying envelope over to the young mistress.

Edith smiled knowingly as she sashayed over to her cousin, who was busy dreamily gazing down the length of her new dress. "Margaret," Edith called to her, "someone has sent you flowers."

Margaret looked up at once, curiosity quickly turning into glad recognition as she saw the profusion of yellow roses. "They're from John!" she declared as she admired them in Edith's arms, unable to move from her position while the seamstress efficiently pinned the hemline.

"And there's a note," Edith said with a rising lilt, smiling at her cousin as she gave her the envelope. "I will have Ellen fetch a vase for these flowers," Edith remarked as she gently laid the blossoms on the vanity and left the room to find the maid.

Margaret swiftly opened the envelope to read the note contained within while she stood fastened to her place as the seamstress's captive subject:

For my darling rose from Helstone, who brightens and beautifies every place where she is set,

I pray that such a beautiful rose will flourish in my dark and dreary city, for I cannot live without her enchanting and cheerful presence now that I know such a flower exists.

My days are filled with the routine tasks that I have performed for many years, but my thoughts are filled with you – when I wake, at my desk, when I walk through my home, I dream of the day when you will be mine, when you will wait for me at the end of my day to greet me, filling my home with light and happiness. My heart aches for my dream's fulfillment. Will you not come home to me soon?

In two weeks, we shall declare our vows before the world, but I have already declared my heart to you. I only wait to tell the world of it, so that everyone may know that we are bound as one and will not be drawn asunder.

I am forever,

Your John

Margaret was moved to tears by his ardent longing, and felt a similar ache rise up in her breast for him. How she wished she could go to him and fall into his arms so that he would know she longed for him as well! She missed everything about him – his strong presence, his silken voice, and the sense of humor that had begun to develop between them.

She remembered the letter she had received two days ago, in which he had teased her that he was now her proper pupil, already crossing swords with convention as she had often taught him. He had been pleased to tell her that he had asked Nicholas to be his groomsman, and she was touched to know that he had done so. What would his mother and Fanny think, she wondered?

She felt a strong affinity for this wonderful man who would soon be her husband. He had a good heart, and she admired him for following the mandate of his own conscience in defiance of the blind dictates of society. He was far from the cruel taskmaster she had first assumed he was.

Edith and Ellen returned with a vase of water. "There must be two dozen roses," Edith remarked with satisfaction as she assisted Ellen in arranging the flowers.

"It is two weeks before our wedding," Margaret replied as an explanation.

"Well, they certainly are lovely," Edith commented as stood back to admire them as she finished setting them on a stand placed near the window.

"And you, my dear Margaret - you look beautiful!" Edith enthused as she finally turned her attention to her cousin. "It is so pleasant to see you in something other than black. I am very impatient with your dull mourning clothes," Edith admitted with a look of exasperation for the limiting custom.

"It is lovely, isn't it?" Margaret agreed enthusiastically, as she met her cousin's admiring gaze.

"Yes, I am very glad you decided to have something made for the occasion. I would not have wished you to marry in one of your old gowns," Edith honestly admitted, knowing her cousin's minimal interest in fashion. "It was very generous of Mr. Bell to send you the money for a trousseau," she added. "I, for one, am very grateful to him, as I intend to have a grand time helping you spend all of it!" Edith proclaimed, her eyes sparkling with eager delight as her cousin laughed appreciatively.

Mr. Thornton stood on the scaffold overlooking the vast weaving shed. He had always been impressed with the view, and he still was, but now whenever he was inclined to contemplate all that he had accomplished, the mill was not the first thing that came to mind. News of his impending marriage had filtered through all of Milton, for as he had made the rounds these past few days, he had been aware of the workers' covert glances in his direction. And yesterday, his banker had congratulated him on his engagement.

Mr. Thornton pulled out his pocket watch. He had never paid much attention to the postal deliveries before, but ever since Margaret had left Milton with his heart in her hand, he had learned when to expect the sorted post to be delivered to his office.

He descended the iron stairs and hastened to his private space. Closing the door behind him, he picked up the letters on his desk and deftly searched through them for the familiar handwriting of his beloved. Immensely gratified to find a letter addressed in her hand, he sat down to savor the pleasing gift of her communication.

My dearest John,

I received the gorgeous roses that you sent to me today – I adore them! I will not only think of Helstone, but of you when I look at them. They brighten up my room so beautifully that I am tempted to gaze upon them all day.

Thank you, my love. You have always been so very thoughtful and kind. I will never forget how you brought mother such lovely fruit during her illness, and how faithfully you visited father when he needed the comfort of your company.

You spoil me with such gifts, and I hardly know what I have done to deserve them. I am the one who owes you a debt of gratitude for protecting me from the inquest, and loving me despite having every reason to doubt my character.

I wonder how I am the one blessed to receive your sweet attentions? I am the most fortunate woman in all of England. Did you know that your mother once told me that all of the girls in Milton sought your hand? I wonder how it was you were able to evade such pervasive interest! No matter, I am very glad of it.

Although I did not originally consider it to be so, I now believe that moving to Milton was one of the most fortunate events of my life because it brought me to you. I can no longer think of my life without you, and I cannot wait to spend the remainder of my days with you.

I forgot to mention in my last letter that I would like to bring Dixon to Milton with me. Will you tell your mother, so that she can make the proper arrangements? And perhaps you should also tell her that I plan to invite Nicholas and Mary to dinner straight away! You would not dare, would you? I am funning you, of course. I am still very apprehensive of your mother's opinion of me. I do not wish to upset her unnecessarily at the outset, but I hope she will learn soon enough that my intentions are sincere.

You requested that I tell you of our lodging plans. I have written to the Thompsons, a family of whom I was very fond in Helstone, and they are very happy to help us. You see, I remembered that they always went to the sea in the summer, and I thought they might let their cottage whilst they were away. Granted, it will not quite be summer when we arrive, but they have graciously decided to be accommodating. They are happy to allow us the use of their home while they visit family in London. They assured me that it was not an inconvenience, but that they had planned to visit family in London for some time.

I hope you will like it, John. It is a lovely cottage, more like a country home, surrounded by rolling fields and a few great trees, near a small forest and winding brook. I thought it one of the loveliest places in the village, next to the old vicarage, of course.

I have arranged for you and your family to stay at the Lennard Arms Inn before the wedding. Nicholas and Mr. Bell may stay there as well.

I will stay with my London family at the Thompson's cottage the night before our wedding.

It is only two more weeks, John! Although I must admit this week has passed very slowly without you, it has nevertheless passed, and we are that much closer to the date when we shall meet and ne'er part.

As always, I regret that I am not with you. The only place I truly wish to be is in your arms.

I am forever yours,

Margaret

Mr. Thornton let out a slow breath as he closed his eyes to think of how it had felt to hold her tight against him. How he wished that London were closer, so that he might visit her every week!

Although he had many duties to attend to, he could not resist the temptation to immediately make a reply. No one would know that the Master busily scribbling at his desk was not addressing business accounts or customers, but was writing a letter to his one true love.

∽⧬∾

Margaret spent her days continuing to tend to the details of her wedding and enjoying the company of her family. Edith kept her busy with fittings and excursions to various shops, while Margaret found that there were more letters to write.

She eagerly awaited John's response to her recent letter and attempted to appear unconcerned when the post arrived everyday, but she could not keep her eyes from wandering to the sofa where her aunt would sit slowly sorting the day's delivery.

On Friday, as Margaret stole glances at her aunt, she was thrilled to notice her aunt pick up a letter and slowly direct her gaze across the room. "Margaret, you have another letter from Mr. Thornton," Aunt Shaw told her.

"Thank you, Aunt Shaw," Margaret replied, her heart quickening in anticipation as she serenely rose from her seat to retrieve the letter. Excusing herself from the parlor, she escaped to the privacy of her room to read her lover's message.

My darling Margaret,

I am glad the flowers I sent you gave you such pleasure. You cannot dissuade me from spoiling you if I so choose – in this, you will remain powerless to move me.

How can you believe that you do not deserve such gifts? You astonish me with such words, for it is I who cannot fathom the miracle that has befallen me – that you should love me. I had thought you too beautiful and refined for one as plain and unpolished as I.

As for the girls of Milton, I had no knowledge of any designs on me. I fear my mother is too boastful on my behalf. I have never loved any woman before: my life had been too busy, my thoughts too absorbed with other things. I had no thought for love or marriage until you came to Milton and demanded my attention with your blunt opinions of our Northern ways. Now I love, and I will love.

Let us speak no more of debts or inequities between us. I only wish for us to love each other openly. I cannot take payment for doing that which I could not avoid doing - for loving you as I do. And although I dismiss your debt to me, I will gladly accept your freely given kisses and unbidden caresses!

Mother has adjured me to tell you that there is to be a ball in Milton come June that we are bidden to attend. I am told that you may wish to acquire a new gown for the occasion and need fair notice. Fanny and Mother insist that it will be a fine opportunity to introduce you to Milton society as my wife. Generally, I am not favorably inclined towards such events, but I will take great pleasure in presenting you to Milton society. *Will you accompany me? I must confess that I look forward to seeing you dressed in your finery. I have not forgotten the way you looked at the Masters' dinner last summer – I was aware of your presence in the room at every moment, and though it would have been unseemly for me to do so, I could have stared at you all evening. Did you know, my darling, that I was quite in love with you even then?*

I have told Mother that you plan to bring an entourage of servants with you and that you desire another wing be added to the house for all the belongings that a Southern lady needs for comfort and luxury. (I have not, I promise, but I could not resist saying so.) You must not worry about my mother. I believe it may take time, but she will learn to enjoy your company.

The cottage sounds like it will be a wonderful haven. I look forward to living a country life during our wedding holiday. I have long wished to see the place where my rose came from, and will enjoy seeing the beauty of nature through your eyes as you show me the places that you have spoken of before.

Margaret, it still amazes me to think that you will marry me - that in twelve days you will be my wife. I cannot describe the happiness I feel, when for so long I thought you would never be mine.

I love you, and long to hold you close to my heart and never let you go. Take care, for when we meet again, I shall never let you go.

Forever yours,

John

Margaret felt her heart fairly burst with love for him. She was overcome with gratitude for this wonderful blessing - that she had found such happiness in the love of this man. She had not dreamed such perfect joy was possible.

She immediately sat to write her reply.

My darling John,

My heart is filled with love for you today. Do you know how much happiness you have given me? My words can only tell you but a portion of how I feel. I wish to show you, John, how much I cherish you – and I will do so every day when we are married. I wish to make you so very happy. No one shall have a more loving wife than you.

I would love to attend the ball with you! I am not especially fond of such grand events, but I shall delight in being with you, and proud to be acknowledged as your wife – I only hope I will pass muster. My only regret is that I cannot dance with you, for it would not be appropriate for me to join the festivities after such a recent loss as mine. Will you save a dance for me when the evening is over and we may be in private?

Perhaps I should take pains to wear a plainer garment at the ball, as I was not aware that I could be such a distraction to you. How is it possible that you could be in love with me at the Masters' dinner when it seemed every word we exchanged before then had been in hopeless disagreement? I did not know that you loved me, John. But I do recall that you also looked very handsome that evening, and that I was impressed with your easy authority over the other men. Perhaps I was falling in love as well, but I did not consider it possible we should make a suitable match.

I have not much news to tell, only that I am counting the days until we meet in Helstone. I, too, look forward to spending a week with you in the countryside, but I would be happy anywhere, as long as I was with you.

With all my heart,

Margaret

⊰⊱

Arriving near the elegant draper's shop that Edith favored in the West End, Margaret and her cousin alighted from the carriage. "Will you remind me once more what is our purpose this time?" Margaret asked her cousin. "I am certain I have already acquired a very fine wardrobe. I believe I shall be the best-dressed woman in Milton with all these new clothes," she commented, unfamiliar (her cousin thought) with the diligence and constant attention required to be fashionable.

"That is precisely the point, Margaret!" Edith exclaimed with a tinge of exasperation. "You will be a lady of considerable standing in Milton society, will you not?" she asked. "You will need to look the part. You will no longer be a vicar's daughter, but the wife of a prominent businessman in your city," she counseled her cousin. "I'm certain you would wish to enhance Mr. Thornton's position by your grace and fine taste," she added as they walked to the shop.

"I wish to honor him in any way that I am able," Margaret honestly admitted. "But I am quite certain that he pays little heed to matters of appearance," she commented.

Edith looked at her, recalling her cousin's pitiable wardrobe when she had arrived in London. "Yes, it seems he would adore you no matter what you wore," she remarked with some wonder. "However, perhaps you will be so fetching in your new dresses, he will be enticed to come home early from the mill," she suggested, her eyebrows rising slightly as she casually advised her cousin on how a woman's wiles may be employed to her advantage.

"Edith!" Margaret gently scolded her as a small smile escaped from her lips as she considered the possibility.

They entered the shop. The noise from the streets was at once hushed as they took in the sight of the large selection of fabrics, ribbons, lace and other luxuriant materials. It was a grand store, perhaps double the size of the simple draper's shop in Milton.

Edith led them to the ready-made section for undergarments and nightclothes. Elaborating the fact that Margaret should have everything new, she recommended that the bride-to-be acquire all new undergarments and a few new nightgowns.

"This is a very lovely nightgown," she assessed, holding a cap-sleeved, white nightgown with a modest scooped neck bordered with fine lace. She held the gown against herself, showing how the ruffled hemline stopped several inches above the ankles.

It was Margaret's turn to raise her eyebrows as she looked over her cousin's selection. "It is very lovely, but doesn't it seem a little....improper?" she asked carefully.

"'Proper' is of little use when you are alone with your husband, Margaret," Edith remarked in a quiet tone, not wishing to be overheard.

"Edith!" Margaret exclaimed again, embarrassed by her cousin's implications. She felt the color rise to her cheeks, as she furtively glanced around to make certain no one was listening.

"Look," Edith called her attention to another garment she had selected. "If you wear this dressing gown with it, it would make a very respectable pairing," she commented.

"It is beautiful," Margaret agreed as she noticed that the sleeves' ruffled edges were interwoven with lilac ribbon at the cuff.

"And it's cotton!" Edith announced in triumph, teasing Margaret for her recent penchant towards anything made in that particular fabric.

After successfully purchasing the chosen items, they headed home to Harley Street.

After staring absently out the carriage window a few moments, Edith turned nervously to her cousin, who sat across from her. "Margaret," she began uneasily, "has my mother spoken to you yet of...married life?" she falteringly inquired, her eyes asking more than her words conveyed.

Margaret unconsciously held her breath as she comprehended Edith's meaning. "No," she replied, slowly letting her breath out as she stared at her gloved hands.

"Are you aware of...of what is required?" she asked uncomfortably, glancing only briefly at her cousin, who was still examining her folded hands.

Margaret regarded her cousin before replying. "I...am not altogether certain, no," she replied haltingly.

"I did not wish you to receive the same speech which my mother gave

115

to me, that is all," she endeavored to explain. "You see …I have come to disagree with her opinions," she offered. "I know that the Bible says we are to suffer sorrow in childbirth. But I don't believe it says anything that would suggest that it is wrong to enjoy the attentions of your husband," she confessed as her face turned pink in embarrassment.

"Oh," was all Margaret could manage to reply, not completely certain she understood what Edith was implying.

"You see, Mother suggested that one's wifely duties were to be borne bravely as if they were a great hardship," she explained, looking distractedly at her hands as she fidgeted with a wrinkle in her skirt. "But I have found that it can be quite pleasant to accept your husband's attentions," she confessed, glancing at Margaret to ascertain her reaction to her candid remark.

"Oh," Margaret breathed once more, feeling the tension in her stomach release a little.

"Do you not feel something ….wonderful when he touches you?" Edith ventured to inquire.

Somewhat startled by her question, Margaret considered how she felt when he held her close and the pleasant, strange stirring of sensations she felt when he kissed her. "His kisses leave me quite incapacitated," she admitted with a blush and a small smile. "I don't know how to describe it, really, but I feel something very…strong within me," she stammered in an attempt to explain.

Edith smiled reassuringly at her cousin. "It is perfectly natural to have such feelings, Margaret, when you are in love," she told her. "It is right to feel this way with your husband," she counseled. "And I believe…well, I am quite certain your Mr. Thornton will be very gentle with you," she added quickly. "You need not be frightened on your wedding night," she amended, relieved to have advised her cousin to be unafraid.

They remained silent a few moments, before Margaret bravely spoke up. "But you have not explained…." she began, but could not finish, feeling a rush of warmth come to her face.

"Oh," Edith said, realizing her omission. She quickly looked out the window, wondering how to begin.

With a profusion of averted glances and flushed faces between them, Edith was able to convey by delicately worded implications the conjoining of a man and woman that only marriage sanctifies.

Momentarily dumbfounded by this complete revelation, Margaret remained silent the remainder of the trip, much to Edith's relief.

After the footman helped them carry in their packages, Margaret was glad to escape to her room for a while.

She was greeted by a new arrangement of yellow roses on her vanity.

She smiled to see them. *Of course,* she thought, *it is Monday.* In exactly one week, it would be her wedding day. Would he send a roomful of roses on her wedding day, she wondered?

She walked over to the flowers and drew one out to smell its fresh fragrance. Holding the flower in one hand, she opened the envelope laid next to the vase.

My darling Margaret,

When you receive these flowers, it should be one week until our wedding.

One week. I don't think I have ever have wished a week to pass as quickly as I wish this one to pass. I have waited patiently, although I do not think I ever really knew what patience meant before. It has been a torturous pleasure to imagine you in my embrace these past two weeks and I have often feared I might follow my impulse to take the train to London once more, but my reasoned logic forced me to stay so that I might prepare to take my planned wedding trip.

I cannot imagine a sweeter heaven than to remain in Helstone with you for the days after our wedding. With no binding schedule or intruding company, we shall be free to be with one another every moment. I believe such a promised joy as this will propel me through the remaining days before I board the train south to meet you at last.

I remain, and will always be, entirely yours,

John

How could she remain anxious with such a tender love as this, she thought? She had never felt more secure than when he had held her in his firm embrace. It was the only place she wanted to be.

She sat down on her bed, holding the rose and his letter in her hand, as she thought again of his kisses and the increasing exhilaration she had experienced as his kisses had grown stronger and more desperate. Was this how it would feel to be loved by him - in the marriage bed - she wondered? If so, she could not be afraid of him, but would welcome his intimate attentions. Her heart fluttered in her chest to consider it. She knew she would be nervous, as anyone might be to experience something which was at once so new and of such great magnitude, but she realized in her heart that all would be well.

She wished to be close to him - that was all she really desired. She loved him. That was all that really mattered.

She smiled and brought the rose to her face once more to smell its sweet fragrance.

Chapter Ten

It was a pleasant Sunday morning in London. In Richmond and Hampstead, gentlemen and their families were donning their spring finery to be seen at church. In Bethnal Green, the working classes were enjoying their day of respite from their drudgery, as the womenfolk began early to prepare for the anticipated evening meal.

At the Harley Street residence, all was not as usual. The occupants within were busily preparing for their departure to Helstone. Dixon assisted Margaret as the young mistress made her final selection of the garments that she would take with her and those that would be packed and sent to Milton during her absence. Edith and Aunt Shaw finished packing their overnight bags, and Maxwell sent for a carriage to arrive after luncheon.

The family arrived at the station early in the afternoon and boarded the Southampton train at Waterloo.

Having, at last, nothing to do but sit and reflect, Margaret took a deep breath as she contemplated the reason for all this hectic activity – she was to be married tomorrow, to the cotton manufacturer she had once thought of as thoughtless and contemptible. She had never been so wrong, for she had discovered that beneath the exterior of his stern bearing, he was truly gentle and kind - the most selfless and upright man she had ever had the privilege of knowing.

Tomorrow, he would be her husband. She felt a shudder of anticipation deep within her. She had never felt such powerful feelings before; though she was honestly and fervently drawn to his good character, there was something about his physical presence that electrified her. She had not wanted to admit it before, but she now realized that she had always felt so.

She was apprehensive and exhilarated at the thought of seeing him after being apart these past weeks. Margaret wondered how it would feel to be with him again – to hear his voice and look into his piercing blue eyes. She hoped that they would quickly resume the comfortable familiarity they had attained during his London visit, so that her nervousness might cease.

Edith recalled her to her present surroundings, meekly asking if she would hold Sholto for a few moments. Margaret smiled at the boy and settled him on her lap before she began to encourage him to notice the various scenes passing by their window. It would not be long until they arrived, she thought with exaltation, and she would see her beloved once more.

⬯

Mr. Thornton awoke at dawn and eagerly rose to begin the day. He had slept well, knowing that this day would be unlike the rest – that all the preparations and purchases, all the arrangements and endless waiting that had gone on since she had first named the date would be past. Every plan would be set in motion the moment he set foot on the southbound train.

His trunk was already packed, and he knew his mother would be ready to leave on schedule. He only hoped that Fanny and Watson would be punctual in meeting them at the station.

As he finished buttoning his shirt and began to tie his cravat, he gazed absentmindedly at himself in the mirror, amazed and grateful that this day had finally arrived. He was content: anxious to be on his way, but profoundly satisfied that his arduous patience would be rewarded – he would see her today, and tomorrow she would be his wife.

His wife – he was suddenly caught up in a wave of incredulous wonder at the import of the word. As he glanced at his reflection again, he was astounded that such a rough and plain-looking man as he had won the affections of such a beautiful creature. At times it was almost incomprehensible to him, that he, who lacked the education and refinement of a well-bred gentleman, would marry a girl of such exquisite grace and upbringing. He promised himself that he would never take for granted his great fortune.

He donned his frock coat and gathered up his bag. His eyes rested a moment on the serene expanse of his unruffled bed. *The next time he slept in it, he would not be alone.* A shudder of anticipation coursed through him at the thought. Taking one last sweeping glance at his room, he stepped into the hallway and closed the door.

Fanny and Mr. Watson arrived none too soon, breaking the nervous tension of the groom-to-be, for he had been anxiously searching the gates for their arrival. Fanny immediately consumed her mother's attention as she chattered on about how exhausting it was to prepare for such a journey.

Watson approached Mr. Thornton to properly greet him. "I've not had the opportunity to congratulate you, Thornton," Watson remarked jovially as he reached out to shake his brother-in-law's hand. "You've picked yourself a handsome lass," he approved with a knowing grin. "She's not backward in coming forward, that one, is she?" he remarked derisively as he raised his eyebrows. "I believe you may need to show her who's master," he hinted with a conniving wink.

Mr. Thornton bristled at his brother-in-law's vulgar insinuations. His eyes flared in anger as he attempted to maintain a bland composure. "I believe you will find that Miss Hale and I are in agreement on most matters," he retorted coolly in an attempt to repulse his pretentious remarks. "And I am certain she will know her place in my home," he added with confidence, steadily meeting Watson's eyes.

Indeed, Mr. Thornton hoped Margaret would know her place as his wife. She would be free to speak her mind and do what she wished. She was much more to him than a pretty adornment to be used for his comfort and pleasure. He shuddered to think of her in the clutches of a man such as Watson. Such boorish men would never comprehend the kind of marriage he envisioned.

He did not wish to dominate her – he would not wish to crush the very spirit that had attracted and enthralled him. No, that is what he feared most: that by holding her captive in this city, within his selfish grasp, she might wilt – her lively soul might lose its radiance and become a mere shadow of its former brilliant self. He could never bear to be the cause of her unhappiness.

He wished to possess her, yes, but not in the vile way she had implied when she had so vehemently rejected him. He wanted her, in every way – for he was a man of flesh and blood like all the rest - but he would never impose himself upon her. He needed her to love him, to look into his eyes with trust and respect, if not outright desire. He wished to possess her heart so that she would come to him willingly, not out of obligation.

He hoped that they would freely communicate with one another, so that no weeds of discontent could grow to choke the blossoming beauty of their love. He hoped that they would prove to be a help and comfort to each other, so that together they might banish worry and bring hope and joy to whatever lay ahead.

The gathered family boarded the train, taking their seats for the long journey south. When the train lurched forward to begin its steady advance, Mr. Thornton felt his heart lurch in exhilaration as well. With every mile they travelled, he would be that much closer to the realization of his fondest dream – to make Margaret his own.

As soon as the London visitors were comfortably settled in the cottage, Margaret broke away to go outdoors, eager to enjoy the freedom of the open fields and take in the sights of the countryside she had known so well. The fresh air was invigorating and she was amazed at how green everything looked. It had been nearly two years since she had left Helstone, and she had forgotten how lush it truly was.

She stood for a moment on the pebbled pathway through the front garden, smelling the lavender plants that swayed in the breeze. She smiled to recognize white peonies, Sweet William with clusters of burgundy flowers on its leafy foliage, and pink and purple sweet pea blossoms dotting the ground throughout the garden. How wonderful it was to be surrounded once more by the beauty of nature!

She instinctively began to walk in the direction of the vicarage, curious to see if the passing months had wrought changes to her childhood home.

Before reaching the familiar grounds, however, she was pleasantly surprised to see Mr. Bell approaching her. Meeting in the lane, she greeted him warmly, "Mr. Bell, I did not know you had arrived already."

"I arrived some time ago. I have taken my lunch and have had an afternoon rest," he informed her. "I was told the walk to your cottage was not quite a mile, so I thought I would give these old limbs some useful exercise and come to see you," he explained with satisfaction. "Now, then, where were you off to, if I may inquire?" he asked interestedly, having already conjectured the possible purposes of her foray to the village.

"I was on my way to our old home. I have not seen it in some time," she told him, a hint of nostalgia softening her tone.

"Ah, of course," Mr. Bell responded sympathetically. "Shall we go together, then?" he asked with an affectionate smile.

Margaret smiled at him and inclined her head in agreement before ambling down the country byway with her father's old friend. It was a perfect day to be out walking: the air was clear and slightly cool, while the sunshine warmed everything it rested upon. A slight breeze rustled the grasses and leaves as the sky spread a canvas of dazzling blue against drifting clouds of purest white.

Leaving the lane, they crossed a field to reach the far boundaries of the property so familiar to Margaret. She eagerly took in the view, her eyes sweeping the distance to see the dark, pointed roof of her former home jutting above the greenery of the surrounding brush.

Searching the periphery of the grounds, she caught sight of a man approaching from afar, progressing towards them as he walked along the hedgerow. She held her breath as her eyes focused on him, recognizing at once the purposeful gait of the man she loved. *He was here!* A quiver of sensation rippled through her body to see him. Even from a distance, he exuded strength and vigor: his bearing was powerful and steady as his long, lithe legs brought him ever closer.

Her face began to glow with joy as she rushed forward to meet him, drawn like a magnet to his presence.

Suddenly aware of movement ahead of him, he looked up to discover her hastening towards him. His body froze to see her there, and he drew in his breath as his eyes hungrily devoured her beauty. The sunlight seemed to illuminate her, casting a golden sheen on her auburn hair even as her face shone with a bright smile of tender affection. His heart constricted with emotion to realize that such an expression was for him alone.

He raced toward her, and when he reached her, glided his hands along her forearms to grasp her firmly at the elbows, wanting nothing more than to cast aside the restricting limits of propriety and crush her to him. He longed to feel her body pressed to his.

She in turn grasped his arms to steady herself, reveling in the feel of his firm hold. His legs were nestled in the folds of her skirt and their bodies were inches apart. Their hearts quickening within, they strove to maintain an appropriate distance from each other, but their eyes communicated the yearning that each felt for the other.

Mr. Bell lingered discreetly behind, ambling slowly about to allow the lovers a few moments of privacy.

"When did you arrive?" Margaret breathed at last, still beaming with the glad surprise of finding him here.

"We arrived not long ago. Fanny wished to rest, but I wished to see where my rose came from," he answered, his eyes still roving over her, noticing the fullness of her lips and the alluring shape of her form in her fitted dress.

Eschewing her mourning clothes, she wore a new gown of lavender muslin with creamy lace spilling from the open sleeves and lining the modest dip of her neckline. The fullness of her skirt and the narrowness of her waist accentuated every curve of her womanly figure.

"You look lovely," he murmured as he brought his gaze back to hers.

She bowed her head demurely, before looking up with a mischievous smile. "Is that what you wish to tell me after three weeks absence?" she teased, her eyes sparkling.

He smiled, amused by her taunting rebuke. Her playful tone was intimate and beguiling, inciting him to respond with a candor that bespoke his honest desire. "What would you have me tell you? That I have not stopped thinking of you since I left you in London? That I should like nothing more than to take you into my arms and show you my affection, were it not for the strictures of propriety which force me to hold my distance from you?" he asked her pointedly, his voice becoming scarcely more than a vehement whisper. The very words he spoke inflamed his passion, and the muscles in his arms throbbed with tension as he strained to keep his distance. He felt like a tiger crouched in readiness to spring, but manacled by unseen chains.

Speechless, she was lost in the searing gaze of his blue eyes, and her pulse quickened at his ardent words.

"Thornton!" Mr. Bell announced his approach, "I see you have managed to escape from the city. How do you find Helstone?" he inquired curiously as the couple moved to stand side by side, Margaret fondly clinging to her fiancé's arm.

"From what I have seen thus far, it is truly beautiful," he answered respectfully. "But I expected no less," he added, glancing with a smile at Margaret.

"Where were you headed?" Mr. Thornton suddenly thought to ask, directing his question to Mr. Bell.

"We were just walking, really. Will you join us?" Margaret responded.

"I believe my mother wishes to speak to you," her fiancé replied, recalling something his mother had said before he had departed the inn.

"Oh," Margaret answered. "Shall we go to the village, then?" she asked him.

"I believe she wished to visit you at the cottage," he clarified.

"Then I should return," she said promptly. "Will you accompany her?" she asked hopefully, not wishing to leave him.

"I will," he promised with an affectionate smile.

"Until later, then, Thornton," Mr. Bell said, bidding him a temporary farewell. "I will see your bride back to her home away from home," he assured him.

"I am obliged to you, thank you," he replied with a lopsided grin and gave a quick nod of his head.

"I will see you soon," he gently spoke to Margaret, loathe to leave her.

Margaret simply nodded with a wistful smile, her eyes revealing her reluctance to be parted from him.

Mr. Bell turned to go, leading Margaret away toward the farther fields from whence they had come. After a few steps, she turned to look back, her luminous eyes searching for another glimpse of her beloved.

He had not moved, but forlornly stood watching her go. She gave him a radiant smile of affection. His face illuminated to receive such a gift and he smiled back before she turned once more to resume her course.

Mr. Thornton and his mother arrived later that afternoon at the picturesque stone cottage. Mrs. Thornton was introduced to Edith and Maxwell, while Dixon went to make tea. Every seat was taken in the drawing room, and the conversation veered from the convenience of train travel to the spring weather.

After tea, Margaret led Mrs. Thornton upstairs to her room to view her wedding gown and to speak in private as the elder woman wished.

"Was Fanny able to rest?" Margaret inquired politely. "John mentioned that she was weary from her journey," she explained as they entered the light and airy bedroom. At its center stood a modest-sized bed with a white Matelassé coverlet and a headboard of carved oak. The afternoon light warmed the honey-colored wooden floor and brightened the clean cotton curtains adorning the window. The wallpaper added gentle color to the room with a vertical pattern of pale blue stripes and rose garlands.

"I am sure she is quite well, thank you," Mrs. Thornton answered, disinclined to discuss her daughter's seeming frailty.

"I brought something I thought you might like," she continued somewhat gruffly as she unfurled a sheath of fine lace that she had wrapped in cotton. "It is my wedding veil. I thought perhaps you might like to wear it. The lace is from Brussels," she offered simply as she carefully laid it out on the bed. Looking to Margaret, she suddenly noticed the wedding gown hanging on the open wardrobe door behind her, a veil of lace carefully draped over the top. "I see you already have one... I should have thought..." she stammered uncomfortably.

Margaret was filled with anxious hope, touched that her future mother mother-in-law had offered such a gift. The young bride hastily intervened as she glanced at the veil she had bought.

"While I do already possess a veil, I would be honored to wear this instead — it is a family treasure," she declared earnestly as she reverently examined the veil, gently running her fingertips over the beautifully patterned edging. "Thank you so much for thinking of me," she said with grateful enthusiasm as she looked up at the elder woman.

Mrs. Thornton was moved by the girl's reaction. Gazing on her with newfound appreciation, she discerned that Margaret's grace was not an outward affectation but composed of sincere kindness and consideration of others.

"Were you wed in Milton?" Margaret asked interestedly as she gently placed the heirloom on her head and admired it in the mirror of the vanity table.

"Yes," the older woman answered proudly. "It has not been worn since," she added with a tinge of melancholy.

Margaret turned quickly to look at her. "Did not Fanny wish to wear it?" she asked in some surprise.

"No," she replied, averting her eyes. "Fanny did not think it suited her dress," she remarked with some embarrassment that her own daughter had dismissed the offered heirloom. "She wore my wedding jewelry instead," she explained with a weak smile.

"I shall also wear my mother's jewelry," Margaret remarked. "But I shall be pleased to have something from John's family to wear. Thank you very much for bringing it to me," she enthused with a sincere smile.

"You are welcome," Mrs. Thornton replied as a gentle smile formed on her lips. She was surprised to find herself warming to the girl her son had chosen.

"Margaret," Mrs. Thornton said solemnly, wishing to speak to her a moment while she had the opportunity. "My son has suffered much," she began firmly, "and while he is strong, he has a tender heart. I hope you will carefully tend to it," she implored quietly, gazing steadily at the young woman who would soon be her son's wife.

"I shall desire nothing more than to tend to him. I do not take for granted his affections," she answered earnestly and honestly, without hesitation, unabashed to admit her feelings to the woman who had long cared for her betrothed.

"Very well," she replied with a twitch of a smile, satisfied that Margaret's answer had been sincere. She turned to leave, having finished her task and being unable to comfortably continue any further discussion of a sentimental nature. "We must get back to prepare for dinner," she commented politely before they headed for the door.

⁂

A long table was set with country elegance at the Lennards Inn. Mrs. Purkins, the innkeeper, had used her own fine china and silver for the special occasion. A beautiful arrangement of wildflowers filled a porcelain vase, and tapered candles in polished brass holders lit the damask covered table.

Arriving before the scheduled hour, the London family was introduced to Fanny and her husband as everyone casually mingled before dinner.

Mr. Thornton was impeccably dressed in his usual black frock coat, and wore a patterned gray waistcoat with a burgundy neckerchief. He sought out Margaret immediately with a warm glance and a gentle smile, making her stomach flutter to recognize once more how especially handsome he looked in his formal attire.

He made his way toward her as she removed her shawl and handed it to the porter, revealing a silk gown of midnight blue that fell just off the shoulders and gently sloped downwards to a point in the front. Stunned by her beauty, his smile vanished as he drank in the sight of her alabaster skin, his eyes searing her with barely veiled desire.

Margaret was confused to see his smile dissipate and wondered if something was wrong. With slight trepidation, she charmingly held out her hand to him as she had at the Master's dinner almost a year ago. He gently grasped her fingers and raised her hand to place a lingering kiss on the back of it, regarding her all the while with a smoldering look that took her breath away. His lips curved upward with a gratified smile as he lowered her hand but did not release it.

"You look beautiful," he declared in a deep voice for her alone, recalling with a mischievous glint in his eye how she had rebuked him for similar words hours ago.

She accepted his compliment with a beaming smile. "I only hope I will not be too distracting," she teased, her eyes twinkling.

"I am certain the conversation will not be half as alluring, but I shall attempt to be sociable nonetheless," he retorted with a devilish grin and a penetrating gaze that revealed his yearning to be alone with her.

Margaret dipped her head coyly, feeling warmth rise to her cheeks to be so ardently admired.

Raising her face, she glanced around the room. "Where is Nicholas?" she asked, suddenly aware of his absence.

"He is here in Helstone, but I believe he is uncomfortable about joining our family gathering this evening," Mr. Thornton gently explained. "He promised to join us for the wedding breakfast. He gives you his warm regard," he relayed, hoping she would understand their friend's reticence to dine with family on such a formal occasion.

Margaret had barely nodded her sympathetic accord when Fanny's shrill voice broke over their private conversation.

"Miss Hale!" she called, "or should I say 'Margaret,' - for we shall be sisters soon," she remarked with her usual giddy enthusiasm. Not waiting for an answer, she continued on. "Who would have thought it? We were all quite certain John would remain a bachelor. 'Married to the mill,' I always said," she remarked with a satisfied smile. "It seems you have been successful in winning his attention," she astutely assessed.

Dinner was announced, saving the couple from the trouble of responding as everyone moved to be seated.

Conversation drifted easily through various topics, as the guests compared the benefits and detractions of country and city life. Inevitably, discussion of the burgeoning city populations led to talk of London and Milton's future possibilities. Maxwell was quite impressed with the prospects of industry on the whole, and Milton in particular.

Margaret was once again impressed by her fiancé's perceptive insights and commanding knowledge of every subject. Regarding him with admiration, she found his gaze often returning to her, and felt his eyes on her whenever she offered her own comments and opinions. Seated across from one another, they had many occasions to share fond glances throughout the evening.

At length, Fanny interjected to say how excited she was to be going to the opera in London after the wedding. "We will stay two nights in London before going home. Mother will join us, of course," she added superfluously. "I hope to see the Alhambra as well. I have longed to see its exotic structure," she enthused.

"The Alhambra," Maxwell repeated pensively. "I believe the building in London is a replica of the original structure in Spain," he remarked. "Is that not right?" he asked her.

"Yes, I believe you are right," Mr. Bell affirmed, noting Fanny's look of confusion.

"Yes, well I should like to see it in either place," she commented blithely, "and London is so much more convenient," she reasoned.

"London is not so far from Helstone, Margaret," Fanny continued. "Perhaps you could make a day's journey to the city while you are here on your wedding trip - there are so many different performances you could attend," she suggested helpfully to her brother's fiancé. "Although it is quite lovely here, I think I should tire of the country after a day or two. I can't imagine what you will do here to entertain yourselves for an entire week," she declared wonderingly, oblivious to the discomfiture her comment caused as Watson coughed distractedly and everyone averted their eyes from one another.

Her head bowed in flushed embarrassment, Margaret floundered a moment before bringing her attention to Fanny with a self-conscious answer. "I believe we will be happy here. There are many places I should like to show John," she replied with stilted cheerfulness, her face still pink with embarrassment.

"I believe Margaret knows every nook and cranny of the village," Mr. Bell announced with vigor, masterfully changing the direction of the discussion. "I'm told she accompanied her father on his visits, but could just as often be found in the countryside with a book or her paintbrush," he added with fond amusement.

Mr. Thornton startled at his last remark and looked interestedly at Margaret for her answer.

"It's true," she admitted. "I am familiar with every lovely vista in the area," she said, grateful for Mr. Bell's astute navigation of the conversation.

The candles flickered low when dinner concluded and the London guests prepared to leave the inn. Mr. Thornton requested the privilege of accompanying them, not yet ready to relinquish his time with Margaret.

The short carriage ride took them out of the village into the countryside where the Thompson's cottage stood a fair distance up the lane. As the London party wound their way up the path, the engaged couple followed, lingering outside the door after the others had gone inside.

The western horizon still glowed faintly with the last vestiges of the day's effulgence while the darker night consumed the eastern sky. The coming dawn of their wedding day was as certain as the order of the universe.

Crickets sounded their evening song of harmony and peace as the scent of honeysuckle and lavender filled the cool, night air.

"We've not been alone all day," Mr. Thornton murmured as he reached out to hold her face between his hands. His thumbs gently caressed her cheeks as he studied her adoringly.

"No," Margaret agreed breathlessly, unable to say more. Mesmerized by his nearness and his soft touch, her senses tingled with the anticipation of his kiss.

He brought his face to hers and gently kissed her lips and this first intimate touch sent a tingling sensation coursing through their bodies. Returning again and again to deliver soft kisses, he felt his long-practiced patience swiftly unravel as his deeper passions stirred to life. He brought one hand down to wrap his arm around her and pull her closer.

Margaret put her arms around his waist, heedless of her shawl which slowly slid off her shoulders onto the ground.

Their pulses raced as their lips met more fervently until their mouths opened to each other. Their tongues mingled with a famished urgency that continued to escalate until they were forced apart to catch their breaths.

"Margaret, I've missed you so much," he panted desperately as his eyes roved over the luminescence of her ivory skin, his face only inches from hers.

"I've missed you, too," she avowed, her eyes pleading for him to understand.

Her innocent yearning enflamed his need for her, and his mouth sought refuge in the tender spot of her neck just below the ear, where the sweet scent of her seemed strongest.

She gasped and held her breath as she felt his lips caress her, instinctively tilting her head to one side to offer him the length of her neck.

The fragrant smell of her and the feel of her silken skin created an elixir of desire, intoxicating his senses. Dragging his open mouth down the column of her neck and across her shoulder, he tasted the skin that his eyes had feasted upon all evening.

She sighed softly as he traced a path back to her neck, and grew weak as she surrendered to the rapturous sensation evoked by his ardent attentions. His warm breath and sensual touch sent shivers down her spine. Grasping his waistcoat to steady herself, she trembled to feel her maidenly resolve crumbling away. "John!" she whispered in faint protest.

He heard her soft, low voice speak his name as the intimate whisper of a lover. He hesitated a moment as his lips gently brushed the base of her throat. He knew he should stop, but he could not relinquish her yet - he had waited so long to love her! His pulse hammered his yearning to know just a little more of her. Trembling, he began to move his lips over the creamy skin tantalizingly exposed by her evening gown.

Spellbound by his advances, she stifled a moan and closed her eyes as she felt his lips approach the soft fullness of her heaving chest. "John!" she called out, her voice cracking as she used her remaining strength. "We mustn't..." she whispered, attempting to pull them both back to reason, away from the looming precipice of desire.

He halted, his body screaming to continue its pleasurable pursuit, and slowly lifted his head to meet her gaze. Unabashed by his impulse to love her, his eyes searched hers with searing intensity.

"John, I...." she began, but found she could not speak as she looked into his eyes. She threw herself into his arms, shaking in his powerful embrace as she recognized that she had not wanted him to stop; her knees weakened to realize that tomorrow he would not have to.

He held her tightly against him, nestling his fingers in her hair and kissing the top her head with gentle fervor. He felt overwhelmed with love for this woman who warmed his soul with her very presence. He would be content to spend eternity in just this way, he thought. "I love you," he murmured in a low, resonant voice that calmed the tide of passion that had swept over them.

"Oh, John," she breathed, hugging him closer, "I love you so much."

They stood, locked in a comforting embrace for several minutes, until Margaret moved. "We need not say good night tomorrow," she reminded him wistfully, wishing she could stay in his arms forever.

The corners of his mouth turned upwards as he recognized her unwillingness to part from him. "I am compelled to leave you this one last time, but henceforth you shall not be rid of me," he warned with a teasing gleam in his eye, hiding his deeper need to know that she would never tire of his presence.

"I shall never wish to be rid of you!" she chided him for saying such a thing.

Smiling bashfully at her reassurance, his downcast eyes glimpsed her fallen shawl. He gallantly retrieved it and carefully covered the expanse of skin that still beckoned for his touch. "Good night, my love," he said quietly as he dipped to kiss her lips once more.

She met his kiss, and slowly and tenderly moved her lips in concert with his for one moment more until they both pulled away.

"Good night," she replied.

He stared back, stunned at how easily her gentle kiss had set him afire. He gave her a wistful smile with a slight nod of his head before she turned to open the door and disappeared within.

He headed back down the path to the waiting coach, glancing up at the endless expanse of glittering stars. He could not suppress the smile that slowly spread over his face as he felt the world opening up to him. His future - their future - lay bright before them. Anything was possible now that Margaret would be by his side.

His only task now was to sleep, so that the morrow might begin.

Margaret awoke after dawn to the peaceful sounds of spring. She rose and walked to the window, sweeping aside the curtains to greet the day. The sun was beginning its ascent into the sky, sending filtering rays of sunshine through the branches of the grand oak where a gathering of birds merrily chirped their morning conversations, unconcerned that this day should hold special significance.

Margaret drew a deep breath of contentment and smiled as she took in the scene before her. Today was her wedding day. It would be perfect.

As a young girl, she had dreamed of this day as she supposed all girls did: that on her wedding day she would look and feel like a beautiful princess, gloriously adorned, and that her husband would be handsome. But as she grew older, she discovered that she did not dwell on the subject as much as other girls did. She had not been like Edith, who had vividly imagined all the details of her wedding since she was eight years old.

In fact, Margaret realized that she had not given much thought to marriage in the past few years. Certainly, the idea of it had been somewhere in the periphery of her thought, but she had been too involved in her surroundings, absorbing the world around her and learning new things, that she had not felt the need of anything or anyone to make her happy. The girlhood fantasy had grown dim to her over time. She contemplated that someday she would marry someone with the qualities that she most admired, someone who was intelligent and kind, who did not shirk obligation and duty, or pretend to be something he was not. She had been certain she would recognize such a man if she should meet him.

She had not seen it in John – not at first. She had thought him cold and heartless, as her prejudices had warned her upon arriving in the northern city she had never desired to visit, much less live in.

Over time, she had slowly learned - was reluctantly forced - to see him for who he truly was. It was his kindness and honesty that had won her - and his love. He had loved her quietly and persistently without her even knowing it. She had been overwhelmed to discover his true feelings towards her, and even more overwhelmed to slowly realize that she could not quit thinking of him.

He was everything she had ever wanted in a husband, and more. She could not imagine marrying anyone else. She could not help loving him; it seemed so natural that they should be together. Yes, this was why she was so happy today – it would be the most natural thing in the world to marry him. Nothing else could feel so right, so good.

She was still quietly standing at the window when Dixon knocked on the door to begin the first preparations of the day.

Mr. Thornton's hands rested on the windowsill as he leaned forward to gaze out the open window of his room in the old farmhouse inn. He could see the steeple and slate roof of the church where he would be wed. Why call it a morning wedding, he thought derisively, when it would be closer to noon before it began? He had been ready for almost two hours now and had yet almost another hour to wait.

He was discomfited and perplexed to be so agitated this morning. He had fallen asleep without much difficulty last night, feeling relaxed and happy, so he was surprised to find himself becoming increasingly restless and anxious as the morning wore on. He could not rationalize it. He did not question his decision - he had never been more certain of his intentions in his life.

It did not help that he could hear the high-pitched twitter of his sister's voice from across the hall as she made her preparations for the coming event.

He heard a gentle rapping on his door. "Yes, come in!" he called out more curtly than he had intended.

"Mother," he acknowledged with a cursory glance as she let herself in, but then jerked his head to look at her again. He was stunned to see that she was wearing a fine new dress with long-fitted sleeves and white lace collar - in a flattering shade of pale green. "You look very well," he complimented her, his countenance lightening as he took in the sight of her. He had not seen her in anything but black for nearly twenty years.

"Today my only son gets married," she declared proudly with her chin aloft. "I will rejoice with you," she announced determinedly, as her face scanned his handsome features with affection and pride. She reached out to hold his face in her hands, her heart filled with poignant yearning to tell him how much she loved him, how much he had meant to her all these years. "John..." she began, but could not find the words as tears threatened to fall from her eyes.

He took his mother's hand gently in his and gave it a tender kiss. "Thank you, Mother," he said softly in a low, comforting voice. His eyes attempted to convey all that was left unspoken between them: how grateful he was for her unswerving guidance and support during those long years of deep trial, and how much he appreciated her steadfast devotion and loving care.

Hannah dipped her head to regain her composure and brought it back up to look at him with renewed admiration. "Are you ready?" she asked, busying herself with the superfluous task of straightening his white cravat. He looked resplendent in his deep blue frock coat, white waistcoat and pale gray trousers.

He let out a heavy sigh, "I have long been ready, and have been biding my time," he informed her with exasperation as he began to walk the short length of his room, her words seeming to renew his impatience.

She smiled inwardly at his restlessness. He was a man of purpose and could not abide idleness. He was ready to begin the day's events and needed something to occupy him. "You should take a walk to pass the time," she suggested.

"I have already been out, Mother," he told her wearily as he crossed the room again.

"Then go out again," she directed firmly, "you will do no one any good wearing out the carpet here," she told him, giving him a pointed look as a hint of a smile crossed her face.

He smiled ruefully and gave her a peck on the cheek before he headed out the door, leaving Hannah to stand contemplatively a moment before checking on the progress of her daughter's preparations.

Mr. Thornton was descending the stairs to the main floor when Higgins appeared.

"Higgins!" the restless groom greeted him, glad to see his friend.

Higgins looked dashing in his gray and black gentleman's attire, although he chafed at the snug neckerchief that pulled at his throat.

"I thought I'd see if I could be of any assistance," he explained. "I reckon it's my duty to see that you keep to your time," he said with a slight grin "and I know a man can get himself all in a dither awaiting his hour to arrive," he sagaciously remarked.

Mr. Thornton gave a hearty laugh at Higgins' astute assessment of his own unsettling behavior this morning. "Then perhaps you could join me for a turn about the village. My mother informs me that I am of no use here," he replied in good humor.

"Glad to be of service," Higgins quipped as they headed for the door.

Dixon finished pinning a few orange blossoms in Margaret's hair as Edith rushed into the room to see her cousin before the carriages arrived. After carefully arranging Mrs. Thornton's veil on her head as the finishing touch, Dixon stepped back as Margaret stood from her seat at the vanity to view herself in the long mirror by the wardrobe.

The full skirt and fitted bodice of her gown was of a soft white silk overlaid with fine lace, the neckline being cut open in the front even as tulle and lace rose to surround her neck in the back. Her long, slender sleeves were sheer tulle with a pattern of lace at the cuff, making her hands look small and delicate. The veil's scalloped edging fell just above her elbows at the sides, and sloped downwards to cover her back.

"Oh, Margaret, you are a picture of loveliness!" Edith enthused with a wistful smile, feeling happiness for her cousin's joyful day, but feeling the impending emptiness of her absence from the London house. Aunt Shaw entered the room to admire her niece in her full bridal regalia.

"She's as beautiful as her mother was," Dixon commented, blinking back the tears. "Would that your mother could see you now, Miss Margaret," she added solemnly. "She wore those very pearls," she added with nostalgic importance.

Margaret brought her hand to the string of pearls around her neck in remembrance of her mother. The pearl drop earrings she wore were also her mother's.

"You look beautiful, Margaret," Aunt Shaw agreed, feeling hopeful that her sister would have been happy for Margaret this day.

"Thank you. Thank you all for your help to me," Margaret replied with sincere gratitude for her family and her mother's faithful servant.

Maxwell called out from the parlor below to inform them that the first coach had arrived.

"Mr. Bell should arrive momentarily. We will see you at the church. Don't be late, and don't forget your bouquet!" Edith ordered before leaving the room with the others.

Margaret was glad to have a few quiet moments to be alone. The hustle around her had begun to dismantle the serenity she had maintained all morning.

She glanced fondly at the roses John had sent to her this morning – a dozen were yellow and another dozen a creamy white. Edith had bundled several of each together with a satin ribbon as an elegant bridal bouquet.

Margaret picked up the note that he had sent and read it once more.

My darling Margaret,

My heart has been soaring every since you promised to be mine at the station four weeks ago.

All my hopes will be fulfilled when you give me your hand at the altar today. I can imagine no greater happiness than to be wedded to you, my love.

No man could love you more than I, and no woman could be more treasured.

I am forever yours,

  John

She felt her stomach tighten in excitement to think that even now he might be standing at the church, waiting for her.

Mr. Bell arrived to escort her in lieu of her father and absent brother. "You look radiant, my dear," he professed with vigorous sincerity as he helped her into the carriage. He was honored to perform this service for his friend, and very pleased to see how happy Margaret looked. He would not have felt comfortable giving her away to any ordinary man, but was confident that Thornton would encourage and protect those special qualities in Margaret that made her so unique.

When they arrived in the village, Margaret asked if they might walk the last part of the way, and they alighted from the carriage to set foot on the walkways she had known so well. The bells of the church were pealing as they approached, and Margaret smiled to see that Edith had strewn flower petals along the path nearby as well as on the granite stairs leading up to the heavy wooden doors of the church.

Stepping inside, she was overcome with memories of her father. She stopped to quietly speak to her godfather. "I feel father's presence so much in this place, I fear I may cry," she confessed worriedly.

"You will do no such thing," he stated with conviction. "Your father would wish you to be gloriously happy today, and you will honor his memory best to think of him with joy," he firmly counseled. "Your father thought the world of Mr. Thornton. He would be gratified to see you marry a man of such sterling character," he remarked confidently.

His words struck a chord within her, and she relinquished the feeling of sorrow in exchange for warm memories of love and happiness. "Thank you, Mr. Bell," she said, giving him a look of grateful admiration.

The organ announced the bride's arrival and Edith beckoned to them from the nave's entrance. "It's time," she announced simply with a reassuring smile before turning to reverently precede Margaret down the aisle in a simple gown of pale blue, her bonnet adorned with delicate white flowers.

Margaret took a deep breath and glanced over everyone gathered within before Mr. Bell led her down the aisle. Her heart quickened to catch a glimpse of her intended standing with Nicholas by the altar, but she determined that she would acknowledge those in attendance as she passed them before settling her attention on him.

She noted a few of the older villagers who had heard that the vicar's daughter was getting married, sitting near the back. Dixon watched her proudly from a middle pew as tears streamed down her cheeks. She held Sholto firmly in her stout arms.

Maxwell and Aunt Shaw smiled warmly as she progressed toward the front, and Maxwell gave her an encouraging wink as she glanced at him.

She saw Fanny and her husband to the right, and noticed at once something curiously hopeful about Mrs. Thornton's entire demeanor, but could not think on it further as she drew closer to her place at the altar.

Mr. Thornton was riveted at the first sight of her, when she had appeared at the back of the church. Apprehensive earlier about maintaining control of his emotions, he now cared not that his feelings were on display as he watched her slowly glide toward him.

She was unutterably beautiful, her innocence and purity striking him to the core. He was still in awe that she had chosen him – that the girl who had so haughtily refused to shake his hand would now confidently place her hand in his for her safekeeping.

Arriving at her place at last, Margaret raised her eyes to see her beloved and was arrested by the look of love in his eyes. He took her breath away. She had never seen him look so strikingly handsome before – the blue of his coat gave an intensity to the blue of his eyes, so that she felt she could see the purity and depth of his soul as clearly as one can see infinity in a cloudless sky.

They scarcely heard the vicar's words as he began the service, so bound up were they in the presence of each another, yearning for the moment when they should be allowed to touch.

They answered clearly and unequivocally to the vicar's request for their consent to marry, promising to love, honor, and keep each other as long as they both should live with a deeply felt, "I will."

Mr. Bell then happily performed his duty in presenting the bride, giving Margaret an encouraging smile and a kiss on the cheek before sitting in the front pew to observe the proceedings.

Instructed at last to take Margaret's hand, Mr. Thornton looked to his bride with wonder and inexpressible affection as he moved to offer his hand to her.

When she put her hand in his, a shiver of joy ran through her to feel the comforting warmth and strength of his touch. She felt she had found her rightful home. The world closed in around them, so that they seemed alone before the minister as they began to repeat their sacred vows.

His eyes reverently and tenderly fixed on his bride, Mr. Thornton enunciated his solemn promise: "I, John Thornton, take thee, Margaret Hale, to my wedded wife, to have and to hold, from this day forward, for better for worse, for richer for poorer, in sickness and in health, to love and to cherish, till death us do part, according to God's holy ordinance; and hereto I plight thee my troth." His voice was low and steady, catching briefly with emotion at the word "cherish." He finished with an endearing smile that illuminated his face as he noted the tears filling Margaret's eyes.

A lump formed in Mrs. Thornton's throat as she heard her son speak and saw Margaret's face glow with genuine adoration. She hoped that the girl's devotion would endure.

Margaret's voice wavered with emotion as she began her vows, but it grew steadily stronger as she felt the conviction of each word with every fiber of her being. "I, Margaret Hale, take thee, John Thornton, to my wedded husband, to have and to hold from this day forward, for better for worse, for richer for poorer, in sickness and in health, to love, cherish, and to obey, till death us do part, according to God's holy ordinance; and thereto I give thee my troth." She finished with a loving smile for her beloved, who had listened with rapt wonder to hear her dulcet voice promise herself to him.

They gazed at each other in shared awe at the profound bond that was being created between them as he slipped a ring of gold on her finger and made his final vow. "With this ring, I thee wed, with my body I thee worship, and with all my worldly goods I thee endow: in the Name of the Father, and of the Son, and of the Holy Ghost. Amen."

They knelt to receive a blessing, and then stood in silent wonder with their hands clasped together as the vicar pronounced them man and wife.

When the service had finished and they had signed the register, the organ sounded a majestic conclusion as they bounded down the aisle arm in arm in a jubilant euphoria that the feat was accomplished – they were married!

The church bells pealed once more as the couple emerged into the sunlight. Mr. Thornton wrapped his arms around his wife's waist and lifted her off her feet, spinning them both around in a dance of exaltation.

Margaret laughed at his exuberance as she clung to his arms.

He set her down and kissed her just as the others began to appear.

Higgins approached the newlyweds first, noting with great satisfaction that their smiles could not be broader.

"Congratulations, Thornton. I've not seen a more beautiful bride," he appraised. "I'm glad to see you both so happy," Nicholas told Margaret after giving her a congratulatory kiss. "I'll be anxious to see you in Milton again…. Mrs. Thornton," he emphasized with a merry smile and a twinkle in his eye.

Margaret rewarded him with a beaming smile, dizzy with happiness to hear herself called by her new name.

As her husband's mother approached, Margaret suddenly realized the reason for her changed appearance – she was not wearing her usual somber attire, but looked vibrant and youthful in the pale shade of green that she had chosen. Hannah Thornton held her son's beaming face in her hands and gave him a kiss before arriving in front of her new daughter-in-law with a happy smile.

"Mrs. Thornton, you look well!" Margaret enthused, as her eyes conveyed approval of her new dress.

"My son is very happy, Margaret. I will rejoice with him and you," she declared, giving her a formal but sincere kiss of congratulations. Margaret thrilled to feel her mother-in-law's genuine joy on their wedding day.

Fanny's felicitations were somewhat reserved. She was uncertain if she should shake hands with Higgins, for she felt slighted that John had not chosen Watson to be groomsman, but had instead asked the troublesome union leader to stand by his side! She was shocked that Margaret had her brother so thoroughly wound around her little finger. Fanny had also been hurt this morning to find that her mother had made John's wedding an occasion to abandon her habitual attire, when she had only worn dull gray to her own wedding several weeks ago.

The wedding breakfast back at the inn was a convivial event for the small group. The newlyweds were lost in a haze of ecstatic joy over their newfound status as husband and wife and the time passed quickly.

An open carriage arrived to spirit the bride and groom away and everyone gathered outside to say their final farewells. Nicholas admonished them to take care of one another and promised to do his best to care for the mill in Thornton's absence. Edith's eyes filled with tears as she hugged her cousin good-bye, while Hannah held her son in a tearful embrace for a brief moment before he assisted Margaret into the carriage. Margaret noticed Dixon's face wavering with emotion as the servant watched her mistress depart with her husband.

Maxwell called out that they should take a lengthy drive so that the cottage would be vacated on their return.

Mr. Thornton drew his wife close and draped his arm around her as they rode through the village. "Are you happy, Mrs. Thornton?" he asked her with a radiant smile.

"I am, Mr. Thornton," she answered simply, looking into his eyes and giving him an equally bright smile in return.

Once outside the village proper, the newlyweds exchanged smiles and stole kisses from each other as they intermittently gazed at the passing scenery of the countryside. The last lilac blossoms of the season diffused their fragrant aroma from leafy bushes along the roadside as the lush green grass of the heath waved in the breeze.

Mr. Thornton was startled when Margaret suddenly called out to stop the carriage. "What is it?" he asked, his brow crinkled with concern.

She turned to him with a reassuring smile. "I would like to show you a favorite place of mine," she announced, her face alight with joyful anticipation to share her delights with him.

He happily assisted her out of the carriage and instructed the driver to wait for them as he followed her past a thicket of elderberry and hawthorn bushes to a gently sloping embankment bordering a shallow brook.

She stopped at a clearing of low grasses. A few giant rocks stood guard near the brook, whose smooth stones had been polished by the water's flow for hundreds of years. A wooded forest began on the other side, creating a secluded feeling to the open spot where they stood.

"Isn't it lovely?" she asked hopefully. "I used to come here all the time in the summer to wade in the water," she told him as she moved closer to the water's edge.

Mr. Thornton broke his fascinated gaze from his bride to take in the scene around him. "It is beautiful," he acknowledged honestly, though he was presently more taken with the beauty of his wife than that of the surrounding view.

When he turned to see Margaret once more, she was slipping her feet out from her satin slippers. He watched entranced as she carefully lifted her skirts and petticoats to step onto the flat stones that were submerged in the flowing water. "Oh!" she exclaimed, "it's cold!" She giggled softly to herself and then looked to her husband. "Come!" she beckoned him with such an innocent and joyous smile he could not resist.

He shook his head in disbelief as he sat on an obliging rock to remove his stockings and shoes and quickly roll up his trousers.

He drew in his breath quickly to feel the water rush over his feet as he stepped in the brook near her. "Very cold," he declared.

She smiled at him, and something turned over deep inside of him. She was gloriously radiant - stunningly beautiful - as she stood there, holding her wedding gown up to wade in the stream like a young girl. *This was his wife*. His days would never be dull and dreary again, but would be filled with the wonder of her joyful spirit.

He stepped forward to twine his arms around her waist and reverently lowered his face to hers, irresistibly drawn to her lips - the rushing water and the occasional lark the only sound around them.

He kissed her for all that she had meant to him in the past and for the joyous promise of all that lay ahead of them, and she felt his kiss unleash all the possibilities of the future as their souls melded into one.

It was a sight to behold, but there was none to view it. The cotton manufacturer from Milton and the vicar's daughter from Helstone stood kissing mid-stream in their wedding finery, the afternoon sun beaming down upon them. The open sky and the glories of nature were their only witnesses.

Chapter Eleven

Mr. Thornton's feet grew numb from the stinging cold of the flowing water, but his heart was warm with love for the woman he held in his arms. He slowly released her from his tender kiss. "Is this how we shall pass our holiday?" he teased her, awed by her ability to constantly surprise him. "Will you show me something of your world every day, so that at length I shall become a carefree country dweller?" he pressed, as he gazed at her adoringly, her face only inches from his.

"Have you never waded in a stream?" Margaret asked curiously, detecting something in his tone that revealed a childlike wonder to explore all things new.

He shook his head with a measure of embarrassment to confess that he had never experienced such a simple pleasure. The river in Milton was deep, and dirty with years of use, and he had seldom visited the countryside.

Her heart went out to him for the years he had worked hard, while others his age had played. He had spent his years in a city with little opportunity to escape his structured confines. Margaret was at once determined that he should know the joy of living in the country, where nature dominated the patterns of everyday life and the constructions and regulations of men were less in evidence.

"Then, yes, it shall be my duty to show you everything wonderful about living here," she declared confidently as she regarded him with affection.

He smiled at her determination and kissed her fervently for her compassion, eager to begin at once the glory of her tutelage.

Mr. Thornton carefully guided her by the waist, as the lovers stepped out of the brook onto the grassy bank. Margaret held up her skirts until she was safely on dry land.

They headed back to the coach, Margaret with wet silk stockings in once-dry slippers and Mr. Thornton in his bare feet, casually carrying his shoes by his side.

Seated in the open carriage once more, they grinned at each other in the shared secret of what they had done as Mr. Thornton brought her snugly against him with a strong pull of his curved arm. She rested her head comfortably on his shoulder as they drove a little further into the countryside before turning around to head to the cottage.

At last, they arrived at the country home that would be their private haven. The driver carried in the groom's trunk as Mr. Thornton helped his wife out of the carriage.

As the couple reached the door, Mr. Thornton swept his bride off her feet to carry her over the threshold. Margaret gasped in surprise, but happily wrapped her arms around his neck. The last time he had held her thus she had seemed lifeless and fragile – a tenuous dream of love and happiness. Now, she was alive and vibrant – and promised to him alone.

Stepping into the cottage, he felt the impulse to continue straight up the stairs and into the bedroom to claim his privilege as her husband, but stopped in the foyer at the foot of the stairs. He was resolved to wait until the time was right. He did not wish to appear overbearing.

"I believe you are supposed to carry me over the threshold of our home," she emphasized playfully, enjoying the demonstration of his strength and the feel of his arms about her.

"I must take every precaution to ensure my great fortune," he replied with mirth as he reluctantly set her down, keeping fast hold of her waist.

Margaret smiled in response but dipped her head timidly, suddenly conscious that they were now alone, and the hours before them unscripted.

"I should change into my day dress," she faltered, her gaze still cast downward. "I'm afraid my dress is a little wet," she explained with a wry smile as she brought her gaze back to his.

He faintly nodded his assent as he attempted to ignore the beguiling images already forming in his head, and watched forlornly as she made her way up the stairs.

"If you need any assistance…" he heard himself call out to her, at once realizing with a measure of mortification how his offer should appear.

She halted at his words, and it suddenly dawned on her with a rush of anxiety that without Dixon, she would indeed need his help to get out of her wedding dress. "Yes," she stammered breathlessly, still frozen in her tracks. "I will require your assistance," she finished, her heart beginning to beat wildly as she continued up the stairs.

His heart clattered in his chest to hear her response, stunned by her request. He stood motionless for a moment as his widened eyes watched her slowly ascend to the upper floor. Stirring himself at last, he quietly followed her.

She was removing her earrings, her hands trembling nervously, as he walked through the door. She unfastened the clasp of her necklace as he stood just inside the doorway, silently scanning the room that they would share. At once pleased with its charm, he glanced at the uncluttered arrangement of simple furnishings, his gaze drawn inevitably back to the bed that was prominently placed in the center of the room.

Margaret felt his eyes follow her as she bustled across the room to the wardrobe, the rustling of her skirts and petticoats announcing their encumbering presence.

He waited patiently for her direction, not quite believing that he should be there, waiting to help her undress. He watched as she pulled a dress from the wardrobe and hung it on the open door. He felt a pang of painful compassion as he recognized her nervousness.

Finally, she turned to offer her back to him. "The fastenings are all in the back," she explained, attempting to sound composed, as if this was a normal routine and not an extraordinary occasion.

He crossed the room to her, feigning a calm demeanor which belied his apprehension. He was already unsteady at the mere thought of his task, and was uncertain of the strength of his resolve to complete it in the manner that she would expect.

He gingerly began to unfasten the small hooks at her neck, silently cursing his fingers as they began to tremble slightly. The delicate fabric fell away as he worked, exposing first her neck and then a portion of her back. As he bent lower, the air was infused with the scent of jasmine and the silken skin of her neck only inches from his face. His eyes drank in the vision before him. Unable to resist her allure any longer, he bent even lower to place a delicate kiss on the curve of her back.

She drew in her breath at the touch of his lips and closed her eyes in breathless expectation.

Sensing no resistance, he interspersed light kisses from her neck to her back, following his hands as he continued to unfasten the hooks down to her waist. Every brush of his fingers sent tingling shivers down Margaret's spine.

She began to pull at her cuffs to free her arms from the slender sleeves, and he moved to assist her, gliding his hands across her back and over the curving slope of her bare shoulders, allowing the dress to slip to her waist. The feel of her soft skin and the suggestiveness of the gesture made his heart pound with his desire to experience more of her, his resolve melting in the fervent heat caused by her loveliness.

Powerless to resist the tantalizing smoothness of her bare skin, his hands caressed her shoulders and arms as his mouth found the curve of her neck and followed the gentle slope to her shoulder.

Margaret felt her insides quiver at his touch, her pulse racing at his intimate advances. When he gently slid his hand over hers, she whirled around to face him, her eyes plaintive with longing.

He took one glance at her and clasped her to him, melding his mouth over hers with a fervency that excited her, even as she trembled in his fierce possession.

He grasped her tighter, claiming her with his mouth and tongue, desperate to be at one with her. He felt himself slipping into the abyss of his darker desires, his self-control vanishing as her arms wrapped around his neck.

He tore his lips from hers to look into her eyes. "Margaret," he panted, "will you lie with me?"

"I am yours, John," she whispered, gazing at him steadily so that he might know that her very soul belonged to him.

His eyes flared with the recognition that all that had hitherto been forbidden was now his.

He returned his mouth to hers, kissing her tenderly as his hands trembled to loosen the fabric ties of her corset.

She moved her hands to his chest and slowly pushed his lapels to urge the removal of his coat, causing him to groan in heady anticipation of her willing participation.

He broke away from her to release himself from his blue frock coat, casting it off to land on a chair before returning to his delicate task. No sooner had he resumed his attention to the lacings of her corset, than he felt her fingers moving to free the buttons of his waistcoat.

He could scarcely breathe. The thought that she should desire him promised a bliss so profound that he found her fastidious gesture an excruciating torture.

He gently removed her hands from their purpose and kissed each in turn, and they silently communicated with one another with their eyes.

She moved to pull her dress up over her head, her helplessness in the daunting task tacitly requiring his assistance. With his help, the silk slid easily over her torso and brushed over her hair, loosening the pins.

He laid the dress carefully over the chair, and began to unbutton his waistcoat even as she undid the fastenings of her crinoline and petticoats. They quickly undressed in silence, stealing glimpses of each other, in awe of what was happening.

At last, he stood wearing only his trousers, as she still wriggled to slide out of her corset, clad in a sleeveless cambric slip. She removed the pins from her hair, and her auburn tresses tumbled past her shoulders.

Her breath quickened at the sight of him. Her eyes roved over the chiseled form of his chest and the muscled shape of his arms. His presence was commanding, and yet she detected something of his vulnerability. She ached to touch the broad expanse of his skin, and yearned to feel his strong possession of her.

His heart beat thick and fast as he moved to close the distance between them. He took her into his arms and kissed her.

She quivered to feel the press of his bare chest against the thin fabric of her slip, and willingly opened her mouth to him to experience his deeper kisses. Tremblingly, she placed her hands against the smooth surface of his back.

His passion rose quickly, sending his hands to explore the curves of her body now unbound by layers of feminine accoutrements.

She melted as his hands slid over her breasts and down to her waist, his palms stroking the curve of her hips in aching slowness.

He tugged at the fabric at her hips, desperate now to remove all boundaries between them.

She disengaged herself from him and looked into his eyes. Without a word, she moved to the bed and deftly removed her slip with one fluid motion, dropping it to the floor. She pulled back the covers and climbed into bed. As she did so she recalled something of what Edith had explained. With her knees bent slightly to steady herself, she sat waiting for him as she slowly brought her eyes to his.

She looked to him like a goddess, for truly, he had only seen such a vision depicted in paintings and sculpted in marble, never in living flesh. His pulse hammered and he swallowed hard at the realization that she revealed her beauty to him alone. Her soft, shapely form was presented for his pleasure.

He swiftly stepped to the bed and sat on the edge next to her, his eyes exploring the glory of her until they met her own. He stared in wonder and sank his fingers into her hair to grasp her neck and pull her toward him. He kissed her tenderly at first and then more ardently until, tremulously, he pushed her back onto the pillows. Breaking contact with her mouth, his lips quickly grazed her throat. He continued to trace his course downward, taking into his mouth the pink flesh that tantalizingly rose to meet him.

She cried out in pleasurable surprise, arching her back instinctively to give him more of herself and raking her fingers through the hair at the nape of his neck.

Inflamed by her reaction, he moved to cover her with his body, cautiously lowering his full weight upon her. He continued his blissful ministrations as she moaned softly beneath him, until he could take no more.

He brought his face to hers, both of them aflame with desire.

"Margaret, I only mean to love you," he rasped, forewarning her of his urgent need. His body ached for its fulfillment.

"I know," she softly assured him, looking lovingly into his eyes.

He searched her face with tender adoration before lifting himself off the bed to remove his trousers.

She glanced modestly away for a second but brought her gaze back to him again in breathless wonder of what should be revealed to her. A quiet gasp caught in her throat as she glimpsed the measure of his full manhood before he climbed over her again.

He brought his face to hers for a gentle kiss, his body quaking with emotion, before moving to find his way within. Slowly but firmly, he seated himself inside of her. A soft groan escaped his lips as he felt her warmth surround him. He stilled a moment to see her wince, and then lowered himself to gently kiss her forehead before he began a slow, rhythmic movement.

He lifted his head and hovered over her, closing his eyes in the rapture of the sensations overcoming him.

Margaret watched his face in fascination as his rhythm quickened, tensing in uncertain anticipation as she felt the weight and strength of his taut body. She let her fingers explore the contours of his muscled arms as his movements increased in intensity until he suddenly cried out his pleasure and was still. She felt him shudder his relief before he collapsed upon her breast.

It was done. They had truly united as husband and wife. Overwhelmed by the significance of what they had done, and astounded by the power her body had to please him, she felt tears spring to her eyes as he began to cover her face with gentle kisses. She was gloriously happy to consider the great love that had engendered such an event, and felt a joy beyond measure to know that she had pleased him. Hot tears streamed down her cheeks as she wrapped her arms tightly around his neck.

He continued his soft caresses until his lips met with the wetness on her face. At once alarmed, he moved to lift himself up. "Margaret, I have hurt you!" he declared with great concern, his eyes filled with worry.

She stayed him with a tight clasp, holding him close. "No, no!" she quickly assured him, her eyes entreating him to believe her. "I am happy," she whispered as a smile warmed her face. "I am so happy, John," she repeated as she gently caressed his neck and shoulders with her small hands.

His heart melted to hear her words. Satisfied that he had loved her well, he felt a profound joy to know that she rejoiced to receive his passionate attentions. Amazed that she should love him so, he rolled them both to their sides and drew her into his loving arms, nestling her head under his chin. "My Margaret," he murmured into her hair as they clung to each other. He stroked her back and whispered her name again before they both drifted into a peaceful sleep.

The sun slowly descended in the sky as the lovers slept, filling the room with the dimmer glow of late afternoon.

Mr. Thornton woke first, opening his eyes to find Margaret sleeping in his arms. He studied her face with reverent fascination, afraid to move lest he wake her. Her lips were slightly open, curved in a faint smile. She looked so peaceful; his heart swelled with love for this precious woman.

He was in awe at the thought that she had entrusted her care to him. He had never felt more determined to protect and keep her from any harm. He moved his arm carefully to brush aside a wisp of her hair that had fallen across her face.

She stirred slightly and her eyes fluttered open.

He watched as recognition slowly illuminated her face and she smiled at him.

He smiled in return, his heart twisting with the poignancy of her smile.

"Have we slept long?" she asked groggily, unaccustomed to napping in the middle of the day.

"An hour, perhaps," he surmised.

"We should get up," she commented as she began to fully waken, stretching her limbs out from the entangling company of his own.

"Should we?" he countered, his blue eyes questioning hers with a lustful gleam, not willing to relinquish such warm and intimate contact.

She smiled bashfully at his reply. "We cannot remain....indoors all day," she protested, her luminous eyes responding to him.

Mr. Thornton held his tongue, for at this moment he felt that he would like nothing more than to spend the entire week in this very location, but he did not wish to overwhelm her with his insatiable need to be close to her. "Perhaps we could linger a little longer," he suggested hesitantly as he buried his free hand in her hair and captured her lips with his in a tender kiss. Unable to resist the inviting feel of her soft lips, he returned for more, enraptured by the spell of her willing response.

As their kisses deepened, she began to rub the palm of her hand over the subtle contours of his chest, unaware of the frisson of desire she aroused in him.

He groaned to feel her delicate hands move sensuously over him. Moving his hand, he started his own exploration of her body – running his hand down her neck and over her shoulders to brush the sides of her breasts, her hips, and her thighs. She made muffled sighs of approval as he continued to caress her body with his hand, until his need could no longer be denied.

He rolled her beneath him and, breaking contact with her lips, gave her a steady look of love before entering her slowly again. He breathed a low sigh as he filled her to the hilt, and stilled a moment before moving with slow, steady strokes.

His gentle pace relaxed her and the love she saw in his eyes melted the tension from her body. She slid her hands along his back, reveling in the smooth expanse of his skin as his steady rhythm encouraged her to surrender to him, letting her feel the sensations beginning to build deep within her.

He lowered his head to hungrily kiss her mouth, and ran his fingers over the fullness of her breast, causing her to grip him tighter as she lost herself in a surge of ecstatic sensation. She was only faintly aware of the sounds she made as he intensified his movements in response.

At last, she cried out her rapture as something within her burst and spilt a warm flood of pleasure throughout her body. She heard him cry out his rapture in turn, and stilled as the feeling within her ebbed, her body quivering in response.

Margaret opened her eyes to look at him, astounded at what had happened to her. Searching his face for his reaction, she saw him regard her with wonder. "I did not know…" she began meekly, questing him with curious eyes.

"Nor did I," he acknowledged, amazed and delighted that her pleasure should rival his own; they smiled in shared secrecy at their new discovery.

They lay comfortably in each other's arms for a time, reverently exploring the features that innocently fascinated them. Margaret reached out to touch his face, gently running her hand over his roughened cheek and jaw while Mr. Thornton languidly pulled the silken tresses of her hair through his fingers.

"I should make tea," Margaret offered at length, noting the day's ebb by the light coming in the window.

"If you wish," he replied, allowing her the freedom to do as she pleased.

She rose from bed and hastily donned the slip that was crumpled on the floor. "Will you not dress?" she asked with a casual lilt, self-consciously aware of her husband's eyes on her.

He smiled guiltily but secretly rejoiced to indulge in the simple pleasures of married life. "I will," he promised with some reluctance, for he was loathe to leave the place that seemed such a haven of warmth and delight.

❦

After a spot of tea in the kitchen, they moved outdoors to leisurely walk the surrounding property of their temporary home. The sun cast ever-lengthening shadows across the grass while a few crickets could be heard sounding the evening's preamble.

Behind the house was rolling heathland - a low stone wall the only mark of man's presence. A few large oaks grew near the house, where a chicken coop and a few other structures were strategically placed for the occupants' use.

The grandest oak stood majestically on the eastern side of the house, its larger branches thicker than lesser trees and stretching out to reach far beyond its solid source.

The view from the front of the cottage was expansive, revealing miles of grassy heath and distant copses. The edge of a wooded forest lay to the east and a dirt lane led west to the village.

As they wandered the front garden, Margaret delighted in pointing out her favorite flowers and colors, which seemed to her amused husband to be every last one.

The sound of an approaching horse and cart led them down the path to greet one of the village farmers, whose wife had sent along dinner for the newlyweds. Margaret asked him about his family and kindly thanked him for the thoughtful service. She had been told in advance by Mrs. Purkins at the inn that some of the villagers would assist them in such a manner – as a gift to the old parson's daughter.

After they ate and cleared the kitchen table, Margaret washed and put away the dishes while her husband started a fire in the parlor.

They spent the rest of the evening snuggled closely together on the burgundy sofa, reminiscing about their grand day. They punctuated their conversation with kisses until, at length, their tender kisses become the only conversation between them.

The firelight cast a warm glow in the darkness of the quiet room.

"Perhaps we should retire," Mr. Thornton suggested, breaking the silence in a voice taut with kindling desire.

Margaret rose from her seat in agreement and, without a word, preceded him as they both climbed the stairs to their bedroom.

The newlyweds woke early the first morning of their holiday, but did not rise from their bed until later.

Margaret was the first to rise, and entered the kitchen to prepare breakfast for her husband. She noted that dried herbs hung from the wooden beams above the window at the porcelain sink. A black-leaded stove stood in the large inglenook fireplace, and the gray flagstone floor held a sturdy wooden table with spindle-backed chairs.

She was tending the kettle at the stove when John appeared. He wrapped his arms around her waist from behind and nestled his face into her neck to kiss her.

"Good morning, husband," she delighted in greeting him with a broad smile, her insides flooding with a warmth of happiness.

"Good morning, my wife," he responded with equal satisfaction, reveling in the freedom of holding her whenever he wished.

"If you will fetch me some eggs, I will make you breakfast," she offered.

"Eggs?" he repeated quizzically, uncertain of how he should oblige her.

She turned to face him. "The chicken coop is out the back, if you will recall. You should find some fresh eggs there," she directed him patiently, recognizing his unfamiliarity with such a task.

He looked hesitant, but turned to go out. She smiled to think of the Master of Marlborough Mills standing amongst the chickens at his wife's bidding.

When he returned with a handful of eggs, she noted with tender amusement that he looked pleased with himself. He had rolled up his shirtsleeves, and she recognized how relaxed and handsome he appeared without his long, dark frock coat. It will do him good to spend the week here, she mused happily.

The couple strolled arm-in-arm towards the village later in the day, intent on buying various sundries for a picnic lunch. The day was warming quickly as the noon hour drew close, and the long grasses had lost their morning dew.

She led him through the familiar fields that led to her old home as he remarked on the seemingly endless open verdure. "Did you ever visit the country as a child?" she asked curiously.

"My grandmother took me to the country a few times when I was a young boy. I believe we visited her sister there," he told her.

"What do you remember about it?" she ventured to ask.

"Running," he answered simply. "I don't believe I'd ever seen such open space. I would just run for running's sake," he recalled happily.

She smiled at his answer, trying to imagine the little child from the city running to his heart's content in the open fields. "Fred and I would race each other. He would always win, unless he pretended to fall," she remembered fondly as they approached the outlying property of the parsonage.

"Here," she announced and set down her empty basket. "We would race to that old tree over there," she said, pointing to a thick elm many yards away.

"Ready? Go!" she called out playfully and, to his astonishment, began to run in the direction she had indicated. She looked back with a smile to see if he would follow and laughed to see his startled face as he made a start towards her.

She was no match for him with her long skirts and short limbs and he soon caught up with her and pulled her flush against him as she laughed and caught her breath. Her playfulness incited his ardor for her. He studied her face with adoration and desire before regaling her with a powerful kiss.

She held her hat on and willingly accepted his attention before he relinquished her lips. "I should remind you that we are on the parson's property," she chastised him for his impropriety, her eyes sparkling with mirth.

"If you will not run away from me, then perhaps I should be able to control myself," he responded with a warning tone, holding her fast by the waist.

"But I would not have any fun," she protested as she suddenly wrested free from his grasp and darted across the grass once more.

He stood stunned for a second before dashing after her.

This time, as he reached for her, she swerved out of his grasp and forced him to change direction. She laughed at his quick turn-about, but could not keep her advantage.

When she attempted to evade him yet again, he was prepared for her feint, and snatched her by the wrist. He pulled her against him forcefully and held her firmly in his grasp as she laughed at her game.

My God, how he loved her! The combination of childlike innocence and womanly seduction he found in her threatened to drive him mad.

"You are a vixen, do you know that?" he declared vehemently, restraining himself from consuming her with kisses.

"And you married me," she responded to implicate him in her defense, still somewhat breathless.

"I did," he said, giving her a piercing stare that bespoke his deep affection. "And I shall never regret it. You are my heart, Margaret. I cannot be without you," he confessed with utter honesty, his playfulness vanished.

Margaret was at once serious, moved by his ardent admission. "And you are mine," she replied before leaning in for a kiss. At once tender and passionate, their kiss lingered longer than either had intended. Finally relinquishing their sublime contact, they stared at each other in silent adoration.

Remembering their purpose, they resumed their stroll toward the vicar's house on their way to the village.

"You must have many fond memories of your life here. It is a beautiful place," Mr. Thornton commented.

"Yes, there are memories everywhere," she said wistfully, recalling how happy her childhood had been. As she walked near a sunny knoll, the painful memory of Henry's proposal came back to her. He had found her lying in the sun in this very place. How she rued the day that her childhood had seemed to come crashing to a halt!

Mr. Thornton noted the look of sadness that crossed her face. "What is it?" he asked with gentle concern.

Margaret startled to be so openly read, and answered vaguely. "I was just remembering something," she said.

"It was not pleasant. Will you tell me?" he pleaded softly.

She looked at his tender expression and decided to relent. Perhaps it would feel better to confess all that had happened in the past. "Before my family left for Milton, Henry visited me," she began as she stared at the grass in front of her.

"Mr. Lennox?" he asked with some surprise, his interest piqued.

"Yes. I was not aware that I...I had no idea that he..." she stammered, not knowing how to tell him what had transpired.

"He had feelings for you," her husband quickly guessed.

"I suppose so. I..." she hesitated, still looking down in discomfort at the memory of it all.

"Did he ask for your hand?" Mr. Thornton inquired, recalling now the bristling manner in which Henry had received the news of their engagement in London.

"I believe he would have, but I stopped him from speaking," she explained meekly as she looked slowly over to him, remembering distinctly how she had done the same to him.

The memory of his own failed proposal came flooding back to him and he recalled the bitter sting of her rejection when she had refused to hear him out. His world had collapsed into utter despair when she had snuffed out his hope and wounded his pride with her angry words.

It salved his pride even now to realize that she had attempted to be forthright in dealing with her suitors – that she had been unwilling to contemplate marriage without first feeling love.

"You had no feelings for him," he stated more as a fact than a question, but still yearning to hear her confirmation.

"No, not in that way," she explained awkwardly.

The corners of his mouth edged upward as the implication of her statement filled him with joy - she loved him as no other.

"You are smiling," she noted with surprised curiosity.

"How can I keep from smiling, when I have won the affections of one who had a practiced habit of breaking men's hearts?" he asked teasingly.

"I did not!" she protested defensively.

"*My* heart was definitely broken," he insisted, although he still wore a smile at having roused her to such a staunch defense.

"And have I not mended it?" she asked gently as she tugged at his arm, at once repentant for her words that day.

"It has mended remarkably well, but now I shall require your frequent attention to ensure that it remains so," he informed her with a teasing smile.

Leaving the village later, Margaret led them on a long walk to a grassy clearing near a forest where they might eat their picnic lunch. A lone tree served as their shade as well as a backrest as they took turns reading Burns' poetry to each other. Margaret reveled in the comforting sound of his velvet voice as she leaned against him and closed her eyes, his arm wrapped around her waist.

After it had been her turn to read for a while, she began to wonder if he was listening, for he was lying down with his eyes closed, his head comfortably situated in her lap. She brushed the hair over his forehead lightly with her fingers to elicit a smile from him and assure herself that he was still awake.

At length she let him nap whilst she dozed a little herself. When he finally stirred she woke as well and they arose to leave.

Margaret was eager to take her husband into the forest for a unique display of nature's beauty. She was certain that he had never seen the bluebell woods so popular to those who lived in the country. It was a singular treat of spring to go bluebell picking in the forest. The delicate blue bell-shaped flowers would cover the ground of the forest this time of year.

As they began to follow a narrow path into the old forest, she informed him that there was something she wanted to show him, but did not explain any further. When a blue carpet of flowers appeared in the near distance, he was intrigued, and as they drew closer the scene was enchanting. Sunlight filtered readily through the young leaves of the trees and the floor of the forest was covered with the vibrant blue flowers as far as the eye could see.

"It is truly stunning," he remarked in amazement as he took in the sight. "I did not know the woods could be so beautiful," he admitted.

"The flowers remain only for a while in the spring. You have to know when to come," she told him, pleased that he was appreciative of the view.

"I've never seen anything like it," he said, still in awe of the scene around him.

"I am very glad you like it. I don't imagine many people in Milton have ever seen the like," she commented.

"No, I am certain they have not," he agreed. "Thank you for showing it to me. I feel I have been shown a great secret, which many mortals may never discover," he remarked.

"Perhaps," she replied. "Shall we pick just a few for remembrance sake? They don't last very long, I'm afraid. They will wilt quickly," she remarked as she bent down to carefully collect a small handful.

They enjoyed the freedom of reading and conversing at their leisure in the parlor at evening time. The fire was lit once more to chase away the chill of the cool night air. Eventually, they found themselves cozily situated on the plush sofa staring quietly at the fire as they held hands. Margaret smiled to note the sparkle of her engagement ring in the firelight and marveled again at the gold band around her finger.

"The bluebell woods were so lovely," she recalled happily, staring into the fire. "I am glad that you were able to see it," she added as she turned to look at him.

Mr. Thornton concentrated on the way her lips moved while she spoke, and his mind wandered as he remembered the feel of her silken skin against his. His breath deepened as he anticipated the pleasures that awaited them at evening's end.

"You are not listening to me," she gently accused him, feeling the warmth of his searing gaze.

"You mentioned something of the woods," he responded, rousing himself to remember something of what she had said.

"I was endeavoring to remind you of the beauty of nature, Mr. Thornton," she scolded him with a teasing gleam in her eye.

"And I was reveling in it," he declared ardently, his eyes scorching her.

She felt heat rise to her face to be so admired, and bashfully averted her eyes.

He gently lifted her chin up with a curled finger, and she raised her luminous eyes to his.

"You are beautiful, Mrs. Thornton," he stated in a low, resonant tone. He stared at her steadily so that she might know the depth of his sincerity, before leaning forward to taste the lips that beguiled him so. He kissed her gently at first, and then more urgently, until he swiftly slid his arm under her knees and lifted her off the seat.

She quivered in anticipation of his passion, and draped her arms willingly around his neck as he carried her to their bedroom.

The angled rays of the early sun illuminated the curtains and warmed a patch of the wall in the bedroom. The birds had already begun their morning songs when the lovers stirred in their bed.

A pattern had emerged by their third day together. The newlyweds lingered in bed to enjoy the newfound pleasures of married life until mid-morning. Then, after a late breakfast, they would head out for a walk and picnic in a scenic spot. Evenings were spent in the parlor, talking and reading before they headed to their room at night to blissfully reacquaint themselves with each other after the long day's respite.

Mr. Thornton was enthralled to be a married man who spent every possible moment with his beloved. He was enamored of his new wife and could not get enough of her. Secretly, he feared she would soon grow weary of their frequent lovemaking, leaving him to suffer alone the pangs of desire.

Margaret thought herself well-suited to married life. Wondrously happy, she enjoyed the company of her husband and found the pleasures of the marriage bed to be to her liking.

By the time the couple emerged from the cottage in the late morning on Wednesday, clouds had begun to gather on the western horizon. The eastern sky was still blue and inviting, however, so Margaret led them east to sit near the brook that they had frequented on their wedding day.

The air was comfortably warm and a breeze sent small clouds scurrying across the sky as they ate their lunch. After reading to each other for a while, they both fell asleep on the soft grass.

Margaret awoke to a strong wind and the sound of the fluttering pages of the book lying near her face. The sky had darkened with gray clouds and she knew rain was imminent.

"John!" she woke him with a small shake of his shoulder, "it's going to rain," she warned.

They were both up in an instant to hurriedly gather their things and briskly make their escape. They were in sight of the cottage when the first ponderous raindrops fell. Breaking into a run, they dashed toward the broad oak as the rain began to fall faster, pelting them with droplets from the sky. The branches of the tree offered little coverage by the time they reached it, and they began to laugh as they ran the short distance to the front of the cottage.

As Margaret opened the door, the book in the crook of her arm fell to the stone steps. Mr. Thornton bent down quickly to retrieve it, spilling the contents of the basket he carried to the ground.

Stepping into the house, Margaret covered her mouth in surprise at his sudden misfortune, but began to laugh as he scrambled to pick everything up in the pouring rain.

Finally sweeping inside and shutting the door behind him, he set the basket down and grasped her arms. "Are you laughing at me?" he queried, with a tone of warning, a smile on his lips.

"You are all wet!" she declared, trying to stifle her laughter, but decidedly unsuccessful.

"You are wet as well," he reminded, noting with smoldering eyes how her blouse clung to her shapely form.

"But you are truly soaked," she countered, suppressing a giggle to see his hair and clothes dripping wet. "You should change clothes in the kitchen..." she began to instruct him before he silenced her with a kiss.

He pulled her against him as his tongue stroked hers, hungrily kissing her as if he would devour her for her guileless enchantment.

She held her arms away from him to avoid his wet clothes but soon succumbed to the seduction of his kiss and willingly wound her arms about his neck.

He groaned to feel her submit to him and slowly forced her to step backwards to the wall, pressing her against it firmly with his hips so that she should know his purpose.

She whimpered in response, feeling the firmness of his intent through the layers of clothes between them.

He scooped her off her feet and carried her upstairs, impatient to feel her beneath him again and to hear the high-pitched moans she always made that drove him wild with desire.

Mr. Thornton deposited her upright on the bed and swiftly took off her boots, while Margaret began to undo the buttons of her blouse. He stood to unbutton his wet clothes with alarming dexterity, casting the wet garments to the floor one by one as he peeled them off his body.

Margaret stood by the bedside, hurriedly working to free herself of her skirt and petticoats, her wet blouse already on the floor.

He approached her with decision, and the look in his eyes told her to lie down. As soon as she had done so, he hovered over her and, cinching up her chemise with several determined tugs, he grasped her drawers by the sides and pulled them over her hips and off her body.

Having removed all restraints, he thrust into her, groaning in relief to be at one with her. His firm and steady movements inflamed her desire even as he brought one hand up to undo the buttons of her chemise, desperate to have access to all of her.

She assisted him in freeing her bosom and he swooped down to taste and tease her until she lay back on her pillow in helpless surrender.

Lifting his head at last, he propped himself over her and worked with passionate abandon to bring them to completion, until they cried out their rapture in near unison.

She held him to her as their bodies quaked in the subsiding sensation of their union, the sound of their rapid breathing and the pattering rain filling the silence of the room.

He brought his lips to hers and gave her a gentle kiss of contrition. "I fear I was too rough with you," he apologized, his eyes filled with tender concern.

"I have no complaints," she replied with a knowing smile, running her hands along the columns of his muscled arms as he hovered over her. "Do you love me so much?" she asked, partially in jest, teasing him for his uncontrollable passion.

"I love you so much, I sometimes fear for my sanity," he answered in all seriousness. "And now…" he said, as his eyes roved over the glory of her natural beauty, "now it is much worse," he confessed helplessly with a sigh.

Her eyes warmed with loving affection, but she spoke with a light tone. "For better or for worse?" she quipped with a smile.

He could not help but smile back. "Yes, for better or for worse," he declared, rewarding her comment with a kiss.

The rain came down in torrents while Margaret hung up their wet clothes to dry in the scullery and John started a fire in the inglenook fireplace and lit the stove.

They talked about the storms they remembered and childhood fears as they sat drinking tea in the warm kitchen.

A loud crack and a following thud drew them hastily to the window to discover that a branch from one of the oaks had fallen. Margaret remarked with humor that they now had a story they could both remember.

Though the drenching subsided, the wind continued to rage outside throughout the afternoon and into the night.

Evening time found them once again in the parlor. Margaret leaned comfortably against her husband's shoulder as she sat thinking. Mr. Thornton perused the pages of a book on the Renaissance that he had selected from the cottage shelves.

"John," Margaret hesitantly began as she sat up straight to ask him something of import. "You never speak of your father. Will you not tell me more of your past?" she gently pleaded.

He closed the book and stared into the fire, his face somber with gathering memories.

"Father told me what happened," she cautiously revealed. "I admire you for all that you did," she encouraged him. "I don't know anyone who would have done what you have."

"I would not wish anyone to experience what I have," he replied quietly, his gaze still fixed ahead of him.

She acknowledged his emotions with respectful silence for a moment, before speaking again. "I see no shame in your past. It was not of your doing. You were only a child," she consoled him, conjecturing that his reluctance to speak was borne of the embarrassment that poverty engenders.

He blinked at her words, but still did not speak.

"What was your father like?" she ventured to inquire with some trepidation.

To her surprise he answered readily, though still directing his gaze to the fire. "He was a good man. He made a terrible mistake and was not strong enough to accept the consequences," he replied evenly. "I hated him for it," he remarked with no trace of the bitter emotion that he had held. "I hated him for his cowardice and what he did to my mother," he explained calmly, finally looking to his wife for her reaction.

She regarded him with great compassion. She could lay no blame upon him for the bitter feelings he had held in the past. Instead, she was impressed that he had not succumbed to it, but had seemed to have risen beyond it. "You have forgiven him?" she presumed.

"Yes," he answered simply. "It was not his intention to harm us, but I very much regret his selfish choice," he admitted solemnly.

Margaret was silent a moment before she spoke. "You said he was a good man. What do you remember of that?" she inquired, endeavoring to remind of him of his father's redeeming qualities.

A hint of a smile lightened his expression as he thought on it. "He told me stories many nights before I went to sleep – grand tales of adventures in faraway places," he related. "His voice was deep and soothing," he recalled.

Margaret smiled to hear his boyhood recollections. "And your mother...were they happy together?" she asked tentatively.

His smile vanished at the poignancy of the question. "Yes, I believe so," he answered. "I can remember that my mother used to laugh," he told her, his eyes growing distant. She watched as a faint smile came to his face at the memory of it, and then observed it fade into solemn stillness again.

Her heart went out to them both – child and mother – for all that they had endured. She resolved that she would remember to be kind to her mother-in-law even when the elder woman was cold and unsmiling. Margaret knew that she owed a debt of gratitude to Mrs. Thornton for all that she had borne and done to raise such a fine son.

Both were silent as they watched the dancing flames of the fire.

She ardently hoped that she could be a comfort and help to him in all his endeavors. She did not wish for him to bear his burdens alone any longer.

"John, I wish to be an aid to you. Promise me you will not hide your worries from me. I could not bear it," she implored. "I wish to be a comfort to you, as you have promised to be to me," she pleaded softly.

He looked to her with a measure of wonder and affection. "Margaret…I do not wish to keep anything from you. There will be no secrets between us," he vowed.

She gave him a faint smile of satisfaction.

"You have suffered great difficulties and have worked hard to overcome them," Margaret remarked gently. "I fear you have not known much of joy these many years," she surmised sadly.

"No, I own that I have not," he admitted ruefully, reaching for her hand.

She turned to face him with feeling, wishing fervently that he should now only experience the good of life. "You deserve every happiness, John," she declared as she gently stroked the strong line of his jaw.

He deftly moved her onto his lap and she draped her arm around his shoulders.

"I have found it," he told her with tender honesty, staring straight into her eyes.

Margaret's eyes filled with tears as the looked at him. Her heart ached to love him as he had never been loved before. "Oh, John," she whispered, and hugged him tightly.

They held each other for a long time as the fire crackled and the wind wailed beyond the walls of their safe haven.

Chapter Twelve

Margaret awoke to a room filled with gentle, warming light. Birds chirped, heralding another day.

The wind and rain had passed, and she felt the calm peace that comes after a storm has ceased. It was a simple comfort of nature to know that however fierce the storm or however dark the night, the sunshine of day would return.

Margaret smiled in her contentment. Everything felt new and wonderful now. The former days of trial and sorrow had vanished, transformed into the dawning of a new life where joy and love would reign.

How strange it seemed to be here in Helstone, her childhood home, but no longer a child. She had never before slept without her nightclothes, and yet here she was, unclothed under the covers, lying next to the man who was now her husband. She was a wife, and would gladly bear all the tender responsibilities of care for one who accepted her affections with reciprocal joy.

She looked over to where he lay, facing the wall, and watched the gentle rise and fall of his sleeping form.

She felt her heart swell with unutterable affection. He had shown her love as she had never known before. He did not require her to feign a role of perfect cheerfulness, and expected her to speak her mind. He knew well her faults and encouraged her intellect. She felt a perfect freedom to say and do as she pleased, which she had not felt since the days of her childhood. He did not ask anything of her but to love him, which was the easiest and most pleasant thing in the world to do.

She rejoiced, in turn, to know she played a part in his present restfulness. He had worked so hard and knew so little of easy pleasures. She wished to bring him every happiness and to fill his days with deep contentment.

She wriggled closer to him beneath the bed covers and pressed herself gently against his back. Sliding her hand over his shoulder, she nestled her chin on his neck to bring her lips close to his ear. "It is getting late," she whispered softly, unable to suppress a smile at the thought of his waking to her gentle caresses. "We went to bed late," she recalled aloud.

He smiled but did not open his eyes. "We went to bed early enough," he commented, his voice low and gravelly as he awoke from sleep.

"Yes, but we did not sleep until later," she reminded him with a knowing lilt and kissed the tender skin beneath his ear, moving onto the rough surface of his jaw.

"Mmm…I recall…" he answered with a broad smile at the memory of it, reveling in the feel of her every touch.

"You are becoming quite lazy here," she teased him. "Are you not usually up at dawn?" she asked as she brought her arm down to hug his chest.

He captured her hand and held it fast to him. "Often before dawn. I am at the mill at dawn or shortly thereafter," he replied.

"Do you miss it?" she asked curiously, wondering how often his thoughts tended toward the work he had so diligently managed for years on end.

"Miss what?" he asked, uncertain to what she referred.

"Do you miss the mill? You have seldom been away from it this long," she remarked.

He quickly turned to face her, incredulous at her query. "Miss it?" he repeated with wonder. "How could I miss it when I am so blissfully distracted by such pleasant surroundings?" he asked, taking in the sight of her voluptuous bare shoulders and arm as they laid over the coverlet. His eyes followed the alluring trail of her long, chestnut hair to where the curled tresses splayed and settled over the alabaster skin that was exposed to him.

"I thought you might still think of it. It has been your daily concern for so long," she countered, searching his face for his honest answer.

"It has come to my mind a few times, but I find it relatively easy to dismiss. I am much more interested in my current situation," he informed her with a suggestive smile as his fingers began to play with the tendrils of hair on her shoulder.

"I should make breakfast," she reasoned in an attempt to rouse herself from the certain temptation to remain in bed for longer than would be prudent. "The carriage is to arrive at ten," she reminded him, referring to the journey they had planned to the seaside today.

"Not yet," he insisted in a breathy tone. "There is still time." He found her mouth with his and pulled her closer. First, he wished to love her, to assuage his primary appetite.

The carriage arrived shortly before ten for the newlyweds' daytrip to Lymington, on England's southern shore. The couple had donned their finer clothes for the outing. Mr. Thornton wore his patterned gray waistcoat and traditional black frock coat while Margaret wore a new skirt and fitted jacket of jacquard cotton. Tendrils of dark gray vines and budding flowers were patterned on the mauve fabric, the lace of her chemisette showing at the narrow plunge of her neckline.

Mr. Thornton complimented her on her elegant appearance as soon as the carriage started down the lane. "You have acquired a very attractive wardrobe since you left Milton," he noted with approval. "Your aunt has been very generous," he added with a pleased smile.

"Oh, Mr. Bell insisted on giving me the funds for a trousseau," she informed him, somewhat embarrassed to speak of it.

Mr. Thornton's smile became strained. It pained him to think that Mr. Bell should be a source of benevolence while his present financial standing seemed somewhat uncertain. He hoped his wife would look to him to provide all that she could desire, and yearned to give her all that would befit a woman of her upbringing.

"Edith was very pleased to take me to some fine shops," she added with amusement, implying her relative indifference toward matters of high fashion.

He recovered his smile and took her hand into his, pushing aside any sobering thoughts to enjoy the present company of his beautiful wife.

The ride to Southampton station was short, and the lovers enjoyed the luxury of a few kisses in the privacy of the coach's compartment before heading out into the public eye for the day.

The station at Lymington was bustling with activity as the couple emerged from the train near the quay and headed toward the markets on the High Street. The wide cobbled streets and numerous shops lent an air of importance to the town, and the salty smell of the sea and the sound of gulls crying brought the ocean to its doorstep.

Mr. Thornton took special pleasure in strolling along the streets with his wife happily clinging to his arm. He was proud to openly acknowledge his attachment to such a divine creature.

Margaret enjoyed the close contact with her husband, and was similarly pleased to be seen escorted by a man of such distinction.

Upon making an enthusiastic appraisal of a rose-tinted parasol in a store window, Mr. Thornton insisted they enter the shop so that she could look at the wares. Determined to spoil her for the day, Mr. Thornton delighted in watching his wife examine and select the items of interest to her. The couple left the shop with a few packages and a ruffled parasol in hand.

Margaret was intrigued by the display of pictures in the window of a daguerreotype studio and pleaded with her husband to have their portrait taken. "It would be a lovely reminder of our wedding holiday. Our children and grandchildren should then see how happily we were paired," she appealed to him convincingly.

"Our children?" he repeated, smiling at her, his gaze warm with a suggestive intimacy.

Margaret blushed at his response to her remark, embarrassed to have spoken so boldly of their future. "Yes," she stammered. "I imagine we shall have a family, do you not think so?" she asked haltingly, at last looking timidly to him for his reply.

"I do," he answered, the thought of it stirring his deeper emotions. He walked to the door of the shop and opened it for her to enter.

When they finally emerged from the studio some time later, Margaret stilled her husband to address him. "Will you fetch us a picnic lunch?" she asked pleasantly. "I have an errand which I should like to accomplish in secret," she explained. "We could meet here in half an hour's time," she specified, noting his hesitation. She smiled sweetly at him in expectation of his approval.

"As you wish," he relented, unable to resist her charms, although he was reluctant to part with her in a strange town.

She waited until he had gone some distance away before she darted back into the studio.

They met later at the appointed time and headed toward the boatyards to hire a yacht for an afternoon excursion.

Margaret listened with rapt attention as her husband told her of his trips to Liverpool and Le Havre to sort out cotton deliveries for the mill. He had never been to the sea for a pleasure trip, and was eager to see the sights. She looked at him with admiration and affection as he pointed out the nearby dry docks where the yacht builders were busily plying their skills.

Margaret told him briefly of her family's occasional trips to the sea and the times that Edith and Aunt Shaw had taken her to the coast.

The couple was eventually directed to a mid-sized yacht of gleaming mahogany and polished brass. The captain welcomed them aboard and led them to the cushioned seats of the stern as he called his crew of three men to action. Mr. Thornton watched with great interest the workings of the ship and the crew's dexterous motions as they set sail.

They crossed The Solent and headed for the northwest shore of the Isle of Wight. The steady ocean breeze was invigorating, causing light wisps of hair to dance across Margaret's face. Mr. Thornton put his arm around his bride as they sailed further out to sea, taking in the expansive view of the distant island and the far horizon.

The sight of great sand cliffs of beige and rusty hues entranced the newlyweds as they approached the island's Alum Bay. Great jagged rocks jutted from the sea on the furthermost edge of the island, creating a dramatic vision of the land's rugged endurance midst the waves of the ocean.

The crew steered the ship toward the long wooden pontoon in the bay and docked the yacht alongside to allow the sightseers to disembark. Mr. Thornton assisted his wife as she alighted from the yacht and the couple walked to the shore to see and explore the colored sand cliffs of the bay.

After some time, they returned to the stalls selling trinkets and sundry souvenirs for the tourists who visited the island's famous bay. Margaret was intrigued by the many small glass vials in various shapes that contained layers of the colored sand within. The Thorntons bought several of the souvenirs as gifts and a pair of glass turtledoves for themselves before they sauntered to the pontoon and returned to the tall-masted yacht.

The yacht sailed back east along the shore of the island as the couple watched the cliffs recede in the distance. The couple ate their picnic fare as they took in the scenery of the parallel shores.

Sometime later, Mr. Thornton inquired about the boat and the workings of the crew. He listened intently to the captain's words and asked a few incisive questions before receiving a hearty smile and vigorous beckon by the amiable seafarer to assist in rigging the sail.

Margaret amusedly observed a boyish gleam of adventure light her husband's face as he removed his coat and handed it to her with a smile for its safekeeping. He had missed out on so much during his young life of privation, and it warmed her heart that he took such pleasure in simple things. She watched with admiring interest as he rolled up his sleeves and began to pull the ropes at the direction of the captain.

They sailed past Lymington on the portside and eventually drew close to Cowes on the starboard. "I would take you ashore here to see the gardens at Osborne House, but the Queen's birthday is tomorrow and I imagine there's quite a bit of activity at her favorite residence today," the captain shouted over the sound of the wind and lapping waves on the boat.

Margaret nodded her acknowledgement, and strained to see what she could of the island town that housed the royal family, pleased to know she had come this close to the Queen.

At length, they reached the eastern end of the island and Margaret alternately watched their approach to the isle and the concentrated movements of her husband as he competently assisted the crew in their endeavor to bring the yacht to a long wooden pier serving the town of Ryde. Margaret smiled in knowing admiration at her husband's ability to swiftly learn and master any task.

The couple disembarked and walked the length of the pier to the town on a gentle sloping hill. A golden sandy beach stretched out into the distance, dotted here and there with people strolling along the promenade and children playing near the surf. They found a seaside hotel, and ordered tea and cake as they enjoyed the view from the terrace.

Margaret insisted they walk along the beach, and they left the wooden walkway, taking their shoes off to enjoy the feeling of the sand and waves upon their feet.

They returned at length to the yacht and briefly set sail towards Portsmouth before returning to Lymington. Mr. Thornton sat with his wife as the captain pointed out the various sights of the larger city. A stone gateway, the Sally Port, guarded the harbor's busy entry, where vessels of every shape and size could be found. Wooden warships and frigates lined the docks in the distance. *The Victory*, Admiral Lord Nelson's ship, still in service after all these years, could be seen amongst them, the tall masts of the ship towering above the neighboring vessels.

The sun was descending toward a hazy yellow horizon when they finally arrived at the boatyard. Mr. Thornton and his wife shook hands with the captain and thanked him for the pleasant voyage before they took their leave and returned to the town.

They stopped briefly at the daguerreotype studio to pick up their purchase before finding a restaurant to eat their supper. By the time they emerged again into the street, the sun had set, the western sky ablaze with an orange and pink glow.

They slowly headed for the station to return home, filled with a warm contentment in having shared a day of adventure together.

Margaret leaned heavily against her husband on the train, weary from the day's excursion. Upon reaching Southampton, they hired a coach and returned to Helstone. Succumbing at last to her drowsiness, Margaret fell asleep with her head against her husband's shoulder.

Mr. Thornton carefully secured her to him and reveled in his protective role, ever mindful of the precious treasure that was his wife.

The stars had appeared in the darkened sky and the crickets' chorus was in full swell when Mr. Thornton gently woke his wife upon their arrival at the cottage. He smiled at her drowsiness and, coming around to her side of the carriage, lifted her into his arms and carried her into the cottage and up the stairs, setting her gently on their bed. She began to dress for bed as he returned to retrieve the packages.

She was climbing into bed again when he returned. He quietly undressed to join her. Wearing his nightshirt for the first time, he got into bed and moved to lay his arm over her, kissing her cheek gently as he softly said good night and happily awaited peaceful slumber.

∝∾

The couple awoke some time after dawn and began to reminisce about the previous day's events, Margaret having drawn herself into her husband's loose embrace as they faced each other.

"I have something for you," Margaret suddenly announced with a mysterious smile, recalling the mission she had accomplished in his brief absence yesterday.

He sat up as she slipped out of bed and rummaged through the packages to retrieve the gift that was hidden within the larger package they had retrieved at the shop. She hopped back into the bed and kneeled beside him with an eager smile.

She was like a child at Christmas, he thought, as he took the package from her hands and began to open it.

"It is my wedding gift to you," she declared as he unwrapped the paper from the object within.

It was a daguerreotype of Margaret set behind an oval window in a gold-painted frame. With her hands on her parasol as a cane, she stood at a slight angle, revealing the curvaceous form of her figure. She wore a subtle smile and held a glimmer of love in her eyes, which Mr. Thornton recognized at once. He knew he would treasure the likeness as long as he lived.

Mr. Thornton was speechless as he continued to examine it.

"It is quite pretentious of me, is it not?" she queried. "I thought you might like to have it in your office at the mill," she suggested.

He cocked his head in doubtful agreement. "It may prove distracting," he remarked pensively.

"It is only my likeness. I am not *that* distracting," she insisted playfully.

"You are very distracting," he countered with decision as he snaked his arm around her waist and pulled her against him for a thank-you kiss.

The thin cotton of her nightgown was a flimsy barrier between them, and merely increased his desire to feel the soft, voluptuous flesh that lay beneath. Her tender response to his kiss stirred his deeper longings, but he released her from his embrace and rose from the bed.

He quickly retrieved a small beribboned box from his coat pocket and held it out to her. "I was going to wait to give it to you tomorrow – our last day here," he explained as he handed her the gift.

She undid the ribbon and opened the box carefully to find a pair of earrings within. On each piece, a small pearl sat at the center of a delicate flower of gold and diamond filigree.

She looked up at him with wonderment. "These were in the window at that shop…" she began.

"It seems you are not the only one who can be secretive," he replied with a smile.

"They are beautiful, thank you!" she responded and got out of bed to put them on and admire them in the mirror.

She returned to the bed and knelt by him once again, her feet tucked under her. "They are very fine, John," she thanked him again. "I must look the part of a fine lady now that I am married to the Master of Marlborough Mills," she stated, smiling at him with pride. "I am now glad that I had Edith's help to select my new clothes," she added. "I hope my appearance will be in keeping with your position," she remarked hopefully.

"I may have been drawn to your appearance, but it is the beauty of your character and your striking intellect that made me love you," he replied with sincerity. "However, I must confess I admire you in your new dresses," he told her with a knowing smile.

"I did not think you noticed what I wore," she commented wonderingly.

"I notice everything about you," he replied. "How can I not?" he added as he studied the features of her face for the thousandth time. "I believe I shall be the proudest husband in Milton," he remarked candidly.

She smiled bashfully at his ardent gaze. "I fear the other masters may not hold me in the highest opinion," she admitted as she thought of how his colleagues might perceive her bold, independent manner.

"I believe they will be soundly jealous of my success in securing such a wife," he assured her.

"Perhaps, but you well know that I am likely to voice my strong opinions. I'm certain you were aware of the risks involved in marrying me," she retorted in jest as she grasped his hand.

"I was aware that there were incalculable risks in pursuing you, but I am a man of stubborn determination once I have established a desirable purpose," he admitted with a smile.

"I am glad of it," she readily confessed as she leaned forward for a kiss that quickly kindled their passion for one another.

It was mid-morning by the time the couple ate their breakfast. The back door of the kitchen was open to the view outside. The day was sunny and warm. Large white clouds crawled slowly across the bright blue sky, creating pockets of dark shadow across the green heathland below.

Margaret noted with satisfaction that her husband looked more and more the part of a country man, wearing only his shirt and trousers with his braces showing.

After breakfast, John went out the back to tend to the fallen tree branch while Margaret rose to put the clothes away that still hung in the scullery. When she returned to the kitchen, John was busy chopping the branch into firewood.

She cleared the table and began happily to wash the dishes. The window above the sink allowed her to observe her husband's progress as she heard the steady sound of the axe striking against the wood. She derived a singular pleasure to see him so occupied, and watched with increasing interest as the relentless sun compelled him to remove his shirt.

He returned to his arduous task, and swung the axe with easy vigor and precision.

Margaret's hands stilled as she studied the ripple of fleshly sinew down his back and the contracting swell of the muscles in his arm as he continued his rhythmic movements. She felt a fluttering deep within her and shivered in recognition of the attraction that held her spellbound. Blushing at the images coming to her mind, she quickly resumed her work and finished the dishes as she caught occasional glimpses of the view outside.

She dried her hands and joined him out in the back garden. He smiled at her, but kept on with his work, the remaining segment of the branch only a few feet long.

"Shall I fetch you some water?" she called out over the din of his strokes, noting the sheen forming on his upper body and brow as he worked.

"Yes, thank you," he replied without stopping, appreciative of her consideration.

Margaret turned to the outdoor pump and dutifully filled a pail of water. She turned back toward him, intending to retrieve a cup from the house for his use.

He stopped his work as she approached and stood to face her in anticipation of the refreshment she offered, a pleasant smile on his face.

As she carried the laden pail nearer him, something of his expectant posture triggered in her an impulse to surprise him. Without a moment's hesitation, she grasped the pail's rim with one hand and the bottom with the other and heaved the water onto his unsuspecting form.

The water hit him squarely on the chest, splashing water up onto his face and hair and cascading down his stomach to soak his trousers. He opened his mouth in shock as the cool water dripped off of his body.

Margaret stood in stunned surprise at the sight of him, her hand clasped over her mouth as if some foreign power had impelled her thus and she was but the innocent steward of its wicked purpose.

She watched with growing trepidation as a disbelieving smile crossed his face and a look of revenge came into his eyes.

She turned to run from him, attempting to escape his retribution, but she was no match for him. He quickly caught up to her and, taking hold of her waist, dragged her to the ground with him, shielding her fall as she shrieked in his grasp. He scrambled to pin her down and held her wrists to the ground as he knelt over her.

Laughing uncontrollably, she mustered a protest and called out his name as she studied his face to discern the probability of her quick release.

"You are a vixen!" he accused her with playful vigor.

"You said you should like some water," she laughingly offered as a defense of her action.

"I did not ask to be doused with it!" he countered, eliciting a giggle from her.

"John, you are getting me wet!" she complained, as she attempted to wriggle free from his grasp.

He moved to straighten himself over her, and without warning, suddenly rolled her over so that she lay on top of him.

With a wicked smile, he watched gleefully as she flailed to right herself, shocked to find herself in such a position. Reveling in the feel of her warm body on his, he grasped her arms to capture her, forcing her to prop herself over him, inches from his face.

"John, you are all wet!" she complained again as she felt moisture beginning to soak through her clothes.

"I believe you owe me a kiss for such reprehensible behavior," he stated with decision, ignoring her complaint.

"John!" she pleaded for mercy.

He raised one eyebrow in silent response to her plea, unyielding in his request.

The corners of her mouth curved upward as she relented and moved to kiss him.

He strained his neck to meet her, impatient to release his passion upon her, hungrily entwining his tongue with hers as if he would consume the whole of her.

He thrilled at her quick submission, feeling the weight of her body press into him further as she relaxed. He reached up to hold her fast to him, his hands encompassing her back, and rolled her over again so that she once more lay beneath him on the grass. His heart beat wildly as he continued to plunder her mouth.

"Pardon me, are you all right?" they heard a young voice tentatively inquire.

Mr. Thornton was standing up in an instant, hastily assisting his flustered wife to her feet. A young lad of about eight years of age stood several yards from them, the boy's expression a mixture of confusion and concern.

"We are fine," Mr. Thornton assured him with a flicker of a smile, endeavoring to appear normal as he raked his wet hair off his forehead, feeling heat rise to his face.

Margaret smoothed her skirts and checked the condition of her hair, her face pink with embarrassment.

"I heard the missus scream," he began to explain as an apology for his intrusion. "Thomas Wheatley, sir," he announced. "I've come to tend the chickens and leave a basket of goods at your door. My mother baked this morning," he informed them.

"Tommy, you've grown so! Please tell your mother it is much appreciated," Margaret thanked him sweetly as she swept a loose tendril of her hair behind her ear.

The boy nodded with a smile. "Congratulations on getting married," he politely added.

"Thank you," Mr. Thornton replied before the lad turned to carry out his task.

"To be seen in such a manner...." Margaret remarked with mortification after the boy had disappeared behind the chicken coop.

"He is only a child. He will not think on it," her husband assured her, unconvinced of his own statement. "I suppose we should be glad it was not Mrs. Wheatley herself," he mused.

"Oh, John!" she exclaimed, the very thought of it distressing her.

"It is all your fault," she suddenly turned to accuse him with a hint of a smile.

"*My* fault?" he countered incredulously.

"Yes, perhaps if you had been properly dressed I would not have been tempted to give you an unexpected shower," she explained defensively, giving him a haughty look.

"Then perhaps I should find more occasions to tempt you," he readily replied. "I find your impulsive behavior enchanting," he admitted, his eyes warm with affection.

"Enchanting?" she queried with confusion.

"Yes, and beguiling," he added in a low voice as he locked his arms around her waist.

She placed her hands on his bare chest, beginning to fall under his spell. "You should change your clothes," she remarked softly in an attempt to break the strong pull of attraction toward him. She was as yet uncertain if it was quite right to feel so strongly inclined to follow his every lead. Perhaps it was not appropriate that she be so easily bedded, lest he lose interest in her at some future time.

"Perhaps you should change your clothes as well," he suggested in a sultry tone, his eyebrows raised to elucidate his intentions.

"What about Thomas?" she stalled, thinking it would be polite to say good-bye to him when he left.

"He is not invited," her husband retorted with a devilish grin.

Margaret swatted at him and followed him into the cottage.

It was almost noon when Margaret descended the stairs and opened the front door to retrieve the basket left by the Wheatley boy. She was surprised to find a package from the post sitting on the front steps as well.

She brought the items in and mentioned the package aloud to her husband as he joined her in the parlor.

He raised his eyebrows in feigned surprise and suggested she open it to see, a trace of a smile beginning to play on his lips.

Margaret dutifully obliged, and discovered within the necessary supplies for drawing, including paper, paint tubes, several paintbrushes and a palette board. She looked bewilderedly at her husband, who was now smiling broadly. "You sent these?" she asked in wonderment.

"It was mentioned that you liked to draw when you lived here," he answered simply. "I thought you might like to take it up again," he explained thoughtfully. "I sent for it as soon as possible, I am glad it arrived before it was too late," he added.

"I am not terribly accomplished at it, but I did like to dabble," she answered. "Thank you for thinking of me," she added, rising from her seat to give him a warm smile of appreciation and an affectionate kiss on the lips.

"I will search out every means to please you if I am to be rewarded in such a manner," he answered as he held her waist and leaned forward for a second kiss.

Soon the newlyweds went out the front, and Mr. Thornton set a chair for her where she could draw the cottage, placing her seat just within the shade of the broad oak.

He made himself comfortable and sat on the grass with a book a short distance away.

They quietly pursued their own interests for a long time, until Margaret looked to see him lying on his back with his eyes closed, his book open on his chest.

"You look very comfortable lying there, Mr. Thornton," she remarked loudly with amusement.

"You are welcome to lie with me at any time," he replied suggestively with a devious grin, not bothering to open his eyes.

Margaret snatched an unopened tube of paint and threw it at him with playful determination.

He opened his eyes when the object hit his arm and smiled broadly, chuckling to himself.

He got up and walked over to observe her progress, curious to see her talent. "It is a decent likeness," he remarked honestly of her work thus far. "You have chosen your colors well," he added admiringly.

Thank you," she replied appreciatively and reached up to hold his hand.

They ate a late lunch later in the kitchen, and then ventured out to explore the rolling fields behind the house.

Margaret picked a few violets and buttercups along the way and led them past a grazing herd of sheep toward a neighboring farm.

Mr. Thornton assisted her over the low stone wall as they headed toward a tree swing suspended on the sturdy branch of a tall oak. Margaret alighted on the wooden seat and Mr. Thornton was happy to set her to swinging with several gentle pushes. She told him how she had frequented this swing before, when she had accompanied her father on one of his visits.

Before long, the farmer's floppy-eared beagle came bounding toward them, barking his warning of their intrusion. Mr. Thornton bent low to the ground and extended his arm to placate the dog, and was partially successful in quieting him.

Margaret delighted in watching her husband play with the dog as he crouched in menacing playfulness and then ran with a start, looking back to see the dog race to catch him, chasing his heels.

Eventually they both sat in a tired contentment while Mr. Thornton patted the dog with some affection.

When the newlyweds finally departed the site, the beagle followed them for a little while through the fields until the distant whistle of his master called him back to his home.

When, at length, they returned to the cottage, Margaret continued her drawing and Mr. Thornton read until the daylight faded into twilight.

After dinner they returned outdoors, the warmer night air beckoning them from the stillness of the confined parlor.

They stood down the garden path out the front and gazed at the stars. Margaret pointed out the constellations that Fred had shown her long ago, and Mr. Thornton recounted the facts of the heavenly bodies as he had studied them. He remarked on the clarity of the night sky, lamenting the limited view the smoky skies of Milton allowed of the night's true brilliance.

After some time he wrapped his arms around her and drew her close. "I remember the last time we stood together here under the stars," he murmured.

"Yes...it seems ages ago," she answered a little shyly, recalling the passion that had overtaken them the night before their wedding.

"Not so long ago," he answered in a low voice.

"But much has happened since then," she explained falteringly.

"It has," he agreed as a wave of enchanted joy flowed through him at the remembrance of their first days together.

"Margaret...are you happy?" he asked with a hint of concern, wondering all at once if his demands on her person were too much for her, thinking that her timidity might indicate a subtle reluctance.

"Yes, I am," she answered immediately, taken aback somewhat by his question. "Have I given you the impression that I am not?" she asked bewilderedly as she searched his face.

"No...no," he answered gently. He opened his mouth to say more, but found he could not bring himself to explain further.

"I am truly happy, John," she assured him and pressed her cheek against his chest as she hugged him.

He sighed aloud his rapture to feel her melt into his arms, and slid his hands up along her back to hold her closer as he pressed his face against her hair.

After several moments of blissful stillness, he moved to loosen his hold on her and look into her eyes. He found the answer he sought in her expression and kissed her carefully and tenderly as if it was the first time their mouths had met.

Margaret was astounded at the strong stirring of sensation that his gentle kisses evoked deep inside of her, and yearned for his ardency to increase.

Instead, he withdrew from her and asked, "should I start the fire in the parlor...or do you wish to retire early?" He intended to give her the opportunity to choose what they should do, although his heart pounded with fervent desire.

"Perhaps we should retire..." she replied bashfully, feeling her face flush at the implication of her choice, unable to meet his gaze.

He let out a low sigh of relief at her answer and could not suppress the upward curve of his lips as they walked back up the path to the cottage.

Mr. Thornton removed to the parlor first to extinguish the lamp for the evening, and then climbed the stairs to their bedroom where Margaret was making her preparations for bed.

They undressed and got into their nightclothes in silence. Mr. Thornton finished first, and situated himself comfortably in the bed against the pillows. He watched Margaret sit down at the vanity in her sleeveless nightgown and carefully remove the pins in her hair to allow the long curls of her auburn hair to tumble down her back and over her shoulders.

He felt a rush of aching affection and kindling lust at the sight of her beauty, and swallowed hard.

She brushed her hair for a few moments and then set the brush down to come to bed. She slipped her feet under the covers and sat near him, raising her eyes demurely to meet his gaze.

His breath stilled to recognize the longing revealed in her luminous eyes.

He reached out to take her face in his hands and began to continue the kiss that they had shared moments before. This time, he allowed his ardor to gently build, until he pushed her carefully back onto the pillows as he moved his body over hers.

He intended to love her as he had long imagined – with aching tenderness – so that she would know that it was love that impelled his every motion and filled his heart with the joy of their union.

Mr. Thornton watched his wife as she lay sleeping next to him, her hands tucked under her cheek as if she were a small child in innocent slumber. He marveled at his privilege to observe her thus, and felt the overwhelming sense of contentment that came to him after he had loved her.

She had called out his name this time as she had clung to him - an utterance born of passion and love - and he had felt his entire being shudder at the notion of her need for him.

He felt all the shattered shards of his soul come into alignment. The strain and bitterness of the past had been obliterated by the love of one extraordinary woman whom Providence had sent to cross his path. He reached out to tenderly touch her face as if to ensure she was not a dream – to feel the tangible proof of her existence. He had been alone so long. He wished never to be alone again.

He was happier than he had ever imagined was possible. He felt his life was complete, and yet the future still lay before them, promising untold joy.

He closed his eyes and folded his hands on his chest as a single tear escaped from the corner of his eye and slid down his cheek.

Chapter Thirteen

Margaret set a teapot and pan of water to boil on the black-leaded stove and went to the front door to retrieve a basket of various goods that had been left at the doorstep. She smiled to think of how the villagers had spoiled them with regular gifts of food. She was determined to find out from Mrs. Purkins whom to thank and send the well-wishers a lovely note once she returned to Milton.

She set the table for two and went back to take the tea off the stove, then began cooking some sausage while happily humming a tune of her own invention.

She touched her cheeks with the back of her hand, amazed at the faint heat she still felt in her face and the warm sensation that lingered throughout her body. She was growing quite accustomed to the pleasures of married life, but was still astounded at the power of their impassioned union as man and wife. She wondered how much opportunity for loving they would have once they were back in Milton. Things would likely be very different when John was forced to focus his time and energy at the mill.

Mr. Thornton silently leaned against the doorway of the kitchen with his arms crossed, taking in the sight of his wife at her task. He felt an invigorating glow of contentment from having loved her well. He had enjoyed the leisure of remaining in bed as she had hurriedly dressed to make her way to the kitchen. He smiled at the remembrance of her bashfulness as she slipped out from under the bedcovers.

She was dressed in a simple pale blue skirt and white blouse. He knew that the curves beneath were held in the simplest confinements, having noticed that she eschewed her corset on the days they remained in Helstone.

He would miss the casual intimacy of their life in this place. They were free to do as they pleased, with no one else to observe them. He was loath to remove to the city again and resume a life of schedules and fretful toil under the watchful eye of his mother, the servants, and society at large.

"I think I should like to be a simple farmer," he announced as he crossed the room to wrap his arms around her from behind and press his cheek against hers, reveling in the simple pleasure of holding her.

She smiled at the thought of him in such a role as she enjoyed the comforting bliss of being enveloped in his arms. "You would do well at whatever you chose, and I would be proud to be your wife," she answered honestly. "But you are an important man of industry and belong in the city," she affirmed gently, recognizing his reluctance to leave the country. "I believe you would tire of a simple life of farming. Besides, a mind such as yours is too brilliant to be left in the fields of England. You are far better suited to address the challenges facing industry and propel our nation forward to a grand future," she remarked with easy candor as she moved the sausage about in the pan. "I should not be surprised if you should find yourself working closely with Parliament someday."

Mr. Thornton was astounded at her candid assessment of his abilities. "Margaret, you esteem me too highly, I fear," he replied, modestly doubting her earnest praise. "There are great problems regarding the growth of industry which will be very difficult to surmount," he cautioned. "Yet there is promise as well. I'm afraid I don't have all the answers to navigate the country, much less my own mill, to certain success," he replied with humility.

"I'm certain no one does, but I believe you are apt to discover them more readily than anyone else. You have the wisdom and foresight to make fine judgments, John. I have seen it. I have confidence in your every ability," she declared with solid conviction. "Farmer, indeed," she added quietly to emphasize how ludicrous it would be to have such a man tilling the soil.

Mr. Thornton was struck silent as he considered her generous appraisal of him, her intelligent insight, and her hope for progress. Truly, with Margaret by his side, he felt he could face any challenge. However, he still felt a twinge of guilt to be taking her away from the idyllic countryside of her youth to the gloom and ceaseless turmoil of the city.

"It is so peaceful and quiet here. The sky is clear and bright, and everything is so green," he remarked fondly of the area she had long called home. "I can now see why you loved the South so much."

"It is lovely here," she agreed. "I'd forgotten how green it really is," she added, turning the sausage over in the frying pan.

"I cannot help but think that I am removing you from the place where you belong," he confessed with regret.

She swiveled around to face him. "I belong with you!" she stated firmly, forcing him to meet her gaze so that he would discern her sincerity. "I do not wish to be any place else," she declared, taking his hand and intertwining her fingers with his.

He gazed at her with wonder, moved by her fervent devotion.

"Have you forgotten the message I sent to you from Nicholas?" she asked pointedly, wishing him to know her words were not merely a device to comfort him.

"I could never forget it," he replied, his voice low with reverent emotion at the memory of receiving her coded message of affection. His entire life had changed at that moment – when he had learned that he did not love in vain.

"My heart belongs to you, John. That is what my message was meant to convey. Surely you understood. My heart belongs in Milton because that is where you will be," she explained as she searched his face to ensure he understood her meaning.

"Margaret," he could only whisper, stunned into silence by her ardent avowals.

She turned back to the stove, the sizzling sound of the cooking meat recalling her to her task. She turned the sausage over once again.

"Even if we removed from Milton someday," she confessed, her back to him, "I believe I shall always have a special place in my heart for it. I learned so much there; it is where we met."

Recovering himself to action, Mr. Thornton turned her around again to face him. "I only wish for you to be happy," he declared, his blue eyes piercing hers.

"I am looking forward to going home," she told him with a sweet smile. "I wish to begin my new life as Mrs. John Thornton of Marlborough Mills," she added proudly, although she felt a twinge of anxiety at the thought of proving herself worthy of the title. One of the things that she had learned was that her husband's character had proven more honest and compassionate than her own. "I intend to treat you very well, you shall see," she promised with a twinkle in her eye. In truth, she wished to make amends for all the pain that her foolish words and deeds had caused him.

Her words went straight to his heart, filling him with the hope for their continued happiness. He did not speak, but brought his lips to hers to show his grateful affection.

When he finally released her, she removed her loving gaze from his, and handed him a long-handled fork. "Will you make the toast while I boil the eggs?" she asked with a gentle smile. She knew he would not mind carrying out such a simple task.

They spent their last day in Helstone at their favorite spot – the clearing by the brook where they had gone on their wedding day. Wishing to recapture all the enjoyment of the past week in one single day, they brought a picnic lunch and stayed a long while. They read to each other from Tennyson this time, and the sound of the gently flowing water lent an air of poetic tranquility to their voices.

Margaret breathed deeply and closed her eyes as she listened to her lover speak. The sweet aroma of the grasses and meadow flowers filled her with a pleasant peacefulness.

At Margaret's turn to read, Mr. Thornton was quick to situate himself in the position in which he had become accustomed when they read to each other outdoors. Margaret was amused at his eagerness to recline on his back with his head upon her lap, and felt a glow of joyous contentment in lovingly tracing the contours of his face and lightly combing his hair while she read.

At length, Margaret gently ousted him from her lap so that they could eat their lunch. She brought the basket near to where he sat and began to lay out the fare.

"Is there no place in Milton where we could retreat for a little picnic?" she asked, wondering how they might be able to continue some of the simple pleasures that had become a part of their routine.

"Not unless you should like to eat in the park, near the graveyard. It is not terribly private, I'm afraid," he responded, doubtful that they could find anything similar in privacy or beauty in Milton.

"I shall have to think of something," she muttered to herself, as she placed slices of bread and some cheese out on a napkin.

"Will you single-handedly change my well-established, reclusive habits?" he teased her, watching with amusement as a smile formed on her lips.

"It will be my duty as your wife to ensure that you eat properly and find some time for enjoyment," she informed him with authority, as she pulled out sweet apples from the basket and set them down.

"I can think of a very satisfactory way to spend my leisure time," he responded in a sultry tone, unable to suppress the corners of his lips from curving upward as he watched for her reaction.

Margaret blushed at his implied preference, and was unable to meet his gaze as she busied herself in refolding the napkin in her hands. "I was referring to finding the time to read or make conversation, or perhaps even to take a short walk about," she shyly clarified. "However, I am not averse to pursuing any diversion that you might suggest," she added somewhat boldly, although her pulse quickened and her voice lowered as she openly admitted her willingness to give herself to him.

Her timidity concerning their intimate relationship enchanted him. He felt a tug of guilt for having teased her with his subtle suggestion, but could not regret doing so when she reacted so beguilingly.

He moved to sit next to her and lifted her chin to gaze into her soulful eyes. "I should hardly call you a diversion. You are my whole world," he stated unequivocally, the veracity of his admission striking him even as he spoke the words. For truly, everything that he accomplished or for which he strived from now on would be for her, because of her.

His words washed over her like a powerful wave. As the magnitude and depth of his love overwhelmed her, she struggled to comprehend how she should deserve the privilege of being cherished by such a man.

He leaned closer to kiss her, cupping her face in his hand and gently urging her forward to meet him. As their lips brushed together, a tingling shock coursed through him, and he plied her lips for more. She opened her mouth to him, and he hungrily sought her tongue with his own. Her tongue stroked his in answering yearning, and a scorching heat raced through his veins and stirred his desire.

The impulse to take her right there under the open sky grew stronger as their kisses became more fevered with an urgency neither of them wished to control. She reached out to cling to him, her small hand gripping the back of his neck as her fingers raked through his hair.

He groaned in aching desire to meld himself completely to her. She was his wife; it was his right. But he could not subject her to the risk of their being discovered by some hapless wanderer. He must wait. There would be time later.

Against all the urgings of his body, he disengaged himself from her. His breath was ragged from the passion he longed to unleash upon her. Could she possibly know the power she wielded over him? He looked into her eyes and despaired of ever making her understand what she meant to him – how much he needed her, how incessantly he yearned to bind himself to her so that he might feel complete.

"I love you," he managed to say, his voice wavering with emotion. How meager the words seemed in his attempt to convey everything that he felt for her. He would need a lifetime, he thought, to make her understand.

As he pulled away from her, Margaret felt bereft. Light-headed from the intensity of their amorous bond, she was amazed at how easily she surrendered herself to him, wanting desperately to feel his possession of her. How incredible it seemed that she should now feel so, when she had formerly cringed at the thought of being owned by any man, her independence always screaming forth its rightful claim to life.

Now, she felt no danger of losing her identity and longed to submit herself wholly to him. She felt a powerful sense of security in his care - she never felt safer than when she was in his arms. She experienced something of heaven in his kisses - suspended from the ties of earth - when they cleaved to each other, and longed for the more transcendent moments of blissful union - when they were no longer two separate entities but moved and breathed as one. She wondered if he felt something similar.

"John, I did not know I could love someone as much as I love you," she endeavored to explain. "I've no words to tell you how I feel," she honestly admitted.

His heart swelled with the wondrous joy of being loved by her, and he bestowed a lingering kiss on her lips as an answer to her confession.

When his lips removed from hers, their eyes communicated their adoration and wonder for a moment before Margaret bowed her head under the intensity of his gaze.

"We should eat," she reminded him softly, endeavoring to return them to the enjoyment of their surroundings.

When they had finished their meal, the newlyweds strolled hand-in-hand to the stream and watched the flowing water swirl and ripple over the shallow bed of stones. Mr. Thornton led his wife to a spot where a rock broke the path of the stream and deftly crossed to the other side. Holding his wife's hands aloft as she stepped onto the island of stone, he helped her cross the water to him.

They wandered through the woods for a while, hand-in-hand, to see if they could find more bluebells. Although they were unsuccessful in their venture, Margaret delighted in the sight of the yellow primroses and the growing ferns, easily recalling the days of her childhood when she explored everything on the forest floor.

When they returned to the clearing, Margaret took up her drawing once again, wishing to take back to Milton a picture of the place that had become even more special to her because she had spent time there with the one she loved.

John sat near her with a book, curious to read an American author's work – *The House of Seven Gables*. He savored the luxury of reading in such a beautiful setting, knowing full well the days ahead would afford no such pleasure.

After a time, the sound of little voices broke the silence and grew louder as three young children appeared in the clearing from the path behind the hawthorn bushes.

"Hello," Margaret warmly greeted them, the sight of the children bringing to mind the wonderful memories of her own carefree days as a child.

"Hello, we've come to play here, if that's alright," announced a young girl. "I'm Rachel, and this is my brother Edward," she said, gesturing toward a boy a little older than she.

"My name is Lydia," piped up the littlest one, a pretty girl with unruly curls of golden hair that floated and bounced with her every movement. "What are you doing?" she asked curiously as she noticed the drawing that Margaret had started.

"My name is Mrs. Thornton, and this is my husband," she began properly with a twinkling smile for both the children and her husband, who was fondly watching the encounter unfold. "I'm making a drawing of this place so I will not forget it when I return home," she kindly answered the girl's query.

"Oh," Lydia replied simply. "Well, we are going to play in the brook. Good-bye," she called out as she bounded off with her siblings toward the water.

"You have a very easy manner with children....Mrs. Thornton," John remarked with admiration. He had taken great pleasure in hearing his wife introduce herself to them with her married name.

"I've always been fond of children. They are so honest and are quite perceptive," she explained.

The couple turned their attention to the children, who were quickly shedding stockings and shoes to gather near the stream.

Margaret happily returned to her drawing with plans to add new subjects into her work.

Mr. Thornton was intrigued by the children's antics and eventually went to watch them try floating various leafs and sticks downstream. He crossed the stream again to rummage through the forest floor, handing Lydia a piece of bark for a boat that would surpass her siblings' best finds.

Margaret amusedly observed her husband take off his shoes and stockings just as Edward excitedly announced the discovery of a salamander. Mr. Thornton was curious to see the specimen, and helped the children search for them, squatting in the shallow stream and gently lifting stones with Lydia to find a few more.

Tired of their hunt at length, Rachel announced a game of tag to which her brother readily agreed. Lydia soon found the disadvantage of her shorter limbs and called out her frustration. "It's not fair, you're too fast for me," she protested.

"Come, I can help you catch them!" Mr. Thornton encouraged her, crouching down to allow her to climb on his back. Lydia squealed her delight in quickly overtaking her brother and sister on the back of her faithful steed.

Margaret's heart lifted to see her husband run and play with them. It would be a great crime if this man were not a father, she decided. A warm sensation rose from her belly and flushed her face at the thought of bearing his children.

When he had had enough, Mr. Thornton abdicated his playful role and sat with exhausted relief near his wife.

Margaret beamed at him. "It seems you are also very good with children," she commented.

He smiled at her observation. "I believe there is a part of me which still wishes to be a child," he admitted with candor.

"I think we all ought to have something of a child's heart inside," she suggested with sincerity. "I'm certain it would make the world a better place," she added thoughtfully as she gazed at the children who had returned to the stream again.

They all left the clearing together by mid-afternoon and walked the lane toward the village. When they reached the cottage, the children called their good-byes and waved vigorously as the newlyweds turned to walk up the path through the front garden.

"They are such lovely children," Margaret noted as they approached the door. Mr. Thornton opened it and allowed her to pass inside before him without a word. He set down the things he had carried as his wife continued to chat about their outing.

"Lydia was so delightful. She was having such a grand time riding on your back. I wished your mother could have seen you. You were quite a sight," she began, but was swiftly silenced as he drew her into his arms and kissed her soundly.

He had longed to kiss her for some time, and could no longer wait. Their encounter with the children had only made him love her all the more. The glorious smiles she had bestowed upon them and her peals of laughter had filled his heart to bursting with joy to have such a woman as his wife.

Margaret returned his kisses with equal ardor, the powerful yearning to experience all that he could give her coming over her once again.

His kisses were unyielding, and she melted against him as she was consumed by his ardent passion. They moved simultaneously against each other, trying to fit as tightly as the barrier of their clothing would allow, both inflamed with their urgent need to become one.

He tore his mouth from hers. "Margaret, I need you," he panted with his forehead resting on hers.

"Please," she weakly pleaded, unable to say more, her own need painful in its intensity.

His eyes flared as he recognized her desire. Scooping her into his arms, he raced up the stairs.

They remained in bed long afterward, comfortably lying in each other's arms, legs entangled, as they talked about their week and laughed at Fanny's silly remark that they should not find anything to do in Helstone. When their conversation faded into silence, their hands began to slowly caress the other with a tenderness that conveyed everything they felt; there was no need to speak a word.

When their gentle exploration of each other grew bolder, they surrendered themselves to the fulfillment of every desire until the late afternoon sun sank toward the distant copses and the lovers were languorous and completely spent.

After a time, Margaret entreated her husband to walk to Helstone with her. Knowing the day was quickly fading, she wanted to see the village one last time and suggested they eat their dinner at the inn. She teased and cajoled him for his reluctance to get up and kissed him lightly, first on the nose and then on the forehead, just where she had so often seen his brow furrow.

They strolled slowly down the lane, enjoying the view of the greenery all around them. They detoured past the parsonage, and Margaret showed him where the yellow roses would soon blossom in profusion, and pointed to the window of the house that had been hers.

They walked the path to the church, and stopped near the arched entrance to secretly kiss in remembrance of their wedding only days before.

Mrs. Purkins was delighted to see them at the inn, and bade them sit in a quiet corner where they were served a delicious dinner of roasted lamb and vegetables. For pudding, she brought them trifle made with strawberry jam and garnished with sliced almonds.

The sun had nearly set when they emerged from the inn. The hedgerows, trees, and gardens of the village were cast in a golden glow as the sun made its final descent. The heathland was bathed in brilliant light. The blossoming gorse and distant heather were iridescent with yellow and orange hues that seemed to infuse the earth with a heavenly presence.

When they reached the cottage, the sky was darkening and the moon was more visible. Mr. Thornton stilled her on the garden path. "Thank you for bringing us here," he said with tender affection as he held her hands in his. "I have enjoyed every moment of our time in this place," he added over the crickets' quiet chirping.

"I thought you would enjoy it," she remarked with a sweet smile. "It has been a glorious week, has it not?"

"It has," he agreed, his gaze warm with the thought of all that had transpired. He gave her a lingering kiss on the lips before they continued up the path.

They relaxed in the parlor, enjoying the quiet time to themselves. When John rose to tend to the fire, Margaret also arose to bring them some tea.

After a considerable time had passed, Mr. Thornton grew curious about where his wife could be and sought her in the kitchen. A lamp on the table chased the darkness into shadows; the kettle was steaming, but the room was empty. The open door to the back led him to step outside into the cool night air.

"Margaret!" he called gently, expecting her quick reply as his eyes scanned the darkness for her figure. A pang of worried fear involuntarily built within him when no response was returned. He walked hurriedly behind the house, beyond the canopy of trees to where the open sky and rolling hills began.

"Margaret!" he called again, more fervently.

"I am here," she called out in reply, and the sound of her voice sent a flood of relief through him. "I came out to see the stars," she added as he walked toward her.

He wrapped his arms around her from behind and they both looked up at the splendor of the heavens. The view was magnificent; the earthy smell of the grasses and sweet aroma of the gorse pervaded the air as the night sky glittered with endless stars.

"You will miss this place," he said quietly into her ear, noting how her face looked to the sky with wonder.

"Yes, I cannot help it," she admitted. "I will miss the open space and the quiet peace of nature," she mused. "What will you miss?" she asked curiously.

Mr. Thornton took a deep breath as he thought about it. "I have grown fond of hearing the crickets at night," he offered. "The stars are incredible here, and I shall miss the vibrant color of everything. And I shall miss the freedom of being able to kiss you in the parlor whenever I wish," he finished, kissing her neck for good measure.

"John!" she mockingly protested, giving his arms a squeeze.

"Perhaps we can come back here next year," he mused, knowing how much it would mean to her.

"Do you really think so, John?" she asked enthusiastically, turning to face him in her excitement at the possibility.

He smiled broadly at her reaction. "I don't see why not. If the Thompsons are amenable and we are fit to travel, I cannot think why we should not return," he reasoned.

"Oh, John, it would be wonderful!" she enthused as she wound her arms around his neck to show her approval of his proffered plan.

"It would be," he agreed, rewarding her affectionate gesture with a tender kiss.

They returned to their tea and enjoyed the fire in the parlor until orange embers glowed in remembrance of the fire's former glory.

The newlyweds went upstairs to bed, knowing that sleep would be essential for the long journey that awaited them on the morrow.

After Margaret had donned her nightgown and brushed her hair out, she climbed into bed and happily snuggled next to her husband. "Have you ever shared a bed?" she asked, considering how accustomed she was to their cozy arrangement as she slipped under covers and sank her head into the pillow next to his.

"When I was a boy, my cousin sometimes came to visit," he answered as he laid down to face her. "He always managed to kick me while he slept," he added with a wry smile.

Margaret giggled at the thought of it.

"Have you always slept alone?" he asked her in turn.

"When I first went to London, Edith and I shared a bed. We were sometimes naughty – staying up late and giggling under the covers," she relayed.

"When did you move to London?" he asked curiously, knowing little of her upbringing there.

"When I was eight. I lived there about ten years," she replied with a slightly somber tone. "I went home for holidays, of course, and spent quite a few weeks at home in the summertime," she added more brightly.

"You were quite young to leave your family. You must have missed your parents, and Helstone," he wisely surmised.

Margaret avoided his gaze. "My mother thought it would be a great opportunity for me to take my lessons and learn the social graces in London," she answered shyly. "You see, my mother was from a very fine family, the Beresfords. She was the belle of the county, I've been told. When she fell in love with my father, her family was convinced that she would marry beneath her if she married Papa. But I believe they were happy," she concluded as he listened with fascination to every detail she revealed.

"I'm sure my education was very fine, although my music and dance lessons were not as successful," she continued with a telling smile. "I lived in London until Edith married, the summer before we moved to Milton," she related.

"You must have had many suitors," he remarked only half in jest, for he imagined that she would have attracted the attention of many London gentlemen.

She blushed at his remark. "Oh, it was Edith who was generally fawned over. I was never very good at batting my eyelashes and making silly conversation," she confided with a self-conscious smile. "I don't believe anyone took great note of me."

Mr. Thornton was struck by her humility, perceiving that she had never considered herself to be very beautiful. "I cannot believe you were not noticed. You took my breath away when I first saw you," he confessed tenderly. You are the most beautiful and extraordinary woman. You will always be, to me," he promised in a soft voice as he gently combed his fingers through her hair.

She closed her eyes as his comforting words and soothing touch bade her to relax in his encompassing care.

Mr. Thornton continued his gentle ministrations, marveling at the precious beauty of his wife's face until he noted her breathing had deepened and her lips parted slightly in peaceful sleep.

Margaret woke the next morning to a gentle nuzzling in her hair. She smiled to feel feather-light kisses upon her temple. "Good morning, fair princess," her husband greeted her, his voice caressing her as readily as his lips. "We must leave this enchanted place for distant lands," he announced quietly.

"Mmm...." she replied as she stretched lazily and took a deep breath. "I shall happily accompany my prince to his castle far away," she answered in kind as she reached to slowly trace her hand along the curve of his shoulder.

"I think I should prefer to keep you here indefinitely," he replied in a muffled voice as he bestowed kisses on her neck, the heady scent of her and the soft feel of her skin on his lips beginning to intoxicate him with desire.

"At the cottage, my lord?" she queried somewhat breathlessly, tilting her head to allow him further access to the length of her neck, quickly succumbing to his seductive ministrations.

"In this bed," he replied ardently. He was not yet willing to take leave of the place which held such significance to him – for here is where his fantasies and dreams of love had become a magical reality, more wonderful than he had imagined. Here she had truly become his wife, and he had claimed and reclaimed her irrevocably as his own. He could not forget the time they had spent in breathtaking discovery of one another, and the astonishing power and pleasure they had found in their active union.

She smiled amusedly at his amorous remark, his serious intent sending a thrill of exhilaration through her body. "Will you hold me captive here, then?" she boldly taunted as she wound her arm around his neck.

"Yes, for a while," he answered, bringing his face to hers. "I promise I will treat you mercifully," he managed to jest as a devious smile swept over his face.

"Not too mercifully," she responded softly, a brazen glint in her eye.

Stunned by her reply, he gave her a heated stare of astonishment, before covering her mouth with his own to make her a prisoner of his passion.

The lovers eventually relinquished the blissful sanctuary of their matrimonial bed and rose to prepare for their journey north.

Mr. Thornton donned his trousers and made his morning ablutions, the cool water splashed on his face sending a slight chill over his still unclad chest.

Margaret frequently cast her eyes in her husband's direction as she began to put on the many layers required for a lady's formal attire. She sought help from him in cinching her corset and buttoning the back of her black silk dress, the return of her mourning clothes signaling their imminent return to society.

Mr. Thornton took pleasure in assisting his wife to dress, keenly aware of the privilege temporarily afforded to him in Dixon's absence.

He began to pack his things in his trunk and was drawn to watch his wife taking up a similar task as she carefully folded and placed her garments in her open trunk. The realization of what the future held came to him forcefully – she was coming home with him! Their days together here had been something of a fairy-tale existence. It still seemed a thing incredible to him that she should become part of his everyday life at Marlborough Mills, where the harsh world of struggle, lack, and inequity would constantly clamor outside their door.

He crossed the room to stop her progress and take her hands into his. "I still cannot believe you are coming home with me," he told her simply, the feel of her delicate hands in his accentuating the contrast between the very different worlds that they came from – the breach of which would be mended by the comingling of their lives.

She smiled at his disbelief, remembering how his letters had described similar sentiments. "I will come home with you," she assured him with a loving glance. "However, I must confess I am a little nervous today. I have seldom been inside your home. I am afraid the only memory I hold is that of waking from unconsciousness to find myself in your drawing room," she admitted shyly, avoiding his gaze.

He took hold of her arms and drew her closer. "I hold only pleasant memories of you in my home," he replied honestly.

"Oh, John, I should not have told you to face the crowd, it was foolish of me!" she blurted out. "To think of what could have happened…" She felt a shiver of fear as she contemplated how close he had come to danger.

"And what of you? Margaret, you were struck down trying to protect me!" he reminded her, shuddering as he remembered how he had almost lost her. "You should have stayed inside for your own safety."

"John, I could not stand idly by when it was I who had driven you to action," she answered, her eyes even now revealing the terror that had come over her when she had seen men with rocks and clogs, ready to unleash their frustrated fury on the man who represented all that was unjust in their eyes. She realized now how her heart had impelled her to his rescue, although her mind would not admit the true impulse of her action.

"It is all well now," he comforted her, seeing her distress at the memory of that pivotal event. "We are together and all is well. I wish you to feel at perfect ease in your new home. Will you rewrite your memory to match mine?" he implored, "for I would not erase it. It was a treasured instance of our discovery of one another."

"Do you really think so?" she asked, her eyes searching his for the truth.

"I do," he answered without compunction, and gave her a tender kiss on the lips.

The carriage came soon after they finished packing, and the newlyweds left the cottage with mixed feelings of nostalgia for their week in Helstone, and exhilaration at beginning their life anew in Milton. Margaret watched the passing scenery with particular fondness as they headed toward the station in Southampton. Before long, they were on their way, settled beside each other on the train, the metal squeaking and groaning as the wheels began to propel them slowly forward to Milton – and home.

Chapter Fourteen

The newlyweds spoke little as the train traveled through the countryside, content to gaze out the window together. A small smile played on Mr. Thornton's face, the satisfactory thought of bringing his bride home never far from his mind.

When London was finally behind them and the longer portion of their trip loomed before them, they broke into easy conversation. Margaret asked about the mill and the cotton industry, and Mr. Thornton happily explained everything she inquired about, wisely avoiding any lengthy descriptions that might be beyond her scope. Instead, he gently allowed her to direct the lesson with her inquisitive interest.

When the afternoon drew long, and they wakened from the indolent haze of a peaceful doze, restlessness began to take hold of Margaret. She felt a fluttering of nervousness in the pit of her stomach as they grew nearer to their destination. Her anxiety was born of uncertainty - she would be taking on a whole new role as mistress in a home still foreign to her.

She would not be returning to the small, comfortable home in Crampton with her father, but would be expected to run a household where the large rooms seemed austere and cold, their perfect cleanliness and arrangement suggesting that the occupants within engaged very little in true living. She did not want to disrupt the efficient system she was sure Mrs. Thornton had in place, but she knew that there would inevitably be differences in opinion between them. Margaret did not look forward to being under careful observation, and hoped her mother-in-law would graciously accept any changes she made. Although she wished to please the woman who had so long cared for her beloved husband, her first priority would be to make the house a warm and inviting place for John.

Mr. Thornton sensed the change in his wife's demeanor and inquired after her thoughts.

"It is nothing, really," she said as she endeavored to make light of her feelings, "I suppose I am a little anxious to become mistress of such a grand house. I do not wish to disturb the harmony of your home. I'm certain your mother has taken great pains to make everything run very smoothly," she added worriedly.

Her husband smiled and gently squeezed her hand in reassurance. "It is your home now. I wish you to do as you see fit. I'm certain my mother can assist you in learning the household duties, if need be," he assured her.

"Please, I wish for you to feel at home in my house. You will not worry yourself to please me – I forbid it," he gently mocked her uneasiness with his command. "I will be happy so long as you are in it," he promised, looking into her eyes to convince her.

His words calmed her, but could not entirely erase the uneasiness she felt at the notion of finding her place in the established order of his domain.

When the gray cloud of Milton's smoky factories could be seen in the distance, Margaret's anxiety transmuted to exhilaration. She looked eagerly out the window to watch the city come into view, overjoyed to be coming home at last. Although her memories of living there were mixed, she felt the excitement of starting afresh. A whole new world promised to open up to her in a city she found teeming with activity and the promise of progress.

They alighted from the train and Mr. Thornton signaled a porter.

"Mr. Thornton, sir," the boy acknowledged, bowing slightly after receiving his instructions and hastening to his task.

Margaret took her husband's arm with admiration, and gazed at him with new eyes, seeing now the Milton master and magistrate who commanded the respect of the city. She took a deep breath, feeling a swell of pride to be his wife.

He gave her a warm smile and escorted her to a waiting cab.

Hannah Thornton stared out the window overlooking the gate. Certainly they would arrive before the afternoon grew too late. She had spent enough time waiting, and wished for events to reveal whether her concerns were justified or only the self-imposed fears of a mother who selfishly clung to the past.

She had been a jumble of emotions since the wedding, as various waves of unexpected and overpowering feelings had swept over her throughout the week. John's marriage had affected her more deeply than she cared to admit.

He had been so exultingly happy – the vision of him on his wedding day had never left her. She had wept bitter tears that night, alone in her

London hotel room, as it dawned on her how long and quietly her son had suffered from loneliness. She saw with startling clarity how vain she had been to suppose that her steadfast devotion and care would ensure his happiness. She had loved him fiercely and bolstered him at every turn in his rise to success, but she realized her own inadequacy in providing for him the gentle, sweet affection that would allow him to unburden himself of his unsettled feelings. Although she could not help feeling a twinge of jealousy, she hoped that John had found the affection he needed in Margaret's care.

She had been greatly moved to see Margaret glow with tender adoration for her son. Whatever reasons she had had for rejecting his suit all those months ago had long vanished. Mrs. Thornton could only rejoice to think how much John deserved to be loved in such a manner.

The restless widow left her vigilant post to reclaim her seat in the dining room and take up her sewing. She hoped all had been harmonious for the newlyweds during their stay in Helstone. She was afraid that they might run too early on into some disagreement that would upset their peaceful cohabitation. They were both very strong individuals, but Margaret would need to learn to respect her husband's decisions if she expected to bring him any lasting happiness.

Mrs. Thornton had had ample time to consider why John had been attracted to Margaret. Observing her own daughter earlier in the week had given her much to contemplate as she realized how different Margaret was compared to most women of her age and social standing.

Her two days in London with Fanny had been tiresome. She had enjoyed the opera itself, but disdained the ostentatious dress and mannerisms of those attending. The lackadaisical habits and superior positions of easy wealth that she observed only rekindled her contempt for the South.

Fanny's giddy enthusiasm for everything London had to offer had been almost intolerable, and Watson's silly indulgence of her every whim had increasingly annoyed her. Their insipid behavior contrasted strikingly to the thoughtful and intelligent manner that both John and Margaret seemed to carry. Neither her son nor his wife seemed to be interested in mere amusement or self-indulgence. She could see now how unthinkable it would have been to see her son paired with a flighty girl whose head was only filled with the occupation of society's latest drivel or fashionable pursuit.

Unable to concentrate on her embroidery, Mrs. Thornton stood and walked to the side table, brushing away an imaginary speck of dust from the corner surface and straightening the candle in the wall sconce to a perfect upright position. She wondered how Margaret might try to change the house. Her home in Crampton had been humble, but

Margaret had lived in London with wealthy relatives and might have ideas of how to transform this house into something resembling a grand southern home.

Mrs. Thornton was uncomfortable with the thought of having her daughter-in-law in charge of the house that she had run these many years. Besides being left to insipid idleness, she was afraid that Margaret would attempt to implement southern ideals of comfort and leisure, which would be unseemly here at Marlborough Mills – the center of Milton's standard for industry and efficiency. She could imagine how unsettling the differing opinions between them could become, disturbing the harmony of the home.

She walked to the window again to watch for the couple's arrival. At the very least, she mused, Margaret would need to be kept from any flamboyant purchases at the outset, and be shown a reasonable household budget. The elder woman wondered if John had told her yet of the financial strain the strike had caused. Margaret would need to know that her spending would be limited until such time as the business recovered – *if* it recovered.

It was difficult to imagine that fate would send her son to ruin, but Mrs. Thornton could not dismiss the gnawing fear that circumstances would not improve. Would Margaret stand by her son if he could not bring the mill back to profit? The girl had stoutly endured her own portion of difficulties – moving to Milton, her mother's death, and her brother's misfortune. She hoped her devotion to John would prove just as strong and that she would bring him some sense of hope if events turned downward.

Beyond all her selfish concerns - wondering what place and usefulness she would have now – her overriding concern was that Margaret should bring John happiness. Mrs. Thornton would care nothing for what Margaret did or did not do, if only she could know that the girl would bring him enduring happiness. She could not bear to see her son brought to desolation again.

She trembled to think what would become of him if Margaret became resentful of her marriage or if she fled to her London relations in times of difficulty.

Mrs. Thornton's better judgment told her that the girl was made of stronger stuff than to flee her troubles, but her mother's heart still worried that John might have to suffer great heartache once more.

Her reverie was broken as she observed a coach stop outside the gate. In truth, for all her musings, she did not know what to expect. She only knew that they had been remarkably happy on their wedding day. She fervently hoped that nothing had changed.

When they reached the gates of Marlborough Mills, Margaret felt all the wonder of this momentous event. This would be her new home. Her stomach twisted with anxious hope that she should be worthy of her calling to be mistress of such a place.

Mr. Thornton was fairly bursting with exuberant joy to be bringing his wife home at last.

Before they reached the door, Jane opened it to admit them. Margaret moved to step forward, but Mr. Thornton swept his wife off her feet and carried her over the threshold.

"John, we shall be seen!" Margaret complained, aware that there could be passers-by now that they were in the city.

"Then let them take note that the Master of Marlborough Mills is now happily married," he replied with a wide grin.

Jane smiled discreetly in amusement to see the master in such high spirits.

As Mr. Thornton carried his bride to the stairs, Margaret protested his obvious intent to mount them with her firmly in his grasp. "John, set me down! What would your mother think?" she asked him, aghast at his willingness to appear so unguarded in his jubilation to bring her home.

Mr. Thornton smiled at her embarrassment and set her down, clasping her hand as they mounted the stairs together.

Hannah Thornton awaited them in the dining room, a subdued smile lifting the somber picture of her rigid pose as she watched the newlyweds enter the room.

"Mother," her son greeted her warmly and gave her an affectionate embrace.

"Margaret," Mrs. Thornton welcomed her daughter-in-law to her new home with a light embrace and a kiss on the cheek as custom required.

"How was your journey?" she asked politely of their long train ride.

"It was pleasant enough," Mr. Thornton replied.

"I trust you enjoyed your stay," his mother commented kindly, her eyes falling on her daughter-in-law.

"Yes, it was very lovely, thank you," Margaret replied, casting a timid glance at her husband who was smiling broadly at her answer.

The warm glances and smiles between them did not escape Mrs. Thornton's notice. They were obviously very happy and seemed well adjusted thus far to their new relationship as husband and wife. She was glad of it. Fanny's acclimation to married life had been much more difficult. Mrs. Thornton was greatly relieved to perceive that Margaret would not require her counsel in such private matters.

She would be very interested, however, to see how well the new couple made the transition to the very real pattern of life that would begin when John resumed his work at the mill tomorrow.

"I know the journey was long, and travelling by train can be quite dirty. Would you care to wash the dust off?" the elder woman directed her question to Margaret. "I would be happy to show you to your room," she offered hospitably.

"Yes, of course. Thank you," her son's wife answered kindly.

"There are some letters of urgent importance on your desk in the study," Mrs. Thornton told her son as he made ready to follow them. "Mr. Williams insisted that you be notified as soon as you returned," she clarified, giving him a pointed stare.

Mr. Thornton shot a worried glance in his mother's direction, having hoped to judge for himself Margaret's initial reaction to the living arrangements his mother had established. He knew, however, by the look she had given him that she wished to escort Margaret alone for propriety's sake.

He sighed inwardly as he relented, allowing his mother's judgment to prevail for the moment. He falteringly convinced himself that after such a week of blissfully intimate companionship, Margaret would surely understand that the living arrangement his mother introduced would be a superficial nod to custom.

"I will be up directly," he assured his wife in apology for taking his leave of her.

Margaret nodded sympathetically before turning to be led through the dining room. She studied curiously the painted portraits on the wall as she followed her mother-in-law up the stairs, feeling a strange elation to be ushered up to the private quarters of the house.

"This is John's room," the elder Mrs. Thornton announced as she began down the hall, indicating a thick wooden door to the right. She seemed proud of the many stately doors in the long corridor. "John had a new convenience installed here last year," she remarked, indicating a door on the opposite side. "Fanny was very pleased with it. John wished us to have every modern comfort," she added with obvious affection for her son's thoughtfulness, although she seemed indifferent to the luxury provided.

"And this is your room," she announced with satisfaction, having arrived at the next door on the right and opening the door to usher her in.

Margaret smiled politely in acknowledgement although she struggled with the surprise at being given her own room. She attempted to hide the disappointment and confusion she felt coming over her. The comfortable arrangement at the cottage had led her to assume that she would share John's bedroom. She chastised herself for not considering the alternative.

Of course she should have expected to have her own quarters in such a spacious home. She was certain Mrs. Thornton was proud to offer her son's wife every privilege befitting his wealth and standing.

It was a beautiful room, not at all like the somber, colorless rooms in the formal living space downstairs. Rose and white peonies blossomed in small clusters against a sea of green on the papered walls. A moderate sized poster bed was adorned with a dusty pink coverlet, and the furniture and floors were the warm color of dark honey. Margaret detected the faint smell of beeswax polish on the furniture as she walked into the room.

Her eyes lit with recognition to see her mother's dressing table, and a quick scan of the room revealed other objects that had been lovingly placed to make her feel at home. Her heart warmed as she recognized her husband's hand in such a loving gesture.

She felt a stab of sorrow at the thought that John might be comfortable with such an arrangement. Perhaps it was enough for him to know she was nearby and could be visited whenever it was convenient. He would be very busy now, and she would not wish to interfere or tire him unnecessarily. Although she felt her reasoning was sound, the unsettling thought that she should be left alone at times continued to undermine the peaceful contentedness she had found since marrying.

She had found such perfect happiness in their companionship in Helstone. She had never felt so connected to anyone before. But now, as she stood in the middle of the room, she felt gloom closing in around her at the notion of being separated from him. She had thought that they would be different – that they would not live by the traditions set by others – but instead would create a close bond by spending time together. Her sadness was compounded by the fact that she was expected to be grateful for such a lovely room.

Mr. Thornton frowned at the correspondence laying open on his desk. It seemed that fortune would not smile on him where business was concerned. A buyer whose product was nearly finished was attempting to rescind a portion of his order, while another buyer was outlining a promising contract that would be difficult to meet on schedule with the inventory on hand.

A familiar pall of dread began to descend upon him as all of the challenges of operating a struggling mill faced him once again. The insidious tentacles of fear began to wind themselves around him, infiltrating his peace of mind.

Mr. Thornton roused his thoughts and stood up from his desk with decision. He refused to allow any troubles from the mill to mar his happiness today. Tomorrow would come soon enough. He gathered the papers from his desk and left the confines of his study.

His heart lightened as he bounded up the stairs. How glorious it was to know that she was here, ensconced in the private quarters of his own home!

Upon entering his bedroom, he shrugged off his frock coat and laid it over a chair. He pulled at his cravat as he crossed the room, having grown accustomed to removing the constrictive piece of requisite silk once he was alone. He sighed in disappointment that she should not be here in his room, remembering the sweet bliss of her constant company at the cottage.

He was resolved to allow her the opportunity to choose how they should live here, although his heart yearned to be with her at every moment. He knew she had been happy sharing a room at the cottage, but the wedding trip was over. He was uncertain what she would expect concerning their sleeping arrangements now that they were back in Milton. Perhaps she would wish for a respite from the unceasing demands he had made on her person. He sighed again to think of sleeping alone once more.

Mr. Thornton strode to the back dressing room that connected their rooms, pausing to determine if she were alone. Hearing nothing, he knocked lightly at her door. "Margaret?" he asked quietly to seek admittance, anxious to observe how she liked the room that had been carefully prepared for her.

"Come in," she called out instantly at the sound of her husband's voice, anxiously hoping she could hide her uneasiness from him. She did not want to appear ungrateful for the generous place intended to welcome her to their home.

He entered quietly, giving her a warm smile to see her standing in the middle of the room. She smiled back, the sight of him releasing some of the tension she had inadvertently been holding since she had stepped into the room.

"Is there any trouble?" she asked with concern, referring to the matters of the mill his mother had mentioned.

"Nothing that cannot wait another day," he answered furtively with a twitch of a smile.

"How do you find your room?" he asked hopefully, thinking of the items that had been removed from her parents' home for her personal enjoyment. "Did you recognize your father's desk at once?" he asked, obviously eager to know how much it pleased her.

"Oh, John, I noticed everything you had brought here- my mother's dressing table, her jewelry box, even my pressed flowers from Helstone," she enthused her appreciation for his thoughtfulness as he moved to take her hands in his. "Truly, it is a lovely room, you have been so careful to make me feel at home. I am very grateful for it," she thanked him earnestly, smiling at his joyful enthusiasm.

But, as her eyes alighted on the bed meant for her use, her sorrowing heart could no longer feign cheerfulness. His very happiness caused her doubts to descend upon her again. She wondered if he truly wished to sleep alone, and her face mirrored her hurt and confusion.

"Margaret, what is it?" he asked in dismay, noting at once her discomfort. He felt panic rise within him at the notion that she should already be unhappy in her new home. "Is something wrong? You may change anything you wish if all is not as it should be," he offered, hoping her displeasure was of no great magnitude.

"No, no. It is very beautiful. It is more than I expected. Truly," she assured him, endeavoring to smile convincingly.

"Then what is troubling you?" he asked in desperation, fearing that she should be unhappy to be returned to Milton, despite her best intensions.

Margaret was embarrassed at her churlish behavior, but felt helpless to hide her emotions from him. She was loath to appear ungrateful for the gracious welcome she had received into his home, but could not avoid relaying something of what she wished for. "It is nothing. I suppose I had grown fond of our cozy room at the cottage," she confided shyly, hoping he would not think her too forward in expressing her desires. "But I'm certain I will grow accustomed to this new arrangement and be a good wife to you," she promised, her disappointment evident in her pained expression.

His heart sank at the thought that she should feel shunned by him, but his hope soared to recognize her yearning to be close to him.

"You wish to share a room together – to share a bed with me?" he asked tentatively, wanting desperately to believe that her desires matched his own.

Margaret blushed at his earnest questioning, and averted her eyes a moment before lifting them to discern what he expected of her.

"You cannot believe that I wish you to be separated from me," he spoke fervently, his eyes questing hers as he pulled her closer to him and encircled her waist with his broad hands. "This is my mother's doing. She was insistent that a woman of your stature have her own room," he explained. "I thought you might like to use it as a sitting room, but surely you must know that I want you to be with me….in my bed," he clarified, his voice tinged with an earnest pleading, intent that she should understand his desire to be with her every possible moment.

His last words were spoken with an insistent urgency, causing her to briefly avert her eyes as a fluttering sensation stirred deep within her. She felt a joyous relief to know that he had no intention of loosening the tight bond they had forged during their week together in Helstone.

She returned his gaze and slid her hands around his neck. "I wish to be with you, John," she answered in hushed tones, unabashed at her simple confession.

Her honest admission sent a shiver of joy through him. He could think of no greater happiness than to know that her yearning to be with him rivaled his own unceasing longing to have her near. He drew her to him and held her tightly, holding her head to his chest. The warmth of her embrace flooded his soul with a contented peace.

At length, he moved to hold her arms and look into her eyes. "You must promise never to hesitate to come to my room. It is yours as well. I wish there to be no boundaries between us," he explained. "Come, let me show you," he offered, taking her hand and leading her through the dressing room passageway to his own bedchamber.

As she stepped through the door, Margaret nearly staggered at the opulent colors of the room, feeling as if she had entered the domain of a powerful regent. Rich tones of a deep red were gilded by golden-colored fringe on the heavy valence curtains, and the darker red of the wall was broken by vertical stripes of shining gold. An enormous bed took precedence with a large carved headboard against the wall. The thick, sateen coverlet of the bed was the color of red wine with simple swirls of golden thread patterned throughout.

Her eyes surveyed the arrangement of the room, taking note of the dark wood wardrobe, a dressing table and mirror nearer the bed. A mahogany desk was placed in the far corner with a few books, inkwell and quill ready for use. Everything was in its place; there was no clutter of objects to display wealth or heritage. In fact, the simplicity of the room was well hidden by the grandeur and majestic elegance of the rich fabrics and deep-toned colors, as well as the impressive size of the bed.

Margaret could not suppress a small smile from spreading across her face. She saw Mrs. Thornton's hand behind the regal style of the room. She held her son in the highest estimation – certainly, he was a prince among men in her eyes.

"It is very fine, John. I shall feel like a queen when I enter this chamber," she stated candidly.

Her husband smiled at her remark. "And shall I be consort or king to your majesty?" he inquired humorously, placing his hands around her waist once more.

Margaret hesitated, feigning serious consideration of the matter with a tilt of her head. "I suppose you ought to be king, seeing as you have an empire to rule," she answered with some reserve, unwilling to relinquish the possibility of her sovereignty.

"Are you to be at my command, then?" he asked with a suggestive arch of his eyebrow, enjoying immensely the unfolding exchange between them.

"Am I not already?" she brazenly responded, winding her arms around his neck and gazing at him with open adoration.

A warm wave of sensation swept through him at her willing submission, sparking the desire to assert his power and prove her complete surrender.

He kissed her hungrily for her enchanting behavior, starving for her kisses after the long ride to Milton.

After a moment of sublime silence, Margaret reluctantly fought to pull away from his intoxicating kisses before all ability to resist him was lost. "I believe your mother wished us to join her for tea just now," she reminded him somewhat breathlessly, still reeling from his amorous demands.

His body rebelled against the abrupt cessation of sensual pleasure, but his mind grudgingly perceived his social obligation to his mother. "Perhaps we could be a little late," he rasped, unwilling to release his wife from his grasp just yet.

"John! It would not be kind to keep her waiting," she chastised him with a knowing smile, her pulse still recovering from its rampant pace. "I will tell her you will be down shortly," she offered, realizing he had not had time for a moment's peace since they had arrived home.

The drawing room was empty. Margaret moved to stand by the window overlooking the mill, wondering if her husband often stood here surveying all that he had worked so hard to establish.

The magnitude of what he had accomplished in the face of adversity was staggering, and yet he did not carry an air of superiority or flaunt his wealth or power. She wondered if he knew how truly amazing he was. No man could compare. She admired his humility, but would never allow him to forget what he was capable of, and would fiercely defend him if she heard a disparaging word against him.

The stillness of the mill yard was haunting, recalling to her mind the ominous day when it had been teeming with desperate strikers; she remembered clearly the thundering noise of their angry protests spurring them on to a frenzy of uncontrolled fury.

How naive she had been to assume that a few words of reason would calm the storming crowd. She cringed to think of how she had reprimanded the powerful Master – sending him like an errant schoolboy to rectify his mistake.

She had been greatly humbled to realize that there were no simple solutions to resolving the long-embroiled conflict between masters and the working class. She had eventually come to admire his honesty and willingness to address the inequities that plagued the workers' lives. Perhaps together they could learn to improve things for the benefit of all concerned.

Mr. Thornton came into the room silently and turned to find his wife standing at the window. His heart twisted with emotion to see her there, and he remembered the brief moment when they had stood there together in the charged atmosphere of fear, when she had seemed to take charge of him to compel him to face the rioters.

And it was at that window he had stood alone the following morning in bleak despair, when the hope of claiming her love had been shockingly wrested from his grasp. The pain of that memory now dissolved as he moved to gently close his arms around her from behind – she was now decidedly his.

He looked with her at the view outside and endeavored to see it as she might. "All is still today, but tomorrow it will not be so. I hope you will become accustomed to the noise. I know it is a far cry from the quiet fields of Helstone," he apologized.

"It shall be like music to me," she answered succinctly in a quiet voice, her gaze still resting on the outside scene.

"Music?" he repeated quizzically, looking to her for an explanation of her cryptic words.

She turned to face him with decision. "I am as proud of you as your mother is, John," she stated defiantly. "The sounds of the mill will only remind me of everything that you are," she declared.

"Margaret, do you think so highly of me? I am afraid I am not worthy of such praise," he exclaimed, incredulous that she should so strongly affirm her faith in him.

"I have not met a finer man than you, John. I only hope that I will not tarnish your good name with my headstrong ways and outspoken manner. I wish only to bring you the high esteem which you deserve," she earnestly confessed.

"Margaret, do not mock my own deep feeling of unworthiness," he countered, staring into her soulful eyes.

Their heartfelt exchange was broken by the sound of approaching footsteps.

Mr. Thornton moved to stand next to his wife, but did not relinquish contact with her, keeping hold of her hand as his mother walked into the room.

Noting the couple at the window, Mrs. Thornton felt impelled to inform her daughter-in-law of the stark reality that the morrow would bring. "Tomorrow you will see for yourself how it is to live by the mill when it is in operation. You may find the noise distracting. Fanny was never able to become accustomed to it," she warned.

The newlyweds smiled knowingly at each other.

"I am certain I shall get used to it. I think I may even come to like it," Margaret replied with a polite smile.

Mr. Thornton gave his wife's hand a gentle squeeze.

Mrs. Thornton momentarily stared at the couple, only too aware that her words had sparked a renewal of some shared secret between the two. She felt the discomfort of being excluded from their confidential communication, but reminded herself that that was as it should be. She must learn to accept that John would share many confidences with his wife.

She led them to sit where Jane had placed the tea tray on the low table and asked them if Helstone had experienced good weather during their stay.

The Thorntons enjoyed the refreshment of tea and scones, and inquired of their time away from Milton. Mrs. Thornton mentioned her appreciation for the fine opera, but remarked that she had no interest in visiting London with Fanny again, briefly explaining that she was not as impressionable as her daughter to the sights of the city.

The newlyweds revealed that they had spent much time outdoors, it having rained only one day during their sojourn. Mr. Thornton expressed his desire that his mother should see the drawings that Margaret had made, and encouraged his wife to show them to her later.

After the tray had been collected, Mr. Thornton moved to fetch the *Milton Guardian* from a side table and sat back down next to his wife on the sofa. Wordlessly, the elder Mrs. Thornton moved to her favorite chair to take up her embroidery. Noting his wife's restless quandary in finding herself in an unfamiliar situation, he offered to show her his study, where she could select something to read.

Leading her to a room tucked away from the more formal living spaces, Mr. Thornton relished the opportunity to usher his wife into a room that was seldom frequented by anyone but himself. He extended his arm to indicate she was welcome to his burgeoning collection of books and she noted at once many of her father's books neatly arranged on a bookshelf behind his large oak desk.

"You have acquired father's books!" she exclaimed with unconcealed enthusiasm, eventually bringing her wondering gaze to her husband for his explanation.

"I thought you would appreciate maintaining possession of such a fine collection," he responded, grinning widely at her obvious delight. "I was able to purchase them for a very reasonable price," he revealed. "Mr. Bell was kind enough to allow me the opportunity to choose whatever I liked before putting everything up for auction. I hope I have chosen well, as I had you in mind as I did so," he confided with tenderness in his voice.

She rushed to throw her arms around his neck to confirm her appreciation of all he had done. "Truly, you have chosen everything that I held especially dear. I am at a loss for words at your thoughtfulness. I don't believe I should ever be able to repay you," she told him truthfully, her heart swelling with love for the man before her.

"I am certain I can think of ways…" he could not resist teasing her with a twinkle in his eye.

She only hugged him tighter as an answer, laying her head near his shoulder. "Thank you," she said simply in gratitude for the gift of his thoughtful kindnesses toward her.

He gladly held her in his embrace until she pulled away to make her selection, remembering the reason they had come to his study.

The couple returned to the drawing room, and spent time quietly reading as the afternoon light began to grow fainter.

Mrs. Thornton felt a pervading contentment to have her son home again and enjoyed the silent companionship of her newly extended family.

After some time, Dixon appeared to announce that a bath had been prepared for the new mistress, and Margaret excused herself to follow the stout maid upstairs.

Mr. Thornton watched his wife leave the room before returning to his paper, endeavoring to quell the alluring images already beginning to form in his mind.

Margaret smiled to herself as she soaked in the large copper bath. She felt indulgent, enjoying the luxury of her new surroundings. No wonder Fanny enjoyed this room's conveniences. Margaret had never sat in a tub that allowed her to stretch her legs out in front of her, nor bathed in a room with every modern comfort.

She had married well. She cared not one jot for the fancy titles and respected lineages to which her aunt paid homage. She had married John for love, and was respectfully aware of the privileges afforded her by such a match. He had worked hard to obtain his current position in society, and was able to provide his family with comforts that many only dreamed about. She admired him above all others, and was unutterably grateful to have found her true love in such a man.

She felt a strange exhilaration to be bathing in his house. It would take some time to get used to considering this place her home. She still felt more like a guest than the new mistress of the house. But it was just as well, she thought, since she had only just arrived. She would become accustomed to living in this grand house with time, but for now she would enjoy the newness of everything.

Dixon helped her dress for dinner, informing Margaret that the dinner hour was strictly observed. "That woman runs a tight ship, I tell you. I'd not like to get in her way," her mother's faithful servant remarked dolefully. "I only arrived here yesterday, but she's been soundly determined to make sure every thing was perfect before you came home. If I didn't know better, I'd say she was anxious about handing over the reins. But I know she'd not let a young lass like you get the better of her," Dixon commented with an air of confidence in her judgment. "Although I get a strange satisfaction in thinking that the old dragon is afraid of my young miss," she sniffed in humor as she helped Margaret put on her undergarments.

"I'm sure it must be difficult for her to give up her position, when she has run the house for so many years," Margaret replied sympathetically, wincing slightly as Dixon gave a vigorous tug to the lacing of her corset.

Dixon raised her eyebrows, somewhat surprised at the young mistress's compassionate response. "Well I hope you'll not let her rule the roost. It's your proper place now, as the Master's wife, to run things around here," she brazenly reminded the new bride.

"I am well aware of what is expected of me, Dixon. I'm sure things will work out for the best in due time," she replied, endeavoring to assure herself with the words she had spoken.

Margaret was in a festive and playful mood, choosing to wear the gown that she had worn at Mrs. Thornton's dinner party nearly a year ago. After Dixon had set her hair up elegantly and left the room, Margaret stood to admire herself in the great oval mirror by her wardrobe. She smiled deviously, remembering her husband's confession of how he had felt about her that evening. She felt a twinge of apprehension to appear before her husband in this garment, knowing that he would appreciate the way she looked.

Gathering her courage, she opened the door to the connecting dressing room and walked serenely into his bedroom.

Mr. Thornton was buttoning his collar and saw the movement of her figure in the mirror. He smiled brilliantly as he turned to greet her, pleased that she had taken the liberty to enter at will as he had insisted.

His eyes lit with a torrid recognition of the evening she had worn the dress, captivating him with her beauty.

"You remember my gown?" she asked coquettishly, as if she were not aware of the affect it had on him.

"I think it unlikely I could ever forget," he replied huskily, his eyes still roving over her as the memories of that summer evening flooded back to him. "You offered your hand to me that night. It was the first time our hands met," he recalled reverently as he drew closer to her, his hair still damp from bathing. "You were stunning – are stunning," he declared. "I could not stop thinking of you, and your touch, for many days," he admitted.

Margaret stared at him with wondering eyes, astounded by his revelation.

"I did not think a simple handshake would have affected you so," she stated curiously.

"You enchanted me with your handshake," he told her. "And the vision you presented..." he began, unable to find the words to describe what a glorious torment it had been to keep his eyes from following her all evening. His scorching gaze studied the alabaster skin revealed by the low neckline, which gently dipped from shoulder to shoulder.

Margaret's heart quickened, as she comprehended his desire.

"I did not think such beauty should ever be mine," he breathed, gently brushing the back of his curved finger along the silken skin exposed to him, sending a rippling shiver throughout her whole body. He lowered his head to daringly nestle a kiss in the tantalizing hollow revealed by her décolletage.

Margaret gasped. The warm breath from his open mouth and the feel of his lips upon her skin threatened to undo her. She felt her knees weaken from the sensual intimacy of his gesture.

He brought his lips to hers and she openly received him.

They kissed slowly, with deliberation, reveling in the bliss of belonging to each other. When at last they relinquished their contact, they stood silent a moment, struggling to regain their composure.

"Shall we go to dinner then?" Mr. Thornton asked at length, recovering his sensibilities.

Margaret nodded, still uncertain if her legs could carry her safely down the stairs.

Before dinner was served, the newly married couple presented Mrs. Thornton with a gift. She looked at them in some surprise as she accepted the package. Margaret observed a flicker of a smile cross her face as she opened it.

It was a framed daguerreotype of the son who had been the reason for her existence since her husband's death. It was a close portrait, revealing only the upper portion of his tall frame. His chin was held slightly aloft in a proud pose, but a slight trace of a smile softened the hard look.

Mrs. Thornton was speechless. She ran her fingers over the glass as she studied the picture, blinking away the tears that threatened to form in her eyes. "It is a fine gift. Thank you," she said simply, finally looking up with a smile of gratitude. "And what of Margaret?" she thought to ask, wondering why Margaret was not included in the image.

"We had a portrait taken of both of us," Mr. Thornton informed her.

"I thought perhaps we could find a suitable place to display it in the house," Margaret offered.

Mrs. Thornton gave a small smile of approval as the first course was served – Yorkshire pudding with onion gravy.

Mr. Thornton told his mother much about their day in Lymington as he ate heartily of the beef roast dinner, and Margaret commented on his newly acquired talent for sailing and chimed in to speak of the Queen's proximity when they had passed the island.

Mr. Thornton endeavored to keep his gaze from constantly falling on his wife, for his mother's sake, enjoying the company of the two women he loved most in this world.

Mrs. Thornton was pleased her son had enjoyed his stay in the country and had found adventure during their small venture to the sea.

After a sumptuous dessert of lemon cheesecake, the company removed to the drawing room to settle their stomachs and take up their respective habits of leisure.

Before too long, Margaret announced that she was tired from the long day's journey, and would retire for the evening, bidding her mother-in-law a pleasant good night.

Mr. Thornton glanced somewhat anxiously at his wife and responded that he would remain a few more minutes before he also retired, hoping she would wait for him.

Margaret nodded with a gentle smile and climbed the stairs to her room.

Dixon assisted her mistress out of her dinner dress and brought Margaret's nightgown to her, the traditional white gown draped over her portly arm.

"I think I should like to try my new green ensemble tonight, Dixon," Margaret gently informed her, as she walked to the wardrobe to open a drawer and pull out the garment she wanted.

Dixon raised her eyebrows at the sight of the silky fabric and its gauzy accompaniment as she began to help Margaret into her chosen night wear. "I hope you won't catch your death of cold in such a gown," Dixon chastised her, noting how exposed her arms and neck would be in such a garment.

"It is nearly June, Dixon," she countered. "This is from a very fine shop in London. Edith thought very favorably of it," she informed her, defending her choice. Margaret remembered with an inward smile how Edith had practically forced her to purchase the ensemble against her own maidenly sensibilities, insisting that Margaret would appreciate it later. She was grateful for her cousin's foresight.

Dixon shook her head in disapproval as she looked over the young bride.

Margaret wore an emerald green satin sheath that scooped generously in the front from the thin straps of her shoulder and flared to a fuller skirt as it reached her ankles, revealing matching satin slippers embossed with golden thread. Her bare arms were covered by a long, decorative peignoir of sheer tulle and lace that was loosely tied with a single ribbon at her waist.

"I'm quite certain that a husband needs no encouragement, Miss Margaret," Dixon warned. "Especially a man recently come home from his honeymoon," she huffed in exasperation that the girl might not fully comprehend what men had on their minds. "In fact, if I were you…"

"Thank you, Dixon, for your concern," Margaret hurriedly interrupted, "but you will have to leave me to my own judgment. It is my first night in my new home. I wish to wear something new for the occasion. That is all," she said in an attempt to justify her decision.

Dixon heaved a sigh, and bit her tongue. She hoped the young bride knew what she was doing, tempting her husband with such flimsy garments. What had ever happened to proper modesty? She shook her head at the audacity of these modern young girls.

Margaret allowed Dixon to brush her hair, but stopped her from braiding it into the plait she had always worn as a maiden. "I've become accustomed to leaving my hair undone at night whilst in Helstone," was all she offered as an explanation for her preference.

Dixon huffed again at this statement, well aware of the penchant most men had to see a woman with luxurious, long hair. She only hoped that Margaret did not indulge the master's every whim. It was not meet that a woman should be so anxious to please her husband in the bedroom.

Finding her usefulness at an end, Dixon wished her mistress a reluctant good night and left the room.

Margaret walked over to the long mirror by the wardrobe. She was pleased with how elegant she looked, and lifted her chin slightly in defiance of Dixon's opinions. She would feel like a queen on her first night here. She smiled at her reflection as she imagined John's reaction to her appearance. She delighted in the thought of captivating his attention.

Her heart beat a little faster as she slowly approached the passageway to his room, feeling a little like a lamb approaching a lion's liar.

Mr. Thornton paced the length of his room. How long did it take for a lady to undress? he wondered impatiently. In truth, he had only recently prepared for bed, but found he could not keep still as he waited for her.

The thought suddenly struck him that perhaps she was waiting for him to come to her. What was the protocol for such an arrangement? he asked himself, having never considered how other couples managed such delicate matters. He approached the door to the dressing room, but turned again upon reaching the threshold of his open door as another thought came to him. Perhaps she was truly exhausted, and had decided to sleep in her own bedchamber tonight. His heart sank at the notion of finding himself alone tonight.

Walking to his desk again, he sat down, determined to find something to occupy his distracted mind. He would wait a little longer before checking on her.

No sooner had he seated himself than he noticed the movement of her figure as she entered the room.

He stood up abruptly. "Margaret, I..." he began, before becoming mute as he took in the sight of her. His ardor rose, fanned by her alluring beauty in such a garment. He was keenly aware that it was worn to please him.

"I was beginning to think that you would keep to your room," he stammered at last, his eyes roving slowly over her body.

"There *is* a very serviceable bed in my room," she teased as she closed the gap between them, enjoying the power she had to stupefy him.

He smiled at her taunting words. "I promise my bed can be much more serviceable," he replied in a sultry tone as he moved to grasp her waist, the silken fabric inviting him to slowly slide his hands along the small curve of her waist.

She gently wrested herself from his grasp and sauntered over to the bed. "It is a very large bed. It seems a pity that it has been used by only one person," she remarked saucily as she perched herself beguilingly on its edge, unaware that such a simple gesture would stir his deeper emotions.

Mr. Thornton was spellbound. Her words recalled to him the countless lonely nights he had spent in that very bed. The poignancy of her seduction only increased his aching need to have her in it. "I will not confess how long I have dreamed to have you in my bed," he told her, his low voice wavering with the longing he had secretly held for many months.

"I am not yet really in it," she contested brazenly, capturing his gaze with her own honest longing as she rose.

He watched transfixed as she threw back the bed covers, took off her peignoir, slipped out of her nightgown and climbed into his bed.

"Now I am in it," she announced with a beguiling smile, observing with devious delight his astonishment. "Will you come to bed, Mr. Thornton?" she beckoned him.

He needed no further invitation, but joined her under the covers in a matter of moments. Elated by the very presence of her in his bed, his pulse quickened in expectation of finally utilizing this familiar place of repose for something other than sleeping.

He reverently explored the feel of her skin with his hands, marveling again at all that was his. He covered her face with tender kisses before tasting the honeyed sweetness of her compliant lips, and drew her further under his power with deepening kisses that spoke of his love and burgeoning need.

At last, he claimed her as his own in the city where they had met and fallen in love, transforming all the bitterness of their past into the triumph of their sweet union.

❦

Margaret hugged her husband's arm and lightly kissed his shoulder as he lay sleeping next to her. She was exhausted from the long day's events, but found she could not sleep.

The excitement of her new surroundings and the anticipation of creating a whole new life whirled in her mind, keeping sleep at bay as she wondered what the morrow would bring.

She was eager to be shown the entire house, and wondered what Mrs. Thornton would tell her about running it. Margaret hoped she would remember everything her mother-in-law explained.

Now that she was back in Milton, she hoped to find the time to visit Mary and the Boucher children. She looked forward to seeing Nicholas again, too.

But most of all, she imagined how slowly the day would pass before John came home in the evening. She hoped that his work would not give him undue trouble, so that he might be able to keep a regular schedule. She had not spent even an hour away from him since their wedding day. She worried that she had become too accustomed to his company and would miss him terribly before the day grew to a close.

She closed her eyes and listened to the steady sound of her husband's soft breathing. The comfort of his presence soothed her at last into a sound sleep.

Chapter Fifteen

Along the dim alleyways and squalid streets of the darkened city, a gray-headed man with a lantern made his rounds, tapping the bedroom windows of the factory workers with his long, weathered stick. Inside, the languid sleepers grudgingly rose to throw on their workaday clothes and head for Hamper's, Slickson's, Thornton's and the like. Their day of rest would be a mere memory until the whistle blew at four on Saturday.

In the stately house at Marlborough Mills, the Master woke to the gray light of early dawn. He turned to see his wife sleeping beside him, her hand gently curled over his arm. Her hair sprawled over her pillow and spilled onto the space next to him. A warm smile spread over his face – this was just how he imagined it should be.

Contrary to his every inclination, he forced himself to carefully extract himself from her sleeping grasp, and rose from the bed to prepare for his day. He knew it was the only way he would get to work on time.

He quietly set about getting dressed. As he passed by the bedside, his eyes fell on the pile of green satin and lace lying crumpled on the floor. A stirring of desire rushed through his veins as he remembered her enthralling seduction last evening and the passion that had followed. He studied the shape of her sleeping form beneath the sheets before allowing his gaze to rest on the pink fullness of her gently parted lips.

He shook his head briefly and took a deep breath to bring himself back to his present duty. It required every ounce of his practiced willpower to continue with his routine. How he had enjoyed the blissful leisure of their mornings in Helstone! But there was much to accomplish now; he could not let his mind be overtaken by the sweet pleasures of marriage. It should be enough that she would be waiting for him when his day's work was over.

He was tying his cravat in the mirror when he heard her stir and he turned to watch her wake. She sat up and propped herself upon one arm, modestly holding the sheet to her chest as she did so.

"You are already dressed," she complained groggily, accustomed to their usual languor.

"Unfortunately, our holiday is at an end and I must return to my work," he said gently.

"I understand," she replied, endeavoring not to sound disappointed. "But since you are master, if you should occasionally be a little late, there would be no one to mark your time, would there?" she asked curiously.

A lopsided grin formed on his face at her astute assessment. "No, there would not," he agreed.

"Even if I dressed quickly, you will surely be finished with your breakfast by the time I am ready," she calculated bleakly. "May I not at least have a good-bye kiss before you depart?" she asked hopefully.

More than willing to comply with her request, he sat on the edge of the bed and leaned over to oblige. As she leaned forward to meet him, her covering fell away, but she heeded it not as she received his tender kiss. She moved to cover herself again as he withdrew, but his eyes quickly ravished her loveliness before she had accomplished her purpose. His bed had never looked so warm and inviting.

Mr. Thornton stood up and decisively removed the cravat he had so meticulously tied moments before. He cast the black silk to the dressing table.

"What are you doing?" she asked in surprise as she observed him unbutton his shirt with swift precision.

"As you so conveniently pointed out, there is no one to mark my time," he answered smartly. "So, I have decided to be late today," he informed her, giving her a look of warning for her culpability in disrupting his iron schedule.

She giggled quietly to herself at how easily the Master had changed his mind and sank back onto her pillow to happily await her husband's return to bed.

Mr. Thornton gave his mother a quick peck on the cheek after downing his breakfast, and left the house with a decided spring in his step. The daunting work that awaited him could not damper his spirit today; the world was at his command. The woman he loved so desperately was now his and she boldly trusted his ability to overcome any adverse situation. He yearned to earn her continuing respect and bring the mill back to resounding success so that she might be the proudest wife in all of Milton.

He turned his head to look up at the window of his bedroom. The promise of her nearness lifted his heart with an uncommon cheerfulness. As he opened the latched door to the factory, the corners of his mouth upturned in a contented smile.

❦

Hannah Thornton was alone at the breakfast table when Margaret arrived. "I hope you have not been waiting long," the new wife remarked a little nervously as she took a seat next to her mother-in-law.

"John has not been gone long; he said you would be along shortly," she answered, eyeing the girl to discern her predisposition to the early morning hours. "Did you sleep well?" Mrs. Thornton asked politely, noting that Margaret looked perfectly alert, her face a healthy pink.

"Yes, thank you," Margaret responded, slightly flustered to be speaking about the time she had spent in bed.

Mrs. Thornton regarded her daughter-in-law carefully. She wondered if John would make a habit of being late now that he was married, but quickly allowed that they had only recently returned from a week's holiday. Adjustments to normal life would need to be made.

Mrs. Thornton had a second cup of tea while Margaret breakfasted. "I thought you might like to have a tour of the house, and then perhaps you might care to learn of the household duties," she suggested a little formally, uncomfortable with the singular occasion of renouncing her role as mistress of the house.

"Yes. That sounds like a very reasonable plan. Thank you," Margaret readily replied, awkwardly endeavoring to be agreeable without sounding over zealous to assume her mother-in-law's position in the house.

As they went on their tour, Margaret was impressed by the attention to detail evident in every household task. The kitchen was spotless, notwithstanding the cook's current endeavors, and the scullery spacious and well organized. The furniture in the spare bedchambers was covered in white sheets, but dusted weekly nonetheless.

After she had met all the servants and been shown the entire house, Mrs. Thornton led her daughter-in-law back to the drawing room where she began to enumerate the various tasks that were generally taken up on Mondays. Margaret carefully ensured that her countenance appeared receptive, but her attention began to wane and she unconsciously looked toward the window overlooking the mill.

"Excuse me, Mrs. Thornton," she gently interrupted. "But does Mr. Thornton usually come home for lunch?" she inquired, realizing she had no idea of his regular routine.

"Not always, no. It depends on how busy things are at the mill," she explained.

Margaret's eyes grew distant as she thought of how she could ensure a brief reunion and escape the stillness of the house. "I think I should like to bring him a picnic lunch today, if it would not inconvenience you," she announced with tempered enthusiasm at her idea.

Mrs. Thornton was silent a moment. She swiftly recalled how unpredictable Margaret could be. It was just like her to think of something impractical. Surely it was not her place to be seen gallivanting about the mill any time she pleased as if it were a mere appendage to the house. Did she not realize that John had work to do?

She sighed inwardly at the girl's impertinence in seeking her husband out, but recognized with some appreciation how fondly she must be thinking of him. Although Mrs. Thornton would miss the possibility of her son's company mid-day, she admitted that he was often forgetful in taking his lunch.

"Of course," she said evenly with a slight twitch of her lips. "I'm sure the cook can help you find something appealing," she kindly suggested.

The clamor and continuous motion of the surrounding machinery was familiar to Mr. Thornton - the sound and activity of his mill was comforting in its constancy. He surveyed the floor almost unconsciously, as he had done for so many years. Everything was the same as it had always been. His week's absence had not been noticed by the relentless pace of industry. The days spent in Helstone would already seem to him a distant dream were it not for the tenacious hold he kept on the memory of all that had happened there.

Nothing could ever be the same now that she lived here with him. Although he walked in the same paths and followed the same routine, he was markedly changed. The sublime thought that she would be waiting for him at the day's end filled him with an indescribable joy.

He let out his breath in consternation and furrowed his brow as he took long strides past the working looms. As beautiful as she was, there was a time and place to enjoy such pleasant thoughts, and now was not the time. He reminded himself that the mill required his full attention. He was perplexed to discover that he could not concentrate on his work, the beguiling vision of her lying in his bed constantly coming to the fore. He remembered the way she had invitingly wrapped her arms around him this morning, the intoxicating feel of her smooth skin on his, and the entrancing sounds of her approval of his amorous attentions.

Mr. Thornton was suddenly aware that Higgins was matching his stride and looking at him expectantly. "Did you ask me something?" the Master queried with some confusion.

Nicholas refrained from teasing the Master for his distracted state, but could not suppress a knowing grin from spreading across his face. "I were asking you if you've ordered more cotton. We'll be ready for it by Thursday next," he explained.

"It should come. I have seen to it," the Master answered in a concerted effort to sound business-like. "I'll be in my office if you need me. Just come in if the door is closed," he instructed with a flicker of a smile, feeling a little flustered to be caught off-guard.

Nicholas nodded and watched the new husband leave the weaving shed. He remembered how it was to be so thoroughly in love. Those first few weeks and months of marriage were a special time he would never forget, and he was glad to see that Thornton was properly besotted with his wife.

The whistle blew for the lunch break and workers filed out of Milton factories in droves, but the time was unheeded in the quiet of the Master's office. Mr. Thornton carefully dipped his quill in the ink before setting it to paper again. Having decided on the proper course of action, he concentrated on the response to the correspondence that had been set aside for his attention.

"Come in," he answered to a rapping on his door. He was not disturbed by the interruption, having been consulted on numerous matters throughout the morning.

Margaret quietly entered the office and closed the door behind her, not wishing to disturb her husband, whose head was still bent over his work.

"Margaret!" he exclaimed in welcome surprise as he took a brief glance in her direction. He rose from his desk immediately, his correspondence forgotten.

"I thought you might have time for a small picnic," she invited him with a sweet smile, "although the scenery is not quite enthralling," she said good-humoredly as she approached his desk.

"On the contrary, I find the scenery quite enchanting," he responded with a telling smile, his admiring eyes meeting hers.

Margaret smiled demurely and set her basket down as he approached her for a gentle kiss.

Her arms twined possessively about his neck, Margaret gazed admiringly at her husband, feeling a secret thrill to have kissed the Master in his private office. The last time she had been in this room, she had known only his name, and had been impatient to meet the man who deigned himself too important to meet with her. Now here she was, hanging on him adoringly as if her entire life revolved around him, which it did. He was the central figure of her whole world, and she would never forget her great fortune in finding such a man.

"Sit down, and I will serve you lunch," she gently directed him.

Mr. Thornton watched her as she set things out. Fascinated by the delicate movement of her hands, he remembered how those same hands had glided over his back only hours before. The presence of her in this staid and solitary place beautified and enlivened the whole room; he could hardly believe she was truly there with him.

Unable to resist any longer, he stood up and moved forcefully round the desk to take her in his arms. He pressed her against him and kissed her thoroughly, wanting to taste something of the passion they had shared earlier in the morning. She met his yearning in her answering kiss.

"You will be the ruin of me!" he declared vehemently when at last he tore his lips from hers.

"Whatever do you mean?" she asked, taken aback at his accusation.

"I am not able to concentrate on my work. Instead, I find myself thinking of other things," he explained, giving her a knowing look.

"What can be done about it?" she innocently posed, her eyes dancing in delight at his perturbation.

He moved his lips nearer her ear. "What I wish to do about it requires you to be in our bed!" he warned her, his sultry tone sending a shiver up her spine.

"John!" she called out in mock protest. "Perhaps we could discuss this problem when you come home from work today," she suggested more seductively, her soulful eyes communicating her meaning.

His eyes darkened in recognition of her intimation. "Perhaps I should come home early today," he answered, his voice weakening at the thought of what would await him at day's end.

She smiled at his eagerness. "I know you are very busy," she acknowledged coyly as she rubbed her hands slowly along the front of his waistcoat. "Perhaps we could schedule a meeting this afternoon. Say, at half past four?" she offered with a casual lilt as a small smile formed on her lips.

The door opened suddenly and Higgins took a step into the room.

Margaret wheeled around to see who had discovered them, and each party wore a look of surprise.

"Sorry," the intruder apologized and began to retreat.

"Have you not heard of knocking, man?" the Master brusquely ribbed him, relieved to find it was only their trusted friend.

"You told me...." he began defensively before noting the devious smile growing on the Master's face. "I see you keep right busy through the lunch hour," he responded with a mischievous gleam in his eye.

"Nicholas, it's so good to see you," Margaret interrupted, clasping her friend's hand in greeting.

"It's good to see you back in Milton, Miss Margaret. Or I suppose I should call you Mrs. Thornton," he remarked with a grin.

"You may call me Miss Margaret or Margaret, whichever you like. I'm sure we are all well aware of my title without fuss of words," she assured him, glancing at her husband who smiled broadly at her comment.

"How is Mary?" the new Mrs. Thornton inquired.

"She keeps busy, what with the children and the workers' kitchen. You should come to lunch at the kitchen someday. She's a good cook. The Master here will vouch for that much," he offered.

"I would love to visit it, I've heard so much about it. Maybe we could eat lunch there tomorrow," she proposed hopefully, looking to her husband for his approval.

Mr. Thornton gave his wife a warm smile. Indeed, it was she who had impelled him to open his mind and consider the ways in which masters and workers might work together.

"We will see you tomorrow, then," Margaret said eagerly.

Nicholas nodded and moved to leave. With his hand on the doorknob, he paused a moment to gain the Master's attention. "Had you not heard of a lock?" he quipped with a pointed look. His eyes twinkled with delight at the happy couple before he closed the door and was gone.

Mr. Thornton felt heat rise to his face and shook his head at his employee's audacious wit as the edges of his mouth curved into a smile.

Margaret looked to her husband somewhat guiltily and began to set out their lunch once again.

After Margaret had departed, Mr. Thornton worked tirelessly all afternoon, his focus on the papers surrounding him. As he strode down the narrow pathway between the clattering looms, he pulled out his pocket watch to discover that it was nearly four o'clock. The Master suddenly became a jumble of nerves as he realized how close the time was to the meeting his wife had proposed.

Williams halted him as he made his way to his office, presenting a small dilemma for the Master to solve. Mr. Thornton listened impatiently and delivered his judgment more harshly than he was wont. He gave a nod of apology to his overseer before hastening to his office.

He sat down to look at the ledger opened on his desk, telling himself not to waste precious time. His eyes glossed over the figures, but his mind was no longer compliant to his will. He looked up at the clock to see that it was now twenty minutes past the hour. His fingers toyed with the quill in his hand as he wondered whether Margaret had been in earnest about meeting or had merely been jesting.

He put the quill back in the holder with decision. If she were expecting him, he would not want to disappoint her. If she had only been teasing him, he could find out quickly enough and be back to work in a matter of minutes. He thrust his arms into his frock coat, left his office, and walked briskly to the house.

Mrs. Thornton raised her head from her task at the sound of quick footsteps up the stairs. "What brings you home at this hour?" she asked, surprised to see her son walk into the room where she had been quietly sewing.

Mr. Thornton searched the room for any sign of his wife. "Where is Margaret?" he asked distractedly, ignoring his mother's query.

"She is upstairs. She said she had several letters she wished to write," she dutifully answered, perplexed at her son's agitated behavior.

He turned at once toward the stairway. "Thank you," he thought to reply before he bounded up the stairs.

He entered his room and took off his coat, his heart beating faster in anticipation of what he should discover. He walked to the dressing room and paused, fairly convincing himself that he had come on a fool's errand. He took a breath to renew his determination and walked through the doorway into her room.

"I came home to see if..." he began before he stopped in his tracks to see Margaret sitting at her desk in her sheer green peignoir - wearing *only* her peignoir.

"Yes?" she prompted him as she stood shakily, feeling embarrassed by her seductive ploy now that his virile presence filled the room.

He stood transfixed a moment before stepping forward to stand in front of her, his eyes riveted on the sight before him. His heart beat erratically in his chest at the thought that she should desire him, having lured him to her bedchamber in the middle of the day. He reached out to untie the ribbon that loosely secured the garment and reverently parted the gossamer fabric to reveal the creamy flesh that lay beneath. His eyes hungrily drank in the vision of her as he slid his hands to settle on the curve of her waist, the feel of her smooth skin sending tremors of desire coursing through him.

Margaret felt her skin burn under his scorching gaze, and her eyes studied his in breathless fascination. Something deep within her fluttered in response to the feel of his warm touch.

He released his hold on her and tugged decisively at the binding fabric at his neck.

Margaret's pulse raced and she felt her knees grow weak as she watched him unbutton his waistcoat, his eyes locked on hers. She headed to the bed to sit down. There would be no turning back now.

She removed the peignoir and settled herself on the hitherto unruffled surface of her bed. Her breath caught in her throat at the piercing stare he gave her as he approached her, and she willingly lay down to welcome him.

Their afternoon meeting was efficient and rather quick, but the results proved satisfactory to both parties involved.

Sometime later, Mrs. Thornton lifted her head again at the quick steps of her son descending the stairs. "Is everything all right, John?" she asked apprehensively, wondering if some unsettling news had impelled him to come home unexpectedly.

"Everything is well, Mother," he answered, glancing briefly in her direction before continuing hurriedly to the mill. He felt his face flush at his mother's curiosity.

Mrs. Thornton sighed and leaned back in her chair. She reminded herself that she would not be privy to all of her son's goings on, now that he was married, and resigned herself to the fact that he had Margaret to turn to. She could not help feeling a tug of jealousy that he should not confide in her any longer.

Margaret kept to her room a while longer to accomplish her original task in writing a few letters. When she had finished, she joined her mother-in-law in the drawing room, where the elder woman sat with her embroidery. Margaret took up her father's copy of *Aristotle* and attempted to concentrate as they waited for John's arrival home.

The young wife stole glances at her husband's mother and wondered how she could stand the tedious boredom of her constant needlework before remembering that her mother-in-law had likely spent many years of fretful toil as she raised her son to his current success. She would be grateful and proud that her son could provide her such a position of leisure in her later years.

The sound of voices and carts outside in the yard filled the uncomfortable silence in the room until at last Margaret heard the footsteps of her husband coming up the stairs. She fought the urge to jump up and run to him and instead rose serenely from her chair to greet him.

"You're home!" she exclaimed with tempered zeal as she reached out her hands to him.

"I am," he agreed as he took her hands in his and gave her a chaste kiss on the lips, reveling in such a warm welcome. The newlyweds communicated silently a few moments, sharing secret smiles and loving glances before John greeted his mother and excused himself to wash for dinner.

The evening passed pleasantly without event. After dinner, the family spent quiet time sitting in the drawing room as John read the *Guardian* and Margaret took up her book again. Feeling her attention lapse and her eyes grow weary, Margaret announced that she would retire, and bid her mother-in-law goodnight before giving her husband a smile and climbing the stairs to her room.

Mr. Thornton remained with his mother for a time, revealing more of his concerns about the mill's recovery. "If we do not receive more orders in the next few weeks, I don't see how we can continue to operate through the winter," he admitted with a long sigh.

Mother and son spoke briefly of the possibilities that would extend the mill's operation before they ended their conversation and Mr. Thornton headed upstairs. He felt a pervading gloom begin to descend upon him. He had wished to provide Margaret a secure position in society and share with her the bounty of his labor. His heart sorrowed to think of how highly she esteemed him. He did not wish to disappoint her confidence in him.

Alone in his room, he began to undress for bed. He longed to feel the comfort of her arms around him tonight, but in his self-effacing mood he wondered if she truly wished to come to him this evening, or if she would put aside her own inclinations to please him.

He was dwelling on such thoughts when he turned to see her come into the room. She wore the simple white gown she had worn in Helstone.

"You look surprised to see me," she noted curiously.

"I thought you might have had your fill of me today," he said with a wry smile.

"I don't think I could ever have my fill of you," Margaret declared tenderly as she walked over to him and wrapped her arms around his waist. "I do not wish to be apart from you unless it is necessary," she assured him, looking lovingly into his eyes.

Her words washed over him like a gentle rain, removing the silt of his doubts and fears to reveal the true beauty of her pure affection. "Nor I, you," he replied quietly, marveling at her very existence in his life.

Margaret detected something in his expression that told her he was deep in thought. "What is it?" she coaxed, wanting him to share his concerns.

He smiled a little timidly and began to explain, "When I dreamed of marrying you, I loved you so deeply that I thought I should be the one that would do most of the loving. I did not think it possible for anyone to feel as I did. Now, I am amazed to find that you love me in equal measure," he confessed, regarding her so tenderly that she felt her heart ache with the love she held for him.

"I do love you. I did not know how much I could love until I found you," she admitted, staring into the depths of his soulful blue eyes.

"Margaret," he whispered in awe. Her name had been a melody in his mind for so long - it had been mere weeks since he had first discovered that she cared for him. He still marveled that she should be here with him, that heaven had somehow seen fit to bestow such a treasure upon him.

"My Margaret," he murmured as he gently lifted her chin to bring her lips nearer to his own. He kissed her with tender affection, allowing his lips to graze hers. He shuddered in fascination at the pleasure that coursed through him as her lips met his in eager response.

He pulled away to stare at her. Her eyes shone with adoration and her face glowed with beautiful longing.

She grasped his hand and led him slowly to bed. He watched as she lifted her nightgown off her body and climbed in. Her eyes silently beckoned him to her and he swiftly answered her call.

They made love with luxurious slowness, unabashed to meet each other's gaze as their bodies moved in silent surrender, freely following the impulses that flowed so naturally from their hearts.

When at last they had each called out their rapture, Margaret settled into her husband's arms. Mr. Thornton held his wife close, kissing the top of her head with great tenderness as her fingers gently caressed his chest.

He continued to cradle her in his arms, and when he heard her breathing slow, indicating sleep, he brought her hand to his lips. He kept her small hand within his grasp and held it to his breast as his contentment slowly coaxed him to sleep.

The faint morning light gave form to the shadowy objects in the Master's bedroom.

Mr. Thornton placed a gentle kiss on his wife's temple. "Do you wish to rise with me this morning, or shall I leave you to wake later?" he asked her softly as his fingers played with silky strands of her hair.

"Mmm....will you mind terribly if I do not join you for breakfast?" she asked sleepily as she turned on her side and brought her knees up to curl comfortably on the bed.

"Not at all. I don't see why you should wake so early, love," he answered, giving her one last kiss on the cheek before getting out of bed.

Mr. Thornton took great pleasure in allowing his wife to rest while he stealthily prepared for work in the darkened room. He felt a certain contentment in knowing that she was safely cared for as he watched the gentle rise and fall of her form a moment before he slipped out the door.

Margaret came downstairs some time later to an empty breakfast table. She pulled the cord for the maid, feeling somewhat uncomfortable to be alone in her new home.

Mrs. Thornton greeted her as she finished her tea. "Good morning. Did you rest well?" she asked politely.

"I did, thank you," the young bride replied. "Do you mind if I do not meet you for breakfast every morning?" she inquired thoughtfully.

"Not at all, I have grown accustomed to waking early to see John off, but I don't believe it is necessary for you to wake quite so early," she answered. Mrs. Thornton had to admit that not everyone was fit to rise before dawn, and actually relished the idea of being able to keep the tradition of meeting her son for breakfast.

"I thought I might show you the household accounts this morning," Mrs. Thornton announced rather stiffly, anxious that the girl understand that even in such a house, economy was still imperative.

"Oh...yes, of course," Margaret replied with slight hesitation as she rose to follow the elder woman to the dining room. She dreaded the thought of going through the lists and figures with the attention to detail and serious attitude that seemed to be her mother-in-law's greatest strength.

"Fanny wished to join us for tea this afternoon, if you have no other plans," Mrs. Thornton added as she sat down to the table where the household ledger stood open for their review.

"No, that will be lovely. I'm sure she will wish to tell us more about her trip to London," Margaret perceptively replied. "Oh, but I do have plans for lunch once again. I am to dine in the workers' hall with John today," she told her mother-in-law as she sat down in the chair next to her.

Mrs. Thornton was silent a moment. "I'm certain a lady of means would not be seen in such a place," she declared as gently as possible, knowing that the girl would resist any strongly-worded judgment.

"I'm sure that it cannot be an affront to anyone if I accompany my husband to see his accomplishments," Margaret answered calmly, hoping her mother-in-law would see her point of view.

Mrs. Thornton did not consider such an experiment to be an accomplishment. She had not approved of John's effort to create a kitchen for the hands when he had already been busy enough keeping the mill running after their spiteful strike. She knew that it was her son's association with the Hales that had impelled him to attempt such a profitless venture. They had thrust their philosophical ideals upon him, convincing him that he had a responsibility to ease the burdens of the working classes. Did not John already do enough for these people in giving them ready employment?

"I know you would not wish to stir up unfavorable talk in Milton society. Such experiments are not altogether appreciated here," Mrs. Thornton explained in a level voice.

Margaret bristled at such an insinuation. "I am aware that it is uncomfortable for those in good standing to consider the plight of the poor and sickly; it is an unpleasant subject indeed. But I have no intention of abandoning my efforts to aid those in need just because there may be idle parlor talk about it," she declared with barely contained passion.

"You must do as you see fit," Mrs. Thornton replied succinctly, defeated and growing increasingly uncomfortable with the emotions displayed by her daughter-in-law.

Margaret drew a deep breath to release the tension that had been building within her, relieved to find their conversation at an end.

Mrs. Thornton let out her breath in exasperation and then began to calmly point out how she kept track of the monthly expenses. When she later commented lightly on the wisdom of economizing, Margaret was compelled to ask a rather sensitive question that had been a source of niggling concern for her.

"Excuse me for interrupting, but may I ask if things are still...precarious concerning the mill?" she falteringly queried. "My father told me that Mr. Thornton was very troubled about the mill - that it was difficult to resume business as usual after the strike," Margaret explained, looking to her husband's mother expectantly for her response.

Mrs. Thornton surveyed the girl with more respect. She was surprised to discover that Margaret was not as ignorant to the mill's troubles as she had assumed. She gathered, though, that John had still not spoken to her.

"Business has not recovered yet, so we need to be cautious with our money," she answered simply.

Margaret nodded understandingly. Her heart went out to her husband, who was quietly and nobly trying to reestablish the success that had been his before the unfortunate strike.

She politely listened to her mother-in-law's dry account of the state of their finances, when it dawned on her that there might be a way to compromise with the woman beside her.

"Mrs. Thornton, if you will allow me to interrupt you again," she began, "I hope you will not think that I am shirking my duties—for that is not my intention--but I wonder if there might be a way to divide the duties of running the house between us for the time being. It would allow me to learn everything more slowly, and I believe that it would not displease you to assist me in ensuring that all is done in good order and economy," she finished, hoping to come to an agreement that would give her more time to escape the confines of the house and allow her mother-in-law to maintain a sense of pride and accomplishment in her home.

Somewhat taken aback at the young woman's forthright proposal, Mrs. Thornton considered her idea thoughtfully. "I think that might work well, Margaret," she finally answered, the corners of her mouth lifting slightly in a placid smile.

Margaret was relieved when lunchtime came. She put on her black bonnet and went outside to meet John at his office. Margaret took his proffered arm, and the couple made their way to the dining hall her husband had helped create.

The din of the room silenced and then broke into loud clapping when the Master entered the hall with his new wife on his arm. Margaret bowed her head demurely as the men whooped and hooted, attempting to ignore their shouts of "Kiss 'er for us" and other ripe comments that came from the raucous crowd of grateful workers. Those in attendance swore that the usually stern Master turned a shade of pink at all the attention.

Mr. Thornton smiled bashfully and raised his hand in an effort to quiet the men as Nicholas came over to greet them. Higgins motioned to the men to cease their rowdy accolades and the noise of the hall swiftly lowered, though it was still abuzz with talk as lingering eyes remained on the Master's wife.

"Miss Margaret!" Mary exclaimed as she embraced her friend.

Higgins led them to a place near the wall. A white tablecloth covered the drab table and a pewter vase of bright wildflowers brought a breath of spring to the dull interior of the wide space.

Mary served the Master's favorite stew and Nicholas joined his friends to eat his lunch.

"There's naught at Hampers or Slicksons that would show their fealty to the powers that be. You've gained the trust of the men, Thornton. It's not just the lunchroom. You've insisted the hands do quality work, telling them that their jobs depend on it. They're proud to do their best for one who is honest with them," he remarked candidly. "There's not a worker in the other factories what would not like the chance to work at Marlborough Mills," he added with some pride.

Margaret beamed to hear such an assessment of her husband's reputation.

Mr. Thornton nodded humbly at Higgins' evaluation and gave his wife a grateful smile. "I had hoped the other masters might take note. Not all endeavors are measured strictly in pounds and shillings."

When Margaret entered the house, Jane announced that a package had arrived and was waiting for her in her room. She hurried upstairs, wondering who had sent her a gift.

Dixon was in her bedchamber, putting away clothes. "It's from Spain," she announced with a broad smile as she saw the mistress head for the package placed on her bed.

"Frederick!" Margaret exclaimed as she hastened to open the carefully wrapped box. She pulled out a beautiful folded fan and opened it with a gentle movement of her wrist. The black silk fabric was decorated with a delicate pattern of yellow roses and edged with lace. "Isn't it lovely? It matches the lace mantilla that Dolores sent me earlier this year," she remarked enthusiastically to her long-time maid.

"It's an elegant piece, Miss Margaret," Dixon agreed, happy to see that Master Frederick had sent a wedding gift to his sister.

She returned to the box to look for a note and discovered not only a written missive but also another gift. She pulled out a bottle of sherry. "Oh, this is probably meant for John. Frederick knows how difficult it is to find fine sherry in England."

Eager to read what her brother had written, she opened the folded paper.

My dearest sister,

I hope you will enjoy these gifts from my sunny home in Spain. I am sorry to have missed your wedding in our beloved Helstone. I am certain that you were a lovely bride. How I should have liked to walk you down the aisle! I am grateful that our father's friend was able to take my stead.

Please give my regards to your Mr. Thornton. Your fond words regarding him have convinced me that he will take good care of you.

Dolores and I have such news to tell! We are expecting our first child come January and are fairly bursting with joy! Dolores is doing marvelously well at present, although she is often more tired than normal.

I hope, dear Margaret, that you find yourself as happily married as I. You deserve every happiness after the trials you have faced these past months.

Dolores joins me in sending our love to you and yours.

Love,

Frederick

Margaret handed the note to Dixon and admired her fan again before sitting down to write her brother a return note of thanks.

Fanny arrived for tea on schedule and sat down in the drawing room with great aplomb, fidgeting with the flounces of her new powder blue gown as she settled in her chair.

She smiled at her new sister-in-law, eager to dispense the accumulated wisdom of her many weeks as a married woman. "Did you enjoy your wedding holiday?" she asked with a light tone of formality as she watched her mother leave the room to fetch the maid. Without waiting for an answer, she leaned forward to speak more intimately. "I know it can be a bit of a shock to adjust to married life," she began sagely in a lowered voice. "Between you and me, I find men to be rather beastly the first week or two. It is best to feign some kind of discomfort - they will soon lose interest in coming to you," she advised. "It is our duty, after all, to tame such unseemly desires," she added, lifting her chin proudly as she leaned back in her chair again.

Margaret managed to nod faintly in acknowledgement of her words, suppressing the smile she felt pulling on her face. She giggled inside at the thought of how shocked Fanny would be to know the secrets of her marriage, and how little she wished to tame her husband's desires.

Mrs. Thornton's return rescued Margaret from receiving any more marital counsel from her well-intentioned sister-in-law, and Fanny began more trivial conversation while Margaret poured the tea.

Fanny was elaborating on the difference between the grand shops of London and Milton's best stores when Mr. Thornton entered the room.

"John!" Margaret exclaimed, almost jumping up from her seat. "I did not know you might join us," she admitted, her eyes shining with open affection as he took her outstretched hand and leaned over to give her a peck on the cheek before sitting down next to her.

Fanny managed to smile politely, but her eyes shifted uncomfortably to witness such a display of affection from her brother.

"I cannot stay long, but I came to see my sister," he explained. "How are you, Fanny?" he asked, giving her a ready smile.

Fanny straightened herself and smiled to receive her brother's attention. "I am well, John, thank you," she responded. "Did you enjoy your stay in the country?" she asked in return, wondering how her brother had managed so much leisure time, when it seemed he had spent his whole life working.

"It was a very pleasant trip, I should like to return there every year," he answered honestly, startling both his sister and mother with his response. Margaret smiled demurely as her husband gave her a fond glance.

"Well, I wouldn't have guessed you would appreciate the long hours of leisure. I've never known you to do anything but work and read your books," Fanny replied, looking to her mother for confirmation of her opinion.

"I found it quite relaxing to enjoy my day without schedule," he countered. "The scenery was beautiful and the company very enjoyable," he added with an irrepressible smile.

Margaret pinked at his candid remark, and moved to pour her husband a cup of tea.

Mr. Thornton watched her with a swell of great satisfaction. He had long imagined how pleasant it would be to see her pour tea in his own home. Now that she was his wife, it would be his privilege to observe her graceful movements every time he took tea here.

Fanny regaled her captive audience with a lively description of her hotel room and the impressive opera hall in London and shared her disappointment in finding that the Alhambra in London housed a dreary science museum. Mr. Thornton managed to extricate himself from the drawing room and return to work before she was able to enthuse about the upcoming ball.

Margaret listened politely if not interestedly as Fanny began to speak animatedly about her involvement in planning the grand affair, elaborating every detail with an air of great importance. She breathed a sigh of relief when Fanny announced that she needed to return home to ensure that the cook had diligently followed her instructions for dinner.

Hannah saw her daughter to the door and returned to take up her sewing. For once, Margaret was glad for the silence, and took up her book to pass the time until dinner.

Later that evening, Margaret walked into her husband's room to show him the gifts that Frederick had sent. Mr. Thornton rose from his desk to meet her and commented favorably on the fine gifts, although he was vastly more interested in the way his wife looked in the green satin nightgown that she was wearing.

"Frederick and his wife are expecting their first child," she informed him in a quiet voice, feeling a slight flush of embarrassment to be speaking of such things with him.

"They must be very pleased," he readily replied as he studied his wife with fond affection, wondering how long it might be before they also could rejoice in such a blessing. The thought of her carrying his child caused his heart to ache in tender longing.

Margaret only nodded, unable to meet his warm gaze. Her heart fluttered at the thought of presenting him with similar news.

"I wished that you could have met him," she blurted out, endeavoring to divert his thoughts. "It was a shame he could not attend our wedding," Margaret remarked wistfully, thinking of her brother's forced exile.

"I have not asked before, but perhaps now you could tell me how he happened to be involved in such an unfortunate situation," her husband suggested cautiously, leading her to sit next to him as he pulled a chair near his desk.

"Well, from what I understand, the captain was a rather vicious man and did not like Fred in the least," she began as they both took a seat. "One day a sailor took a fatal fall from the upper riggings when he tried too hastily to follow a rigorous and importunate order by the captain. Fred took great offense that the man had died in such a vain manner and gathered enough of the other men to overthrow the captain's rule," Margaret explained. "Unfortunately, the captain survived his abandonment at sea and most of the men involved have been tried and hung. Fred escaped with his life, but it was very hard on my parents to know that they would never see their son again. He only managed to stay a few days here in Milton before we felt he must take flight," she told him with a sorrowful expression at the remembrance of those dark days.

Mr. Thornton listened attentively to her explanation, but kept his judgment on the matter to himself. He recognized at once that Fred shared the same spirited sense of compassion as his sister, and although he had acted foolishly in defying authority, it had nevertheless been done with unselfish intentions. He would not argue the point with his wife, knowing her fierce loyalty to her brother, but could not help but be disturbed to remember how Frederick's situation had put Margaret in danger because of the inquiry.

"I am sorry for the sorrow it has caused you and your family. It was a most unfortunate occurrence," he sympathized truthfully as he took her hands in his.

"How did you manage the rest of Fanny's visit?" he asked in good humor, changing the subject to a more amusing topic as he stood from his seat.

She smiled knowingly at his question. "I have not quite decided what she enjoys most: visiting places of grand repute or telling others about it," she remarked with a slight sigh of exasperation as she also rose.

"Not everyone can be as sensible as you," he chided, drawing her closer for a fond kiss on the lips before releasing her again to undress.

Margaret grew pensive. Fanny's earlier comments had given her much to think on. She had begun to wonder if perhaps it was not quite appropriate to give in to their physical desires quite so often. After all, John was a magistrate and prominent businessman, and she was considered to be a lady of refinement.

"John?" she said tentatively as he hung up his shirt and waistcoat in the wardrobe. "How often do other couples..." she began, but could not continue, unable to find the words that would explain her meaning. She felt her cheeks burn in embarrassment.

He turned to her interestedly. "What makes you ask?" he queried softly, at once perceiving her intended question, given her flushed face and averted eyes.

"Fanny mentioned something..." she faltered, her eyes cast downward.

"Fanny?" he interrupted in surprise, coming over to her and gently grasping her waist. "I hope you do not take seriously anything Fanny might have to say about such things. I'm afraid it is rather apparent that she did not marry for love," he remarked, curious to know what was disturbing her.

"It's just that I thought....that maybe we should not ....that perhaps it is not considered proper...You are a magistrate..." she stammered, feeling all the more flustered by his nearness. Her eyes scanned the planes and contours of his bare chest as he held her in his grasp, and her hands ached to touch him. She took a deep breath to steady her resolve. "I do not wish to influence you unduly. I want to be a good wife to you - in every way," she explained anxiously as she briefly glanced at him.

His heart lurched in horror at the notion that she should think herself remiss in her desires. He took her face in hers to look into her eyes. "You are everything a man could wish for in a wife," he assured her fervently. "Do not stop loving me, Margaret. I could not bear it," he earnestly pleaded.

"Surely you do not wish to follow the strictures of society's opinions on such private matters," he stated more calmly, endeavoring to relieve her mind from any formulated judgments she may have heard.

"No," she answered, timidly avoiding his gaze.

"How much loving we shall do is of no one's concern," he assured her, his velvet tones coaxing her to dismiss all her unspoken worries. He pulled her closer, encircling her waist with his strong arms. "Is it?" he breathed, willing her to look up at him as he studied the tantalizing softness of her skin.

"'No," she whispered as she slid her hands slowly up over his chest and rested them around his neck, finally daring to raise her eyes to his. Their eyes locked in a shared understanding – their love could not be bound by custom or restrained by propriety. No one else would ever know how fiercely they longed to be as one.

Margaret melted under the intensity of his gaze, the depths of his crystal blue eyes mesmerizing her.

"Come," he beckoned, his silken voice caressing her very soul. "Let me show you my love," he entreated, gently capturing her mouth with his and pulling her closer in his firm embrace.

Chapter Sixteen

The evening of the ball had finally arrived. In the finer homes of Milton, women preened and pouted as servants pinned flowers and ribbons in delicately coiffed hair, the battles with corsets and crinolines behind them.

Dixon stepped back after placing a decorative piece of black lace and violet ribbon in Margaret's hair. The young mistress stood to admire herself in the oval mirror. She wore a gown of violet silk overlaid with delicate black lace. Her full skirt accentuated the form-fitting bodice, and satin roses ran along the modestly sloping neckline from shoulder to shoulder. Long, black gloves adorned her arms.

"Even in your mourning dress, you're sure to show those crusty Milton folk what a true lady looks like. You'll be the envy of all those northern girls with all their finery," the proud servant crowed.

"Dixon," Margaret gently protested in response to the servant's effusive praise and condescending judgments on Milton society. "It is not my intention to surpass all others. I only hope I am well received so that my husband may retain his high standing," Margaret related.

"Humph!" Dixon scoffed. "He is the one who is lucky to have married such a well-bred girl as you. For all his money and power here, he is a tradesman nonetheless - not a gentleman's son. Why, you are far..."

"Dixon!" the young bride called out sharply. "You will not speak that way in this house. I have not yet met a gentleman who has accomplished half of what my husband has, and there is no one that I regard more highly," she declared with conviction. "Perhaps I am strongly persuaded by my affections, but it is I who feel most grateful to have married such a man and I will not hear a word against him," she announced decisively.

The loyal maid pursed her lips and reluctantly nodded her acquiescence. "I'm certain you will only raise his stature here. You could hardly do otherwise, Miss Margaret," she assured the new wife.

"Thank you, Dixon," she answered before the servant bade her good evening and departed.

Mr. Thornton looked out the drawing room window, his hands clasped behind his back. Darkness had not yet taken over the gray haze of the cool spring evening. He did not relish the thought of spending the night making pleasant conversation and being compelled to dance with women who held little interest for him. The contrivances and formalities of such affairs held little enjoyment; he vastly preferred to spend a quiet evening with his wife.

He smiled to himself. This occasion would be different, however. Margaret would be there with him. He would take great pleasure and not a small measure of pride in presenting his wife to his acquaintances. He was certain there could be no finer lady in attendance.

He turned around at the sound of someone entering the room, and stared in wonder as his wife glided toward him in the dwindling light of the room. Would she always have the power to move him so, he wondered? She was indescribably beautiful - the sight of her lustrous skin and the soft curves of her feminine form made his heart begin to pound.

Margaret was equally impressed with her husband's appearance. She drew in her breath at the sight of him and released it slowly as he approached her with a warming smile, her eyes examining the full length of him.

He was impeccably dressed in a white waistcoat that cut low to reveal a crisp cotton shirt and white cravat. The black dress coat trailed elegantly behind him and lay open in front, making his legs appear endlessly long. His boots were polished and gleaming and the white gloves he wore added an air of elegance to his every movement.

Did he not know how devastatingly handsome he was, she wondered as he gathered her into his arms? She could not resist sliding her hands along the surface of his broad chest to finally rest her hands behind his neck. He smelled of cologne and sandalwood soap, and as he pressed her firmly to him she fairly swooned at the recollection of the intimacies they shared.

"You look dazzling. I will be loathe to leave your side this evening," Mr. Thornton uttered earnestly as he began to nuzzle her neck just below the ear, drawn by the scent of her perfume and the alluring smell of her freshly washed skin.

"I believe you will be expected to socialize with others, Mr. Thornton," she reminded him teasingly. She quivered as his mouth trailed downward to taste the curve of her neck.

"John!" his mother shouted, more in surprise than in reprimand, as she walked into the room.

Mr. Thornton startled and lifted his head at once, but only slowly turned to face her, unavoidably feeling like a guilty child.

Mrs. Thornton's eyes shifted uncomfortably a moment before addressing him more calmly. "Perhaps you could check to see if the coach is ready," she astutely directed.

He moved to carry out her order, relieved to be given temporary escape.

"You look very well, Margaret," Mrs. Thornton complimented the blushing young woman before her. "Although I'm certain you don't need me to tell you," she added dryly, remembering what she had just witnessed.

Margaret blushed anew and bowed her head slightly. "Thank you," she answered. "You also look well," she offered. Mrs. Thornton wore the dress she had worn at the dinner party last summer, a simple gown of dark silk with ruffled lace along the neckline from shoulder to shoulder.

Mr. Thornton returned to escort the ladies of the house to the carriage, and the Thorntons of Marlborough Mills were soon off to the Milton Ball.

The new town hall was impressive. Looking more like a cathedral than a house of government, its arched doorways were carved in stone, and ornate stained glass windows adorned the walls.

After leaving their wraps in the cloakroom, the Thorntons climbed the sweeping marble staircase to enter the main hall that would be the evening's ballroom. Margaret's eyes were drawn to the high, painted ceilings and glowing bulbs of the large gas-lit chandeliers. Huge paintings in gilded frames hung above oak paneled walls. Magnificent profusions of flowers were stationed around the hall on columned pedestals and an enormous fireplace of carved marble stood majestically along the wall. Gentlemen and ladies conversed and greeted each other with eager formality on the gleaming wooden floor, and the buzz of their mixed voices filled the hall with expectant energy.

Mr. Thornton escorted his wife toward a gathering of masters and their wives, while his mother moved across the hall to speak to an acquaintance from church. Margaret recognized the men and women from the dinner party of a year ago. How things had changed since then!

"Thornton!" Mr. Slickson called out upon seeing his colleague approach. "We have heard of your recent news. Congratulations on your marriage," he offered as he eyed the new Mrs. Thornton with appreciation.

"Thank you," Mr. Thornton said graciously. "May I introduce my wife?" he stated with unhidden pride.

Margaret bowed her head to each person as introductions were formerly made among the congregated wives and masters.

"Ah!" Mr. Slickson noised as a dapper young man appeared at his side. "Allow me to introduce my nephew, Albert Slickson. He has been at university in London and is staying with us to study our industrial town, is that right?" he asked him.

"Yes, Uncle," Albert answered politely, his green eyes shifting slightly in discomfort. The scholar carried himself with the practiced dignity of youth, his bearing swift and purposeful. Much more handsome than his near relative, his light hair and alert countenance was borne on a fine frame of medium height that exuded strength and vigor.

"This is Mr. Thornton of Marlborough Mills and his new bride," Mr. Slickson introduced his nephew to the newcomers.

"Very pleased to meet you," Albert announced with sincerity, bowing to the Master and his wife. He gave Margaret a pleasant smile, feeling an uncommon affinity with the woman who was nearer his own age.

The men drew Albert and Mr. Thornton aside with them and began to discuss how business was conducted at Thornton's mill, leaving the ladies to find their own topic of conversation.

"They never tire of talking business and are forever tied to their work," Mrs. Hamper remarked with an exasperated sigh to Margaret. "I'm afraid your husband may be the worst of the lot in that regard. His experiment in providing a workers' kitchen no doubt takes up even more of his time," she warned the new bride.

"I support such efforts," Margaret replied politely. "I believe that mitigating the differences between masters and workers will only benefit everyone. Surely, if the workers are satisfied that they are well-treated, they will not feel the need to strike," she proposed hopefully.

"I'm certain that is a matter best left for our husbands to decide. After all, what do we know of the ways of business?" Mrs. Slickson asked with a casual shrug of her shoulders.

"But is it not our Christian duty to aid those in need when it is within our power to do so?" Margaret countered, barely containing the ire she felt building inside at their indifference.

"Yes. Well, it was nice to see you again, Mrs. Thornton," Mrs. Slickson blithely excused herself with a slight nod of the head as she and Mrs. Hamper turned to greet a friend who had recently entered the room.

Margaret sighed, despairing of ever finding a kindred mind in the female ranks of Milton society.

"I could not help overhearing," young Mr. Slickson interrupted her solitary stance, stepping nearer to her. "You are disposed to improve the lives of the lower classes?" he inquired respectfully.

"Yes, although it does not appear to be a favorable subject here in Milton," she answered, somewhat taken aback at his forwardness in approaching her.

"It should be. It is a subject dear to the heart of our own Prince Albert. There are more forward thinkers in London, I believe, than in our more remote cities, I'm afraid," he commented thoughtfully with an approving smile. "You are not from Milton, I gather?"

"No, I'm from Hampshire. I also lived in London for many years," she answered.

"Indeed," he acknowledged with a growing admiration.

A few steps away, Mr. Thornton, seeing his wife abandoned by the company of wives and newly engaged by the young university student, extracted himself from the increasingly invasive inquiries of his colleagues.

"Thornton is as cool as they come. You cannot get beneath that steely exterior," Mr. Hamper remarked to Watson and Slickson as the new husband departed.

"Perhaps he's not as cool as he appears - it would seem he prefers a little fire in his bed," Watson snidely remarked with a wily smirk. The men chortled in smug agreement.

"Your wife has told me she is from Hampshire," Albert remarked to Mr. Thornton as he joined them. "How did you manage to find her?" he asked good-naturedly.

"She moved to Milton with her family," he answered rather stiffly, uncomfortable with the young man's easy familiarity.

Fanny descended upon her brother's small group. "It is time to arrange your dancing partners for the first set," she shooed the men away with a fluttering of her hand. "Margaret, I am so pleased you could come to our soiree despite your circumstances," she welcomed her sister-in-law. "Is not the hall magnificent?" she enthused.

"It is sure to be a grand affair, the setting is marvelous," Margaret praised as she noted the grand sweep of her sister-in-law's skirt. Fanny wore a silk gown of yellow, covered with innumerable layers of gauzy white tarlatan, which were adorned with small flowers, and ribbons of almost every color. She was a veritable walking garden, Margaret thought, as she noted Fanny's penchant for all things ostentatious.

"Oh, Eva!" Fanny called out melodiously to her friend who had just arrived, motioning for her to come nearer.

Margaret turned to see Miss Dallimore accompanied by a middle-aged man, who, although not blessed with grand looks, was evidently pleased with his privilege in accompanying the lovely young woman. Miss Dallimore looked very fetching in a light and airy gown of pale pink tulle and lace, her dark blonde hair adorned with delicate white flowers.

"Eva, you will remember my new sister, Margaret Thornton, formerly

Miss Hale?" Fanny introduced her brother's wife.

Eva and Margaret nodded to each other with polite smiles. The two women had met before at the Thornton dinner party.

"Mr. Holsworth," the gentleman in attendance introduced himself to Fanny and Margaret. "Very pleased to meet you," he added with eager grace.

Eva gave a meager smile. Her father had selected Mr. Holsworth as a probable suitor after Mr. Thornton had become unavailable. One of her father's bankers, Mr. Holsworth was a kind man with relative wealth, but his awkward comportment and unappealing appearance left much to be desired in Eva's estimation.

Fanny reminded the newly arrived couple to get Eva's dance card, as the music would begin soon.

Turning her attention to her sister-in-law again, Fanny began to describe the great effort involved in preparing the hall. She began to explain her role in selecting the flowers and the refreshments, but excused herself with some haste as she noticed several distinguished newcomers enter the room.

Relieved to be alone for a moment, Margaret watched as Miss Dallimore and her escort greeted Mr. Thornton, who was attempting to find his way back to his wife. When he reached her at last, the trumpet sounded the signal for the first set of dances to begin. Mr. Thornton sighed aloud.

"Don't worry about me; I shall keep myself occupied well enough. You mustn't be seen catering to me all evening," Margaret advised him, giving his gloved hand a gentle squeeze as she smiled lovingly at him.

He nodded in reluctant agreement and left her side to seek out his first dance partner.

The band struck the first chord of the opening promenade and a grand scene of moving couples commenced to dominate the floor. Margaret observed with some amusement the patient smile on her husband's face as he led the mayor's daughter in measured steps. The rather plain-looking girl was obviously very pleased to have found herself escorted by the redoubtable Mr. Thornton.

Margaret watched the first few dances, receiving an apologetic glance from her husband at every break. She smiled at his attentiveness.

"What a shame that the most glorious women in the hall should be relegated to the role of elegant wallflower! I would lead you to the dance floor in rebellion of this tired nonsense of endless mourning if it were not for the ludicrous tattle it would provoke among the so-called refined of our class," Mr. Bell declared as he sidled next to his goddaughter.

"Mr. Bell! I didn't know you would be here!" Margaret exclaimed, her eyes shining in delight to see her father's friend.

"Yes, the Ladies Society insisted I should make an appearance. I thought it a decent excuse for coming to see you," he answered with his usual charm.

"You need no excuse to visit us. Please, won't you come to dinner tomorrow evening? Will you stay at Marlborough Mills?" she asked earnestly.

"I would be delighted to dine with you tomorrow evening, and I thank you for your invitation to stay, but I have already made arrangements to stay at the hotel," he answered. "I'm afraid I turn into a rather irritable old codger when it gets late, and would not be very good company after dinner," he explained with a half-wink.

"I don't believe you could be poor company, but will allow you your freedom to leave us shortly after dinner. I'm pleased you can come," she responded warmly.

Upon noticing the entrance of a distinguished older gentleman and his wife, Mr. Bell directed Margaret towards the couple.

"Ah, Mr. Bell, it's good to see you here! Welcome. Welcome to our fair city," the gentleman greeted his old colleague.

"Thank you, I make my appearance now and then," he responded. "Margaret, may I introduce you to Mr. and Mrs. Nathaniel Benson? Mr. Benson is one of the earliest investors in industry here in Milton. A very astute fellow, I must add," Mr. Bell informed her as she bowed her formal greetings.

"Allow me to introduce my goddaughter, the new Mrs. Thornton of Marlborough Mills," Mr. Bell added with pleasure.

"Mr. Thornton has married! I had not heard. You have married recently, my dear?" the affable fellow inquired kindly.

"Yes, just a few weeks ago," she answered, vaguely aware of the pause in the music.

"Well then, I wish you every happiness. Mr. Thornton is a fine man of great determination and uncommon wisdom. I've watched him carefully for many years. I see he also has excellent taste in the finer things in life as well as a keen eye for business," Mr. Benson stated with alacrity. "And speaking of the man, here he is," he added heartily.

Margaret turned eagerly to see her husband approach, and they exchanged a brief glance.

"Mr. Thornton, I have not seen you for some time," the wealthy Milton investor amicably greeted him.

"Mr. Benson, Mr. Bell," the younger man acknowledged respectfully. "I was out of town recently..." he began.

"So, I have heard. You are recently returned from your wedding holiday, I gather. Congratulations, my fellow. I'd begun to think you quite oblivious to the charms of the fairer sex - utterly consumed by your dedication to industry. No doubt, as in all things, you were only persistent in your quest for perfection," Mr. Benson remarked in good humor.

"Indeed. Just so," Mr. Thornton readily confirmed, observing in a glance how beautifully his wife blushed; her feminine grace at once enthralled him and ignited in him every manly desire. He wanted nothing more than to carry her off to some private place so that he might give her just reason to blush.

"Here you are!" Fanny declared as she bustled to her brother's side, flashing her most charming smile at the Bensons and Mr. Bell for her intrusion. "Are you not engaged for the next dance?" she casually reminded him as the first strains of a waltz sounded from the band. Her eyes shifted somewhat nervously, having sought her brother on behalf of her friend, Eva Dallimore, who was waiting for her promised partner some distance away.

Mr. Thornton introduced his sister before reluctantly excusing himself to find Miss Dallimore.

As Mr. Bell continued to chat with Mr. Benson, Margaret watched as Miss Dallimore smiled prettily at her husband's bow and proffered arm. Her eyes followed them through the swirling crowd of colorful gowns and black suits as they moved across the gleaming floor, turning and gliding in perfect accord with the music.

They made a very elegant couple, Margaret considered as she noted how Eva's fair colored dress and light hair contrasted strikingly with her husband's dark frame and similarly dark hair. She was impressed with how well they danced, and wondered with an admiring smile if there was anything he could not do.

Her smile vanished, however, as the couple came closer into view. Miss Dallimore's countenance displayed her particular delight in finding herself in Mr. Thornton's formal grasp. Margaret felt a strange surge of jealousy grip her as she recognized that Eva still held a tendresse for her husband, recalling in a flash how Eva had cloyingly grasped John's arm at Fanny's wedding. Studying her husband's face, however, she felt a measure of satisfaction - he wore a practiced smile of gentility.

"Margaret," Mr. Bell interrupted her thoughts, "shall we see what sumptuous fare is available in the refreshment room?" he invited.

"Of course," she replied kindly, taking one last glance at the dancers before taking her godfather's arm to be led to an adjacent room.

Mr. Thornton was not the only one to notice Margaret's retreat from the ballroom. Across the hall, Slickson's nephew watched the graceful figure of the manufacturer's wife while he made conversation with some of Milton's elite.

In the large refreshment room, guests milled about two long tables festooned with draping cloths and laden with cakes, biscuits, sandwiches, and tea and lemonade. Mr. Bell assisted Margaret and then helped himself to the abundant offerings. As Mr. Bell became involved in a conversation with others, Margaret eventually meandered to the far side of the room, sipping a glass of lemonade as she studied a grand portrait on the wall.

"I am sorry you cannot dance," a friendly voice addressed her. "I offer you my sincerest condolences. I understand your father died recently," Albert Slickson spoke solemnly as Margaret turned to see him.

"Yes, it has been only two months past," she replied with some hesitation, feeling a little disconcerted to be singled out by him.

"He was a parson?" he continued, having already acquired as much information about her as could be garnered by his uncle and other companions.

"Yes, and a scholar. He gave lectures and took on private pupils while in Milton," she added with a measure of pride.

"Indeed, then I gather that you must be very well learned yourself. And as a parson's daughter, you naturally have an interest in improving the lives of those less fortunate in rank and wealth," he remarked thoughtfully. "Not to help justice in her need would be an impiety," he quoted an ancient philosopher.

"I believe Plato is correct," Margaret readily answered. "It seems to me that the greatest injustice in this present day is to keep the poor ignorant. If they might be schooled - learn to read and write - their lives might be much improved. My father always lived by Aristotle's maxim - 'All men by nature desire knowledge.'"

The young man was suitably impressed and stared at her momentarily in rapt admiration. "Yes, I quite agree," he answered with a warming smile. "And have you begun any charitable works toward that end?" he asked interestedly.

Margaret was struck by his question. "No, not at present. I have only recently come into a position which might offer me the opportunity to do so," she responded, reflecting quietly on his suggestion.

As the music stopped in the ballroom, Mr. Slickson glanced at the open doorway. "If I may be of any assistance in your endeavors, I hope you will notify me. I would be pleased to be part of such a noble cause," he said, turning to her again. "If you will excuse me, I believe I am obligated to the next dance," he explained before gallantly bowing and taking his leave of her.

The next voice that broke her chosen solitude gave a sparkle to her eyes and sent a warm thrill through her veins. "How is it that you are unattended?" her husband asked with some concern as he approached her unsuspecting figure.

"May I not seek a little respite for myself?" she answered in good humor as she quickly turned to him. "I am very glad to see you. You have been very busy so far this evening. You perform very gallantly for one who professes to dislike such affairs," she complimented him with a gleam in her eye.

"You approve of my talent for deception?" he retorted smoothly with a crooked smile.

"Are you sure you do not derive any pleasure in dancing?" she countered. "Your dancing partners seemed to enjoy themselves immensely," she teased.

"Did they? I did not take notice. There is only one woman I wish to have in my arms," he told her, his eyes blazing with the ardor he must suppress. His fingers twitched in his desire to touch her.

He let out a slow breath. "May I get you another drink?" he offered.

Margaret accompanied him to the refreshment table, where her husband inevitably came upon people of his acquaintance. Mr. Thornton introduced his wife to the town judge and his wife and a local barrister.

Sometime later, after Mr. Thornton was called into service again on the dance floor, Margaret headed for one of the many seats supplied around the hall's periphery and found herself suddenly face to face with Miss Dallimore.

"Mrs. Thornton," the beautiful businessman's daughter greeted Margaret with stilted kindness. "I hope you are enjoying yourself. Your husband seems to be a rather popular dance partner this evening," she remarked.

'Yes, I have noticed. He seems to be very well known in Milton," she replied politely.

"Yes, it is a shame that the strike has put his business at risk. He was the most eligible bachelor in Milton for many years. Why, I even had eyes for him myself at one time. It is a wonder he never married until now," Miss Dallimore commented smugly.

"I would not judge a man solely on his wealth or success in business. It is far more important to consider his character and purpose of heart. Mr. Thornton is a man of substance. Perhaps he had not the fortune of finding anyone of his kind here in Milton," she readily retorted with a light tone of forced pleasantness.

A subtle smile played on Margaret's lips as she observed the belle of the ball stiffen and thrust her chin into the air before turning away to find more agreeable company.

Margaret was content to listen to the lilting music of the quadrille band as she watched the company of elegantly dressed men and ladies dance several polkas and a Schottische. Her mother-in-law joined her before long, taking the seat next to her.

"The ball is well attended," the Mrs. Thornton commented. "I am certain Fanny will be pleased," she added.

"Yes, it seems to be a great success," Margaret responded. "Everything is beautiful and the people are very kind," she remarked magnanimously.

Mrs. Thornton nodded her agreement, pleased that her son's wife appreciated the city's grand affair.

The music faded and the dancers dispersed before the next set was called.

Mr. Thornton approached his wife and mother with a broad smile.

"Are you free for a time, Mr. Thornton?" his wife inquired, teasing him for being so often on the dance floor.

"I am. However, I came to seek another dance partner," he answered with a mischievous gleam in his eye. "May I have the honor of the next dance, Mrs. Thornton?" he asked his mother.

Mrs. Thornton startled, her eyes darting to her son's face and then quickly falling to her lap. "Don't be ridiculous, John. I'm sure there are many young ladies who may need a partner," she reasoned in her discomfort to be called to dance.

"There may be; however the two ladies whom I most prefer and admire are before me. Am I to be denied the privilege of dancing with either?" he asked earnestly.

Mrs. Thornton took a deep breath. "Very well, if you insist," she relented as the corners of her mouth edged upward and she stood to take his proffered arm.

Margaret's face glowed with admiration for the man she had married as she watched him lead his mother around the ballroom in an elegantly spirited polka. Her heart warmed in delight to witness mother and son enjoying themselves, a beaming smile enlivening her mother-in-law's usually staid countenance.

When the dance finished, her husband and his mother were swallowed up in the surrounding company, and Mrs. Thornton was persuaded to join in the quadrille that soon formed. Margaret's lips twisted in slight irritation to see her husband paired once more with Miss Dallimore, whose smiles seemed a hint too charming. Mr. Thornton cast a warm glance at his wife before the music began, and Margaret returned it with a knowing smile. She would not give Miss Dallimore a second thought.

"There you are!" Mr. Bell declared as he walked over to where Margaret was sitting. "I have come to say good night. I feel my endurance for social pleasantries coming to a rapid end," he explained with a wry smile.

"We will see you tomorrow, then, at dinner," she reminded him as she stood to walk with him.

"Yes, of course. I look forward to it," he responded. "I am pleased to see you looking so content. Yours must be a happy home," he added with fond attention for her well-being.

"Yes it is. I...we are very happy," she confirmed, as a sense of deep gratitude welled up inside her, misting her eyes.

"Good. I am glad I have lived to see you so well settled. Your father would be very pleased indeed," he affirmed with conviction.

The tears that had begun to form fell unbidden from her eyes at his words.

"Oh, dear! I see I have caused you to spring a leak," Mr. Bell joked in his consternation to have made her cry.

A quick puff of air escaped her lips as she laughed in spite of herself, embarrassed to have become so emotional.

"Come, come. Let us find some fresh air," he insisted as he handed her his handkerchief and began to lead her away from the ballroom.

Mr. Thornton caught sight of his wife's hurried departure and was at once unsettled to note that she was dabbing her eyes in some distress.

Mr. Bell escorted his goddaughter to a darkened room away from the grand hall and stood awkwardly by her, uncertain how to aid her recovery. Margaret took several deep breaths and assured him that she was fine.

It was not long before Mr. Thornton appeared in the doorway and briskly made his way toward them.

"Ah, Thornton!" Mr. Bell called out in relief. "I'm afraid I'm not any good with women's tears. I will say good-bye to you both and leave you to tend to your bride," he said, rapidly extricating himself from the situation.

Mr. Thornton politely nodded his acknowledgement before turning his entire attention to his wife. "Margaret, what is it?" he asked gently, his brow creased in concern.

"It is silly, really," she said apologetically, smiling as she blinked away all remnants of her tears.

He waited patiently for her to explain, his countenance still bearing a serious expression.

"Mr. Bell reminded me of how happy I am," she offered, looking to him to see confusion still cloud his face. "And then he mentioned father...." she added, unable to continue.

Mr. Thornton let out his breath as his face softened in understanding. "You loved your father dearly," he said softly.

She nodded her head and moved closer to be gathered into his comforting arms, sobbing again as she remembered poignantly how her father had admired her husband.

"Although we know not how, perhaps your father knows of us and is happy," he whispered near her ear, gently gliding his gloved hand along her back as his chin nestled in her hair.

She nodded and stepped back to compose herself.

Mr. Thornton moved his thumb across her cheek, tenderly wiping away a glistening tear. The distant strains of a gentle waltz filled the silence. "Come, dance with me," he invited soothingly, placing his hand at the small of her back and holding his hand up for her acceptance.

Her somber features brightened a little as she lifted her eyes to his. She hesitated a moment, looking toward the door to ensure they were alone.

"Just for a moment," he gently coaxed her and smiled as she slowly placed one hand on his shoulder and the other in his waiting hand.

They moved in seamless harmony around the shadowed room, the rhythm of the music flowing through them to make limbs and feet the scribe of a force beyond themselves - expressing something astonishingly beautiful with an inherent ease. Captivated by the joyous exhilaration of their synchronized motions, the world around them was a blur - nothing else existed. They beheld in each other's eyes for a moment the sublime reason for being alive - a love that set everything in motion and transformed their earthly existence into a symphony of joy.

Reluctantly, they came to a stop as the final chord dissolved into silence.

They remained transfixed for a moment longer, staring into each other's eyes, unwilling to relinquish their close contact until Margaret bowed her head and took a step back upon hearing voices in the hall. "We should return to the ball," she suggested quietly.

As they neared the brilliant lights of the grand hall, a man of distinction who seemed to be followed by a small gathering, greeted Mr. Thornton. "Mr. Thornton, how is business faring this year?" the gentleman asked with confident ease.

"It seems it will take longer to recover from the strike than I had hoped," Mr. Thornton answered somewhat elusively. "Allow me to introduce my wife, who has only recently moved to Milton from Hampshire," he cordially offered with a telling smile as Margaret nodded her greeting. "Margaret, this is Mr. Edward Wilkinson, our local member of Parliament," Mr. Thornton informed her.

"I am pleased to make your acquaintance, Mrs. Thornton. And how do you find Milton?" Mr. Wilkinson asked curiously.

"I have found the pace of life here quite invigorating and am hopeful that such an industrious spirit can forward much progress. There is opportunity for improvement almost everywhere one looks," she answered forthrightly, at once capturing the attention of all those hovering near the politician.

Mr. Thornton observed in bemused admiration as Margaret continued to discuss with Mr. Wilkinson what might be done to improve the plight of the poor working class.

From a more distant location, Albert Slickson noticed with some surprise the animated conversation that seemed to be taking place between the enchanting Mrs. Thornton and Milton's Member of Parliament. His eyes lingered upon the scene until he was called back into the discussion in which he was supposedly engaged.

As the evening grew closer to an end, Margaret once again sat with her mother-in-law to watch the dancers take advantage of the final set of dances. As she observed another young lady smile with barely veiled adoration in her husband's arms, she considered the truth of what Hannah had bragged of long ago - that John was sought out by all the girls of Milton. Margaret had seen the glances her husband received as he made the rounds of the hall, and she had felt herself the subject of uncomfortable study by various women all evening.

She was not in any way disturbed, however. She felt secure in his affections, and could only rejoice in wonder that she had been the one to win him.

⟶⟶⟵

Mr. Thornton hastily pulled off his gloves and lit the lamp just inside the door, ushering both his wife and his mother through the darkened house and upstairs to their rooms. He escorted his mother to her bedchamber and returned to open the door of his room for his wife to enter, only too glad that Dixon had been dismissed for the night.

"I believe that went well," Margaret stated, taking a deep breath of relief that the evening was over.

"Yes," Mr. Thornton answered as he set the lamp on the dressing table and moved to his wife's side. He had watched her from afar all night. Arrayed prettily among the others, she had stood out to him as a paragon of beauty and grace. No one could compare with her.

"Fanny should be pleased, it was a grand event," she added as her husband tugged at her long gloves, helping her slip them off.

"Um-hmm" he murmured distractedly as he brushed his hands lightly over her neck and into her hair, removing the pins and watching the tresses tumble free. He remembered how enthralled he had been by her beauty when she had first appeared to him in a similar gown - at his mother's dinner party the summer before. How eminently touchable she had appeared and how unattainable she had been! His body ached to claim her now.

"I believe you know the entire city," she chattered, as he continued to remove every pin from her hair. "I hope I passed muster as your wife," she continued on, her pulse quickening at his quiet determination.

"You more than passed muster," he replied in a low voice as he lightly brushed his lips over her temple as the last tendril of auburn hair fell to her shoulders. Indeed, he had seen the eyes of many men linger upon his wife. It had been an exquisite pleasure to introduce her as his, affirming aloud to every acquaintance throughout the evening that she belonged to him.

He gently turned her around and swept aside her long tresses to unfasten her dress. Letting his hands travel the length of her arms, he coaxed the dress off of her, causing Margaret to shiver from the rapturous feel of his touch. He bent to kiss her neck as his fingers moved dexterously to loosen her corset.

Margaret closed her eyes in anticipation of his continued seduction, and gasped as his hands slid slowly over her shoulders and trailed downward to capture the fullness of her soft flesh, cupping and exploring the contours of her feminine form as she sighed in pleasure.

"There are too many layers of a woman's attire," he whispered huskily in her ear, eager to have the whole of her revealed to him.

Unable to speak, she nodded in agreement and reached her hands behind her to aid in undressing herself.

He helped her out of her dress and burdensome crinoline before beginning to remove his own clothing, piece by piece.

They met at last in the bed as he drew her to him, kissing her with deep and longing kisses, marveling that it should be he and he alone that she would allow into the secret chambers of her heart and body.

The lamplight cast shadows over the darkened room and the sheets rustled as they commenced their lovers' dance.

Early the next afternoon, the Master of Marlborough Mills and his wife took their Sunday promenade through the park, enjoying the simple freedom of wandering the outdoors together. A breeze stirred the grasses as they climbed a hill overlooking the city. Patches of blue appeared behind the gray pall of the sky, and the dirty chimneys cluttering the horizon lay dormant, allowing the air the chance to clear.

"I've been thinking," Margaret began, breaking the silence between them as they walked. "There are so many children here that are not going to school. You have taken an interest in Tommy Boucher's education, have you not?" she inquired about Higgins' young charge.

"I have," he answered with a wily smile, wondering what new venture his wife was concocting.

"Well, there are so many others like him - they all ought to have some schooling. Why should they not have the opportunity to learn? It is not just," she reasoned with compassion.

"Will you single-handedly change the world, Margaret Thornton?" he asked, stopping for a moment to lift her chin with his curved finger and tenderly examine her face.

"I cannot stand idly by when there is so much that could be done for those around me. Are we not commanded to love our neighbor?" she asked as they resumed their walk, her arm in his.

"I see that you are your father's daughter," he mused fondly with admiration. "What is it you wish to do?" he inquired, surmising that his wife might be formulating some scheme in which to aid the poor.

Margaret hesitated, uncertain how her husband would receive her ideas. "I thought I might be able to organize some kind of regular education for a few of the children. Perhaps we might find someone to teach them to read and make a school of sorts. I could start it, and maybe take a few hours in the morning to go to Mary's where some students could be assembled. I would still have time to tend to my household duties in the afternoons," she hurried on before looking anxiously to see her husband's reaction.

Mr. Thornton could only smile at her ambitious enthusiasm. "It is a just cause," he answered succinctly. He took a deep breath. "There are many factors to be considered in such an enterprise, however. Will you allow me to think on it?" he asked her expectantly, giving her arm a fond squeeze.

"Of course," she agreed, understanding her husband's rightful need to think carefully of every contingency. She trusted his good judgment and was willing to admit that her impetuous ambitions might benefit from his patient deliberation. She gave his arm a loving squeeze in return and looked up at him admiringly as he gave her another affectionate glance.

Dinner with Mr. Bell was a very pleasant affair. Margaret listened with rapt attention as the Oxford scholar, Mrs. Thornton, and her husband recalled the past events and circumstances that led Milton to rise to its present state of industrial enterprise. She felt a swelling of pride to think of Mr. Thornton's important place in the grand scheme of things, and took even greater satisfaction to hear more of his untiring efforts to claim his role in leading the city to progress and growth.

As they discussed the possibilities of the future, she entered into the conversation, expressing intelligently her hope that the next stage of development would include sharing the benefits of progress with the whole of society. She reasoned that there could be no permanent improvements in stability and growth until the masses felt their contributions equitably rewarded and were offered a chance to rise according to their own efforts. She concluded that education would be essential if any true progress were to be made in Milton and England at large.

Hannah Thornton stared at her daughter-in-law in wary surprise and was nonplused to see that both men had listened to Margaret's speech with perfect equanimity and consideration.

"I believe our Margaret has a point. Very well reasoned, my dear," Mr. Bell declared with a measure of pride.

Mr. Thornton said nothing but gave his wife a look of admiration.

"I believe married life suits you, Thornton. You look very content," Mr. Bell remarked with candor after the women had withdrawn from the dining room.

"It would be difficult to be unhappy with Margaret near," he replied honestly in an even tone, the corners of his mouth edging upwards in an irrepressible smile.

"Quite so," Mr. Bell agreed approvingly as he studied the newly married man's face. "And Margaret is looking wonderfully happy," he added thoughtfully.

"Thank you," Mr. Thornton answered quietly with a swell of joy. "It is my highest privilege and greatest pleasure to care for her," he revealed openly.

"Yes, of course, I know it is. She is in very capable hands, I might add. There is no one else I would have entrusted her to," Mr. Bell responded respectfully. "Be that as it may," the wealthy landowner continued, "sometimes circumstances that are beyond our control beset our earnest endeavors." He paused to assess the look of cautious apprehension that the younger man now wore. "I'm sure you know what I am speaking of," Mr. Bell added.

"I believe I do, but..." Mr. Thornton began.

"Yes, well, I have not yet given you and Margaret a wedding gift, and I would very much like to offer you something that would be useful. I would be pleased to give you £500 to do with as you will," Mr. Bell announced with decision.

Mr. Thornton hesitated uncertainly, his brow furrowed in momentary contemplation. He was torn between the desire to prove himself fully capable of handling his own affairs and the temptation of being able to pay off his debts with such a sum.

His mind quickly rebelled against the notion of bolstering his business with money intended to be a wedding gift. After all, he had not yet explored every avenue to revive the mill – he still had hope of recovery. With patience, wisdom, and fortuitous circumstances, he might slowly regain his former position of security.

"I thank you for your concern and great generosity, but I cannot accept such a grand sum as a gift. I believe £100 would be generous enough, and we would both be very grateful," he responded with sincerity.

Mr. Bell nodded his head in acknowledgement as he pursed his lips, sympathetic to the younger man's desire to retain a sense of honor by seeking his own fortune amid trying times. He only hoped that Thornton would not let his pride become a stumbling block to maintaining control of the mill. "Shall we rejoin the women, then?" he suggested with vigor, setting their awkward discussion squarely behind them.

Mr. Thornton moved aside the paneled doors that divided the living space and Mr. Bell joined the family in friendly conversation a while longer before thanking his hosts for an enjoyable evening and taking his leave.

Early one morning the next week, Margaret arrived at the breakfast table to find a gorgeous array of yellow roses in a crystal vase. Smiling at the sight, she picked up a note that was propped against the vase and opened it eagerly to see what her husband had written.

My darling wife,

Did you think I would forget your birthday? No one else could be more grateful than I for your entrance into this world. My life has been transformed by your presence - I wake every morning in joyous wonder to find you by my side.

I hope that your day will pass pleasantly. I am thinking of you (whether or not I should!) and feel a comforting happiness to know you will be waiting for me at day's end.

Will you dress for dinner this evening? I have made special arrangements that I hope will please you.

With all my love,

John

Margaret bent to smell the lovely blossoms, beaming at the thought of her husband's thoughtfulness. She stepped to the wall to pull the cord for her breakfast. She knew it would be a pleasant day.

Later that evening, Margaret stared dreamily out the window at the back of her room. She had spent the last hour bathing and dressing with Dixon's help, preparing for the upcoming evening with her husband. She had decided to wear the dark blue gown she had worn the night before her wedding.

It was well after six o'clock when Margaret heard her husband come into his room. Roused from her pleasant daydreams, she stepped eagerly through the dressing room to greet him.

A warm smile lit his face at her entry into the room. He was changing into his silver-gray waistcoat. "You received my note?" he asked in a knowing lilt.

"Yes, I have been waiting all day for you to arrive home. How utterly mysterious of you to leave me in suspense for so long!" she chastised him, a teasing smile spreading over her face.

He approached and gave her a conciliatory kiss. "Anticipation can be enjoyment in its own right," he responded with a sultry glimmer in his eyes.

She gave him a look of feigned reproach for his improper insinuation, and patiently waited for him to tie his gray cravat and don his coat.

When Mr. Thornton escorted her to the dining room, Margaret was confused. The table was set elegantly for two and long tapered candles had been lit, although daylight had only just begun to diminish. She cast her husband a quizzical glance.

"Mother is staying with Fanny for the evening. We shall have the house to ourselves," he explained, studying her hopefully for her reaction.

Surprise changed to glad acceptance as she realized they were not going out after all. Margaret looked to her husband with fond appreciation, her countenance expressing her delight at this unexpected arrangement. "We are dining here?" she asked to confirm his intentions.

"Yes," he answered simply as he took her wrap and helped her to her seat.

A dinner of roast duck and all the trimmings was served - a favorite meal of Margaret's. The couple ate leisurely, talking freely of things that only concerned themselves.

After the dinner plates had been cleared away, Dixon surprised Margaret by presenting the dessert that had always been served on her birthday - a strawberry sponge cake dusted with powdery sugar. Margaret's eyes glistened at the memory of her summers in Helstone and the sad realization that last year she had celebrated her birthday with both of her parents. Her sorrow dissipated, however, as she looked at the beaming face of her husband - this birthday would be very special for it was the first one she had spent with him.

When they had finished eating, the couple removed to the drawing room to read to one another as they had so often done in Helstone. Margaret leaned comfortably against her husband as they situated themselves on the sofa.

When it was Margaret's turn to read, Mr. Thornton bemoaned the fact there was not a sofa long enough for him to fully recline. Borne of his strong impulse to receive the attentions he so fondly remembered, he suggested they could sit on the carpeted floor.

"But the servants, John!" Margaret protested, aware that the house was not entirely vacant and that their activities might be viewed.

"They have been dismissed for the evening," he informed her, his eyes pleading for her to comply with his simple wish.

Margaret could not deny him his pleasure, and settled herself on the carpeted floor with childlike glee, her gown and petticoats rustling as she coaxed them into place and leaned against the sofa. Mr. Thornton laid his head on her lap with a triumphant smile on his face.

Margaret laughed at his stubborn determination to gain her attentions and laughed again at the thought of how shocked his mother would be to find them in such an unrefined arrangement.

Margaret thoroughly enjoyed watching her husband relax as she ran her fingers through his hair and gently caressed his face with her free hand as she read to him. When, at length, her legs began to tingle under his weight, she reluctantly moved them, ousting him from her lap.

Mr. Thornton felt a deep settled calm pervade his entire being. "Thank you," he murmured as he assisted his wife to her feet and gathered her into his arms. "Perhaps Mother should visit Fanny more often," he remarked, wishing they could often be so informal.

"Perhaps we could retire early on occasion and read in bed," she answered ingeniously with a subtle arch of her eyebrows as she slid her arms around his waist.

"That is why I married you. You are more clever than I," he responded in a low voice as he stared at the pink fullness of her lips and brought his face closer to kiss them.

"I don't know about that," she said as she pulled back slightly from him, "you were very clever today - surprising me with flowers and a private dinner," she continued, her eyes dancing with playful delight.

A spark of recognition crossed his face at her words. "I've almost forgotten your present," he informed her before walking over to fetch her lace mantilla. "Come with me," he invited, offering his arm.

She looked at him in surprised confusion but allowed him to lead her outdoors and toward the mill. "My gift is at the mill?" she asked in wonderment as they approached the factory door.

"You will just have to wait and see," he responded, relishing the opportunity to draw out her curiosity.

He turned on the lamp on his office desk and almost laughed at her bewildered expression. "I did not have time to bring them to the house," he explained as he indicated a large cloth-covered crate on a table against the wall.

Margaret walked over to the table. "This?" she asked him with wondering eyes.

He nodded, and watched her face carefully as she slowly pulled back the covering.

She cast aside the cloth more quickly as she recognized the items before her. "Books.... readers and blackboards for the children!" she exclaimed with growing excitement as she searched the contents of the container. She whirled around to face her husband who was smiling broadly at her enthusiastic reaction. She threw herself into his arms to thank him. "I had so hoped you would approve!" she confessed, giving him a quick kiss for his support of her intended endeavors.

"I cannot deny you your wish when your purpose is so noble. I believe we can prepare one of the derelict buildings near the canteen to house a school," he told her, enjoying her grateful attentions.

"Truly?" she queried in disbelief. "You are a most wonderful husband!" she announced, giving him another kiss in her excitement.

This time he did not relinquish her lips, but moved to capture her mouth with his and kiss her soundly, drawing her closer as their kisses deepened.

Pulling back at last before he lost his self-control, he reminded himself of their location and the purpose of the evening. "We should return to the house. The evening is yours. We will do as you wish," he told her calmly even as his pulse still hammered and his body ached with desire.

"I believe I can think of a suitable activity," she replied saucily as she smiled and stretched up to kiss him again.

It was the very next day that Watson sent a messenger to Marlborough Mills: speculations in America had ended poorly and word was circulating that local and neighboring businesses would be severely affected, dampening trade and throwing the Exchange into certain turmoil.

Mr. Thornton's face drained of color as he stood motionless in his office, unknowingly dropping the hand that held the written note. In the next moment, he snatched his coat and left to find his banker, determined to know the whole truth.

His banker confirmed his fears. The shipping houses in the neighboring port were in financial ruins, sending a rippling of doubt and fear throughout the entire area and greatly affecting business in Milton proper. Credit would be insecure and men who had recently felt themselves safe might see their fortunes tumble.

The beleaguered Master returned to the privacy of his office with a heavy heart and sat absently in his chair in stunned silence. The words and implications of the dreaded news whirled in his consciousness until at last he sank his face into his hands in despair, wondering how he would ever explain this to Margaret.

Chapter Seventeen

The partial moon afforded little light, occasionally peeking through thinning gaps in the clouds that hovered over the city. Margaret shivered in her nightgown in the grand bed, and pulled the burgundy bedcover up to her chest. It was unseasonably cold for June; she wondered if she should have asked Dixon to start a fire.

She shifted the pillows behind her and leaned back to read again in the quiet of the night. Her eyes glossed over the words in the book for a moment but then slowly drifted to the empty desk in the shadows. The lamp next to her was a comforting presence, illuminating the area around her with color while fending off the encroaching darkness of the room.

She missed him. For several days now, he had come home to dinner but had returned to his office immediately afterwards to take care of 'pressing matters.' He was pleasant as usual and had spent a leisurely Sunday with her, but Margaret sensed that all was not well. His eyes lacked a certain sparkle and his smile seemed at times tinged with sadness.

She hoped he would come home soon. She had long understood from Nicholas that Mr. Thornton sometimes worked late, and she had fully expected that there might be times in which his work would require much more of his attention. From comments she had recently heard, she worried that his work would slowly consume him until he was ragged and worn.

Perhaps it was time for her to ask him what he faced. She knew her husband was well used to struggling alone, and she truly understood that it would be a sore matter of pride for him to speak of the mill's failings. If he only knew how much she wished to aid him! She did not want to be protected from any harsh news - it was much more tolerable to know the truth, however treacherous, than to be left ignorant for sympathy's sake.

Bringing her attention again to the book in her hands, she attempted to read while she waited for his return.

Margaret woke sometime later to find the book had haplessly fallen onto her lap. She lifted her head dazedly and looked around as it dawned on her that her husband had still not come home. She flung off the bedcovers and swiftly walked to the mantle of the fireplace, where an ornate clock of wood and brass told her it was well past one o'clock.

She let out a sigh of distress at the thought of her husband still bent over his desk long after the looms had ceased their clatter. Turning with decision, she fetched the lamp on the bedside table and hastened to her room to find her warmest dressing gown.

⚜

Mr. Thornton was indeed bent over his desk as he poured over ledgers and account logs, endeavoring to discover how long he might be able to keep the mill in operation. He desperately hoped to discover a way to keep the mill running so that fortune might have a chance to turn its path and bring him new orders and an opportunity to rebound.

He rubbed his brow as his tired eyes strained to add the figures in front of him. He knew he should have stopped long ago, but he had kept telling himself to continue on a bit more. He found it difficult to cease as the facts of his present situation became clearer with every calculation.

In his state of wearied concentration, he did not hear the footsteps along the dark corridors of the empty mill, headed towards his office. He looked up in surprise as his wife opened the door, carrying a lantern and wearing a shawl over her blue flannel dressing gown.

"Margaret! What are you doing here? Is everything all right?" he asked, suddenly concerned as to the reason she had sought him out.

"Everything at the house is fine, except that my bed is empty," she assured him. "Will you not tell me what it is that takes you from your rightful rest?" she asked, her eyes pleading.

"I did not want to worry you," he began, looking down at the papers in front of him, his brow furrowing at the notion of sharing his unsettling news.

"Then you have failed miserably," she said unequivocally, lifting her chin in defiance of his reasoning.

He startled at her sharp words. His head snapped up to search her face for her meaning as his eyes filled with painful uncertainty.

Seeing his distress, her expression softened. "I have already been worrying - not for the mill...for you," she said softly, caressing his roughened jaw with an outstretched hand. "How can I be a helpmeet to you if you will not share your burden? Let me care for you," she implored, her eyes kindling with tender affection.

Mr. Thornton let out a sigh. How he had longed to give her every comfort - and now she would care for him! Still seated in his chair, he reached out to encircle her in his arms and buried his face against her, feeling the comfort of her soft form, her very fragrance a balm to his soul. "I had wished to care for you," he said softly, feeling acutely the discouragement of being thwarted from providing her the life he had envisioned.

"Am I not cared for?" she asked as she cradled his head, tenderly holding him close to her while running her fingers through his hair. "I have no fear of want. I already possess everything that I desire," she told him truthfully. At her declaration, he held her closer.

She released her hold on him so that she could see his face. "Will you not tell me what is troubling you?" she implored once more, her eyes searching his.

He stared at her before casting his gaze toward the papers on his desk. "Trade is bad," he said simply, his voice deep and solemn. The dark stillness of the mill seemed to echo his gloom.

Margaret felt her body tense in apprehension at his tone, but she was determined to know everything. "How bad?" she probed as her throat went dry. She felt her heart drop at his silence as she waited for his answer.

He looked up at her, his eyes reflecting the sorrow and pain of losing what he had so long worked to build. "Very bad. I fear the mill will be forced to close. There is little hope of recovery now," he told her, feeling a mixture of relief and anguish to have revealed the depths of danger into which his business had sunk.

Margaret was momentarily stunned. Flailing for something to say, she reached to grasp his hand. "Surely there must be some hope. If the mill could be kept going a little longer, trade might again improve," she suggested desperately, unwilling to believe that all her husband's efforts would be for naught.

He looked at her somberly. "The weather has been cool, and there are not as many orders coming in. I will extend operations as long as I am able. That is precisely what has required all my attention. But I also need to know at what point I must stop, so that all my obligations might be paid," he explained.

"Could you not borrow money until trade improves?" she asked awkwardly, despite her certainty that her husband would have already considered every possibility.

"The banks are very hesitant to lend now," he answered gently, sympathetic to her desire to offer help.

He sighed aloud. "There was a speculation offered me some time ago," he mused in his discouragement. "But I did not think it prudent to risk everything for uncertain gain," he confessed, looking to see her reaction.

"I cannot believe that you would be tempted by such schemes, John. What good would all the riches be if you had compromised your principles?" she exclaimed wonderingly.

He let out a breathy sound of amused relief and pulled her down to sit on his lap, a smile spreading across his face. "Do you know me so well, Margaret?" he asked in amazement. "Will you stand with me even as my honest endeavors are reduced to no effect?"

She took his face between her hands and gazed at him with serious import. "Never to no effect, John. All the good you have done stands as a testament of who you are. I am not afraid to stand with you. I know you will do all in your power to stay the storm. We must have faith that there will be recompense for our good endeavors. Circumstances will not change who we are if we continue to hold fast to what is right," she encouraged him, looking deep into his piercing eyes.

Mr. Thornton could only stare back at her in wonder at her steadfastness and faith. Her trust in him gave him a semblance of hope that all would be well, but insidious fear continued to whisper its repetitious refrain of doubt. He did not want to fail her. He clasped her to him and held her tightly, shuddering at the thought of how he could have survived such a trial without her.

Margaret woke early with her husband the next morning and quickly dressed to join him for his breakfast. She wished to show him her support in every way; it would not do to linger in bed at present when he spent so much time at work.

Hannah Thornton was surprised to see her daughter-in-law, but smiled politely as she joined them for breakfast.

Mr. Thornton apologized for his haste after he had eaten and moved to kiss his mother and wife on the cheek.

Margaret took his hand between hers to stay him for a moment. "Will you eat lunch today?" she asked him as a reminder to take care of himself, studying his face questioningly for his answer.

A warm smile spread over his face. "I make no promises, but I will try," he answered as he gave her hand a squeeze.

Mrs. Thornton watched their exchange, noting Margaret's concern for her son, which was written on her plaintive expression. Perhaps John had at last revealed to her how serious circumstances were at the mill, for the girl bore a manner of solicitude more pronounced and somber than before.

After Mr. Thornton had departed, the room fell into silence as the women drank their tea, both reflecting on the daunting tasks which the

Master of Marlborough Mills would face while their day would undoubtedly unfold in much the same pattern as ever.

"I will visit Mary Higgins this morning," Margaret began. "I mean to help some of the workers' children get an education," she announced cautiously, deciding she could no longer keep her activities hidden from her mother-in-law's judgment. "Mr. Thornton is aware of my purpose, and approves of my intentions. I will still happily fulfill my household obligations every day," she added to avoid undue censure, "but I will also be spending time pursuing my plans. I will go to the market this morning on my return. Is there anything that you should like me to purchase?"

Being given little opportunity to equivocate, Hannah was taken aback by the girl's directness. "I believe the cook has a small list," she answered, regarding her son's wife with reluctant respect for her adroit ability to accomplish her designs with a commanding sense of purpose and deft diplomacy. She only hoped that John would not fall prey to his wife's persuasive wiles and sanction her every plea without due consideration of the consequences.

Mrs. Thornton was certain that Margaret's ideals were well intended, but she doubted the wisdom and practicality of attempting to solve the long-standing problems of society at the expense of everything John had worked so hard to build up - namely, the mill's success and the un-questioned respect of those in the city.

Margaret enjoyed the freedom of walking the familiar streets and alleyways toward the Princeton district. The squalor and grimness of the place always pulled at her heartstrings, but she had also come to recognize the solidarity and friendliness of the people, which encouraged her to think that their lives were not barren. She perceived in most of them the inherent qualities of man's higher nature that would elevate them above the sordid conditions of their lives and aid them in their determination to better themselves.

She acknowledged women and children she passed, and smiled at their expressions as some of them recognized the Master's wife. It amused her to think of how horrified Aunt Shaw and Edith would be to know of her daily walks. Margaret was keenly aware of the liberty afforded her in marrying Mr. Thornton. She did not know many husbands of similar standing who would allow their wives to wander the more dismal parts of the city all alone. Henry would have sorely disapproved, she felt, shuddering at the thought of being held in a restrictive marriage. No, she was grateful to have found someone who understood her independent nature.

Last night, after they had both returned home, Margaret had suggested that she drop her plans for the school. Her husband had insisted, however, that she should continue despite the circumstances. He reminded her that the supplies had already been purchased and that there was little cost in setting up the room. He was also concerned that she have some occupation that gave her pleasure.

When Margaret arrived at Higgins' humble and cramped home, she helped Mary tidy the main room, gathering little Joseph Boucher into her arms as his surrogate mother quickly swept the floor. Mary was excited to hear more of Margaret's plans to begin schooling some of the children, and told her friend that several other families would like their children to attend.

Margaret walked with Mary and the children to a neighbor's where the children would stay while Mary went to prepare lunch for the workers at Marlborough Mills. The two young women walked together until Margaret parted ways to go to the market.

Sometime later, Margaret emerged from the chemist's shop with a few small packages, her basket already laden with fruit and sundry other items. She sauntered down the high street and stopped to look at flowers for sale by an aging woman in a faded cambric dress.

Further down the same street, Albert Slickson spied the lovely Mrs. Thornton as she bent to smell some lavender and selected a few bunches to carry in her basket. He stepped to the curb at once and, dodging the carts and people massing in the cobbled street, briskly crossed to the other side to catch her eye.

The dashing young student ambled toward Margaret with a feigned nonchalance and waited with civil courtesy for her to recognize him. His inward smile swiftly manifested itself on his lips as her eyes met his and she slowed and then stopped.

"Mr. Slickson," Margaret greeted him politely as he tipped his hat.

"Mrs. Thornton. So pleased to see you again," Albert replied warmly.

"I hope you are enjoying your stay in Milton, learning our northern ways," she commented with good humor.

"Indeed, there is much to note about the difference in the way things are done here. I am inclined to think that such cities of industry as this will propel all of England into the future," he remarked with an air of respect.

"I am pleased that you think so. You will be interested to know that I am beginning a school for the workers' children," she continued, remembering their previous conversations at the ball.

"A capital idea! That is another point I have discerned about the pace of life here: in London we must discuss at great length any grand ideas for progress before they are implemented, whereas here in Milton an idea put forth seems to be immediately acted upon. I am impressed with your swift initiative," Albert praised her. "And is Mr. Thornton involved in your endeavor?" he asked with particular interest, wondering to what degree the Mistress of Marlborough Mills was supervised by her husband.

"He approves, of course, but I'm afraid he is much too engaged with business at present to offer his assistance," she answered somewhat uncomfortably.

"Of course, I understand. There is a dampening of trade currently. I imagine your husband must be very involved in his business as of late," he remarked smoothly.

"Yes, he is," Margaret replied, her polite smile tinged with sadness at the thought of the many hours her husband was forced to spend at the mill.

"I mustn't keep you any longer. I wish you well in your new enterprise. Perhaps I could visit your school to see for myself how such a place can be run," Albert suggested hopefully.

"Of course. Perhaps in a week or two," she responded pleasantly. "Good day."

"Good day, ma'am," Albert replied with a gallant nod and tip of his hat. He walked half a block away before turning discreetly to catch a glimpse of Margaret's retreating figure.

Unbeknownst to either of them, Miss Dallimore had spotted Mr. Slickson and the Mistress of Marlborough Mills upon coming out of the milliner's shop and had observed with great interest the animated conversation between them. She recalled with haughty disdain the rumors that had circulated about Margaret last winter - that she had been seen alone with a man at dusk at Outwood Station.

Miss Dallimore smiled smugly to herself as she casually inspected the wares of the fruit vendor. Perhaps Mr. Thornton should have been more careful in his choice of a wife, she mused.

Margaret busied herself the remainder of the day, spending a good deal of time in the kitchen, much to Mrs. Thornton's surprise. When the young woman had finished her task and given the cook her final instructions, she went upstairs to arrange a few things, take a short rest, and change for dinner.

She sat later in the drawing room with her mother-in-law, eagerly awaiting her husband's return from work. She had requested that he make every effort to come home for dinner each evening. Attempting to read the book in her hands, she listened intently for the sound of his footsteps and sighed in happy satisfaction when at last she finally heard them.

Taking pains to greet him with the restraint required in his mother's presence, she nevertheless grasped his arms and stretched up to give him an affectionate kiss on the lips.

Mr. Thornton reveled in the warm welcome he received as he grasped his wife's waist lightly, feeling the urge to return her enthusiasm with a kiss that would not be appropriate in his mother's view. He would be glad to come home to dinner every night with such attentions as these, he mused, studying his wife's lips for a brief moment before releasing her and greeting his mother.

Margaret accompanied him as he headed upstairs to wash, mentioning that she wished to show him something that she had purchased.

They had only reached the landing at the top of the stairs when Mr. Thornton swiftly took her into his strong embrace and kissed her as he had longed to just moments before. He felt a thrill of lustful desire as she immediately melded to him, putting herself under his power. They kissed as starving lovers, having not come together in several days.

He tore himself away from her to pull out his pocket watch, fairly quaking with ardent desire. "Dinner is at half past?" he asked.

She nodded her accord, breathless from the yearning he had wrought in her.

"We have yet twenty minutes," he answered, his eyes alight with triumphal determination. He scooped her up into his arms without another word and bounded for the bedroom door.

Hannah Thornton waited patiently as her son and his wife arrived at the table a few minutes late. Margaret self-consciously felt to check the pins in her hair as Mr. Thornton helped his wife to her seat. Mrs. Thornton eyed her son as their dinner was served and marveled at how radiantly happy he appeared despite the current circumstances at the mill. She glanced at Margaret, whose distractedness had dissolved into effusive joy as she observed her husband's delight in the meal she had specifically chosen for him.

The elder woman could not help but be glad about her daughter-in-law's evident care for her son. Mrs. Thornton remembered how worried she had been last summer when her son had become distracted with events concerning the strike and subsequent riot, and had had little concern for food or proper rest. She was pleased and not a little relieved to see that Margaret would tend to him during this difficult time when all was uncertain. She was a good wife to him.

Margaret spoke of her plans for helping the workers' children, and Mrs. Thornton listened without comment, taking her son's responses as her cue to keep silent with her own reservations about such undertakings. She did not wish to disturb the evening with her objections.

Margaret smiled when dessert was served and bowed her head humbly when it was announced that the young mistress herself had made fresh gooseberry tarts.

Mr. Thornton looked at his wife with surprise and admiration, feeling a flood of affection for the effort she had taken to please him.

She beamed at his praise and mentioned that she sometimes enjoyed baking, and would especially enjoy it now that she knew it would please him.

When dinner was over, Mr. Thornton was again obliged to excuse himself to continue his work. However, this time he brought his ledgers and papers to the desk in his room as his wife had suggested the evening before.

Margaret stayed in the drawing room with her mother-in-law for a while, but found she could not concentrate on her reading. "Would you mind if I excused myself? I think I should like to write to Edith tonight," she asked her husband's mother.

"Not at all," Mrs. Thornton replied with a sliver of a smile as she looked up briefly from her needlework.

Margaret climbed the stairs with a determination not to bother her husband, and entered her room quietly to write to her cousin as she had mentioned. She described the recent ball as she had promised, but carefully omitted telling her of the recent disturbance in the economy and John's trouble with the mill.

When she had finished, she could no longer bear to remain alone in her room and ventured to see how her husband was faring with his work.

He gave her a smile as she walked into the richly toned room.

She walked over to stand behind him and began to rub his shoulders, feeling the muscles through the thin cotton of his shirt. "Are you comfortable working here?" she asked with a knowing smile.

"I am. It is a great deal more comfortable than my office," he admitted. "The room smells of Helstone," he added, referring to the fresh lavender she had placed in the room.

"It is just as I desired. If you must work, I see no reason why you cannot do so in pleasant surroundings," she reasoned as she continued to work on his taut muscles.

He set his quill down and relaxed in the bliss of her vigorous attentions. "I think you shall quite spoil me," he remarked, his voice revealing the pleasure he took in her care.

"Then I have succeeded as a good wife. I wish to help you in whatever way I am able. But don't let me be a distraction," she added. "Will it bother you if I come later to read in bed?"

"No, I would like your company," he answered truthfully. The bleakness of his accounting seemed mercifully lessened with her nearby. Her presence gave him reason to hope.

"Then you shall have it," she replied and left him to dress for bed, although it was still early in the evening.

She dressed in her nightgown and read in the great bed, in perfect contentment to be in the same room as him. And when he at last turned out his lamp and prepared for bed, she set her book aside and waited for him to join her under the covers. She ran her hand along his darkened jaw and began to rub the muscles at the back of his neck. He gave her a grateful kiss and turned to offer her his back as well, sighing in the comfort of her soothing skills.

At length, she snuggled against him and whispered her affections in his ear. He took her hand, kissed it and held it against his chest as he fell asleep.

⊷

The next week, Margaret began her teaching. The building by the workers' hall had been cleaned and patched by Higgins and other workers after hours.

Upwards of twenty children filled the open room with eager if not altogether clean faces. Some of the children had learned to read a little, but others barely knew their letters. A few of them would work at the mill the latter half of the day. The young Mrs. Thornton hoped to find a suitable teacher for them soon, as it would be daunting work to settle them all in a course of learning tailored to their varying needs. She did her best to discern what each child knew, and by the end of the week had an acceptable routine that kept her students busy learning the basics of reading and writing.

As the morning drew to a close, the children were busy copying on their blackboards the various lessons written on the large board at the front of the room when Margaret heard a noise from the doorway.

"Mr. Slickson," Margaret called out, surprised to see the young gentleman come through the open door.

"Albert, please," he insisted with a broad smile. "I've come to see your school as you suggested," he said, dropping his voice in response to her gesture to be quiet while the children worked.

"Take a look around if you wish," Mrs. Thornton invited, pleased to have someone take an interest in her efforts.

He walked silently around the room, impressed at the children's diligence and good behavior. The room was plain but clean, and the children had no qualms about sitting on the floor for lack of furniture.

His eyes soon returned, however, to the subject that most attracted his attention.

Margaret stood calmly looking out the door towards her husband's office, waiting for the whistle to sound the lunch hour, when the children would depart for the day.

Mr. Slickson thought her face angelic as he noted a faint smile cross her features. The open lace of her black blouse revealed the creamy flesh of her forearms, and the muslin skirt fit snugly at her small waist. He had never met any woman quite like her and was taken with her energetic spirit and obvious intelligence as well as her refined grace and delicate beauty. He had begun to think that he should like to marry just such a woman, if indeed, there was any other that could compare.

He approached her when she at last turned her attention toward him once more. "You have done admirably well in your endeavors, Mrs. Thornton," he praised her with sincerity.

The whistle blew at his last words and the children began to stream out the door. "Good day, Miss," they said politely in turn as she had taught them, before bounding outside to find their parents.

"And you have done all this yourself?" he asked incredulously.

"Yes, I have not yet found a suitable teacher to take my place. My husband is very supportive, but he can hardly afford the time to help me in my endeavors," she answered, feeling slightly discomforted to be alone with him in the room.

"In the meantime, I would like to make a few excursions with the children. I was thinking of taking them to the park next week. They seldom get the opportunity to run and disport themselves as children ought," she explained as she led him out of doors.

Albert's hazel eyes sparkled at her revelation, his mind quickly devising a course of action. "Indeed! You are very solicitous of their needs. I should not have thought of such a thing," he commended her.

"I'm glad you approve," she responded, giving him an appreciative smile.

Albert flashed her a brilliant smile. Glancing at the crowd behind her, he reluctantly prepared to take his leave. "I hope I will see you again soon. I should like to hear more of your enterprise. Good day to you," he said as he tipped his hat before striding with vigor across the yard.

Margaret turned to find her husband coming to meet her as they had planned. She was happy to eat with him at the workers' kitchen on occasion. On those days, she knew at least he was eating his lunch. She smiled warmly as he grew nearer.

He returned her smile and took her arm under his to lead the way to the canteen. "Was that Mr. Slickson's nephew that I saw just leaving?" he asked curiously, his brow furrowed slightly as they walked.

"Oh, yes. He was very interested to see the school," she answered simply with a little pride.

Mr. Thornton nodded his head in acknowledgement but wondered if the school was indeed the only thing the young man was interested in. He glanced unconsciously in the direction where Margaret's visitor had disappeared before turning his full attention back to his wife.

On Saturday evening, Margaret drew a hot bath for her husband using some of the lavender bath salts she had purchased at the chemist's shop. She lit a few candles and snuffed out the lamp, hoping the warmth and dim light of the room would help him to relax before bed.

With a secretive smile, she went to retrieve him, slipping her arms around his chest from behind as he sat at his desk in the study. "Your bath awaits you," she informed him, rubbing her cheek against the stubble of his face.

"Am I obliged to come at once?" he asked teasingly as he brought his broad hands up to hold her own, pressing her hands firmly against his chest in an effort to keep her close to him.

"You are. You cannot be seen with such hands as these at church on the morrow," she chastised him lovingly, holding his hand out to see the ink stains on his fingers.

He smiled wryly at her observation, feeling the poignancy of her care for him. He did not forget that she could have chosen to marry a gentleman, someone who did not have to toil in such conditions as he did to provide her with a comfortable living.

"Then I will come. I would not wish to embarrass you," he retorted as he got up from his chair.

She brought his hand up to her lips and kissed it tenderly in response, looking at him with luminous eyes that spoke more than mere words could convey.

She kept hold of his hand as she led him upstairs and ushered him to the bath. She closed the door behind her and left to return to her room, but returned on impulse a few minutes later to tap lightly on the door.

"Have I forgotten anything? Are you well settled?" she asked through the paneled wood.

He glanced around him, quickly looking for any excuse for her to enter. "I'm afraid the soap is out of my reach," he answered truthfully as he sat in the bath, seeing it on the counter just across from him. He smiled deviously as he heard the door click at her entrance.

She found the bar of soap and handed it to him, acknowledging him briefly before bashfully averting her eyes.

He took the soap with one hand and deftly grasped her wrist with the other before she could withdraw.

"Will you wash my back?" he asked, his eyes pleading for her to stay longer.

She opened her mouth to protest, but could not find a suitable response as she met his gaze. She stood still to communicate her willingness to comply. Looking at the lace of her sleeves she realized she would need to change. She extracted herself gently from his grasp and turned to unbutton her blouse. Folding it gently on the counter, she returned to him in her sleeveless camisole.

She wet the castile soap and lathered his back. Her breath came slow and even as she watched in fascination as her hands slid over the slippery surface of his broad back. She helped him wash his hair next, pouring water over his dark hair with a pitcher as she stared at the back of his neck, longing to feel his skin with her lips. Setting down the pitcher at last, she followed her impulse and glided her hands over his shoulders to his chest, leaning over to place a kiss just behind his ear.

He took hold of her hands and pulled her closer, bringing her almost flush against him. Her heart beat faster at his ardent gesture.

"Come in with me," he requested compellingly, tugging her arm to bring her around to face him.

"I could not!" she declared, shocked at his demand. Having always been banned from a portion of the house whenever Fred or her father were bathing, her sense of propriety was deeply ingrained.

"No one would be the wiser," he gently coaxed her, loosening his hold but maintaining contact with her hands.

Entranced by the imploring intensity of his deep blue eyes, she felt her resolve falter. She took a step back to distance herself a moment, wavering between what her heart wanted and what she had long believed must be indecent.

She glanced again at her husband and mused that he only wished to enjoy her company. She longed to please him. They had already shared every intimacy, she reminded herself. Finding herself at a loss to explain to him her refusal, she began to unfasten her skirt, stepping out of it and her petticoats. She hesitated, unable to bring herself to undress further.

Coming to him in her camisole and drawers, she began to smile at her hesitation. "You are wicked to propose such a thing," she scolded him as she stepped carefully into the bath opposite him, taking his hand to steady herself.

He could not suppress his delight in her concession, and grinned as she scolded him; all the while his eyes avidly took in the sight of her thinly clad form as the fabric quickly soaked and clung to her skin.

Avoiding his gaze, she decided to make herself useful and took up the soap and brush to clean the ink from his fingers.

Mr. Thornton studied her in fascination as she worked, amazed that she should be there with him. He had not thought such a thing possible and had half expected that she would decline his request. She had surprised him once more with her willingness to break with convention.

"There! Now you are fit to be seen with me," she announced with a haughty tone as she finished her task, a glimmer of mischief in her eyes.

"And shall I tell everyone the great lengths to which you will go to see that I am presentable?" he taunted, barely able to contain his mirth at such a proposal.

Her mouth flew open in mortification at the very suggestion and he laughed out loud at her expression.

"You are horrible!" she declared in response, splashing water at him with a flick of her hand.

He laughed only harder at her attempt to punish him and grasping her under the knees, drew her closer to him, desiring to make amends. She feigned reluctance to forgive him, resisting his efforts to hold her by the arms, but his laughter reached to the depths of her heart and she could not restrain her delight in bringing him such joy. She let him pull her closer, and clambered to her knees to situate herself nearer him, giggling at their encounter even as Mr. Thornton began to kiss her in earnest.

They laughed softly between kisses, the sloshing water only amplifying the awkwardness of their amorous movements. Mr. Thornton had never been more enchanted, finding his wife utterly irresistible. Their laughter faded as their ardor for one another grew, and their kisses became more fervent.

When he could stand it no longer, Mr. Thornton hoisted himself and his wife upright and they climbed out of the bath. Quickly wrapping a towel around himself, he handed his wife a towel. She dried herself a little before peeling off her wet garments. Mr. Thornton graciously handed her his dressing gown. He opened the door to furtively scan the hallway. Seeing that they were alone, he opened it wide to allow his Margaret to scamper across to their bedroom before he swiftly followed her.

They hurried to the bed with broad smiles and, dropping their wrappings, delved under the covers to accomplish what had been frustratingly thwarted in the bath.

Remaining in their room for the rest of the evening, they happily languished in each other's arms as they talked, setting aside the worries of the mill for a time.

As July progressed, warmer days punctuated the cooler weather at intervals. On one such morning when the opened windows did little to stir the air, Mr. Thornton stood up from the breakfast table and gave his mother and wife a quick kiss as was his custom before he departed. His schedule had been sternly demanding, but his heart was light in the company of the women he loved.

After her son had gone, Hannah Thornton cast a discerning eye on her daughter-in-law, and watched with knowing sympathy as she nibbled slightly at her toast and dabbed at the eggs on her plate with little interest. This was the third morning that she had not really eaten her breakfast, but had surreptitiously sipped her tea while her husband swiftly breakfasted and departed for the mill.

The elder woman might have assumed the girl was merely tired from matching John's morning schedule so regularly, but when she had risen from the table the morning before with an ashen face and a hasty excuse that she must go to her room for a while, Mrs. Thornton's suspicions had been greatly aroused. However, Margaret had seemed well the rest of the day.

Seated next to her now, she noted that Margaret was again a little pale.

"I found it helped to eat a little, even when it did not appeal," Mrs. Thornton thoughtfully encouraged her daughter-in-law. "Some toast might help settle your stomach," she advised quietly as her gaze met Margaret's surprised and expressive eyes. The young wife looked relieved and anxious all at once to have her secret discovered.

"Thank you," Margaret replied softly, and took a tentative bite of toast as she was bidden.

"Have you told John yet?" Mrs. Thornton probed gently, doubting that her son was even aware of the monthly occurrences that women normally experienced.

"No," Margaret answered, swallowing the food that she had reluctantly taken into her mouth. She took another sip of tea to chase the toast down before speaking again. "I wasn't quite certain myself. I wanted to wait a bit to be sure. I thought perhaps it was the recent heat that made me feel unwell, but I suppose there is no denying it now," she admitted with a short laugh at her own uncertainty.

"The morning sickness will pass before long," her mother-in-law assured her with a kind upturn of her lips.

"Yes, I know. Edith also was indisposed for a short time each morning, but it did not seem to last very many weeks." Margaret replied with a hopeful smile. She did not relish enduring these queasy sensations for any length of time.

Mrs. Thornton noted the girl's wan look with compassion. "Take rest if you need it, Margaret. You must take good care yourself - and of my grandchild," she added with a sparkle in her eye and a warm smile. She placed her hand over Margaret's and gave it a squeeze.

Margaret returned the knowing smile and placed her other hand over her mother-in-law's, feeling a wonderful comfort to receive her blessing and compassion.

⤜⤏

Margaret sat on the edge of her bed, twisting the loose fabric of her white dressing gown into knots. She stood up decisively only to hesitate as she walked to and from the wardrobe to her bed and sat down again.

She chastised herself for being so nervous. She was certain he would gladly receive her news. If only the timing of events had not been so unfortunate! She did not want to add to his burden with news of a coming child.

She smiled to recall how wonderful he had been with the children they had met in Helstone. What a glorious father he would be! She was quite certain he would be pleased to have a family.

Standing up again, she told herself it would do no good to dither about it all night. There was nothing that could be done. She had to let him know - she ached to tell him, to have him exclaim his joy and take her into his arms.

She decided to go downstairs first and fetch him something to eat. Then, she would tell him.

Margaret entered their bedroom later carrying a small tray with a mug of hot chocolate and some biscuits and set it down on a corner of his desk.

He looked up from his work to acknowledge her and glance at her offering. Smiling, her husband wrapped an arm around her waist and brought her to him, settling her on his lap. She smiled anxiously and loosely wound her arms around his neck in return.

"You have been so good to me," he declared with an affectionate gaze.

"Have I?" she answered somewhat distractedly, finding herself staring at the skin at the base of his throat, his shirt casually unbuttoned for his comfort.

"You have," he affirmed, studying the features of her face as she held her gaze downward.

She looked up to him, her eyes wide with anxiety for what she had to say. "John," she began quietly, having gained his attention.

He waited with a faint smile for what she wished to tell him,

268

supposing she had more suggestions for her endeavors with the school.

"I am with child," she said at last, studying him carefully for his reaction.

His smile dissipated in his astonishment, struck dumb by her revelation. His eyes swept to her stomach as he touched her reverently where she would soon swell. "A child?" he repeated, attempting to comprehend what she had just told him as a tremor of emotion began to take over him. She was carrying his child! He would be a father!

"Are you not pleased?" she questioned with concern at his distant gaze.

He jerked his head to look at her in wonderment, coming awake to the feeling of exuberance that was beginning to take hold of him. "Am I not pleased?" he repeated, incredulous that she should ask such a thing. "How can I not be pleased with such a gift?" he asked, taking her face into his hands. "Margaret, I love you. I will welcome with joy any such gifts from our marriage," he stated honestly, his face now beaming with undeniable happiness.

She smiled with glad relief.

"When?" he asked with eager curiosity.

"I believe it will be sometime in February, or perhaps early March," she answered, glowing with the joy of his excitement.

"I see," he replied, thinking how long they had to wait. His face lit with eager anticipation as he thought of announcing their news. "Shall we tell mother?" he asked with an earnest expression.

Margaret almost laughed at his boyish eagerness. "I'm afraid she has already guessed," she replied.

He gave her a quizzical glance.

"I have not recently had much appetite at breakfast," she explained.

His countenance changed instantly to one of concern. "You are ill?" he asked, his eyes full of worry.

"No, no," she assured him. "I believe it is quite common the first few months to feel a little unwell in the morning. Edith had the same complaint," she explained.

"A baby," he murmured in wonder, still overcome by the unexpected news.

"Yes," she confirmed with a glorious smile as she caught his gaze and wrapped her arms around his neck a bit tighter.

"Margaret!" he breathed, crushing her to him, albeit more gently now, afraid he might somehow hurt her. She would bring him every precious thing, all he had thought might never be his to enjoy. He blinked away the tears he felt welling in his eyes. How truly blessed he was! He did not care at this moment what fate would bring. He could weather any storm, as long she would love him.

Tears of relief and joy silently fell from Margaret's eyes as she held tightly to him. He had been pleased with her news. He would tenderly provide for her and any children they might have, she was certain of it. She cared not if circumstances reduced them to a more modest living. She could be happy anywhere as long as they were together.

Chapter Eighteen

The Master of Marlborough Mills scanned past the streaming crowd of workers for a glimpse of his wife. Alert to the noon whistle on Tuesdays, he looked forward to eating his lunch in the worker's hall with Margaret; not only did it divide his day with a needed break, but he relished every opportunity to be with her.

The dry mill yard sent up a fine cloud of dust as innumerable boots and clogs pounded the ground. As the swarm of drab colored figures dispersed, Mr. Thornton caught sight of her. She stood facing him with her arms loosely holding her summer shawl about her shoulders. Errant wisps of hair caressed her face in the faint breeze as she smiled at him, her lips slightly parted and her eyes filled with a tenderness he knew was meant only for him. He felt his heart lift; the care-worn expression and creased lines of his forehead dissolved as he approached the woman he loved.

His gaze was torn between the allure of her shining eyes and her soft, pink lips. Restraining the urge to pull her flush against him and kiss her, he politely offered her his arm to lead her to the canteen. "How was your morning?" he asked upon reaching her, recalling that she had planned to take the children to the park.

"The children had a wonderful time. It was quite a morning!" she happily enthused, pleased that her excursion had been a success.

Mr. Thornton smiled at the thought of his wife watching over twenty-odd children running to and fro. "How did you manage all those children?" he wondered aloud as they reached the worker's dining hall.

"Oh, I was a little worried, but everything came about just perfectly. Mr. Slickson happened by and stayed to help me watch over everyone," she blithely told him.

Mr. Thornton frowned as he assisted his wife to her seat and moved to sit next to her. Mary promptly delivered steaming bowls of stew before them and then retreated.

"Mr. Slickson, the young nephew from university?" he queried in as casual a tone as he could muster.

"Yes, he is very supportive of all my endeavors. He was quite happy to stop and assist in keeping the children from becoming too unruly," she answered with an innocent smile.

"I see," Mr. Thornton replied, noting Margaret's eager expression with tug of tender affection for her naiveté. She did not perceive that her rare beauty and infectious spirit might draw the attentions of other men, instead supposing Mr. Slickson was genuine in his interest in her work. Mr. Thornton wished he could be as magnanimous in his assumptions, but could not shake the growing suspicion that the handsome London visitor was overly fond of his wife.

Margaret's eyes roved over the collection of porcelain objects displayed on the walnut what-not, the towering exotic fern behind the plush ocher sofa, and the carefully arranged clutter of stools, tables, and furniture that abounded in Fanny Watson's extravagant drawing room. Her gaze returned once again to the intricate gold pattern of the Indian wallpaper as she listened to Fanny regale her mother of her plans to redecorate her bedchamber and the adjoining sitting room.

"Have you begun to prepare a nursery, Margaret?" Fanny eagerly asked her, bringing Margaret's attention back to the conversation at hand.

"No, not yet. I'm sure there will be plenty of time to arrange everything," Margaret offered as an excuse. In truth, she still found herself bewildered at times that she was indeed expecting. It had only been a little over a week since she had revealed her condition to John. She would have preferred to keep it private for a while longer, but knew her husband had been fairly bursting to tell his family of his latest news.

"I must confess it is a surprise to hear you will be starting your family so soon. Perhaps it won't be long before I bear similar news," Fanny remarked, a trifle jealous that her brother's wife would be the one to provide the first grandchild in the family. "John seems very pleased. I can hardly believe he will be a father! How exciting that I shall be an aunt! We must go shopping together for the things you will need," she suggested with enthusiasm and then began to tell of the shops that would carry the finest goods as Margaret politely inclined her head and listened.

In the neighboring room, Mr. Thornton declined the proffered cigar from Watson with a polite smile and shake of his head. He was happy to dine at his sister's house on occasion, but dreaded the tedious custom of being sequestered with his brother-in-law while the women withdrew to hold their own conversations. He had little in common with his sister's husband, even though they both had similar responsibilities as masters of local cotton mills.

Watson lit a cigar and gave a few puffs with satisfaction. Turning to the sideboard, he poured a small glass of port and handed it to the father-to-be. "So you are to be a family man! I was just growing accustomed to your being married. The country air in Helstone must have been quite invigorating, eh, Thornton?" he remarked with a suggestive arch of his eyebrow and sly grin.

Mr. Thornton did not deign to respond, recalling with disgust the reason he avoided going to the gentlemen's clubs the other masters so frequently attended. He often found the conversation at such places crude and offensive. "How are you faring in this dismal economy?" he asked his colleague, changing the subject to matters of business.

"I've got the situation under control. I believe I have enough capital at present to wait out this damned downturn, no thanks to my dear wife. She's spent a small fortune on decorating this old bachelor's home of mine with whatever suits her fancy. But, I'll have to keep her spending in check until my investments come through," Watson explained with confidence. With a hint of disapproval, he continued, "I hear your wife has been busy starting up some kind of school for the working poor."

"She has - with my approval, of course," Mr. Thornton replied in defense of his Margaret's ambitious plans. "I am aware of her activities," he added.

"Are you?" Watson retorted doubtfully, pulling the cigar from between his teeth to carefully study his brother-in-law for his gullibility. The stench of smoke filled the paneled room.

Mr. Thornton's eyes narrowed as he stared at his brother-in-law in rising indignation. "What do you mean?" he demanded evenly, the deep undertones of his voice reverberating a warning. His body tensed in foreboding at Watson's tone.

"I'm just saying that I'd not let my wife go gallivanting about as she pleased. I'd keep a tighter rein on that one, Thornton, that's all," Watson cautiously advised, shaking his head warily.

Mr. Thornton's anger flared at such counsel. "Margaret may be un-conventional in her actions, but I trust her implicitly to use her own good judgment in conducting her affairs," he replied with tempered vehemence. A twinge of doubt clouded his confidence as he remembered with chagrin that Margaret could be rash and impulsive when her passions were ignited. Had she done something to cause censure from those with more tepid natures and minds, he wondered?

"Then let me take this opportunity to caution you as a brother that however noble her intentions, it would be best not to be seen so often in the company of that young Slickson dandy," Watson exclaimed, jutting his chin ever so slightly in the air to punctuate his advice.

Mr. Thornton's blood ran cold to have his fears confirmed. Others had noticed it as well: the young man was attracted to his wife. Indignation welled up inside him as he thought of how his wife might be innocent prey to Albert's illicit affections and the scandalous gossip of the city.

"A coincidental meeting in a public park is hardly fodder for tittle-tattle, especially when children are running all about," he countered, increasingly incensed that Margaret should be subject to such talk.

Watson's expression indicated faint surprise that Thornton was indeed aware of his wife's goings on. "I'm not saying there's anything to it, just that there is talk," he retorted somewhat defensively before returning to his cigar with renewed interest.

Mr. Thornton nodded his head in fair acknowledgement of the warning, his defiant stance slowly yielding to his habitual impenetrable demeanor. He turned the conversation to other matters with an impassive expression, but beneath his rigid exterior his mind roiled with suspicion and agitation that Margaret might lie in some danger.

The guests rode home in silence, their inclination for conversation exhausted. Margaret considered the fretful time and energy that Fanny must expend in creating a showcase of her home, while Mrs. Thornton quietly reminded herself of her good fortune in living with John and his wife.

Mr. Thornton's hand gently gripped his wife's as he steadily stared out into the dark. Shaken by Watson's revelations, he contemplated what he should do. Going over in his mind all the times he had seen Slickson near his wife, he was certain that Margaret suspected neither the idle talk about her nor the young man's inordinate attention. He did not want to disturb her with contemptible rumors, nor did he feel a word of warning concerning Albert would be well received.

He decided to let the matter be, although he determined he would keep a vigilant watch for Slickson's appearance anywhere near the mill. Thankfully, it was nearly August, and the London student would soon return to university come autumn. It would be well had he never arrived in Milton, Mr. Thornton thought as he turned his gaze to his wife and gave her hand a squeeze.

As he climbed into bed that night, Mr. Thornton leaned over to brush his lips against his wife's for a goodnight kiss before settling his head on the pillow.

In the darkness, Margaret let out a slow sigh as she found herself once again facing her husband's shoulder. He had not touched her since she had announced her pregnancy. She had reasoned, at first, that he might think her condition too delicate. Perhaps it was; she had no knowledge of such things. But as each night came and they shared a tepid bed, she could not help but ruminate. Did the stress of his work drain him of all desire? Had he somehow lost interest in her? She could not bear to think that the passion they had shared was now over. She fretted for some time before finally closing her eyes and allowing sleep to overtake her.

Mr. Thornton heard the sound of her breathing change, and emitted a long sigh of relief and frustration. She was safely asleep at last. As each night approached, he found himself increasingly agitated. How long he could endure the torment of his longing he did not know, nor did he see how he could discover the knowledge he sought. He did not wish to bring any harm to his unborn child, and worried how he should be expected to refrain from claiming his privileges for the months ahead.

Last night, when she had rubbed his shoulders and pressed her lithe body against his back, he had burned with the temptation to press her beneath him and take her as his wife. Instead, he had taken her hand and held it to him to halt her seductive touch.

He sensed her disappointment in the nightly kisses he bestowed, but he could not trust himself to offer her anything beyond a touch of his lips, knowing how their deeper kisses could ignite him in an instant.

He turned from the sight of her, and prayed that somehow he would be saved from this nightly torture.

Early the next morning, Margaret left the house to visit Mary Higgins. She was eager to tell her friend her news, knowing that the taciturn girl would keep it a secret.

Mary was excited for the young mistress and gave Margaret a quick hug upon Margaret's revelation, an unusual gesture for the generally recalcitrant girl. "Oh, Miss Margaret! You'll be a wonderful mother, to be sure!" she exclaimed. "The Master must be pleased," she surmised.

"Yes," Margaret responded, beaming from the excitement of her friend.

"Oh, you must see Mrs. McKnight!" Mary declared in earnest.

Margaret gave her a curious look. "The midwife Dr. Donaldson spoke to me of?" she inquired.

"Yes, that's the one! She's the very best in the city. Why, even the finer folks call on her. Her husband was a shop owner, but now she lives with her son and his wife in Crampton, not so far from your old house I reckon. Anyway, she's not so grand as to turn up her nose at us working folks, and she's respectable enough to be called to those finer homes out by your way. She saved Mrs. Pritchett around the corner from a terrible time with her first 'un. If you'll pardon me from saying so," she added, suddenly flustered to hint at the pain involved in labor.

"No, no, I appreciate your recommendation. Dr. Donaldson mentioned that she often assists him. I will be interested to seek her out. Thank you, Mary," she consoled her friend with her grateful thanks.

Mary smiled brightly, the trepidation vanishing from her eyes, pleased to have helped the young mistress.

∽∾

The next afternoon, Margaret took the familiar path to Crampton. She felt impelled to seek out the popular midwife after hearing Mary's praise. Dr. Donaldson had also recommended her as a helpful aide and Margaret's interest had piqued when the kind doctor hinted that the midwife could help answer any questions she might have regarding womanly issues. Just a few blocks away from her former home, she climbed the clean gray steps to a painted door and rang the bell.

Upon inquiring after Mrs. McKnight, Margaret was eventually led into a quiet parlor where heavily brocaded drapes kept the room perpetually dim. A thick-boned lady beyond her middle years stood up to greet her, her bright eyes exuding an energy her wrinkled face betrayed. "Adiara McKnight," she introduced herself, her Scottish brogue expressed in the simple utterance of her name.

Margaret warmed instantly to her kindly smile and firm handshake. "Margaret Thornton. I've come to speak to you about having a baby," she explained with a faint blush.

"Of course you have, my dear. I'm pleased to meet you. Mrs. Thornton, is it? You live at Marlborough Mills, is that right? My husband always spoke kindly of Mr. Thornton. Are you recently married?" she inquired straightaway, receiving a quiet nod in response. "Now, sit down with me and let's talk about this baby," she invited with a sweep of her arm toward a comfortable chair.

After the spry elderly lady had asked several questions and explained a little about what Margaret could expect as the months rolled by, Mrs. McKnight gladly confirmed that she would be willing to take the case. Margaret thanked her, having come to trust the woman's forthright and friendly manner.

"Now, are there any other questions you may have?" the experienced midwife asked the young mother-to-be.

Margaret opened her mouth hesitantly before closing it again and cast her eyes to the floor.

"Don't be shy, now, I've been around for quite some time. I have

276

heard everything, my dear," she encouraged her gently.

Gathering her courage, Margaret opened her mouth to speak again. "I was wondering if there is any harm to the baby in..." she began, but could not continue, feeling her face flush at her unspoken question.

Mrs. McKnight smiled knowingly. "It is a very common question, dearie. You wish to know if lovemaking will be harmful to the child. That depends," she said with a lilt.

Margaret's bowed head snapped up to search the elder woman's face, caught off guard by the midwife's unexpected response. Mrs. McKnight's eyes twinkled with merriment.

"It depends on whether you wish to dissuade your husband from visiting your bed, or if you are comfortable with his attentions," she said with a sly smile.

Margaret smiled at her implication, remembering that there must be plenty of women, such as Fanny, that would appreciate an excuse to keep their husbands at bay for a time. "No, I...I am very fond of my husband," she answered falteringly, unavoidably feeling her face warm again.

"Then I will tell you that there is no harm in receiving your husbands attentions. Gentle care will be needed when the baby grows bigger, of course. Let your own judgment guide you and I'm sure all will be well," she candidly advised, showing no compunction in speaking of such intimate matters.

"Thank you, you have been very helpful," Margaret said, flooded with a sense of relief to have been enlightened on a multitude of issues that had been a source of anxious concern.

After saying her goodbyes, Margaret took her leave of the kind woman who felt already like a familiar friend. She took a deep breath as the door closed behind her. She was glad to have come - she felt better prepared to face the coming months with equanimity and joy.

Later that evening, Margaret wrote a letter to her brother at her desk while John poured over his ledger in the main bedroom. She tried to keep herself well out of his way in the evenings until he indicated that he was finished.

She signed her name and put the quill back in the holder. Realizing that it must be getting late, she snatched her brother's letter and walked through the dressing room to the larger room where her husband sat at his desk in the corner looking disheveled and weary, his head propped up with his free hand.

He turned his face to acknowledge her with a faint smile and returned his attention to his work.

Margaret hoped to give him some respite. "Frederick wrote today. His father-in-law has taken him on to help head the family business. He has described the villa they live in. It sounds so lovely. He hopes we can come to Spain someday," she related cheerfully.

"And are we to comply with his every wish?" he snapped with a sting of bitterness, not lifting his head from where it rested in his hand. "He would be in England still if it were not for his foolish impudence," he muttered at the papers before him.

Margaret stood frozen with shock at his words, her mouth agape.

Mr. Thornton cautiously brought his eyes to hers to see the damage he had caused. The look of hurt and confusion on her face tore at his heart. He stiffened in unknown dread as he watched her lips quiver slightly as if she would say something before she turned abruptly and rushed out of the room. He winced to hear the thud of the door as she separated herself from him, the finality of the sound cutting his soul.

What had he done? He closed his eyes in revulsion. Had he become so abhorrent as to lash out at her for her kindness? He dropped his hand to the desk and clenched his fist in anger and disgust - he had always thought of himself as uncouth and unworthy of her, and now he had proven it.

He stood up forcefully from his chair, the screeching wood sending a further chill of discord through the darkened room. Pacing the floor as he gritted his teeth, he whipped himself into a torrent of self-loathing. He had promised to cherish and care for her, and this is what he offered her - a rebuke for her innocent happiness at her brother's good fortune? Was he now set so low that he should resent another's success?

He shook with the frustration and longing that plagued him. He felt sharply the injustice of it all. How hard he had tried to do everything the right way - only to be brought to desolation! He had yearned to prove himself worthy of her, to give her the comfort and security that a woman of her stature deserved.

A sudden fear began to creep over him, halting him in his tracks as he thought of losing her trust and respect. More distressful than the mill's slow demise, was the notion that he may have irreparably damaged the sweet bond of affection that they had so long now enjoyed. The mill was nothing compared to her! He could bear any indignity or hardship, but he could no longer live without her enduring love.

He raked his fingers through his hair as he unconsciously began again to stride back and forth from the window to his desk. He knew he must apologize, and quickly, before any bitterness began to take root in her thoughts of him.

He turned with decision toward the connecting dressing room and, taking a moment to calm himself, gently opened the door to her bedchamber. She stood stiffly from the bed where she had been sitting, and moved several paces away, her back firmly turned to him.

A piercing pain stabbed his heart to see her justly distance herself from him. "Margaret," he entreated with desperate hope as he swiftly came to her side. "Forgive me, I spoke cruelly," he began in earnest.

"Perhaps only too honestly," she reproached him. "I did not know that you thought so ill of my brother," she stated in an icy tone, keeping her face resolutely to the wall.

Mr. Thornton bowed his head in regret for his outburst and ran his fingers through his hair in consternation, not knowing quite how to respond, only knowing that he must explain himself. "I will not lie to you. I believe your brother made a grave error," he admitted.

"For which he deserves to be perpetually punished by his exile!" Margaret finished hotly, tears stinging her eyes as she considered her husband's harsh judgment against her beloved brother.

He let out his breath and struggled to control his voice. "Margaret, listen to me," he pleaded patiently as he gently grasped her arms, forcing her to face him although she would not look into his eyes. "I believe it was unwise for him to defy authority in such a manner, but I cannot condemn his motive. Am I not familiar with such unselfish impetuosity and righteous fervor - a spirit which I am certain he must share with his sister?" he explained, searching her face for her understanding.

Margaret slowly brought her gaze to his, her manner more contrite although her eyes still shone with confusion at his anger.

"I was jealous," he confessed, recognizing the truth of his emotions as he spoke. "I know it is unconscionable and coarse, but I am an uncouth and unrefined man. I do not wish your brother ill. I am weary this evening, and it has been hard for me to bear my frustration. I cannot even offer you the security of maintaining this home, let alone give you all the things that you desire," he averred, his eyes blazing with anguish. "At present, I do not know when we should ever be able to visit Spain," he added softly, releasing her arms in defeat.

A wave of compassion swept over Margaret to see her husband's sorrow. How could she have been so insensitive to announce Fred's happy success in life, when John was struggling to retain all that he had so scrupulously worked to establish? "It is not important, John. I cannot travel now anyway," she replied, taking hold of his hands. "I did not mean to cause you any pain. I did not think..." she apologized, slowly realizing how deeply he must feel his burden as provider and protector of herself and his mother.

"You will forgive me?" he asked for reassurance, bringing her hands up to bestow a kiss on each.

She wound her arms around his neck and pulled him tightly toward her, hugging him. "You work so hard, John. How can I begrudge you when you have only this once lost your temper?" she asked as she pressed her cheek against his shoulder, the warmth of his body and the scent of him filling her with an indescribable feeling of peace.

"Margaret," he murmured with joyous relief, holding her close.

He moved, at length, to look into her eyes. Unable to resist her, he kissed her tenderly.

She tightened her hold around his neck and parted her lips to receive more of him.

He made a low, guttural sound in response, and kissed her with the hunger he had long suppressed. The sensual feel of her tongue entangling with his own inflamed him, sending a hot surge of desire coursing through his entire body.

He pulled away in alarm, remembering her condition and his decision to be cautious, his slow panting revealing the strength of his ardor.

She looked up at him in agonized dismay and confusion. "Will you not love me, John?" she pleaded, keeping her arms tightly wound around his neck.

How he wished to love her! "Is not your condition delicate?" he asked gently, endeavoring to conceal his ardent wish for her to tell him otherwise.

She smiled knowingly. "I spoke with a midwife today. She told me there is no harm in loving until the baby proves to be cumbersome," she revealed, averting her eyes from his intense gaze as she spoke of such intimate matters.

"There is no harm to the child?" he asked her with rising hope in his voice.

She lifted her flushed face to his and shook her head faintly in agreement.

He could not contain the gratified smile that slowly spread over his face. Returning his mouth to hers, he continued the kiss that had ended so abruptly. This time, he allowed his passion to flow freely as the press of her shapely form against him increased his desire.

He whisked her to the nearby bed where they hastily divested themselves of their clothing. The taste of her skin and the feel of her curves under his hands and body engulfed him in sensual delight. When she at last cried out her pleasure, he felt his bliss in hers and cried out in answering triumph.

Collapsing onto her, he began to shower her with kisses, grateful beyond measure for the precious union that they shared.

Tears of tremendous happiness trickled down her cheeks as she clung to him. Despite the uncertainty of the mill, she felt her life was complete. She gazed at him in wonder and love before she closed her eyes and held him tightly against her.

In the days that followed, Mr. Thornton diligently sought to save his mill from failure. He left no stone unturned in attempting to increase revenue, searching all past accounts to ensure payment had been made in full and seeking out old customers who might be persuaded to order again.

He bravely took up the more sobering task of summarizing the expenses that would need to be paid as current orders were fulfilled. He had decided that if no substantial orders were received within a few weeks' time, the mill would need to close its doors before winter.

Margaret worried for her husband's health as his hours remained long and he took little time for leisure except on Sundays. She took pains to deliver him lunch when she feared he would not notice the time, and made his evenings as pleasant as possible when he was within her realm of care.

On more than one occasion she had taken matters into her own hands when the hour grew very late and he was still at his desk. She would rise from her bed to stand behind him and rub the tired muscles of his neck, shoulders, and back. Then she would gently chastise him for staying up too late as she moved to sit on his lap and unbutton the front of his shirt, working her hands over the muscles of his chest. It had never failed to bring her husband quickly to bed and she would gently comb her fingers through his hair after he had fallen asleep, exhausted from having spent his remaining energy making love to her.

She wondered how he could endure like this, and prayed that soon they might know what path lay ahead for them. She did not care if he were no longer Master for her own sake; she loved him too much to lay any conditions on her esteem and affection. It pained her greatly to think how sorely he had worked these past weeks to save all that he had built. She would feel no shame if he were forced to look for other work. She knew he would rise to greatness in whatever he laid his hands to; it was his nature to do all things with astounding ability. She trusted that all would be well, regardless of what fate might devise.

Early the following week, Margaret went to the draper's shop to purchase yards of fine cloth to make clothes for the baby and herself. After stopping at a few other shops, she soon had acquired several packages to carry home. Arranging them carefully, she determined that she could still manage them on the walk home to Marlborough Mills.

Lost in her thoughts as she made her way down the busy sidewalk, she was startled to hear a voice call her name from the street. She turned to see Albert Slickson hurriedly stepping out of a halted cab.

"Mrs. Thornton!" he called once more as he crossed the thoroughfare to her side. "May I offer you a ride in my cab? Here, let me help you," he offered eagerly as he reached to unburden her from her load of parcels.

Margaret had opened her mouth to decline, but as Albert removed the weighty materials from her grasp, she thought better of his offer, recognizing that she was fatigued and that there was yet a good distance to go before she reached home.

"Thank you. I believe I purchased a good deal more than I intended," she remarked in good humor.

"Then I am very glad I happened by," he replied with a dazzling smile as he led her to the waiting carriage, taking the remaining bundles from her hands.

"I am sorry it is not a bigger cab," he apologized politely as he took his seat beside her in the small compartment. In truth, he was very pleased to find himself in such close confinement with her. The feel of her skirts brushing against his leg gave him a rush of excitement at her nearness.

Margaret smiled politely, but felt a strange twinge of nervousness to be alone with him. She brushed aside the feeling in the next instant, reasoning that there could be no harm in taking a short cab ride with a friend. After all, she needed to be more careful with herself now that she was pregnant.

"Are you keeping busy with your school?" he asked as the small carriage moved forward, impatient to establish an easy rapport with her. However, he already knew that she had been keeping her schedule with the children, for he kept himself well informed of the goings on at the mill.

"Yes, and I've taken the children to the museum and library this past week," she informed him happily.

"You have indeed been very busy," he answered with a bright smile. "I hope you have time to take your leisure," he remarked courteously as his eyes took every opportunity to drink in the sight of her.

"Oh, yes, I have much time to myself in the evenings," she assured him.

"I hope your husband is not still working late," he remarked with great interest, wondering how often such a woman was left unattended.

Margaret looked at her hands for a moment, flustered at his question. "He has been very busy as of late, but he comes home as often as he is able," she answered with a forced cheerfulness before turning to give him a polite smile.

Albert returned her smile, struck by the glimmer of sadness in her eyes. He had watched her profile with fascination, studying the movement of her lips as she had spoken demurely of her husband. Now, faced with the haunting beauty of her expressive blue-gray eyes, he was momentarily speechless.

"Perhaps we could assuage each other's loneliness," he implored, his voice low and unwavering. Breathlessly, he brushed his hand over her thigh to reach for her hand, his hopeful eyes studying hers with adoration.

Margaret withdrew her hand as if his had been laced with poison, gasping in surprised confusion.

"You are gravely mistaken if you think that I..." she blurted out, unable to continue as the full realization of what his words portended suddenly dawned on her. "Stop the carriage!" she fairly shouted, her heart beating wildly in horror at her predicament.

"Margaret....if we could only get to know each other," he stammered frantically to explain himself. "I believe fate has brought us together," he declared, his eyes flashing with fervor.

Growing increasingly alarmed, Margaret drew back against the compartment door, her eyes wide with disbelief. "Stop this carriage at once or I shall be forced to make a scene!" she demanded with all the strength her voice could muster.

A look of pain crossed his face before he turned to halt the cab as he was bidden.

Before the wheels had come to a full stop, Margaret opened the door and leaped out of the compartment, snatching the packages that had been at her feet.

Albert raced around to offer her assistance, handing her the remaining parcels. "Please, I mean you no harm. You have captured my heart," he pleaded as she gathered her packages. "I cannot forget you," he called out to her back as she dashed across the street.

Above the pounding of her heart, she listened intently as the wheels of the cab clattered past her and began to grow fainter in the distance. As she approached the familiar gates of her home, she began to tremble uncontrollably.

She entered the dining room with her eyes on the floor in front of her, intent on fleeing to the refuge of her room.

Mrs. Thornton looked up from her sewing. "Margaret?" she called out with some concern, noticing the girl's hurried pace and pale face.

Margaret deposited her packages on the dining room table, studiously avoiding her mother-in-law's inquisitive gaze. "Would you have Jane take care of these, please?" she asked, her voice wavering slightly despite her best efforts to sound at ease.

"Yes, of course. Are you all right?" Mrs. Thornton asked, perplexed at her strange behavior.

"I think I just need to lie down," Margaret answered elusively before turning to go upstairs.

Mrs. Thornton's eyes lingered toward the stairs after the younger woman disappeared, wondering uneasily what was troubling her son's wife.

Margaret flung herself upon her bed as tears of terrified confusion and shame began to fall upon her pillow. How had this happened to her? She had begun to think of Albert as a friend. Had he had ulterior intentions all along? How had she been so blind? Now she had brought shame to herself and her husband.

John! She cried harder to consider what he would think of her, and how ignorant she had been to have caused this turmoil. She had wanted only to bring him the increased respect and admiration of the city; she had never supposed she would bring him degradation and shame! She could not bear to think that she should cause him any more pain.

Her turbulent mind poured over the past and pondered with great trepidation the outcome of the day's occurrence, but she steadfastly avoided recalling the horrible moment when she had been trapped in the small cab with a man who professed to admire her.

Hannah Thornton surreptitiously observed her daughter-in-law as the family ate their dinner. Pale and sullen, Margaret answered when spoken to but initiated no conversation herself and seldom looked up from her plate. The clinking of silverware amplified the stilted silence of their gathering.

Catching her son's eye, Mrs. Thornton could only offer him a collaborative shrug of ignorance as to what bothered his wife.

After dinner, Margaret was guiltily relieved to hear her husband announce that he needed to work in his office again this evening. She felt she could not yet face him, and hoped a reprieve would give her time to sort out her tumultuous thoughts.

Begging leave from spending time with her mother-in-law in the drawing room, she escaped to the solitude of her room, claiming a headache.

Once alone, the full torrent of her troubled thoughts poured out upon her and she sat at her desk with her head upon her arms in a fit of despair. Convinced that she was somehow in error for allowing such a thing to happen, she began to lose all hope of gaining the courage to tell her husband what had taken place. Her heart grieved at the thought that she had failed him - that she had not been able to bear the high standard of character to which he had entrusted her. She felt sick to her stomach at the notion of bringing him more trouble and sorrow.

Choking back tears that obstinately coursed down her cheeks despite her valiant efforts, she prepared for bed as if in a trance, not knowing what to do next or where she should seek solace from the torment of the constant stream of troubling images and imagined scenarios that invaded her mind.

At last, feeling she had no recourse, she climbed into her bed to find relief in unconscious sleep.

Mr. Thornton quietly opened the door to his bedchamber. The light from the lantern he held revealed an empty room. At nearly midnight, he had fully expected his wife to be sound asleep in their bed. Momentarily confused, he sought her, walking through the narrow chamber that led to her room. A lamp still burned on her desk, and he snuffed it out as he noted the sleeping form under the covers of her bed. He moved quietly to the bedside to gaze at the hapless manner in which her arms and hair lay tangled over the pillow. Her face bore no sign of distress in sleep and he studied for a moment with deep love the peaceful face of the woman he had married.

He hoped that she would wake refreshed from whatever had troubled her today. He brushed his fingers lightly along the hair by her temple and leaned over to place a gentle kiss on her cheek. She stirred slightly at his touch and then remained still.

Taking one last lingering look, he left as quietly as he had come in and returned to his room. Trying to ignore the gnawing sadness that began to descend upon him, he prepared for bed. He reasoned that she was tired and might very well need more rest these days, but he could not shake the feeling of loneliness that attended the solemn fact that echoed in his head: this would be the first night he slept alone since the day he had married.

He climbed into bed and turned away from the yawning emptiness of the space beside him, eventually falling into a fitful sleep.

The following morning, Margaret arrived late to the breakfast table. She apologized briefly with a meager smile and sat to join her husband and mother-in-law in the early morning light.

Mr. Thornton sought her gaze, but she only briefly met his eyes with a timid look. He felt his heart sink at her withdrawal. He had hoped to see a sweet renewal of her usual spirit today, and began to speculate with trepidation what could be the cause of her cheerlessness.

He gave his wife and mother cursory good-bye kisses and headed for the door, casting one last worried glance at his wife.

Lost in thought as he crossed the yard to his office, his wife's somber mood threw him into a gloom that was evident in his bearing and expression. He had barely sat down at his desk when Higgins appeared at the door. The Master lifted his chin and narrowed his eyes in curiosity to see his trusted colleague so early.

"I thought it'd be best to catch you before the day gets started," Higgins explained as a way of greeting. "You've been working past your hours, wearing yourself to the bone. Trying to make the best of a bad situation, I reckon. Is there anything else we can do to help?" he asked in earnest, his face a mixture of concern and determination.

Mr. Thornton dropped his gaze for a moment as his eyes swept the open ledgers on his desk. He felt a profound gratitude for the fidelity and hard work his hands had done these past months, occasionally working past their hours without pay to finish an order on time. The Master felt the sting of the mill's failure most acutely for the men and women who depended on him for their very livelihood.

Looking up again, he met Higgins' stare with a somber but steady gaze. "You've done all you can. I'm proud of the men. And I have you to thank for some of that," he commended his friend, hesitating before he continued. "There will not be work for you come November," he announced bluntly, with an inward sigh.

Higgins showed no sign of surprise at this news. "It'll be a sore time to be out of work, come winter," he remarked solemnly.

"I know it," the Master replied, heaving a slow breath at the thought of shuttering the mill just as the bleakest season began it merciless reign.

Higgins surveyed his friend's brooding posture and the deep-set lines of toil and care on his face. The former union leader knew that his employer had done his best to keep the mill running since the strike. Both Master and employee felt responsible in some degree for the welfare of all of the men at the mill. Higgins could not but admire the Master for his perseverance and kind heart. As he had quickly learned, Thornton could not be judged by the stern demeanor that had doggedly been part of his reputation for so long.

"My Mary tells me you're to be a family man," Higgins declared, endeavoring to gain a smile from the Master's face before he departed. "Congratulations, Thornton. There'll not be a luckier child in the country to have such parents as you and Miss Margaret," he pronounced with fond sincerity.

Mr. Thornton's face glowed with an effusive light at the mention of his forthcoming child. "Thank you. It remains a bright spot for me amidst this difficult time," he revealed candidly, gifting his friend with the smile he had sought.

Higgins nodded his understanding. "I'll leave you to your work," he remarked, before turning to go.

Mr. Thornton considered the weighty announcement he had uttered. He had not yet told Margaret his final decision, having only recently come to the inevitable calculation that led him to delineate October as the last month the mill would operate. All creditors and employees would be paid. He would retain sufficient funds to live on for a few short months, but he would need to find employment before long, and give up the house.

He could not find the impetus to tell Margaret, biding his time with long nights at the office and all-too-brief encounters with her. He half hoped that some propitious event would propel him to reveal his temporary secret, so that he would not have the distinct displeasure of creating a moment in which to deliver such unhappy news, news that he dreaded would cause sadness to linger in her soulful eyes.

Margaret kept herself as busy as possible to evade contemplating all things untoward. It was a relief to immerse herself in her work with the children for a few hours, although she occasionally looked over her shoulder in the haunting fear that Albert might stroll through the doorway.

When evening came, she kept to her room for a while as her husband worked at his desk. Eventually, she brought a book to read in their bed, comfortable in her husband's presence as long as his attention was elsewhere.

She closed her book and settled down on her pillow with a tingling anxiety when Mr. Thornton turned out the lamp and began to prepare for bed. When he stole under the covers and leaned over to kiss her, she stiffly received his affectionate gesture but professed to be tired when his attentions pressed her for more. Too ashamed and confused to openly accept his love, she shied away from his passion. She bit her lip to keep from crying, sensing his hurt as he turned away from her.

Mr. Thornton withdrew from her with a heavy heart. Inevitably saddened, he tried to fathom what had made her so unresponsive. She had never declined him before. Beginning to imagine her disappointment in the present state of affairs, he thought she must be weary of his long hours and the unfruitful portent of all his efforts. He despaired at the notion of having to crush her lively spirit with his dismal lot in life. How he had feared to bring her back to Milton - to have such a vibrant blossom wither in his grasp!

He stared in the dark for hours before finally closing his eyes to rest.

❦

Mrs. Thornton surveyed the scene before her at breakfast. She was dismayed to see her son looking haggard as he absently poked at his food. Her suspicious gaze moved to her daughter-in-law, who sat bent over her tea in silence. Margaret's behavior had been peculiar ever since she had returned from shopping two days ago. Something had happened.

Both were decidedly unhappy. She glanced at them again as a burgeoning sense of resolve began to gather in her mind.

Later that afternoon, as Margaret walked swiftly through the drawing room on her return from her teaching, her mother-in-law halted her.

"Margaret, may I have a word with you?" the elder woman called out imperatively but kindly as she put down her sewing.

The young mistress stilled, her heart drumming faster in apprehension. She walked calmly to a seat near her mother-in-law and reluctantly lifted her sorrowful eyes to hear what she would say.

"You've been unhappy. And, consequently, my son is unhappy," Mrs. Thornton announced as fact, looking steadily at her daughter-in-law. "Now, it is not my business to pry into your marriage, but I promised your mother that I would offer you womanly counsel if you needed it. As your mother-in-law, I find myself in a unique position to treat you as my own daughter," she continued, pausing to discern the girl's receptivity. "Will you not tell me what is troubling you?" she asked gently.

Margaret struggled with what she should say, uncharacteristically twisting her fingers in her lap. She desperately wanted to share her anxieties, but at the same time was afraid of the judgment that might be cast on her. She looked at her mother-in-law in momentary helplessness.

"Did something happen the day you went to the draper's shop?" Mrs. Thornton prodded, distinctly recalling the girl's ashen face and distressed behavior that afternoon.

"Yes," Margaret quickly admitted, feeling relief to have confessed that much.

Mrs. Thornton sat back in her chair in partial triumph, and waited patiently for Margaret to reveal more.

"I...was offered a cab ride home...by Albert Slickson," Margaret stammered.

Mrs. Thornton lifted her chin to steel herself for what this would imply, vaguely recalling the young gentleman from introductions at the ball. Her mind raced to imagine what had so upset her.

"He made...advances..." she began uncomfortably, staring blankly at a pattern on the carpet.

"Did he harm you?" Mrs. Thornton asked with alarm, visibly disturbed at her latest revelation.

"No...no...but he was most indiscreet in his intentions," Margaret blurted, the pent-up emotions she had tried to hide now rushing to the fore.

"You did nothing to encourage him?" Mrs. Thornton calmly inquired, fairly certain of the girl's innocence but desiring to hear her admission nonetheless.

Margaret looked at her mother-in-law with horror. "No! I did not know he...I could never...I only love John! I could never bring him any dishonor!" she exclaimed in great agitation, stinging tears coming to her eyes.

Mrs. Thornton moved to the sofa to sit next to the girl and patted her arm to comfort her.

Margaret pulled out a handkerchief from her skirts and dabbed at her eyes. "I should not have ridden with him. If only I had heeded my better judgment, I would not have caused such shame," she berated herself.

"I am certain you were not at fault for what happened," Mrs. Thornton consoled the distraught girl. "I have lived long enough to know that there are men who will act indiscriminately in pursuing what they desire, heedless of a woman's reputation or honor. Unfortunately, I have also perceived that it is a characteristic of our gender to take the blame upon ourselves for such misconduct," she wisely pointed out.

"You must tell John," the elder woman advised after a lengthy pause.

Margaret jerked her head up to face her mother-in-law, a look of pain in her eyes. "I cannot!" she protested. "I cannot bear to aggrieve him with any further trouble. He has already so much to endure," she attempted to reason.

"Surely you cannot keep such a secret from him. Has it not already stolen your happiness, and his?" she appraised.

Margaret considered her words. Indeed, she had been most miserable and it seemed she had made him so as well. She sighed aloud at her predicament. "How can I tell him?" she asked helplessly, looking to her mother-in-law for guidance.

"He is a wise judge. He is a magistrate, is he not? Tell him the truth, Margaret. He trusts you above all others," Mrs. Thornton advised.

"Will he not be angry?" Margaret asked the woman who knew best the history of his temperament. She was concerned that her husband might act rashly upon discovering what Albert had done.

Mrs. Thornton could not hide the slight upturn of her lips. "Indeed, but it will not be directed toward you. I believe you would do best to leave any consequences to John's discretion," she offered simply.

Margaret nodded, falling into a contemplative mood.

The girl's question returned to Mrs. Thornton, and she considered the severity of her son's wrath. His strong sense of morality combined with his fierce devotion to his wife would indeed ignite his fury against a man who had deigned to tamper with Margaret.

She shuddered slightly to think of it. She would not wish to be Mr. Albert Slickson.

⁂

That evening, Margaret allowed Dixon to brush her hair, gaining a sense of comfort from this childhood ritual with her mother's dearest servant. She did not always call upon Dixon, but had felt a need for her stolid presence tonight before facing her husband with the secret she held.

As soon as Dixon had bidden her mistress good night and shut the door, Margaret stood in resolve and walked the length of her room, rehearsing the words that she would use to explain everything to him.

It was not long before she heard his footsteps in the next room. He had come home from the mill at last.

Remembering the simple counsel her mother-in-law had given her, she felt a surge of courage and headed toward the connecting chamber between the two rooms. She felt impelled now to unburden herself of all that she had withheld from him, although she trembled to imagine his righteous anger.

He was hanging up his waistcoat, his shirt already loosely unbuttoned as he was wont to do when he worked late. She noted with a pang of guilt the cautious hope in his acknowledging glance at her, and hoped her confession would remove the uncomfortable silence that had unwittingly evolved between them.

"I must speak with you," she announced quietly and without ceremony as her husband turned from the wardrobe.

He stilled for a moment, tensing at the upward tilt of her chin and solemn tone. He moved nearer to where she stood and sat on the bed with the sinking fear that she would at last voice her unhappiness.

She turned away from the saddened look in his pure blue eyes and took a few paces to begin her practiced speech. "On Monday, I went shopping and began to walk home with quite a few packages. I thought I could manage them well enough, but I was offered a cab on my way. I accepted the ride, thinking I should not weary myself in my present condition," she started, glancing at him to see his brow crinkle in confusion at her unfolding story.

"It was Mr. Slickson..." she began to elaborate, her pulse hammering.

"Slickson?" he repeated, standing bolt upright in agitation. "Albert Slickson?" he thundered, his expression dark with the maelstrom of suspicion the name invoked.

"He offered you a ride in his cab?" he asked, his voice tightening in rising alarm as his mind began to conjure disturbing images of his wife in close confinement with that man.

"Yes," she breathed, her throat constricting as she witnessed the unleashing of her husband's fury.

"Did he touch you?" he asked frantically, his chest heaving with the terrifying notion that Albert had preyed upon her somehow. He instantly berated himself for his failure to protect her from such unwanted attention.

"No!...well, yes....he reached for my hand," she stammered, flustered by the intensity of his inquiries. Her eyes cast about nervously, unable to meet his piercing gaze.

His blood boiled with indignation at the thought that such a gesture had been made toward his wife. How dare that man attempt to claim his wife's affection!

A burning need to know exactly what had transpired gripped him, driving him half wild with impatience. He grasped her firmly by the arms and made her look at him. "What did he say to you?" he demanded, his eyes boring into hers.

She startled at his panicked tone, shivering at his grasp as she tried to remember the words she had endeavored to erase from her mind. "He spoke of being lonely..." she haltingly recalled, her face revealing the distress it caused her to recount the event. She saw his brow furrow at her vague response, and she redoubled her efforts, scouring her memory for the exact phrase he had uttered. "He suggested that we assuage each other's loneliness," she answered at last, feeling the shame and embarrassment his proposal had engendered all over again. She dropped her gaze from her husband's, afraid of what he might think. "I fled from him as soon as I could," she added.

He loosened his hold of her, letting his arms drop in stunned silence as the full import of the words slowly etched into his consciousness. His stomach sickened and his outrage grew at the audacity of the young man - he would have Margaret entangle herself in a romantic liaison with him!

Recognizing at once the depths of the conniving scoundrel's attraction to his wife, Mr. Thornton suddenly paled. "If you had been harmed...." he uttered in horror at the thought of what Mr. Slickson might have done had Margaret not escaped from his presence.

"No, he would not..." Margaret began.

"You would defend him?" he exploded in consternation at her

deference for someone so vile.

"No...I..." she could not answer. Frightened that he should raise his voice to her, she began to tremble in her confusion and shame, wondering still what he must think of her. Her composure crumbled as the myriad emotions she had withheld from him now came tumbling out. "I'm sorry, John. I could not bear to bring you any dishonor. I love you...only you!" she cried as she rushed into his arms, sobbing in her distress over everything that had happened.

His manner softened at once, and he held her as he would some precious object, rare and beautiful, unlike any other thing in the world. How monstrous he had been! He had been harsh and overbearing when she most needed his assurance and understanding.

"You could not dishonor me," he said softly, pressing his face into her hair and breathing the very fragrance of her. "You have done nothing wrong," he assured her, feeling a shiver trace his spine as she held him closer at his words. "All will be well," he blindly promised, not yet knowing what he would do. He only knew that at present, he should gently tend to the woman in his arms.

Mr. Thornton simmered within, though, at the thought of the man who had caused his wife such turmoil. He would deal with Mr. Slickson soon enough.

Chapter Nineteen

The sidewalks of Milton bustled with everyday activity. Just past the mill, vendors and shoppers clogged the streets, and the approaching heat of the noon hour rendered the smells of the marketplace more pungent. Towards the city's more fashionable districts, servants silently slipped past ladies in wide skirts and bonnets to accomplish their errands, while gentleman in top hats walked in tandem discussing business and politics.

Mr. Thornton strode past them all, his unseeing gaze fixed before him. Oblivious to the curious glances of those who stepped aside in the wake of his unrelenting pace, Mr. Thornton continued to brood, his brow creased and his jaw firmly set. His commanding stature and steadfast purpose garnered the attention of all who recognized the stern features of the Master of Marlborough Mills.

Bounding up the polished granite stairs of a fine townhouse, Mr. Thornton rapped briskly on the door of the Slickson residence. He was impatient to confront the audacious young dandy who would attempt to assault his wife.

A slight girl in her domestic cap and apron answered the door.

Mr. Thornton relayed his name and request, sending the maid swiftly back into the house. "I'm afraid Mr. Slickson is not able to come," she stuttered upon her return, the uneasy shifting of her eyes telling the imposing visitor otherwise.

"If he is man enough, he will come to the door," Mr. Thornton enunciated in a booming voice, his piercing eyes dismissing any excuses.

"I am here," a steady voice answered from within. The terrified maid hastily retreated, relieved from taking any further part in the unfolding hostility. In the next moment, Albert Slickson stepped forward to the doorway, jutting his chin upward in brave defiance.

Mr. Thornton's eyes narrowed as he regarded the London student with disgust. "You would dare disrupt the harmony of my home with your vile attentions," he fairly spat, the anger he had held for so long now spilling out.

"I'm certain I do not know to what you allude," Albert responded elusively, looking at the Master with proud disdain.

Mr. Thornton grasped Slickson violently by the shirt and forced him to meet his own ferocious glare. "You know very well of what I speak!" he hissed, livid that the dastardly boy would deny his guilt and cast him as a jealous fool.

"I will caution you to stay away from my wife," he continued as he released his firm hold, his face dark with barely controlled rage at such provocation. He unconsciously clenched his hands.

Albert smoothed his ruffled shirt to regain his dignity and hardened his gaze. "And might I suggest that you spend less time at the mill. If you are unwilling to tend to your lovely wife, then someone else will," he smugly advised with a discernible smirk.

Mr. Thornton's eyes flared. Swinging his fist back with astounding agility, he struck the young man's face with a stinging smack, sending him to the floor.

"May I suggest, Mr. Slickson," he began, his chest heaving with seething fury, "that you remove yourself from Milton? I wish never to see your face again. Do I make myself clear?" he demanded through his teeth, his growling voice a threat.

Mr. Slickson answered not a word as he attempted to right himself, holding his injured face with his hand.

With one last penetrating glare, Mr. Thornton spun around to descend the stairs. His hand throbbed as he pounded the sidewalk with vigorous steps. A sense of satisfaction rippled through him, giving his body palpable release from the tension he had held. But close upon the heels of this euphoria came the taunting words of the young rogue he had just abandoned.

Had he been negligent in caring for his wife, he wondered? Irritated that the inflammatory remark had stung him as intended, he endeavored to shake it from his mind. But as his long strides bore him through the city, the invasive suggestion of her loneliness crept into his thoughts. Had he been so busy with the mill's pressing concerns that he had overlooked her needs? She had been attentive and understanding these many weeks. She seemed content enough, but was it not a woman's practiced habit to cheerfully tend to others? It pained him to think she might carry a burden of loneliness or sorrow that was kept hidden for his benefit.

The notion that she had slowly become discontented with their marriage haunted him. Did she feel isolated in the large, austere home of which she was now mistress? He knew that his mother offered little in the way of warm company, and his long hours at work had given him but modest hours to truly tend to her. As much as he would like to spend more of his time in her presence, he could not offer her the comfort and attention that a gentleman of leisure might. Surely she had not foreseen her marriage would entail being left alone night after night to amuse herself while her husband toiled in vain to make a comfortable living.

Immersed in his musings, he heard his name called out in earnest.

"Mr. Thornton!"

He turned to find that Mr. Holsworth called out as he approached him from the bank's columned facade.

Mr. Thornton recognized the banker as one of Mr. Dallimore's assistants, the gentleman who had escorted his employer's daughter at the ball. He tipped his hat in polite acknowledgement as he slowed to stand and await him.

"Have you heard the good news?" the banker asked with an affable smile, his face ruddy with the excitement.

Mr. Thornton tilted his head in curiosity, his expression conveying a cautious anticipation.

"The speculation your brother-in-law touted has proved a resounding success! After all these unfortunate affairs of late, this should lift the dour faces of a good many businessmen," he announced with acclaim, oblivious of Mr. Thornton's standing on the matter.

"I'm certain it will," the Master answered politely with no observable change in demeanor. "Good day, then," Mr. Thornton bade the man farewell with a twitch of a smile and a tip of his hat before he resumed his way to the mill.

His heart sank at the implication of the speculation's success. Watson and the other mill owners who had invested in the scheme would now be in a strong financial position to wait out the disastrous downturn of the market. He felt the last vestige of his hope drain away. Marlborough Mills would be considered a risk; all new business would be given to other mills.

Unconsciously, he slowed his pace as he rounded the last corner. His eyes took in the sight of the buildings in which he had lived and worked these many years - a manifestation of his strong belief that with self-discipline and hard work, a man could rise above the fate meted out to him by birth or circumstance. He had striven to give his mother and sister a decent home and an honorable position in society, and had been successful for a time.

Hearing the distant noise of machinery within his mill, he thought of the families that would in all probability go hungry this winter. Now that he knew them as fellow men and not as mere nameless hands, he felt his helplessness more keenly. He had found great satisfaction in working to improve their lives in a way that benefited his enterprise. Such experiments would now be at an end. The other Masters only sought to make themselves more profitable, heedless of any effect on the humanity that toiled within their mills.

He looked at the home of solid stone that housed his bride. How he had longed to have her in it - to share with her the wealth and stature he had spent years attaining! She would not have been in it a year before it was wrested from his grasp. Soon, he would have little to offer her except his name. His heart ached to know if she could be happy still with such a humble standing.

⟨◈⟩

As the afternoon wore on, Margaret quietly stitched the lace edging on the layette for her baby. She stole glances across the room to observe her mother-in-law's fingers deftly working at the intricate embroidery she crafted on the small christening gown.

The young Mrs. Thornton had searched for her husband at lunchtime, to no avail. A clerk who had seen her attempt to enter the mill informed her that the Master had left earlier in the day to tend to important matters.

She had known instantly what he was about, and had felt her body tense in trepidation at the notion of her husband's mission. She had kept silent about it this morning, although she had been sorely tempted to plead with her husband to incur no violence on her behalf. She prayed he would not act rashly, and had given him a plaintive look upon receiving his good-bye kiss, which she hoped would remind him to guard his temper.

When she found herself drowsily closing her eyes, Margaret put her sewing aside and excused herself to take a nap. The elder Mrs. Thornton gave her an understanding nod as the corners of her mouth turned up in a small smile.

Once upstairs, Margaret chose to enter the larger bedroom and, slipping off her shoes, climbed onto the bed to take her rest in the spot her husband usually occupied. Nestling her head in the soft pillow, she breathed in the essence of him that lingered there. Closing her eyes, she took a deep breath to fill her senses with his imagined presence, and felt his love envelope her. She quickly fell into a peaceful sleep.

⟨◈⟩

Making the rounds of the mill, Mr. Thornton took careful note of the men and women bent over the large machines. He felt his sense of helplessness deepen as he realized he would soon no longer be able to pay them for their work. Catching Higgins' eye, he gave a quick nod of acknowledgement before heading to the privacy of his office.

Restless and deflated, the Master removed his heavy frock coat and sat in his chair for some time, mulling over the day's events. He breathed a sigh of weary resignation. Could the day be any worse? He had had enough of trouble and gloom, he thought as he opened the ledger before him and tried to make sense of the figures scripted in his own hand.

He soon realized it would do no good to sit and stare at accounts. He had no appetite for work, and yearned for a reprieve from his discouragement.

Taking up his coat, he headed for the house. More than anything else, he longed to see Margaret.

However, upon entering his home he learned that his wife was taking a nap. Thwarted from his original purpose, Mr. Thornton spoke quietly with his mother in the drawing room. "Watson's scheme has proven successful," he announced impassively, though his face was long and drawn.

Mrs. Thornton discerned her son's despondency but could offer no appropriate response. Solicitous of his mood, she waited patiently for what he would communicate to her.

"We must close the mill by November. We cannot last the winter," he stated as he stared straight ahead, feeling the weight of his every word.

At this moment, Fanny entered the room to proudly convey the news of her husband's new wealth. "Have you heard then?" she queried with a gleam of reproach as she noted her brother's defeated posture. "Now you must admit that you were sorely mistaken to reject Watson's investments. You would have saved your precious mill," she gloated.

Mr. Thornton could not find the words to speak.

Exasperated at her brother's silence, she hurled a biting invective. "You're fortunate to have married Margaret so quickly. I'm sure she would not have you now," she smugly decried before sweeping out of the room.

As effective as a knife, her words stabbed at his heart, bleeding him of his pride and aggravating every unsettling thought. He instinctively revolted against his sister's harsh judgment. What did Fanny know of their love, he wondered bitterly? But the venomous remark crept insidiously through his thoughts like a poison, deadening his self-confidence and infusing a numbing sense of guilt and doubt. Had he selfishly claimed her for himself without consideration for her best interests? Had he dragged her back to this grimy, crowded city only to be joined to him when he fell from his position of wealth and prestige?

Mrs. Thornton reeled at the viciousness of her daughter's verbal attack. Ashamed and confounded that Fanny would glory in John's adversity, she studied her son to discern how deeply he had been afflicted. She knew it was not the mill of which he thought, but Margaret. She did not know how the girl would take such dire news, but from what she had witnessed of Margaret's devotion to John, she doubted Fanny's presumptuous assessment could be true. Surely Margaret would not be so fickle as to withdraw her affection because of his lack of fortune.

She watched uncomfortably as he stirred from his trance-like stare. Glancing askance at his mother, he attempted a meager smile. "You won't much grieve over our leaving this house, shall you, mother?" he muttered in defeat.

Looking at her son with the compassion borne of years of shared struggle, she leaned forward to catch his distant gaze. "No, but it will break my heart to see you lose all that you have sorely earned," she admitted honestly, her voice wavering in emotion.

A flicker of a smile crossed his face and then swiftly disappeared. Broken and defeated, his mood remained solemn. He stood up slowly from his chair, not knowing quite what to do. "I will see if Margaret has awoken," he decided in a quiet voice before heading upstairs.

He longed to see her face, to gaze upon something transcendent that would lift him from the weariness and turbulence of the present. She could brighten any day, no matter how dismal, by her incandescent smile and tender looks. Although he ached for the comfort only she could give, his footsteps fell heavily with dread as he climbed the stairs. The moment of truth he had sought had arrived - he could no longer avoid telling her that the mill must certainly close.

When he opened the door to his room, he was pleasantly surprised to find Margaret propped up on the bed, sitting as if she had just awoken. With several loose tendrils of hair undone from her nap, she wore a look of groggy contentment. The vision of her innocent beauty left him mute with admiring wonder. A smile irresistibly formed on his face as she scrambled off the bed and padded to him in her stocking feet.

"You are home early," she noted happily as she ran her hands affectionately up his chest. Gazing up into his face, she discerned the sadness in his eyes. "What is it, John?" she implored with great concern, her eyes now filled with worry.

"Margaret," he whispered in relief to be with her at last. Taking her into his arms, he gloried for a moment in the sublime feeling of holding her close. The weight of his cares lifted as he breathed in her scent, clinging to her as a man desperate to keep within his grasp his most prized possession.

He loosened his hold, rebuking himself once more for his selfishness. "You would have been more comfortably situated if you had married a gentleman," he uttered in a toneless voice, the words wracking his soul even as they were wrung from his lips.

She drew back from him instantly to search his face, and brought her hand up to caress the cheek of his drooping head. "Do I not have every comfort here? What makes you speak such nonsense, John," she gently chided. She saw hope flicker in his eyes as he brought his gaze to hers.

Unable to dismiss his melancholy so easily, his face clouded with self-condemnation. "I should have told you the mill was failing before we married," he confessed, his brow creased at the thought of his perceived indiscretion.

"I knew you were facing troubles. Father spoke of it before he died," she relayed, noting the faint look of surprise on his face. "Surely you know that I care little about society and wealth. I have married the finest man in Milton; that is all I care about. I should not have been happy marrying anyone else. Who else can tolerate my stubbornness and impetuous behavior?" she teased him as she slid her hands around his neck.

"I have brought you hardship, when I had wished to protect you from any more suffering," he continued, endeavoring to explain his feelings of failure and unworthiness.

"I feel no hardship. Do you not come home to me every evening? Have I lacked for anything? I am happy, John. What has troubled you so?" she inquired again, curious to know why his dark mood seemed so impenetrable. She let her hands fall slack from him as she stepped back to hear his answer.

"Watson's speculation has been successful," he revealed, letting his breath out slowly.

"I'm sure Fanny will be pleased. You are not regretting your decision, are you?" she asked pointedly, wondering still what touched him so sorely.

"No. Had it failed I would not have been able to forgive myself," he answered honestly.

"Then...what?" she prodded.

He could not look into her eyes to tell her. Turning from her, he took several paces to his desk where the memory of all of his recent efforts returned to him in full force.

From this distance, he brought his gaze reluctantly to hers at last. "The other mill owners joined the speculation. They will now be in a superior position to wait out this cycle and take whatever new orders may come," he explained bitterly. "Marlborough Mills must close. We will shut our doors in three months' time."

Margaret was stunned by the finality of his announcement. Instinctively rebelling against such grave news, she opened her mouth to speak, but held her tongue to prevent her husband the further torment of reiterated conclusions. Although it came to her mind, she knew it would not do to speak of the workers' plight at this time. She only wished to assuage her husband's pain, which was discernible in his defeated posture.

"John," she exclaimed as she rushed to him in sympathy and twined her arms around his waist, laying her head on his chest.

He folded his arms around her mechanically, unwilling to allow himself release from his tension until he had told her the stark implications of the mill's closing. "We will be forced to give up the house and move elsewhere," he told her, bitterly discouraged to have failed in providing her the basic security of maintaining their current home.

She moved to look into his sorrowing eyes. "I will not mind moving to more modest quarters. You will rise to greatness once more, I am sure of it, John. I am proud to be your wife, no matter the circumstances. Will you not put aside your worries about me? I am content as long as we are together," she confided, her eyes shining in earnestness. "I could not live without you," she declared, hugging him tight.

A flood of feeling washed over him as he clasped her close, holding her to him as if he would never let go. "Margaret! I should perish without you. How is it that I have found such a love as this?" he exclaimed in incredulous wonder.

"We were brought together, John. Providence has decreed that we belong to each other," she uttered, her faith in God's plan apparent as she held him fast to her.

"We are bound as one," he murmured near her ear, his velvet tones sending a shiver through her body.

"Yes," she whispered breathlessly, wishing only that it could truly be so - that she could stay within his embrace forever. She raised her mouth to receive his kiss.

The years he had struggled alone, the months he had longed for her and the toil of the recent weeks all seemed to lead to this moment when he could taste her lips and know that her soul was his forever. He would never doubt it again.

Their kisses quickly deepened. He pressed her to him strongly and she cleaved to him with equal vigor, desperate to prove her fervent devotion.

Margaret moved her hands to find his cravat and tugged at the silk fabric to unbind his cravat, and swiftly worked to free the buttons of his shirt.

Mr. Thornton quaked. Hot desire coursed through him at the thought of her intent and he answered her gesture with his own urgency, sending his hands up the length of her back to unbutton her dress.

In escalating frenzy, their lips and hands parted reluctantly from one another only long enough to hasten their undressing as they moved toward the bed. Free of all constrictions, they consummated their marriage again with a fevered passion, feeling the depth of their love with every nuanced move and ecstatic touch.

Afterward, they lay closely intertwined in each other's arms, reveling in the simple bliss of being together. Mr. Thornton felt a refuge from the world in the tangled hold of her embrace, and ran his fingers gently over the silken skin of her shoulder in reverent fascination. She would stand with him through every difficulty and love him still, he thought with fervent wonder. Together, they would face every adversity, knowing that their affections would not be changed. He had announced the demise of his present livelihood and offered her no certain position of status or prosperity and yet she clung to him as if she were naught without him. He could not ask for anything more in life. All that he had ever wanted was here in his embrace.

After a time, the dim noise from the mill reminded Mr. Thornton that the workday was not yet finished. "I must return to work for a time, but I will come for dinner and spend the evening with you," he promised. "You have dealt long enough with my absence. Will you mind if I seek to be with you tonight instead of spending time with my desk?" he asked her with a lopsided grin.

She smiled in return. "I have grown accustomed to my solitary evenings, but I will try to accommodate you," she teased, leaning in for one more kiss before he departed.

Reluctantly, he climbed out of the bed and retrieved his clothes from the floor. He tossed to his wife her garments that had been strewn with his, flashing her a devious smile at the memory of what had just taken place.

She smiled knowingly in return and bashfully withdrew her gaze for a moment. She made no move to get out of the bed, but brought her eyes back up to surreptitiously observe her husband as he dressed unhurriedly. Something deep within her stirred as she watched him slide his clothes over the muscled form of his body, until, piece by piece, he was no longer the amorous lover who had shared her bed, but was once again the imposing Master of Marlborough Mills.

Already near the door, he turned to say his good-bye. "Thank you," he uttered with deepest sincerity.

"For what?" she asked curiously, a faint smile coming to her lips.

"For loving me," he answered humbly and honestly, his low voice just above a whisper.

Her face at once diffused with warm affection. "I could not do otherwise," she returned in kind, her eyes shining with adoration.

He took swift strides back to the bedside and stretched himself out to reach her. Their lips met in a gentle refrain, rekindling in each the deeper emotions wrought by their intimate union.

He stood to go once more. "I will take care of you," he promised, feeling a swell of pride in the great privilege of being her husband. He would never falter in his responsibility to ensure her well-being, no matter the circumstances.

"I know," she gently responded with a sweet smile.

He could only stare at her in wonder for a moment as the corners of his mouth edged upwards in an irrepressible smile. Finally, he moved to leave. "I will see you later," he acknowledged before disappearing through the doorway and closing the door.

The conversation at dinner that evening was light. Hedging around the subject of the mill and Watson's speculation, Margaret remarked on the lack of rain this summer and the effect it might have on the southern crops while Mrs. Thornton mentioned an encounter in the streets with an old acquaintance of Mr. Thornton's as she had made her way to visit an invalid.

Although there was silence between the interjected talk, Mrs. Thornton was pleasantly surprised to detect no uneasy tension or gloom in her son's manner. Rather, a peaceful calm pervaded the atmosphere of the house. Catching the exchange of a tender glance between her son and his wife, Mrs. Thornton felt a triumphant smile slowly spread over her face. How wrong Fanny had been! She had no understanding of the kind of marriage John had entered into.

A twinge of guilt swept through her consciousness as she recalled the grave misgivings she had had concerning John's choice of a wife. Margaret was unconventional and strong willed, but there was no denying her devotion to John. Although she still felt a tug of reluctance to admit it, John had chosen well. That he could sit here and seem so content when his business stood in the shadow of certain failure was a testament to the happiness he found in his marriage. Certainly, he must have told her of the impending closure of the mill. How graciously she must have borne the news for her husband to be in such happy spirits!

Breaking the silence again, Mr. Thornton related that next week London would begin to move the Crystal Palace to Sydenham Hill. At last a discussion had been found which kept the small gathering animated for the remainder of the meal.

After dinner, the couple politely kept company with Mrs. Thornton in the drawing room for a time before excusing themselves to the privacy of their own room.

After changing into their nightclothes, Margaret made preparations to read to her husband, but he gently took the book from her hands and insisted on reading to her first.

Margaret willingly agreed and arranged her pillows so that she might snuggle up against her husband as he began to read the book she had recently borrowed from the library - *Nicholas Nickleby*.

Mr. Thornton was pleased to relax when Margaret announced that it was her turn to read, and situated himself comfortably with his head on her lap.

Margaret became engrossed in the story, alternately rubbing his shoulders and combing her fingers through his hair as she read. He was halfway asleep when she finally stopped and placed the book on the bedside table.

"I have been thinking..." she began auspiciously, fondly waiting for her well-rested husband to stir from his languor before she continued discussing her subject in earnest. "Perhaps Mr. Bell might be interested in investing in the mill. It would give us the needed capital to keep things running. I'm sure he would prefer to see the mill continue to operate under your management rather than to see his property abandoned with uncertain prospects," she carefully proposed, having deliberated for hours as to how she might present this idea to her husband.

Fully alert now, Mr. Thornton studied her as he lay on his pillow. He smiled ruefully at her suggestion. "I believe Mr. Bell's wealth is largely comprised of his holdings of certain properties. I'm not certain he would wish to tie up what capital he has in a loan," he answered doubtfully, although a glimmer of hope enlivened his eyes as he considered the possibility. He had not wished to resort to Mr. Bell for any aid in reviving his business, and had shut the door on that prospect some time ago. Listening to his wife's logical plea, however, he began to wonder if now might not be the time to put aside his willful pride and think of this option seriously.

"I know you wish to prevent the workers' families from starving this winter. Certainly there could be no harm in asking him," she offered meekly as she settled down near to him, propping her head with her elbow rested on a pillow.

"I suppose not," he agreed with a warming smile at her persistence.

"Oh, I knew you would be reasonable!" she exclaimed excitedly, reaching over impulsively to wrap her arms around his neck.

Mr. Thornton swept her into his arms, pulling her against him so that her body covered his. "Are you saying that I have been unreasonable?" he queried tauntingly, a mischievous sparkle in his eye. He smiled brilliantly up at her, reveling in the seductive position in which he had placed her and enjoying the view it afforded him as he peered at the décolletage of her nightgown.

She flashed an equally brilliant smile at his words, remembering his defensive accusation that morning a year ago when she had so foolishly rejected him. "You are the most reasonable man I know," she admitted, "except when your stubborn pride goads you," she added with an impish grin.

He raised his eyebrows at her bold assessment. "*My* stubborn pride? And are you innocent of any such impulse?" he taunted with a twinge of warning in his voice, a devilish smile spreading over his face in expectation of her answer.

"I will readily admit that my southern pride blinded me from seeing who you really were. It took me far too long to realize that the most extraordinary man I had ever met happened to be a cotton manufacturer in Milton," she confided, looking into his eyes with blatant adoration.

Mr. Thornton rolled over to pin her beneath him, his eyes smoldering at her confession.

"I am still stubbornly prideful," she continued resolutely as she felt herself blissfully melt under the power and strength of his weight.

He gave her a quizzical look.

"I am shamelessly proud to bear your name," she added softly.

"Mrs. John Thornton," he murmured, and the utterance of her name increased his desire to demonstrate that she indeed belonged to him.

She nodded her assent, breathlessly submitting herself to the man who dominated her thoughts, reigned in her heart, and commanded her body into compliant response with his every touch. His lips quivered slightly as he stared at her before lowering his mouth to capture hers in an ardent kiss.

Mr. Thornton woke the next morning as if in a new world. For the first time in weeks, he felt at peace. The heavy weight of anxiety had lifted as if it had all been a bad dream.

He studied his wife as she lay in gentle repose, taking in the soft skin of her cheeks, the delicate closed eyelids, the gentle curve of her nose, and the ever-beguiling fullness of her lips. His love for her swelled in his breast, and he knew it was she who had wrought this change in him.

He felt confident now, as he never had been, that she loved him unequivocally. Although it was far from certain whether the mill might be saved, he felt his future was secure. With a renewed sense of purpose, he looked ahead with eager hope.

He moved gently to extract his arm from her sleeping grasp, but she stirred at his motion and rolled nearer to him. He watched as her eyelids fluttered open and she gazed at him.

Wordlessly, she lazily snuggled up against him and settled her face at his throat as she brought her arms and limbs over to nestle alongside of him. The scent of her and the feel of her velvet skin against his body ensnared his senses, and he quickly resolved to remain in bed in order to love her thoroughly.

Mr. Thornton smiled to himself later as he buttoned his crisp cotton shirt, thinking of his wife dressing in the other room. The extra time they had spent in bed only enhanced the exalting feeling of rejuvenation that had overtaken him this morning. He felt ready to tackle every task today with vigor and purpose. He was the most blessed of men: with Margaret as his wife, he had everything in life to enjoy.

Sometime mid-morning, Mr. Thornton made his way to the weaving shed to find Higgins. The Master relied more and more on his friend to provide the information he sought regarding the men's progress and problems. Upon finding him, the Master debated affably with Higgins for a time on the feasibility of finishing an order ahead of schedule. Convinced at length of the answer, the Master thanked his employee for his time and returned to his office.

Higgins observed his friend thoughtfully for a moment as the commanding figure strode back through the working machinery. He was glad to detect a lighter tone in Thornton's manner - the Master had been in a somber mood for far too long.

Not an hour had passed when Higgins looked up from his work to spy a stranger in a gentleman's frock coat and top hat forging his way through the great weaving shed. Dropping his task, Higgins followed the young man, unnerved by the intruder's dark expression.

Floating wisps of cotton in the air dipped and swirled in the wake of the black figure ahead of him. Picking up his pace to trail the man, Higgins' suspicions intensified as the unknown visitor continued unabated towards the carding room and passageway beyond.

The stranger stopped upon reaching the Master's office and reached out and opened the door as Higgins quickly closed the distance between them.

Higgins watched in horror as a revolver suddenly appeared from the man's coat and was carefully pointed with determination.

Time was counted by furious heartbeats as Higgins raged forward, a roaring cry rising from his throat. A cracking shot rang out as he hurled himself onto the attacker. His senses jolted at the exploding sound and his blood froze in terror.

The stranger let out his own startled cry as both assailant and protector fell to the floor with a resounding thud.

Chapter Twenty

An acrid smell filled Higgins' nostrils; he could taste it in his mouth. Ignoring the throbbing pain in his elbow, he scrambled to pin the attacker down with violent thrusts, his teeth clenched in vicious anger.

"What the hell do you think you're doing?" he growled. As he finally met the culprit's eye, he glimpsed the blackened bruise on the scoundrel's cheek.

Higgins did not listen to the man's crazed rants about Thornton or his demands to be released, but instantly turned to shout at the workers who arrived to gape at the scene. "Wilson! McConnell! Hold this bastard. Parker, fetch the police! Quick!" he bellowed, his ears still ringing from the deafening gunshot.

As soon as his coworkers were able to restrain the raving madman, Higgins bolted into the Master's office where a blue-gray cloud of smoke roiled sinisterly at the entryway. He felt his heart thumping, and terrifying images sprang to his mind as he stepped through the blinding smoke.

"Thornton!" he called out hopefully, his eyes wide in desperation.

The Master was at his desk. He brought his head up slowly at Higgins' exclamation, his eyes glazed over with shock. "I'm all right," he uttered tonelessly, his brow knit slightly in dazed confusion.

"My God, you've been hit!" Higgins blurted, rushing to the Master's side at the sight of a crimson stain spreading onto the white cotton. After furtively inspecting the wound on Thornton's arm, he turned his head to bark out orders to the gawking workers gathered at the doorway with bulging eyes. "Get me some cotton! Fetch a doctor! Quickly!"

Higgins carefully guided the Master to the floor and against the wall, where he began to tend to his friend. He ripped the torn cotton sleeve to expose the injury. "Damned if it's not a bleeder," he cursed as he snatched the cotton cloth handed him and pressed it to stem the flow of blood.

"Jonas, get the mistress. She's at the schoolroom," he ordered a young carder, who blinked in alarm at the thought of his unenviable task.

"Hurry!" Higgins scolded as he diligently wrapped the Master's arm with the material from the looms.

"Margaret must not be alarmed," Thornton spoke out from his trance, a look of concern crossing his face. He did not want to cause her distress in her condition.

"I don't think we'd be able to restrain her," Nicholas answered this nonsensical request. "Who was that bastard?" he bluntly asked.

"Slickson's nephew," Mr. Thornton said between shallow breaths. "He had eyes for Margaret," he offered as a brief explanation, his voice tensing now as a burning pain began to rage in his arm. He scowled at the sensation and leaned back, closing his eyes.

"Then he's a fool and an idiot," Higgins sputtered vehemently. "I've never seen anyone more in love than you and Miss Margaret. Anyone with eyes could see it. He's either a blind fool or raving lunatic," he declared as he finished winding the piece of fabric around the wound. "Looks like the bleeding's stopped," he announced with relief as he looked over his work.

The Master only nodded vaguely in response, as his senses began to spin and the sounds around him began to fade.

⸙

Margaret heard the racing footsteps of the messenger before he appeared in the doorway.

"Ma'am, it's the Master. He's been hurt," the young man relayed breathlessly before taking a gulp of air.

Margaret's heart stilled. She paled at what his coming must imply - John had somehow been injured.

She glanced dazedly at her students. "School is dismissed," she managed to say before hastily stepping out the door to follow the anxious messenger.

Horrifying images flashed through her mind as she lifted her skirts to rush across the dusty yard. Her legs trembled unsteadily as she entered the weaving shed, uncertain of what she should discover therein.

As she blindly followed the figure ahead of her, the clanking of the machines was muted by the clamor of her heart. *What had happened? Where was he?* She endeavored to steel herself for whatever she would find, vaguely aware that all eyes were trained on her.

Her pulse raced and her tension grew as they neared the Master's office. A lingering smell of putrid smoke met her nose and she wrinkled her brow in bewilderment. She startled at the sudden outburst of her name, and her frightened eyes flew to a huddle of men further down the hallway.

"Margaret! I did it to save you!" a familiar voice shouted.

She gasped and shuddered as she recognized Albert Slickson as he hollered and writhed to escape the grip of the men who held him. "Unhand me! Margaret, I must speak with you!" He wildly beckoned to her.

Overcome with horror at the notion of what he might have done, Margaret felt a surge of panic as she was finally ushered into John's office.

Her eyes desperately swept the room before falling upon the figure of her husband as he lay next to a ministering Nicholas on the floor.

"John!" she cried out, shaking with terror as she glimpsed his blood-stained clothes. Casting aside all propriety, she fell on her knees and took his face between her hands. *He was alive!* "John...oh John!" she moaned as she drank in the sight of him. Her relief was visceral as she watched him gaze upon her before he closed his eyes and his head fell limp into her hands.

"John!" she called out to him as fear rose up from her belly, causing her nerves to tingle and impelling her to act.

"He took a hit to the arm...lost a bit of blood. He'll come around," Nicholas hastily reassured her as she pulled the weight of her husband against her, cradling his head to her bosom.

"John, I am here," she said in a soothing voice, determined to bring him back to consciousness with her affection and care. "John, I am here," she repeated, gently caressing his face with her hands. She was aware of nothing else around her; her only focus was on the man lying so lifelessly in her arms. How could this possibly be, she thought in a frantic flash; only hours ago, he was so strong and full of life as he made love to her?

Mr. Thornton heard a voice calling to him. At first, it was faint and far away, but with time it grew stronger and more clear. *Margaret!* A comforting balm washed over him. He felt bathed in love, recognizing her gentle touch and the softness of her form. As he yearned to see her, he felt his strength slowly return.

Margaret sensed his slight movement and watched as he opened his eyes. "John!" she exclaimed in tremendous relief, bending over to plant fevered kisses on whatever portions of his face she could reach.

He smiled weakly despite the burning pain; the rain of affection she bestowed on him lifted him momentarily to a higher plane.

"Doctor!" Higgins announced in glad greeting as Dr. Donaldson walked through the doorway.

❧

Hannah Thornton looked up from her needlework as a strange sense of foreboding swept over her. She put her sewing aside and walked to the window overlooking the mill yard, but there was no indication that anything was amiss.

She stared for a long moment, wondering what her uneasiness could portend. She was about to turn away when she glimpsed several figures emerging from the mill. She saw her son coming slowly toward the house, supported by Higgins and Williams on either side, Margaret and Dr. Donaldson trailing behind.

Fear coursed through her. Although her son was prudent, she had always feared that his daily contact with such heavy machinery might someday run afoul.

She stood still a moment to gather her courage before heading toward the door.

As he and his companions entered the house, she found little comfort in her son's assurances that he was fine, and listened with increasing horror as Higgins and Margaret alternately explained what had happened.

The men assisted Mr. Thornton upstairs to his room and then politely took their leave of the Master's house as Margaret and the doctor helped the injured man into his bed.

Dr. Donaldson set about to examine the injury once more. Mr. Thornton sucked in air through his teeth as the doctor gently probed the bandage. "I can give you a bit of morphine to dull the pain," Dr. Donaldson offered his grimacing patient.

"I can manage," the weakened man replied stoically. He watched with dread as the doctor pulled out a flask of whiskey from his black bag. Mr. Thornton grasped his wife's offered hand and held his breath as the physician prepared to clean the wound. His stomach clenched and a guttural cry escaped his throat as the cold liquid made contact with his skin, searing his arm with stinging pain.

When he was through tending the injury, the seasoned doctor told his patient and the two women gathered in the room that the wound should heal well, leaving only a scar. "You are very fortunate in that the bullet only grazed you. The wound is deep, but with a few days' rest, you should be able to return to your daily routine," the doctor pronounced. "But you will need to take extra precautions that you do not aggravate your arm for the first week or so," he expounded, giving the attending women a pointed look. The doctor knew that Mr. Thornton would not easily take to being confined in his activities.

"Thank you, doctor," Margaret gratefully exclaimed as she saw him to the bedroom door.

"I entrust you to his care, Mrs. Thornton," Dr. Donaldson spoke to the young wife in a lowered voice. "He must rest that arm. If the pain does not abate, call me back. Perhaps then he will take some morphine."

Margaret nodded and shut the door behind her mother-in-law and the departing physician, before returning to the bed to sit gently by her husband. Never had he seemed so precious to her. She could not resist running her hand along the side of his face, cherishing every subtle contour and the rough feel of his jaw. "What can I do for you?" she inquired tenderly, desiring to make him as comfortable as possible.

"Water?" he asked simply. His throat and mouth were parched.

When she dutifully returned with some water, she sat by him and watched him slake his thirst.

"I'll let you get some rest," Margaret declared and stood to leave.

He grasped her wrist with his good arm. "Stay with me," he pleaded, his eyes full of tender longing. "Perhaps you could read to me a little. The sound of your voice will help me to sleep," he suggested.

She warmed at his request, pleased to aid him in some way.

When at last he drifted off to sleep, she quietly shut the book in her lap and studied him as he lay propped in repose. The tears came unbidden, coursing silently down her cheeks as she tried to comprehend the fullness of the love that ached in her heart, and how close she had come to losing him. She thanked the Lord for keeping him safe and prayed she should never know life without him.

Later that afternoon, Mrs. Thornton sat in the empty dining room reading the opened Bible on the table in front of her. The events of the day had jolted her, and she looked for reassurance in the words of Psalms and Isaiah. With her son's injury and the impending closure of his business, the future was at best uncertain. She clung to her belief that the Lord would reward the righteous and was comforted to remember that through disciplined and faithful endeavor, she and John had already once proved the Lord's provision. She refused to falter in her faith now.

Fanny burst into the room wailing, handkerchief in hand, invading the quiet sanctuary of her mother's thoughts with a torrent of hysterics. "Oh, Mother, John is dead! What are we to do? How could such a thing happen? Think of poor Margaret - to be a penniless widow with child!" she cried in a fit of despair, her blond ringlets bobbing and swaying with her every move.

"Don't be ridiculous, Fanny. John is not dead," her mother retorted with exasperation, trying to stop her daughter's dramatic frenzy.

"But your message said he received a gunshot wound! To think that my poor brother was shot! What a vile thing to have happened!" she exclaimed with horror.

The elder woman looked at her daughter with a measure of wonder and disgust. "You were not so solicitous of your brother's welfare yesterday," she reproached her youngest child.

Fanny's mouth flew open in hurt surprise. "Mother, how can you say that when Johnny is upstairs dying!" she exclaimed in disbelief at her mother's reprimand.

"He is not dying," she countered adamantly. "The bullet only grazed him. His arm is injured, but the doctor said he should mend well. He's resting now. Margaret is with him," she explained to calm her daughter's overwrought concerns.

"Whatever happened, Mother? Did one of the workers do this?" she asked with an expression of incredulous anger.

"No, it was not one of the workers, Fanny. It's a bit more complicated than that," she answered with impatience. "It was Slickson's nephew. Apparently he had developed an attachment to Margaret," she cautiously revealed, reluctant to offer her daughter any more information than was necessary. She dreaded the notion of her son's name being dragged into torrid rumors of a lover's scandal.

"Albert? So it is true!" she cried out in more hushed tones. "There was talk in town, but I could hardly believe that it would have come to this!" Fanny declared in utter shock.

"Talk? What talk?" Mrs. Thornton demanded, unnerved by Fanny's drivel.

"About Albert Slickson and Margaret...that there is a connection," she revealed with a knowing air.

"What utter nonsense!" her mother declared with irritation.

"But Mother, they have been seen together in the streets and at the park," Fanny continued defensively.

"It is possible Albert sought her out, but I'm certain Margaret took no note of it," Mrs. Thornton interjected.

"But perhaps, Mother, Margaret is the type that is constantly toying with the hearts of the men around her: the man at the station, John, and now Albert," she suggested with raised eyebrows.

Mrs. Thornton recoiled at her daughter's faulty conclusion. "How can you say such a thing! Margaret is a most devoted wife to your brother. I will certainly not listen to such tittle-tattle and neither should you!" she admonished with vehemence, her eyes flashing with indignation.

Fanny opened her mouth but was rendered speechless by her mother's strict warning. Unconvinced of her mother's judgment, she tossed her head in defiance.

"Perhaps you could visit us tomorrow at tea," Mrs. Thornton suggested more quietly. "John may join us then if he is feeling well enough."

"Of course," she agreed compliantly. "Please give Johnny my fondest affections. I hope he will recover soon," she said as she prepared to leave.

Hannah nodded and gave her daughter a faint smile before the girl turned to go. She listened to the retreating footsteps until the room was silent once more. She sighed aloud in worry about the coming storm. The talk about town would no doubt be thick and fast from such a dramatic event. She hoped her son and his wife would emerge unscathed from any malicious gossip.

Shortly after the six o'clock whistle blew, Margaret left her husband to see about dinner.

Mrs. Thornton looked up from her Bible in the drawing room as her daughter-in-law appeared.

"John is resting. I thought I could bring him his dinner tonight," Margaret explained as she headed toward the kitchen. She had taken just a few steps when Dixon came barreling around the corner.

"Miss, that man Higgins is downstairs. He wants to know how the Master is," she informed the mistress of the house with a sympathetic tone and look of concern for the young bride's troubles.

"Nicholas!" she breathed. Of course, he would want to know how John fared! She chided herself for neglecting to send him word of her husband's condition. "Send him up at once, Dixon," she directed. "After all he's done for Mr. Thornton today, it is the least we can do," she added for her mother-in-law's benefit, hoping to dissuade any qualms the older woman might have in admitting the former union leader into their home.

Moments later, Nicholas entered with cap in hand, glancing uncomfortably at the fine surroundings of the Master's house. "I weren't expecting to come in. I just wanted to know how the Master was before I left for home," he explained respectfully to Margaret.

"Please, Nicholas, don't apologize. Mr. Thornton is taking rest. The doctor expects he shall make a full recovery," she related. "Thank you, Nicholas. I should not like to think what might have occurred if you had not been there," she added quietly, a quaver of emotion stealing the fervor from her voice.

"I knew something weren't right when that fellow went by. It was like a voice inside me told me to follow that man," he mused thoughtfully, his brow knit in a serious expression. "I'm glad to hear the Master is doing well. I'll not take up your time," he said, preparing to leave.

"Nicholas," Margaret halted him. She hesitated, trying to think of some small gesture of thanks that could be made for his valiant action today. "Would you and Mary join us for Sunday luncheon? I'm sure Mr. Thornton will be able to join us then," she invited. She felt the watchful gaze of her mother-in-law, but was unfazed by her presence. As mistress of the house, she was entitled to choose her guests.

Mrs. Thornton felt a twinge of uneasiness at the admittance of the former union leader into her home. She quickly reminded herself, however, that her son regarded him as a friend now. More importantly, the loyal worker had undoubtedly saved her son's life.

Higgins cast a nervous glance at Mrs. Thornton. He saw the imploring look in Margaret's wide eyes and understood the meaning of her offer. He could not refuse her. "We'd be pleased to come. Thank you for thinking of us," he responded with meek sincerity.

Margaret's face lit up with childlike joy. "Oh, I'm so glad! Thank you, Nicholas," she answered humbly, her eyes conveying her profound gratitude.

He gave her a friendly smile and a meaningful look before he turned to go home.

⟢⟣

The following day was Saturday. Although Mr. Thornton usually worked, he was forbidden to leave the house.

Margaret coddled and pampered her husband, bringing him meals in bed, reading to him, and spending time conversing with him. Most importantly, she allowed him to nap throughout the day, staying nearby to tend to his every request. Under her prodigious care, he improved in strength and appearance as the day progressed.

Early in the afternoon, the police inspector came to ask the Milton magistrate about the events of the day before.

"Mr. Mattson, it's good to see you, although it is not the most pleasant of circumstances," Mr. Thornton greeted the stalwart policeman with a wry smile. "Sorry to receive you like this," he said, propped upright in his bed, "but my wife will not let me downstairs today," he explained, throwing a loving glance at Margaret who stood some feet away from the bed.

"Very unpleasant circumstances indeed, sir. I was very sorry to hear of it. Congratulations, by the way - ma'am, Mr. Thornton - on your marriage," he said, remembering clearly the couple's odd behavior concerning the inquest many months ago.

Margaret nodded at his felicitations, feeling a slight flush of heat at the memory of her blatant denial of the truth. Surely Mattson must have known the underlying reason behind Mr. Thornton's dismissal of the murder inquiry.

Mr. Thornton thanked him for his good wishes and began to answer the questions the investigator posed about the shooting. Unavoidably, the history of the Master's relationship with young Slickson was brought up, and he was forced to admit his visit to Slickson's residence and the

314

violent encounter that had ensued.

Mattson did not flinch at Mr. Thornton's confession, but raised his eyebrows at the general explanation of Albert's indecent behavior towards Margaret. He sighed inwardly upon hearing the complicated entanglement of events. He knew such a case would be eagerly watched by the whole town and was sincerely sorry to see such an honorable man plunged into such a circus.

Reluctantly, the inspector asked Margaret to confirm everything that her husband had relayed to conclude his inquiries.

"I thank you for your time, Mr. Thornton, Mrs. Thornton. I'm certain that justice will be served. Fortunately, there were many witnesses," he assured them when he was through. "From what I've gathered, it seems Mr. Higgins might have saved your life when he pushed Slickson to the floor. I'm glad he was so observant," he added solemnly before taking his leave.

Fanny bustled into the familiar drawing room of her former home that afternoon with eager importance, pleased to find her mother preparing the polished, low table for tea.

"You're early," Mrs. Thornton noted at the sight of her daughter, who was fashionably dressed in a silk dress of silver blue.

"I couldn't stay away another minute! How is John? I still cannot believe he was injured in such a dreadful manner!" she cried out as she stood wringing her gloved hands.

"He is well, Fanny. He has spent the day in bed. It seems to be doing him good," Mrs. Thornton remarked plainly.

Fanny blinked her eyes and shook her head as she fussed with her skirts and sat down in a cushioned chair. "I cannot remember him ever being in bed all day. This has all been quite traumatic," she declared. "Will he join us for tea?" she asked with great anticipation to see how events had affected her brother.

"Yes, I believe so. I'm sure he will appreciate the change of scenery," Mrs. Thornton answered, noting with chagrin the agitated mannerisms of her youngest child. Her daughter could not remain still for any length of time and was easily excitable.

The anxious guest quickly glanced around to ensure no one was within hearing before she leaned toward her mother to speak in an exaggerated whisper. "Mother, you will not believe the rumors going round about town. They are simply horrid!" she declared, all too eager to share her knowledge with the staid woman before her.

Hannah Thornton let out a slow breath. She had feared just such a thing, and Fanny would revel in the glory of being attuned to society's fascination with the sordid and sensational.

Not waiting for her mother's prompting, Fanny began to reveal what she had learned from the house calls she had made that morning. "Some people have it all wrong, saying that it was John who shot Albert! I corrected them right away, of course, telling them that John would never do such a thing. But you will never guess what they said *then* - that John had discovered that Margaret was carrying *Albert's* child!" she announced, her eyes wide with disbelief.

Hannah's mouth fell open in shock and her face darkened in revulsion. How utterly abominable these tattlers were! She reeled at thought of her son's character and honor being bandied about as trifling amusement for persons who had nothing better to do than partake in idle gossip. Such worthless people had no compunction in sullying the reputation of those above them.

After a moment's reflection, Mrs. Thornton looked inquiringly into her daughter's eyes. "Margaret's condition is not common knowledge, Fanny. How did such rumors start?" she asked, her eyes narrowing in growing suspicion.

Fanny looked away in momentary embarrassment. "I...I didn't mean to let it slip. But I was speaking with Eva yesterday and I told her how horrible this all must be for Margaret, being so newly married and...with child," she said, cautiously bringing her gaze back to her mother's eyes, hoping to be forgiven for her faux pas.

"Oh, Fanny!" the elder woman muttered in disgust at her daughter's careless, easy chatter.

"I was very specific with Eva about keeping it quiet. I can't imagine how it got spread all over town and twisted into such an appalling tale!" she declared in defense of her actions.

Mrs. Thornton let out a sigh. "Some people will never tire in their attempt to bring others down," she surmised with conviction. "The least you can do is deny these ridiculous rumors when you hear of them!" her mother advised with exasperation.

"But, Mother, are you sure there is not any truth in what has been said about Margaret and Albert?" she asked in earnest, her eyes alight with the possibility of scandal.

Mrs. Thornton gazed at her daughter as if she were a complete stranger. Was there no hope that Fanny would ever learn to be sensible and discerning? How easily she believes the worst of all situations! She took a deep breath before answering, "There is not a shred of truth to it, Fanny! Margaret is fully devoted to John. Why, she practically runs to greet him when he comes home from the mill each day. If there is any substance to such talk, it belongs on the side of Mr. Slickson. If you must know, he pursued Margaret but she would have none of it," she firmly declared.

Fanny's eyes sparked at the revealed morsel of truth. She settled back in her chair, satisfied to have learned something of interest. "Did John know of this?" she suddenly asked, her expression alive with impatient curiosity.

"Yes, he was made aware of it," her mother answered in a tired voice.

At that moment, mother and daughter heard the approaching footsteps of the couple in question and Fanny quickly closed her mouth at Mrs. Thornton's warning glance.

Fanny shot up from her seat at her brother's approach, the sight of him with his arm in a sling throwing her into a state of fitful alarm. "Oh, Johnny! Are you in pain? I was so worried you would die! I have hardly had a wink of sleep since I heard of that awful incident," she exclaimed dramatically.

Mr. Thornton smiled patiently at his younger sister's concern. "I am doing quite well, Fanny, thank you. The pain is not so pronounced now, and I am in good hands," he remarked, giving an affectionate glance at his wife as they took a seat together on the sofa.

"My dear sister, how are you?" Fanny continued animatedly. "I am sure you must have been beside yourself with worry. I should not like to think how I should have managed if my Watson had been hurt in such a way! Although I should not even mention it, I cringe to think you might have been left a widow at such a time!"

"It was very frightening, I admit, but I am grateful he was not too badly hurt," Margaret calmly replied, giving her husband a loving glance as she reached for his hand.

The family gathering managed to find other small talk as they took their tea, although Fanny brought the subject of the recent events back into the conversation once or twice. She was fascinated by every detail of the drama that had unfolded in her own brother's mill.

Fanny was encouraged by her brother's healthy appearance, and was glad to learn a little more of the details of what had happened. Throughout the hour she stayed, she took careful note of her sister-in-law's attentiveness to her husband and the sweet, unspoken exchanges between them. She was finally forced to admit that there was no discord between them; they were the picture of marital contentment as they sat closer together on the sofa than was deemed entirely proper.

After their talkative guest had departed, the party remained in the drawing room. Mrs. Thornton relayed the names of the families who had sent their cards to the house that day to inquire about Mr. Thornton's health. She seemed particularly pleased that Mr. Wilkinson, the local Member of Parliament, had sent wishes for Mr. Thornton's speedy recovery along with a firm conviction that the manufacturer's contribution to society would continue unhindered.

Before long, Margaret persuaded her husband to return to his room, concerned that he still needed rest. It had been but a day since he was so grievously hurt and she wished to ensure his complete recovery.

Mr. Thornton took pleasure in following his wife's behest, knowing such secluded time spent alone together was a rare gift to cherish. He would return to his laborious schedule soon enough.

When evening came and the darkness of the room was bathed in candlelight, Margaret put down the book that she had been reading aloud and helped her husband out of bed and into his nightclothes. When his shirt had been removed, he stilled her from retrieving his nightshirt.

"The evening is warm. I will be more comfortable as I am," he explained in a low voice, drinking in the loveliness of his wife as he held her captive in his gentle grasp. He had enjoyed her company all day, but they had only shared a few affectionate kisses.

Margaret avoided his gaze, feeling the warmth of his stare awaken her own longings. The sight of his bare chest only increased her desire to touch him. She was afraid it would not bode well to satiate their desires for one another tonight, knowing he must not strain himself unduly. "I must dress," she whispered as an excuse to escape from him. She was sadly relieved to feel his hand relinquish his hold upon her. Wordlessly, she left to go to her room, the swishing of her skirts announcing her retreat.

When Margaret returned a short time later, her husband looked comfortably relaxed as he sat against the pillows in their grand bed. A white cotton sheet was pulled to his waist, but his torso was left exposed. She was disconcerted to find he was still in a state of undress.

She swallowed as she approached the bed. "Do you wish me to read again?" she asked him with a light tone, endeavoring to sound at ease as she attempted to keep her eyes solely trained on his face.

"Just talk with me," he invited with a voice that made her insides quiver.

She climbed into bed, casually kneeling beside him. "You look well," she noted, for truly he had made remarkable progress today. He no longer appeared in any way pale or weak.

"I am well cared for," he replied with a knowing smile.

Margaret's heart welled with gratitude that he appeared so unaffected from the events of the day before. It could have been much worse. The dark, frightening images she had pushed aside for hours suddenly rushed in to torment her. "If I had lost you…" she stammered, but was silenced by the soft press of his thumb to her lips.

His fingers splayed along her jaw and gently grasped her neck. "Shh, you did not. I am here," he comforted her as he brought her a little nearer.

Still shaken by her morbid thoughts, she thought of her role in the sordid drama of it all. "Oh, John, if I had only…" she began, but this time she was silenced by a tender kiss.

When his lips slowly parted from hers, he looked into the depths of her questing eyes. "Do not blame yourself for what has happened. I forbid it. You are in no way responsible for any of it. Do you understand me?" he demanded, holding her face inches from his own, his piercing blue eyes mesmerizing her.

She nodded her head in meek compliance.

"Good," he breathed, before bringing her lips to his and kissing her gently at first, and then with increasing fervor.

Her hands glided up the molded planes of his chest to caress the strong column of his neck and run her fingers through his thick, dark hair.

Her touch enflamed his need, and they both became lost in the rapturous mingling of tongues as they kissed with slow deliberation.

When they broke apart, Mr. Thornton kept her face close, cradling the back of her neck with his hand. "I want to love you," he declared, his voice ragged with longing.

"We cannot…you are hurt," she protested falteringly, although her own desire ached to be fulfilled.

"I am much improved," he responded eagerly, his eyes fixed on her lips.

"But you will harm your arm. You mustn't," she argued reluctantly as her pulse pounded at the closeness of his mouth and the smooth feel of his shoulder under her fingers.

"There are ways…" he suggested in a sultry voice as he began to lean further back into the pillows.

She watched him nervously as he relaxed, hesitant to follow his lead.

"I will not be harmed," he assured her, discerning her uncertainty. A devious smile came over his face. "On the contrary, I am quite certain you will aid my recovery," he promised as he deftly removed a few pillows from behind him and moved to lay further down on the bed. He grasped her arm and tugged her slightly toward him, his eyes beckoning her.

She could not resist him. Margaret bashfully moved to lean over him, her long hair brushing his bare chest. "Then if you promise me you will not injure yourself, I will do my best to mend you," she answered in hushed tones as an impish grin slowly illuminated her face.

He let out a slow, lusty breath and pulled her down to bring her mouth to his.

❧

The next morning, Hannah Thornton went to church alone, leaving John and Margaret to rest and avoid the swirl of curiosity that would amass in their wake. She bore herself with pride amongst the milling crowd afterwards, taking careful note of those who inquired after her son with sincere concern and those who only mouthed the words and would undoubtedly whisper behind her back.

Upon her arrival home, she busied herself in directing the servants to make the final preparations for their luncheon guests while her son and his wife dressed and came down to receive them.

Nicholas and Mary arrived early, and Margaret happily ushered them into the drawing room.

Mr. Thornton led Higgins to the sideboard at the far side of the room and poured him a glass of sherry, while Margaret tried to make Mary comfortable in the unfamiliar surroundings of the Master's home.

Daunted by the presence of the elder Mrs. Thornton, Mary spoke in a quiet voice when Margaret inquired about the Boucher children, barely lifting her head except to steal occasional glances at the elegant furnishings in the broad room.

When luncheon was announced, everyone removed to the dining room where the pristine linens and glittering table settings elicited a look of wonder from the humble working girl.

As a delicate watercress soup was served, the conversation centered around the success of Margaret's school. Mary listened attentively to her father speak to the Master and his family, awed into silence to be seated sociably with such high company. It had always seemed to her that the Master walked as a god amongst them, and the stern matriarch seated across from her was hardly less intimidating. She was feared by all the workers as the strictest taskmaster.

The young woman blushed when the talk veered to mention the worker's kitchen and Mary's talents as a cook.

"Perhaps you might find work someday in one of the finer homes of Milton," the elder Mrs. Thornton kindly suggested.

Mary's heart beat wildly to be the focus of attention. She gulped before responding. "I would be grateful for such work in the future, but I doubt as I could find work in as fine a house as this. It's a very fine home, ma'am," she added, anxious to compliment the long-standing mistress of the house.

Mrs. Thornton smiled at the girl's words, and felt a pang of compassion for her nervousness. "I've not always lived within such grand walls. My son worked hard to gain this place. We have lived in much humbler homes," she related to lessen the barrier between them. Mrs. Thornton was not ashamed of her history as it related to her son's rise to success, but seldom found it appropriate to mention it in the circles of society in which she now walked.

Noting the girl's startled expression, Mr. Thornton elaborated, "Indeed, when I became the head of the family as a young man, we moved several miles away to Altrincham, where I found work in a draper's shop. That was where I first learned of fabrics, Higgins," he digressed.

Turning his attention to both of his guests, he continued. "We lived, the three of us, in a humble two-room dwelling not unlike the one you currently live in. We moved back to Milton when I was offered a sort of partnership with the former owner of the Mill. I learned the trade quickly and was commended to be Master when my mentor died. It has been nearly ten years that we have lived here," he finished quietly, sharing a small smile with his mother before he returned to his meal.

Margaret studied her husband with adoration. She had only twice heard from his own lips a recounting of his past. She would listen with fascination every time he retold it, for she always learned a little more of his amazing character. For a brief moment, she endeavored to imagine him as his younger self, and wondered how breathtaking he would have been to her even then. She could not love him more fiercely. The humility he expressed in his great accomplishments and power never ceased to astound her. She knew of no other man on earth like him, and when his eyes sought hers a second later, an effusion of warmth spread through her so strongly that she felt her face aglow with deep affection.

Nicholas spoke of his own history, and proclaimed himself to be born for the trade since his father had also worked in the cotton mills of this town, when they had been new and even more dangerous. He related the slow progress he had seen in the mill hands' working conditions over time, and expressed his earnest desire to see more to come. Someday in the future, he dared to hope, he longed to see the children kept from the factories and given a chance to seek their own path in life.

By the time the raspberry trifle was served, Mary began to see the Master and his mother in a softer light. Although she still thought her host a god, he bore more human qualities than before, and the long-standing sober mistress seemed almost kindly at times.

Mrs. Thornton gained new respect for her son's loyal employee. Notwithstanding the fact that he may have saved her son's life, she discerned in him a keen mind and a dedicated spirit. And she could not help but be impressed to learn that he had adopted the young orphan children of a fellow worker who had taken his life in desperation during the strike.

Margaret was pleased that the luncheon had gone well. Mary and Nicholas looked more at home than when they had first arrived, and her mother-in-law seemed to have warmed to the guests from the Princeton district. Most of all, she was pleased to see her husband well and happy, surrounded by those that truly cared for him.

The house fell into a peaceful quiet after the guests departed. The Thornton family remained in the drawing room taking up their own pursuits, as was often their habit. They had not been alone for an hour yet when Jane announced a visitor.

"Mr. Bell!" Margaret happily exclaimed, and rose to greet her godfather as he strode into the room.

"I came as soon as I could," he assured her quietly, taking her hands affectionately.

Mr. Thornton's head jerked toward his wife, his blue eyes questioning her as he also rose to greet the elder gentleman.

She bowed her head somewhat guiltily for just a moment before lifting it again to speak to their guest. "I believe that there are some matters of business that may be resolved with your assistance. I hoped it might give Mr. Thornton some peace of mind, so that he could rest more easily," she meekly explained, hoping her husband would forgive her for her bold action in calling Mr. Bell to Milton.

"I am very sorry to hear of your injury, Thornton," the Oxford visitor related to the man of the house as they shook hands. "You look remarkably well considering the circumstances. What a most unfortunate incident! I'm afraid it's in all the papers. I had hoped your telegram might convey happier news," Mr. Bell hinted with a sly smile.

Margaret blushed at his remark. "Actually, we do have good news. We are expecting our first child toward winter's end," she gladly announced.

"Splendid! Congratulations, Thornton! It warms my old heart to know there will be a Thornton heir. Wonderful news, indeed," he addressed both of them.

"You must be pleased, Mrs. Thornton, to await your first grandchild," he said, turning to acknowledge the elder woman.

"Yes, I am," she replied as a warm smile came to her lips and illuminated her face. She stood up to tend to the Oxford scholar. "Your journey was long. Let me get you some refreshment. I will send for some tea," she offered.

"Thank you," Mr. Bell responded politely.

Margaret gestured for him to sit, and the couple took their seat across from him.

"Mr. Bell...." Mr. Thornton began uneasily. He had not been prepared to present his request for a loan to his landlord.

"Forgive me for being so brusque," Mr. Bell interrupted, "but I believe I have something of interest to say to you," he announced with an air of authority.

"Of course," Mr. Thornton replied with a tilted nod of his head, apprehensive as to what the Oxford gentleman might say.

"I had much time to ponder while on the train, and I have come to a decision," he declared, having the rapt attention of his listeners. "As you know, I have no family to whom I might bequeath my holdings. I have intended for some time now to bequeath my worldly wealth to my goddaughter, Margaret, when I leave this existence," he related seriously. "Now, I don't see any sense in making you wait for me to die. I should much rather enjoy seeing you make use of my money now. I have more than an old man like myself should ever need," he explained.

"Mr. Bell..." Margaret endeavored to meekly protest, but the elder gentleman raised his hand to silence her.

Mrs. Thornton returned just then, carrying a plate of buttered scones.

"Now, then, my decision is made and I will brook no argument. I will sign over the deed to the mill and house to you, Thornton, as caretaker of my dear Margaret," he stated firmly.

The china plate clattered as Hannah set it before her guest. Unprepared to hear such a pronouncement, she stood momentarily in amazement to realize that all her son had worked for would now be given to him. He would be the sole proprietor of Marlborough Mills and all the surrounding property. She sat down in her seat in bewilderment as to how all this had come about.

Mr. Thornton moved to speak, but the wealthy landlord motioned him to hold his tongue.

"Hear me out; I am nearly finished. I have also recently received a very lucrative return on an investment, and I would like to give you £5,000 to help you endure this unfavorable turn in the markets," he graciously proposed.

Mr. Thornton was momentarily speechless. "I don't know what to say..." he answered shaking his head in astonishment.

"Good! Then it is all settled. I will have the papers drawn up as soon as possible," Mr. Bell replied with happy determination.

That evening, after Mr. Bell had dined with them and retired to his room, Mr. Thornton asked for a few private moments with his mother. Margaret went upstairs to prepare for bed.

The drawing room was dark with the glow of lamplight.

"The righteous is delivered out of trouble…behold, the righteous shall be recompensed in the earth," Mrs. Thornton quoted Scripture solemnly as she gazed proudly at her son. "You have been saved twice now, both bodily and now of your worldly endeavors," she declared in reverence for how events had played out. "Your troubles with the mill are over."

"Yes, but there are still matters that are unsettled," he acknowledged humbly. "There will be a trial and there will talk," he said wearily of the days ahead.

Mrs. Thornton sighed in heavy sorrow at his words and looked away in discomfiture. "Yes, there is talk of a connection between Margaret and Slickson," she affirmed.

Mr. Thornton remained stoically unmoved. He had already heard of these rumors and knew they would swell at the news of the shooting. "Thank God Margaret's condition is not known," he uttered with a degree of solace.

Mrs. Thornton bowed her head in grave distress.

He discerned her anguish and his heart sank with dread.

His mother lifted her head, but could not look her son in the eye. "Fanny was careless in her chatter," she revealed.

He closed his eyes in revulsion. "Is she truly so eager to see her family's name ground into the dust?" he sputtered angrily.

"She was sorry for it, John. She will try to make amends," she explained in weak defense of her daughter's doings.

John chuffed a bitter laugh. "Amends? It will be too late for that. You know what they will say," he spoke hotly.

"Yes," she admitted softly. "I'm sorry, John. What will you do?" she asked, lifting her eyes to his.

"What can be done? There will always be such reprehensible people. I will never understand them, but they mean nothing to me. Their words are nothing. We will hold our heads high and continue on as we always have. I care not what others say. I only asked to protect Margaret from hearing such slander. I pray she will not hear of it," he concluded reflectively.

"I am sorry, John," Mrs. Thornton offered again, keenly feeling his sorrow as her own.

Mr. Thornton rose from his seat. "All this shall pass. It will not alter anything. I am happy, Mother," he assured her more calmly, endeavoring to shrug off his worry over what could not be controlled.

Mrs. Thornton's countenance lifted. "I know," she answered him with affection. "You have married well," she acknowledged, giving him a meaningful look.

He smiled warmly at her admission, communicating his appreciation with a sparkle in his eyes as he turned to follow his wife upstairs.

He had barely begun to undress when Margaret glided into the room wearing her green nightgown of shimmering silk. His eyes remained fastened to her as she approached him.

"Here, let me help you," she said as she began to undo the buttons of his waistcoat. He could not contain the satisfied smile that crept over his face as she worked, nor could he resist letting his hand slide around the silky surface of her waist or nuzzling her neck. He took a deep breath to inhale the scent of jasmine that she always wore.

"Behave yourself, Mr. Thornton, while I attempt to tend to you," she mockingly admonished him with a smile she could not hide.

His grin grew wider. "If you wish me to behave, then you should not wear such enticing clothing," he replied, raising an eyebrow.

"I rather felt like celebrating tonight," she said in defense of her choice of nightclothes, a glimmer of mischief in her eyes. "It is not every day one inherits a great fortune," she reasoned as she discarded the black waistcoat onto the dressing table and began to work on his shirt.

"It was bold of you to ask Mr. Bell to come here without consulting me," he feigned a warning.

"I wished to settle things so that you could relax," she explained as she rubbed her hands against his chest and slid them up to work the muscles of his neck in demonstration of her desire to comfort him.

"And look what you have done," he replied with teasing admiration, pulling her close against him.

"You have become the rightful owner of the mill and house. It is just, after all your years of dedication, John. Are you not pleased?" she asked, searching his face.

"How can I not be pleased with all that you have brought me?" he asked tenderly, his eyes burning with the love he felt for her.

"I love you," she whispered with aching sincerity as she threw her arms around him and brought her lips to his.

On Monday morning, Margaret convinced her husband to delay his return to work by a few hours and rest a little longer. And so, for the third day in a row, Mr. Thornton was served breakfast in bed. Although eager to return to work, he could not help but enjoy languishing in bed with his wife in the early morning light.

"Will you tell Nicholas of the mill's new owner?" she asked with a knowing smile later as she helped button her husband's waistcoat for work.

"The papers have not yet been signed. I am not yet the owner of my own mill," he replied with cautious eagerness. He smiled broadly at her words - she knew well how much it meant to him to attain the stature of a landowner.

"Soon you will truly be the sovereign of all you survey," she said proudly as she tugged at his collar and prepared it to receive the encircling black cravat.

"Indeed?" he answered suggestively with arched eyebrows.

She smiled coyly at his teasing reply. "I believe I have fallen under your power some time ago," she openly admitted as she reached up to snugly settle the black silk fabric around his neck.

"I should like to think we have equal rule over the other," he answered affectionately. "At least here in this place. I find your dominance quite enthralling," he hinted teasingly with a wicked smile.

"John!" she scolded him, pushing him away from her for his brazen remark. She blushed slightly at his insinuation.

He pulled her toward him and gave her a conciliatory kiss on the forehead, but could not contain his broad smile at her reaction.

"Will you make any announcements to the workers?" she asked, deftly changing the subject back to the mill as she once again set out to tie his cravat.

"I don't know. I suppose I could have Higgins ask the men to stay a minute after the last whistle," he replied thoughtfully.

"I think that would be wonderful. Could I attend? I should love to hear it," she asked enthusiastically, stepping back to check her work.

"Of course. I will expect you," he answered warmly and gave her an affectionate kiss.

When the whistle sounded later at day's end, Margaret accompanied her husband as they walked from his office to the cavernous weaving shed. The horde of working men and women that surrounded the still machinery broke into applause at their appearance.

The Master was moved by their expressions of goodwill and searched the faces of the crowd with an equal measure of pride and humility at the bond of sympathy that had been forged between master and men.

Mr. Thornton raised his hand and the din quickly quieted. "As you know, business has not been good, and you have surely heard talk of the mill closing. I will tell you what the plans for Marlborough Mills are so that there will be no doubts," he announced with booming authority, looking out over the mass of anxious faces.

"We will continue to make cotton. We will *not* shut our doors. We will all have work," he proclaimed with increasing fervor as the shouts and whoops of the workers began to fill the factory with a roar of jubilation.

The Master and his wife watched with glowing faces the boisterous antics of the crowd. When the mistress threaded her arm through her husband's and looked up to him adoringly, Mr. Thornton turned to her and they both smiled in exalted happiness.

Chapter Twenty-one

From private drawing rooms and stately gentlemen's clubs, to rowdy pubs and simple servants' quarters, the talk of Milton revolved around the shooting at Marlborough Mills and the upcoming trial. In the Princeton district, the workers at Thornton's were not immune to the swell of self-importance that rose in their breasts when they were sought out for their rendition of the events of that day. Most, however, swore by the faithfulness of the Master's wife and decried the sordid rumors that raised the eyebrows of well-coiffed ladies at tea and prompted derisive snickers from men in smoke-filled billiard rooms.

Mr. Thornton and his wife continued their daily routines, unfazed by the whirlwind of tattle about town. Suddenly the recipients of an influx of social invitations, they politely declined most, choosing to attend occasional gatherings to quell suspicious scrutiny with their placid composure and genuine contentment.

Margaret carried herself with quiet dignity, aware that Albert's vociferous rants would have undoubtedly incited a slew of rumors concerning a romantic entanglement. She consoled herself to endure such slander with the knowledge that she was innocent of any inappropriate behavior. She was especially grateful that her pregnancy was not yet evident, for she believed her condition was known only to her husband's family and Nicholas and Mary.

The Mistress of Marlborough Mills walked with a purposeful gait across the mill yard one morning a week before the trial. The late August sun warmed the air as it climbed toward its pinnacle of glory, hidden behind the mottled grays of Milton's bleak skies. Although surrounded by the colorless world of man's making, she smiled in satisfaction at the hope and progress her husband's enterprise represented. She envisioned a shared prosperity, in which both Master and men benefited from the diligent work of the other.

A small flock of children gathered around her skirts as she approached the schoolroom.

"Please, Miss?" asked a young lass as she looked inquisitively into the elder woman's eyes.

"Yes, Nancy?" Mrs. Thornton politely responded as they reached the doorway, glancing at the girl in fond acknowledgment.

"Are you really going to have a baby?" the girl asked innocently, her eyes wide in expectation.

Margaret's smile faded and she grew pale at the inquiry. "Whatever makes you ask that, Nancy?" she queried anxiously, endeavoring to brush off the question as childish curiosity.

"I heard my mum and dad arguing over it. Mum said you was carrying a baby, but me dad said it weren't nothing but foolish blather. Even if you were, says he, there would be nothing to hide about it," she said triumphantly, hoping her father's words would please the mistress.

Margaret felt queasy with dread. "I *am* going to have a baby, Nancy, but it was meant to be kept a secret a little longer," she told the child kindly in a lowered voice.

The girl nodded her understanding and everyone took their place for school to begin.

As soon as the whistle for the noon break sounded, Margaret hastened to see her husband. Distracted and unsettled since the child's unexpected query, she had mentally wrung her hands the past few hours in contemplation of all it implied.

She entered the Master's office and shut the door behind her without a word.

Mr. Thornton looked up from his work, at once alarmed by her sullen appearance and the listless look in her eyes. "Margaret, what is it? Are you ill?" he inquired, his brow knit with concern as he abandoned his desk to come to her.

"No, no," she assured him half-heartedly, only briefly meeting his gaze. "I have just discovered something quite...unsettling," she revealed with sorrow.

Ever alert to protect her from the damage of careless talk, he instantly surmised her discovery. "What have you heard?" he demanded with trepidation.

She looked at him questioningly and a spark of recognition crossed her face. "You knew," she uttered quietly in astonishment.

He glanced away. "I had hoped you would be spared the worst of it," he admitted, a look of painful anguish passing over his face.

"Oh, John," she answered, his words confirming her fears. "How did it become known?" she wondered, wary to know the truth.

Mr. Thornton heaved a sigh. "Fanny was careless in her chatter," he answered, bitterly disappointed in his sister's frivolous character.

Margaret was silent as she considered with dismay what might have been said behind her back these several weeks.

Her stomach churned uneasily at the thought of what her husband must have endured, at the ridicule and snide looks that may have dogged him. "How can people be so vile?" she asked in despair, although she knew only too well from her years in London how those dressed in the latest fashions could hide malicious intent behind pleasant smiles. "Your honor..." her voice trailed off as she was unable to finish her thought.

His eyes flashed with intensity as he grasped her arms and pulled her toward him. "My honor is not touched, and your reputation remains unsullied. Such talk is as the chaff to the wheat. It signifies nothing. What we know is true will be known by all soon enough - that the child is mine," he declared, lowering his voice at his last words as his eyes travelled down to her middle, where the evidence of their union would show.

He noted how beautifully she blushed as he raised his eyes to her face. Possessive desire coursed through him at the notion of the privileges afforded him as her husband. The outline of her soft lips and her translucent, smooth skin beckoned him to taste of her even as the remembrance of all that they had hitherto shared increased his ardor. Carefully, aware that this was neither the time nor place to prove his passion, he enveloped her in his embrace and leaned down to kiss her tenderly.

Releasing her lips from his, he searched her eyes to gauge the effect of his comforting assurances.

She looked up to him with calm trust and effusive adoration. His strength and resolve bolstered her to withstand whatever would assail. She felt anchored in indisputable love, and knew that the raging tempest would soon pass over them, ushering in a sun-soaked tranquility in its wake.

"Promise me you will not let such worthless drivel disturb you again," he implored, wanting to ensure her peace from invasive worry.

She nodded her head in silent assurance, and reached up to entwine her arms around his neck to bind herself to his strong form.

When the morning of the trial arrived, the Court of Assizes was full to overflowing with crowds who wished to see what drama might unfold. Those in the back craned their necks to catch a glimpse of the Master of Marlborough Mills and his wife, who sat serenely in the front row just behind the balustrade. Margaret's arm was nestled under that of her husband, and he held her gloved hand discreetly in his with firm purpose.

The elder Mrs. Thornton sat stiffly next to her son with her chin aloft.

Angled sunlight glanced into the courtroom through half-opened windows, allowing the hand of nature to place this paltry human event in its proper context.

A hush fell over the assembly as the judge entered and the defendant was brought in.

No longer defiant and proud, Albert Slickson appeared uneasy, casting his eyes to the floor.

The judged opened the trial and lay out charges against the young man who had caused such bedlam.

Asked how he pleaded, Slickson brought his eyes up and sought Margaret's gaze only to find her head bowed demurely. "Guilty," he answered in a low voice, gulping to retain a semblance of dignity.

Murmurs erupted from the mixed assembly of Milton's masses.

"I acted rashly with.....greatly deluded intentions," he choked out the words with difficulty, glancing at his father who sternly glared at his son to continue his well-rehearsed speech. "I hope those I have injured will forgive me," he concluded, daring to look at the Thornton family.

Mr. Thornton's expression remained cold while Margaret's eyes flashed briefly toward Albert at his halting confession.

The prosecution was allowed to make its case, carefully delineating the exact nature and circumstances of the attack on Mr. Thornton by questioning the defendant and calling upon several witnesses, including Nicholas Higgins.

Once a clear picture of the crime had been created, the crafty lawyer set out to clarify the motive behind Mr. Slickson's actions. "You said earlier that you 'acted rashly with deluded intentions.' Is that correct, Mr. Slickson?" the prosecutor asked.

The defendant answered in the affirmative.

The warm August air exacerbated the uncomfortable stillness of the room. A few flies buzzed disrespectfully about as well-dressed ladies quietly fanned themselves.

"Will you explain why you went to Marlborough Mills with a gun on your person and deliberately sought out Mr. Thornton?" the lawyer posed with deliberation.

Albert's eyes shifted uncomfortably and his shoulders heaved as he looked nervously to his parents and then glanced again at Margaret with a hint of painful longing. "I was in love with his wife," he answered boldly, jutting his chin slightly in the air in defense of his emotions.

Gasps and tittering whispers burst the tense silence of the courtroom. Margaret shut her eyes in deepening embarrassment as her husband gave her hand a reassuring squeeze.

The judge hammered his gavel for silence and the prosecution resumed its questioning.

For what seemed like an eternity to Margaret, the history of what had passed between Albert and her husband was dragged to the surface. Her heart beat wildly as her husband was called to testify and she listened to him explain his own actions and the reason behind the violence he had inflicted on Mr. Slickson.

Margaret breathed a low sigh of relief when Albert admitted his unsolicited advances and it became clear that she would not need to testify.

The remainder of the trial went quickly, and it was not long before the jury returned with the verdict: guilty on all counts, including attempted murder. The courtroom once again burst into shocked whispers and righteous acclaim.

When the judge had silenced the assembly, he solemnly delivered the sentence. In deference to the defendant's confession of guilt and his admitted remorse for his impassioned behavior, he would be transported to Australia and be required to remain there for no less than ten years.

Albert's mother cried out in anguish; she was relieved that her son had avoided death, but was grief stricken to think her boy would be sent to the far side of the earth.

The courtroom was abuzz with excited chatter as the crowds slowly dispersed. Mr. and Mrs. Thornton sought only to escape the throng, but were hounded with congratulations for justice served and condolences for their hardship. They had just exited the stately building when Eva Dallimore called out to Margaret just as Mr. Thornton became engaged in conversation with another acquaintance.

"Mrs. Thornton! How relieved you must be to have this whole affair put to rest at last. It must have been awful to endure such scandalous rumors," Miss Dallimore offered her false sympathy, smiling politely. A devious twinkle in her eye revealed her secret mirth.

Margaret smiled in return with a defiant swell of mischief. "It was not so grievous, really. My husband and I pay no attention to baseless lies," she answered with a light tone. "It is a small comfort to remind ourselves that such vapid talk only reveals the minds of the speakers. Such people are not worthy of our attention," she remarked blithely, her eyes sparkling in victory.

Miss Dallimore's countenance fell, and she tossed her head back as Margaret turned to her husband once more.

The married couple finally eluded the lingering crowd, but Hannah Thornton was ensnared by a circle of solicitous acquaintances and eventually acquiesced to be taken to tea. Mr. Thornton steered his wife briskly down the streets with a light step. When they had distanced themselves far from the courthouse, the Master relaxed his pace and beamed at his wife. An exalting vigor swept through him to have closed the door on this distressing episode of their lives. He saw nothing but sunny skies ahead of them.

He stepped spontaneously into a florist's shop and emerged with a bountiful bouquet of pink, cream and yellow roses for his wife. Margaret exclaimed with pleasure over his impromptu gift and could not stop smiling at her husband, gloriously happy to see him so carefree.

When they arrived home, Mr. Thornton escorted her up the grand staircase, stopping to kiss her twice. Margaret's happiness bubbled forth in a soft giggle as he halted her the second time to seek out her lips. Upon reaching the landing, he gathered her in his arms and kissed her properly, endeavoring to avoid crushing the blossoms between them.

"I need to put these in a vase," she demurred with a faint blush when he finally released her. "It was very warm in the courtroom today. I will draw you a refreshing bath. Why don't you go upstairs and prepare yourself. I will be up shortly," she promised with a pursed smile at his forlorn expression.

Mr. Thornton reluctantly left his wife's side to do as he was bidden. As he climbed the stairs, a devious smile spread over his lips.

Margaret rolled up her sleeves and tested the water. It was lukewarm - just right for a fairly warm day.

She smiled at the thought of John's exuberance earlier as she went to fetch him.

He startled her by opening the door almost as soon as she rapped on it.

Her eyes roved over the length of him. He stood before her in a satin dressing gown of gold and burgundy paisley with dark crimson borders. Her gaze lingered on the casual twist of ribbon cinched at his waist. What had possessed her to offer him a bath, she wondered? She felt a flush of heat to see his bare legs and feet.

He seemed to enjoy her stupefied hesitation. "Will you help me wash my hair?" he asked hopefully, careful not to sound too eager.

"In a little while," she answered falteringly, uncertain what she was about.

He smiled in satisfaction and proceeded to his bath.

Margaret entered the bathroom a few minutes later after removing her stockings and shoes. She padded quietly into the room and watched as her husband turned his head attentively in her direction.

"I thought you might not come," he confessed.

"I said I would," she retorted.

"I thought you might be afraid of me," he elaborated slyly.

The corners of her mouth edged into a smile. "And why should I be afraid, pray tell?" she asked haughtily.

He smiled devilishly at her taunting inquiry. "Because you cannot resist my charms and my power of persuasion," he responded with a silken voice tinged with a brazen self-confidence. "Because you might find yourself as before and join me in my state of undress," he added audaciously.

Margaret reveled in their game, determined to demonstrate her own prowess. "I am well aware of your tactics, sir. But I believe I have the upper hand as long as I remain decently clothed," she stated triumphantly, her arms akimbo.

"If you are so certain, then come assist me as you promised," he baited her, impatient to have her within his reach.

She moved apprehensively toward the bath and breathed a silent sigh of relief when she reached his side and he made no move to detain her. She bent to retrieve the pitcher to begin her task, when she suddenly let out a gasp of surprise as he grasped her wrist. "John!" she protested as a smile crept over her face. She knew she had been caught.

Mr. Thornton grinned broadly at his conquest and tugged her slowly toward him. "I believe I have the upper hand now," he declared smartly.

"John, let me go! If I am to join you, let me remove my dress," she protested, pulling against him without much effect.

"I'm not certain I can trust you now that you have behaved petulantly. I believe I must show you who is master here," he announced ominously with a wicked gleam in his eye.

"John!" she made one last protest before he pulled her in, seating her on his lap. She scrambled to turn around and assess the condition of her clothes, drenched now nearly to the breast. "You are incorrigible!" she chided him.

He chuckled irrepressibly and moved to offer tangible apologies, but she swatted at his hands as they approached her, and he threw his head back and laughed.

Margaret knew she could not resist him for long; the bass tones of his laughter always warmed her heart. Soon their lips co-mingled and the strong arms of her lover drew her into his power.

When Hannah Thornton swept by her son's room sometime later, she heard the faint tones of laughter coming through the dark, paneled door. She reflected on the day's events as she continued down the hallway to her bedchamber. The corners of her mouth turned upward in a contented smile. They had endured much during these past weeks; she was glad they were happy. Her son deserved no less.

As autumn approached, Mr. Thornton threw himself earnestly into his work. He carefully scheduled the existing orders to ensure that the mill would be in full operation during these lean months, and diligently planned for production to rebound, keeping abreast of every portending change in the industry at home and abroad.

Margaret decided it was high time to host a Master's dinner to celebrate her husband's new status as a landowner, which made him a solid fixture in Milton's business landscape. She proposed inviting Milton's own Member of Parliament, Mr. Wilkinson, as a special guest and her husband readily approved.

The Mistress of Marlborough Mills found great enjoyment and no little amount of pride in carefully planning and arranging the event which she was certain would showcase her husband's prominence in his field of business. She hoped, too, to impress upon Mr. Wilkinson the relative success of the social improvements being made at Marlborough Mills.

On the evening of the dinner, the young Mrs. Thornton was calmly composed as guests began to arrive. Everything was in perfect order. She stood with her husband to graciously greet the masters and their wives in an elegant gown of violet satin.

The entrance of Mr. Wilkinson and his wife made Fanny's jaw drop for a moment and turned the heads of the other guests. Mr. Thornton and his wife warmly received the celebrated guests. The Member of Parliament had not forgotten his conversation at the ball with the vibrant and beautiful Mrs. Thornton, and looked forward to a stimulating evening with such intelligent hosts.

He was not disappointed. The conversation centered on the challenges and the future of the cotton industry in Milton proper and of industry and economic progress in general.

As Margaret expected, her husband was looked to for the final word in virtually every consideration. She could not restrain the corners of her mouth from turning upwards, and endeavored to politely mask the overwhelming pride she took in noting how her husband's conversation garnered the profound respect of all those in attendance.

When talk of the working classes veered to mention Margaret's school and the mill's dining hall, Margaret became animatedly involved in the unfolding discussion as to whether such 'experiments' were a worthwhile venture. During these moments, when the vicar's daughter argued with fervent eloquence for the virtue and practicality in aiding those without wealth, it was the Master's turn to gaze at his wife with a smile of admiration. A glimmer in his eyes and his lingering stare laid bare his open adoration, and all but the least observant were aware of the strong attraction between the master of the house and his wife.

Mr. Thornton was well pleased with the evening, but as he graciously bid his guests good-bye with his wife, he grew more impatient to be alone with the woman who had charmed everyone with her open manner and impeccable grace.

Margaret felt her husband's eyes upon her, bringing a faint blush to her cheeks as she spoke her parting words to the last guests. She turned to face him with an expression of glad accomplishment and he rewarded her with a brilliant smile and effusive praise.

"You are an astounding hostess. I am certain Mr. Wilkinson has never seen such intellectual vigor in the form of such stunning beauty. Truly, you are a wonder," he murmured in her ear as he bound her to him, elated to hold her in his arms at last.

"I believe we make a formidable team when we are not put at odds," she responded, smiling uncontrollably as her husband began to brush his lips against her temple. "Do I pass muster as mistress of Marlborough Mills?" she queried in jest, as his continuing attentions caused a shiver of pleasure to trace her spine.

"You more than pass muster," he answered huskily. "And I should like to show you my fond appreciation," he whispered before straightening himself at the sound of his mother's footsteps as she returned from viewing Fanny's new carriage.

A few weeks hence, Mr. Thornton rose quietly from his bed in the pale, gray light of an October morning. After making his ablutions, he returned to his wardrobe and doffed his nightshirt to put on the crisp, white cotton shirt of his everyday attire. Intent on his task of buttoning the front, he was pleasantly surprised to suddenly feel the warm arms of his wife wrap around him from behind.

"Happy birthday, dear husband," she exclaimed in a voice of drowsy contentment as she pressed her cheek against his back. The scent of sandalwood and the feel of his firm abdomen under her forearms aroused in her a tingling awareness of his manliness.

"Is it my birthday?" he asked casually. A warm smile spread over his face as he reveled in her embrace, covering her arms with his own.

"So your mother tells me. Do you mean to tell me you have forgotten your own birthday?" she asked wonderingly, slackening her hold.

He turned to face her, keeping her arms close about him. "I have not had much interest in celebrating it these past few years," he admitted ruefully.

"Well, it is very important to me, and I shall much enjoy making your day special," she answered defiantly, stretching up to give him an affectionate kiss.

He returned her kiss with his own, and slid his arm around her waist to bring her flush against him. The feel of her curvy flesh under the thin fabric of her nightgown inflamed his desire. "I can think of a very satisfactory way to celebrate..." he suggested in breathy tones upon relinquishing her lips. He forced her to move backward with him as he took a step toward the bed.

Still breathless from his kiss, she felt his thigh brush against her own and felt a fluttering deep within. "You will be late," she countered weakly with a quavering voice.

"It is my birthday, is it not?" he responded with arched eyebrows and moved her further back toward the bed.

Margaret fidgeted excitedly as she and Mrs. Thornton presented John with gifts at the breakfast table.

Mr. Thornton thanked his mother for a pair of dark leather gloves and several new handkerchiefs that she had initialed for him. He could not refrain from smiling at his wife's impatience as he untied the ribbon of a package and pulled back the wrapping to reveal a textured waistcoat in cobalt blue with a fine pattern in copper thread. A matching blue cravat was folded within.

"I think you will look stunning in blue. It brings out the color in your eyes," Margaret explained eagerly when her husband thanked her for the handsome gift.

Mr. Thornton smiled in return, pleased to be fawned over by his beautiful wife.

"Oh, and one more thing," Margaret added, handing him a smaller package wrapped in colorful paper.

Mr. Thornton opened it to find a box of bonbons, each wrapped in thin paper. "I have not been given sweets in many years," he remarked, looking to his wife wonderingly with affection.

"I think you deserve to be spoiled now and then. Now, be sure to take these with you and keep them in your desk. They are for you alone. If you leave them here, your mother and I may inadvertently devour them," she laughingly directed him with a playful glance at her mother-in-law.

He picked the box up as she instructed and, giving a good-bye kiss to both women, left for work with a happy heart.

Shortly before noon, Margaret prepared to leave the house. It would take some time to become accustomed to the increase in her time for leisure after giving up her teaching post. She was happy with the young lady who had answered their advertisement in the *Guardian*. Miss Garrat was a bright, kindly girl whose father owned a shop on the high street. Margaret felt certain she would do an admirable job in forwarding the school in the manner in which it was begun.

As she walked the short distance to the mill, Margaret was grateful that the cooler season required her to wear her woolen overcoat. The covering allowed her to hide for a little longer the ever-increasing swell of her belly. She knew her confinement would begin very soon, and she wished to enjoy her freedom for as long as possible. She nodded in kindly acknowledgement to the polite greetings she received from workers as she passed through to the Master's office.

Mr. Thornton looked up from his desk as his wife entered and closed the door behind her, taking note of the basket on her arm.

"I've brought you lunch," she announced with satisfaction. "Have you eaten any of your sweets?" she thought to ask as she stepped closer.

He closed a partially open drawer conspicuously with a quick shove. "Why do you ask?" he inquired with a playful gleam in his eye.

She walked over to him curiously. "I simply wished to know if you would remember to indulge yourself on occasion," she smoothly replied with an inkling of a smile, her suspicions aroused.

"I am a very plain man, you may need to instruct me in the southern art of indulgence," he taunted as he deftly pulled her onto his lap for a kiss.

The chair creaked in complaint, but Margaret slipped her arm around her husband's neck in willing submission.

A rap on the door brought them abruptly apart. Margaret extricated herself from her husband's grasp and clambered awkwardly to her feet as Higgins walked in. A surprised expression was quickly replaced by a barely controlled grin as the faithful friend recognized the nature of his intrusion.

"Higgins," the Master exclaimed, "your timing is impeccable," he remarked with a bewildered shake of his head.

"I knocked," Nicholas answered in his defense. "Perhaps you should take your lunch at home, Master. The locks don't seem to work here," he quipped with a twisted smile and a devilish glimmer in his eye.

The Master blinked and bit his tongue in embarrassment as Margaret bowed her head in flushed amusement.

"What was it you wished to tell me that was so important? Out with it, man," Mr. Thornton prodded, with a trace of a grin.

"Hanson's loom is not working right. Something is skewed. I've tried my best. I thought you might like to take a look at it before the lunch hour is over," he dutifully reported.

The Master let out a small sigh. "I'll do what I can," he replied but made no indication that he would immediately investigate the issue.

"I'll leave you to your lunch then," Higgins answered with a merry twinkle in his eye. He fumbled with the doorknob on his way out to examine if there was indeed a locking mechanism.

"Off with you!" Mr. Thornton impatiently chased him out with an irrepressible grin.

Higgins contained a chortled laugh at the Master's injunction and speedily departed, closing the door behind him.

Covering her mouth with her hand, Margaret suppressed an embarrassed giggle.

⬥

Margaret stood at the long window of the drawing room scanning the darkened mill yard for the figure of her husband. She wore the violet gown from the Master's dinner several weeks ago, although Dixon had left a few fastenings in the back undone to accommodate her growing middle.

She watched intently for the first sign of him, feeling foolishly like a schoolgirl in her anxiousness. How was it after these many months of marriage she should still feel so hopelessly in love, thrilling at the very thought of him walking through the door? She doubted it would ever change; her longing to be with him throughout the day had not abated since they had returned from Helstone.

She smiled at herself. She was glad that Mrs. Thornton had offered to dine with Fanny this evening for if propriety would allow it, she was certain that she would await him at the window like this each and every day.

Her eyes strained against the darkness until at last she caught her breath to see him emerge from the mill and cross the yard. Her stomach fluttered as he approached the house and she turned away to move nearer the drawing room entrance.

"You're home!" she welcomed him as he appeared through the entryway, throwing her arms around his neck to kiss him.

He received her kiss with some surprise but returned it with swift vigor before turning his head to furtively glance in the direction of his mother's usual seat.

Margaret laughed at his discomfiture. "She's not here. She is dining with Fanny tonight," Margaret answered his unspoken question with a mischievous smile.

He sought her lips again to return her audacity, kissing her thoroughly now that he knew they were alone. "And what are your plans for me?" he asked in a dark, low voice upon releasing her.

"You will have to wait and see," she answered somewhat breathlessly as he towered over her with a glint of lust in his eyes. She gathered her senses and gave him a saucy smile before taking his hand and leading him upstairs.

"I thought it might be pleasant to make a grand affair of your birthday and take you to dinner and dancing at the Westford Hotel," she explained as she climbed the stairs ahead of him. "You have an impelling charm when you are set amidst society; you quite naturally command the attention of all those around you," she continued as they walked down the hall.

She stopped just outside the door to their room to finish her speech. "However, beneath such a gracious and sociable exterior, I am quite certain you are truly a quiet man who much prefers the privacy of his own home," she concluded, gazing at him with affection. With her last words, she opened the door to usher him in.

Mr. Thornton stepped inside, taking in at once the seductively inviting atmosphere. A candlelit table was set for two in the open space beyond their bed, and a fire crackled and spit in the fireplace near the foot of their bed, casting dancing shadows across the crimson walls and over the broad surface of the bed. The thin, golden panels of the papered walls glinted in the wavering light. After surveying the scene with growing rapture, he looked to his wife in wondrous adoration.

"It is just as I should have liked," he murmured, gathering her into his arms to bestow his thanks.

Mr. Thornton nestled closer to his sleeping wife, reveling in the feel of her smooth back against his chest. He lifted his head to kiss the soft skin below her ear, her silken hair catching on his roughened cheek. He slid his hand from its resting place on her arms to gently caress the rounded protrusion of her stomach. He could still scarcely believe his fortune.

How much had changed in a year! He had felt such a profound emptiness on his last birthday, convinced that his future would only count the advancing years of painful solitude. Now he held his wife in his arms every night, and soon they would welcome into their lives the child of their union. The fullness of love that beat within him made his breast ache with indescribable joy.

The glowing embers of the fire dimmed and the darkened room grew cold. Carefully, Mr. Thornton pulled the bedcovers over his wife's bare shoulders and settled himself to sleep next to her.

Trudy Brasure

Chapter Twenty-two

Rain that had been lacking in the summer now descended in torrents, turning the dusty mill yard to mud and hastening the steps of those forced to brave the elements. The sky loomed ominously day after day, heralding the coming winter with little prospect of reprieve. In truth, it was an ideal time for Margaret's confinement, although the perpetual gloom of the darkened sky threatened at times to bring waves of melancholy over her.

The expectant young wife kept her spirits up by occupying her time with pleasurable and practical pursuits. Having now the inclination and freedom of economy to make changes as she saw fit, Margaret carefully set about adding color and vibrancy to the living spaces of the home which seemed more her own with every passing month. Mrs. Thornton gladly relinquished her collection of glass-domed alabaster to make room for more suitable decorations for a home with young children, and watched with growing approval as her southern daughter-in-law made her choices.

Margaret papered the walls in the drawing and dining rooms with patterned tones of rose, gold, and burgundy. She covered the cold, dark tables with richly colored fabrics, and placed beautiful rugs strategically about the main living area. A bookcase and several favorite chairs from the Crampton house were placed in the family drawing room at Marlborough Mills, giving it a more comfortable appeal. Flowers and bowls of fruit adorned the tables; the daguerreotype from their honeymoon was displayed on the back wall with framed depictions of the Hampshire countryside; and books and a few sewing baskets were at the ready throughout the room, inviting one to linger and relax. Mr. Thornton enjoyed his wife's decor immensely, for it seemed to him that she had transformed his home into the warm, welcoming atmosphere that he had so loved in the Hale's home.

Margaret kept a modest social schedule, so that she would not feel quite so housebound. She invited Mary and sometimes Fanny for tea. She also enjoyed having the new teacher, Miss Garrat, come to visit once a week to keep her informed of the children's progress.

Occasionally, when boredom tempted her, Margaret brought out her paints and endeavored to capture on paper the summer landscapes of her childhood home.

Mr. Thornton was ever attentive to his wife's needs and endeavored to be good company for her in the evenings. He brought her magazines and books, and on the weekends took his wife out for walks if the weather was not inclement.

When the holidays neared, Margaret plied her womanly wiles to gain her husband's permission to hold a Christmas celebration for the mill workers. With Mary and Miss Garrat's help, she delighted in busying herself in the planning and organization of the festive event.

On Christmas Eve, while the occupants of the mill still toiled, Margaret and a crew of helpers secretly cleared the dining hall and trimmed it with wreaths made of mistletoe and boughs of holly and ivy. Bowls of punch and platters of mince pies were set on tables along the wall in preparation for the unsuspecting guests.

Mr. Thornton shut down the mill's steam engine three hours early and directed his workers to the waiting hall. Higgins grinned knowingly at the excited chatter of the crowd and caught the Master's eye with an approving nod.

The hall was full to bursting with happy faces as everyone eagerly partook of the bountiful fare and joined in hearty wassailing. The Master and his wife watched with great amusement and eventually clapped in time as many of the workers showed their skills in high-spirited clogging to the music of a fiddle, flute, and drum.

As the celebration drew to a close, the Thorntons stood by the door to wish a merry Christmas to the departing employees whose beaming faces were ruddy with dancing and glad indulgence.

Mr. Thornton conceded to his wife that the event had been a tremendous success and that he had thoroughly enjoyed himself as he escorted her back to the house through the dark and quiet mill yard. The night air was chilly but Margaret's heart was filled with joyous contentment that warmed her soul. Everything around her was beautiful. A thin layer of snow settled on the ground and the deep indigo of the heavens seemed more clear and wide than ever. Candles burned in each window of the house, promising light and warmth within. She hugged her husband's arm tighter and sought his loving gaze.

The Thornton house was filled with guests on Christmas day. Fanny and Watson had stayed overnight after a late dinner on Christmas Eve, and Mr. Bell had come to Marlborough Mills for the holidays. Margaret was glad that her father's friend had decided to accept her invitation. His presence brought a measure of comfort to her, for he felt like family to her now that her parents were gone.

After eating breakfast together, the family gathered by the Christmas tree in the drawing room. A warm fire burned in the hearth, and the mantle was covered in Christmas greenery. Bowls of nuts and sweet-smelling tangerines were set about the room and the dining table was covered with scarlet linen and gleaming brass candlesticks.

Fanny praised Margaret for the beautiful tree, remarking with a hint of bitterness that her mother had never conceded to having a tree before. Decorated with small candles, home-sewn felt pieces, and wooden ornaments crafted in Germany, it was the centerpiece of the room.

Margaret was pleased with her effort to enliven the house with the joy of the season. It being the first Christmas she was mistress of her own home, she thought a tree would be perfect. She knew her mother-in-law had initially been a little wary of her intentions, but the elder woman had helped to sew sequined ornaments for the tree and had admitted that the live greenery about the house was very pleasant. However, it had been the twinkle in her husband's eye that morning that truly satisfied Margaret. She knew that he was pleased with her doings.

Indeed, Mr. Thornton was happy this day. He recognized the joy in his wife's eager expression and knew it was her heart's intent to give others joy. The house had never looked more warm and inviting, but it was her sweet, selfless giving that truly enchanted him. It would be a Christmas he would always remember, the first time they would spend it together.

Mrs. Thornton retrieved the family Bible and read the Christmas story while the fire quietly crackled in the background.

Afterwards, the gathered company opened the gifts that lay beneath the boughs of the tree. Margaret delighted in watching her husband open the gifts she had given him: the deed of ownership framed in dark wood and a larger framed painting of Marlborough Mills which she had secretly commissioned. Mr. Thornton was visibly moved by the thoughtful gift, and was pleased when Margaret exclaimed over the beauty of the sparkling emerald pendant he had chosen for her.

When the last gifts had been opened, Mr. Bell thanked his hosts again for the mahogany cane and fine cheese and wine and explained his plans for giving in return. "I'm sorry, but my gift would not fit under the tree. As a matter of fact, it would not fit in the house. So if you will wait until one o'clock, perhaps you could gather your wraps and follow me outdoors," he explained with a subtle smile of mischief.

"Of course," Margaret answered warmly, as everyone glanced at one another in curiosity.

"Watson and I also have an announcement concerning a gift of sorts," Fanny proclaimed brightly, bringing the attention of room swiftly to her. She cast her eyes demurely to her lap for a fleeting moment before lifting them to glance briefly at her grinning husband. "We are to a welcome a child come summer!" she declared, beaming with pride.

Everyone gave them heartfelt congratulations and Fanny glowed with excitement and bobbed her head at the generous outpouring of felicitations. Mr. Bell remarked observantly that the family's next Christmas would be blessed by the presence of children.

Just before one o'clock, everyone donned their coats and hats to see what the Oxford scholar had planned. When they arrived at the gates to their home, a stately black carriage stood on the street just outside. "Since your family is expanding, I thought you might need a more spacious coach. I hope it will serve you well," Mr. Bell pronounced fondly, giving a warm smile to his goddaughter.

Margaret's mouth fell open and she looked at her husband before turning back to Mr. Bell and giving him a proper hug and a kiss on each cheek. "It is wonderful! I should love to take rides to the surrounding countryside," she declared.

Hannah Thornton looked over the grand carriage with a wary eye. She avoided extravagance, valuing practicality and modesty above mere show. But as she contemplated Mr. Bell's reasoning, she decided the gift made sense. John would soon be a family man and would need such a coach to fit a growing household.

Fanny smiled, although she felt a twinge of jealousy to notice that her brother's new carriage was a little larger than her own and was painted with elegant gold trim whereas hers was merely polished black.

"Shall we all take a ride?" Mr. Bell offered with a sweeping gesture of his hand. The coachman perched out front tipped his hat in willing acknowledgement.

After a short ride through a fine layer of snow on the quiet streets, the company returned to Marlborough Mills. The warm house was filled with the smells of their Christmas dinner, and the family and their guests soon sat down to enjoy cooked goose with all of the trimmings. By the time the flaming pudding was served, the afternoon had darkened. Everyone removed to the drawing room well-sated and spent the dwindling hours of Christmas in happy companionship.

The weeks passed without event during the dark days of winter.

Margaret remained determinedly cheerful despite her lackluster routine, counting her blessings when boredom endeavored to dampen her spirits. When she took into account the many women who were less happily situated, she could not help but be grateful for her dear husband and the splendorous events of the past year which would culminate with the birth of their child.

It was late in February when the Thorntons sat quietly in the drawing room after dinner with a modest fire blazing on the hearth. Mr. Thornton took up the *Guardian* as he was often wont to do while his mother and Margaret sewed yet more tiny clothes for the baby.

Margaret suddenly stilled her hands and, after some hesitation, spoke aloud. "I'm feeling a bit...strange," she announced falteringly, putting a hand to her broad stomach.

The newspaper rustled noisily as Mr. Thornton set it down to intently observe his wife. His mother looked up from her work.

"What is it, Margaret?" Mrs. Thornton asked calmly but with evident concern.

"I have been feeling a tug of sorts every so often in my belly. I thought it would surely pass, but it has not," she endeavored to explain.

Mr. Thornton stood up from his chair and looked back and forth anxiously between Margaret and his mother to discern what this meant.

Mrs. Thornton glanced warily at her son. "Perhaps it would be wise to fetch the doctor. It may well be her time," she stated soberly.

Unable to speak, Mr. Thornton nodded vacantly and cast a worried glance at his wife before turning to carry out his task.

Dr. Donaldson sat for a while to mark Margaret's progress, but when an hour had passed and the pains had dissipated, he announced that the babe was not yet ready to come forth. He explained to the anxious listeners that it was perfectly normal to experience false labor. "All in good time. All in good time," he assured the worried husband, laying his hand briefly on the younger man's shoulder. "Perhaps I will see you in a few days," he suggested to the small gathering in Margaret's room before taking his leave.

Later that evening, Margaret quietly entered the large bedchamber that she shared with her husband. "I'm sorry to have been so much trouble," she apologized as she secured the door behind her.

"There is no need to apologize. You have no knowledge of these things," he assured her.

Mr. Thornton watched transfixed as she padded toward him, her normal gait altered to accommodate the burden of her extra weight. Her long nightgown flowed about her gently with feminine grace.

He thought her more beautiful than ever. Her rounded curves were more evident and her full face shone with a beautiful innocence. She was the essence of purity as she stood before him, on the cusp of motherhood.

He reached out to take her hands in his. "You are beautiful, Mrs. Thornton," he uttered with awe.

"With such a figure as this?" Margaret asked incredulously, laying her hands on her large, protruding stomach.

"Even so," he replied, moving behind her to gather her in his arms. "How can I think otherwise, when you bear the evidence of our love?" he murmured in her ear.

She shivered at his words and leaned back into the comfort of his embrace, feeling safely wrapped in his care. He glided his hands reverently over her rounded form, lost in the wonder of the swollen belly that had ripened with his seed. A stirring of manful pride welled up within him to know that he had given her the babe that lay within. They stood silently for some time in each other's embrace, enjoying the blissful contact of their bodies, before they climbed into bed.

Early the next week, Mr. Thornton woke as usual and dressed for work. He kissed his wife as she lay in bed and headed downstairs for his breakfast where he endeavored to appear to his mother as collected as possible. In truth, however, since the evening of the doctor's visit he was reluctant to leave his wife's side, knowing at any time she might begin to feel true birth pangs.

Mrs. Thornton smiled inwardly at her son's anxious concern as he reminded her once again to call him to the house if there was any change in his wife's condition. She nodded her accord before he gave her a peck on the cheek and departed.

When she at last arose, Margaret took her time getting dressed. It was not in her capacity to hurry anywhere at the present time with such a girth. Dixon helped her don one of the very few gowns she owned that still fit.

The servant sighed at the remembrance of the confrontation she had experienced with her mistress a few weeks previous. Dixon had reminded Mrs. Margaret that it was high time to seek out a suitable wet nurse. She was aghast to discover that Margaret was determined to nurse her child herself. Dixon shook her head at the thought of a Beresford woman falling to such a low-bred practice, but knew it would be useless to argue against the girl once she was decided.

The expectant young wife fondly passed her hands over her rounded belly. The new expanse of her skin was a source of fascination and wonder every day, even though at times it seemed very much a burden.

She said nothing to Dixon to indicate that this morning might be different from any other, but feared that the twinges she currently felt might increase in strength throughout the day. She was determined not to alarm anyone until she was more certain.

Mrs. Thornton drank her tea at the table with her daughter-in-law and noticed that the girl ate her breakfast more delicately than had been her recent habit. The house was quiet as they removed to the drawing room, where Margaret took up a book while Mrs. Thornton resumed her sewing.

Not an hour had passed when Margaret set her book abruptly to the side and sat stiffly upright. "Mother..." she called out in panic.

Mrs. Thornton raised her head at her daughter-in-law's cry. At the sight of the girl's frightened eyes, she put her sewing down. "Margaret...have the pains returned?" she asked.

Margaret nodded meekly, her hands on her belly.

"We must summon the doctor and the midwife. I believe you will have your baby today," she told the girl gently, giving her a reassuring smile.

Mr. Thornton spoke earnestly with Higgins as the dexterous worker tended a loom in the large weaving shed. The Master twisted his head to follow his friend's sudden distracted gaze and spotted his house servant timorously looking about in the unfamiliar clamor of the factory. His face went ashen, surmising immediately what Jane was about, and bolted toward the girl without a parting word to his employee.

Nicholas smiled understandingly at his friend's conduct and prayed that all would be well at the Thornton house this momentous day.

Mr. Thornton bounded up the stairs two at a time to reach the door of his wife's bedchamber. "Margaret, may I come in?" he asked as he knocked, his stomach roiling in desperation to see her before she was swept into the care of the coming attendants.

His mother opened the door, her doubtful gaze assessing her son's temperament. "She's undressing, John, in preparation for the birth," the steadfast matriarch announced to dissuade him.

"May I see her just this once?" he begged with as much patience and calm as he could muster.

His mother relented wordlessly and opened the door further to allow him in.

Margaret stood in the middle of the room in her undergarments, her face blanched in stupefaction at the enormity of what lay ahead.

Dixon gave a disapproving glance at the Master as she made her way to the wardrobe with her mistress's gown.

"Margaret!" he exclaimed as he rushed to her side. Taking her hands in his, he brought them to his lips, unwilling to relinquish his contact with her. "Are you well?" he asked, not knowing what to say.

"All is well at the moment," she replied honestly, a glimmer of a smile breaking through her nervousness.

His every nerve tingled with longing to take her into his arms and protect her from any difficult experience, but he knew his love could not save her from the event that must take place. "What can I do?" he whispered helplessly, knowing that he would soon be whisked from the room as custom and propriety demanded.

"Pray that the birth will be swift and that all will be well. I am certain all will be well, John," she amended as she noted the fear that flashed in his eyes. "We will rejoice together before long," she assured him.

Oblivious to all women but the one in front of him, he gently held Margaret's chin with a curved finger and stroked it with his thumb, staring in wonder at her strong resolve. He bent to kiss her lips tenderly, savoring the touch with an aching heart. He pulled away reluctantly and they gazed at each other without a word until Hannah called her son's name impatiently, and he turned to leave.

"John!" Margaret called him back to her. She pulled out a handkerchief from her camisole and held it out to him, her eyes communicating with his.

He took the small token from her gently and held it firmly in his grasp. Then, studying her face one last time, he turned and left the room.

Mr. Thornton stood at the drawing room window, staring at the large, wet snowflakes that serenely floated past his view. The sight stilled him, giving him momentary reprieve from the unbearable restlessness that had carried him to the window.

He watched the snow collect on the ground, slowly covering everything in a blanket of white. He gazed upward to follow the smoke that bellowed from the mill's chimney and disappeared into grayness. Below, a few carts were loaded and unloaded in the yard. The calm normalcy of the scene seemed to mock his agitation. Today his world would change, but the tide of nature and mankind continued unchanged.

He would become a father this day! For months, he had imagined the joys and cares that would come with fatherhood. He was excited and apprehensive to consider that what had once seemed a dream-like concept would soon be a reality. A powerful and tender love swept through him as he envisioned his wife holding their babe in her arms.

Turning abruptly from the window, he glanced toward the stairway before he began to pace the length of the room. He pulled out his pocket watch to check the time, as he had done so many times before. It had been nearly four hours now since he had left Margaret in her room, and over an hour ago that his mother had come to tell him that all seemed well.

He did not know how much longer he could endure the torture of waiting in ignorance. His uselessness was palpable as he strode aimlessly from fireplace to window and back again. If only he could assist in some tangible way, he would be free of this wretched idleness! He wondered if she might need his comfort, if the pain would overwhelm her.

He longed for a surcease from the turmoil of his thoughts, a palliative to put his mind at ease. Fear poised like a viper, ready to strike at his first move toward the dire thoughts that threatened to undo him. He remembered with disturbing clarity the unworldly screams of a neighbor in labor one dark summer night when his family had lived in rented rooms. The memory of that nightmarish evening, when he had only bravely begun his venture as the head of the family, caused him to shudder.

His nerves tensed and he stopped in his tracks to listen for any discerning sound. The silence of the house exacerbated his anxiety, for he half expected to hear screams pierce the quiet from the floor above.

Gripping the mantelpiece for support, Mr. Thornton hung his head and leaned heavily as he struggled to gain dominion over the fears that began to take hold of him. He could not bear to think of Margaret in pain, and gulped to regain his composure, which he felt was crumbling. Surely the silence was a good omen, he told himself. She was strong and could bear this experience, he endeavored to reassure himself, remembering something of what his mother had said earlier.

Lifting his head again, he saw the handkerchief Margaret had given him still held tightly within his grasp. This small token calmed him, and he walked over to the window to see it in brighter light.

Mr. Thornton examined the finely stitched initials and the yellow rose embroidered on the fabric. He smiled at the 'T' emblazoned next to the 'M'. *The girl from Helstone had taken his name.* His thumb brushed gently over the yellow flower - a symbol of the innocence and beauty which was ever his Margaret.

If he should lose her... He froze in terror at the thought, his hand shaking tremulously as he brought the handkerchief to his face. *No!* He would not allow himself to be shaken with unreasonable fear. He must trust that all would be well. Had she not promised that they would rejoice together today?

He lifted his chin in determined resolve. He would hold on to her words. He had no other choice.

⁂

Margaret held fast to the bedpost as another strong urge to push overcame her; her eyes were wide with amazement at the power of the contractions.

Dixon attempted once more to coax Margaret to lie down as a lady ought, fretting at the indecorous position her mistress had taken when the pains had grown stronger.

Margaret ignored the plea, focused only on gaining some relief from the heavy weight bearing down on her. She had raised herself to her knees, unable to remain prone upon the bed as she had been bidden. She wore a long chemise that covered her properly, even as she clung unladylike to the wooden column of her four-poster bed.

"I'm certain there can be no harm in allowing gravity to assist her," Mrs. McKnight, the midwife, calmly stated to assuage Dixon and Hannah Thornton's evident dismay. Dr. Donaldson quietly nodded his head in agreement.

As the strong sensations eased slightly, Margaret found the coherency to speak. "John! Where is John?" she asked, desperate to feel his reassuring strength. Discomfited looks passed between Hannah and the doctor at the girl's outcry.

"It's all right, Margaret. John is downstairs, as is proper. I will call him here as soon as the baby is born," Mrs. Thornton promised, endeavoring to placate the girl.

"Please call him now," she entreated, the strength of her determination evident in her voice.

Mrs. Thornton's mouth hung open in flustered alarm and she exchanged a horrified glance with Dixon. "Surely it is not necessary..." the stalwart matriarch began.

"Please, or I shall call out for him myself!" Margaret interjected with panic, her warning delivered with clear resolve.

Hannah blanched, mortified at the thought of her son being summoned in such a way. With great trepidation, she turned to do as she was bidden.

"Perhaps it will comfort the girl. It is not entirely unheard of," Mrs. McKnight murmured to Mrs. Thornton as she walked to the door to fetch her son.

Mr. Thornton walked swiftly toward the stairs at the sound of descending footsteps and met his mother's unsmiling gaze with an expectant stare.

"She's asked for you, John," his mother relayed evenly with solemn tones.

An exultant joy swept through him to hear that she wanted him. But as he bounded past his mother up the stairs, a frisson of fear tingled his spine. What had impelled her to call for him, he wondered? Instantly, he thrust aside any clamoring fears to steel himself for whatever scene he would face. He must be the strength she would need.

His hand hesitated on the doorknob for the briefest moment, his heart pounding, before he swung wide the door. All eyes watched the Master as he strode with purpose to his wife's side, his expression one of tender compassion.

Still kneeling on the bed, Margaret released her grip on the bedpost to take hold of her husband's hands. She grasped him tightly and leaned her weight on him as she looked to him with hopeful trust. Their eyes communicated all that needed to be said.

Mr. Thornton staunchly held her up, relieved to be of assistance at last although inwardly he quaked to see his wife so shaken.

"Oh!" Margaret let out a gasp as her body once again commanded every muscle towards its final purpose. Unprepared for her sudden reaction, Mr. Thornton fairly staggered at the strength with which she held on to him.

The next few minutes went by in a haze of noise and confusion, as Mr. Thornton focused solely on holding his wife while the doctor and midwife spoke soothingly to Margaret as she panted and uttered short groans in her travail.

Although it seemed a small eternity to the strained father and mother-to-be, it was not long before Margaret made a final cry of exertion and relaxed her hold on her husband. The midwife exclaimed with joy and in the next moment the sound of a brand new voice permeated the air - the healthy cries of the infant lifting the heavy atmosphere to one of joyous vibrancy.

"It's a girl," Mrs. McKnight announced.

Their child was born! In dazed confusion, Mr. Thornton watched the unfolding activity around him as a distant observer. The writhing infant was spirited away to be examined and bathed by the doctor and his assistant, while Dixon and his mother carefully helped Margaret lie down against the pillows. All the while, the cries of his newborn child filled his ears with stupefying wonder.

Tears streamed down Dixon's face. The girl that she had tended since birth now had a babe of her own.

No one saw the proud new grandmother dab her wrist at her eyes as she witnessed her son's child kick and boldly announce her entry into the world.

Dr. Donaldson walked over to the Master with a broad grin as he wiped his hands on a cloth. He offered his hand to the new father, breaking the man's reverie. "Congratulations. Mr. Thornton, you are the father of a healthy young daughter," he confirmed as the men shook hands.

"Thank you," the flustered Master replied, his face breaking into a wide smile as the heady realization began to settle in his mind - *he was a father now!*

Mrs. McKnight carried the tiny bundle to his wife and helped Margaret settle the babe at her breast. John stared transfixed at the sight, unable to move or speak. Everything he had once dreamed to be impossible was now his - the girl he had thought would never love him had borne him a daughter. Was it possible to receive a more profound blessing than this?

"What is her name?" the midwife gently asked the new mother.

"Sophie...Sophie Maria," Margaret answered with a smile, her voice proudly triumphant despite a trace of weakness. She looked up to her husband to share in her joy.

Mr. Thornton beamed with happiness, and gazed at his wife with tenderness and pride.

"What a lovely name," Mrs. McKnight responded as Hannah and John shared knowing looks.

When the babe had suckled, Hannah brought her sleeping granddaughter to her son and laid her gently in his tentative arms. She smiled fondly at his awkwardness in his new role. "There is still a matter which needs tending to," she informed him. "Why don't you take the baby to your room for a while? I will call you when all is through," she directed him, nudging him in the right direction with a nod of her head.

The snow still gently fell outside, covering everything in white and dispersing the winter's gray. Reflected brightness streamed into the windows, as if the heavens themselves sent their blessings to this very place.

Mr. Thornton stood still near the foot of the bed, gently holding his new daughter. He looked up for a moment to survey his surroundings.

The silence of the room echoed its sacredness, for here was the place where their lives had co-mingled most tangibly and where their love was spent freely. It was this love that had brought new life into the world in the form of the precious child that lay in his arms.

His eyes welled with tears as he studied the tiny infant with reverent fascination. He had never seen anything so beautiful. Marveling at the perfect shape of her tiny nose, a wavering smile formed on his lips as he noted with affection how she resembled her mother.

He had kept his preference a secret; he had not told a single soul that he had hoped for a daughter. He was certain a son would be born to him soon enough, but ever since it had been revealed that a child was growing in his wife's womb, he had dreamed of sheltering a daughter. In watching her grow, he imagined he would glimpse the joyful sweetness and innocent exuberance that must have been Margaret's as a young girl.

He bestowed his first kiss on her forehead and let his lips linger to feel the velvet skin under his soft press. He lifted his head slowly to study her again, amazed that she was finally here.

After some time, his mother entered the room from the connecting door. He turned unabashed to acknowledge her, his glistening blue eyes communicating his awe as he held out the babe in his arms.

Her heart melted to see him thus. "She is beautiful, John," she said, joining him in gazing at the exquisite perfection of the tiny pink face that peeped from the swaddling flannel. She noted with pride the trace of dark hair on the babe's forehead.

"You will be a good father," she told him, moving her gaze to meet his eyes.

"Thank you," he whispered, unable to find a stronger voice.

"Margaret is an extraordinary young woman. She will make a fine mother," she remarked with rare praise.

He nodded his agreement, grateful for his mother's confident assessment.

"Come now, and see your wife," she beckoned him with an affectionate smile.

Dixon swept the babe to the nursery to allow Margaret to rest, and before Mr. Thornton crossed the room, Dr. Donaldson asked to speak privately with him for a moment.

Just outside the door in the hallway, the doctor informed Mr. Thornton that all had gone very well. "Not every woman is so fortunate. Your wife has a very strong constitution. I expect you will have many more children," he remarked candidly, making the Master nod with a flushed smile. "Now, she will need to rest for several days and take care that she does not unduly exert herself in the first few weeks; and, as I tell all my new fathers, it is best to refrain from marital relations for at least a month to allow healing," he solemnly advised.

"Of course," Mr. Thornton quickly agreed with a creased brow, averting his eyes a moment before meeting the doctor's gaze with a serious expression. He would need to be patient in reclaiming his wife's attentions.

Dr. Donaldson offered his congratulations one more time and shook hands with the Master before taking his leave.

All was quiet when Mr. Thornton returned to the room where his wife lay resting with her eyes closed. The recent excitement and activity of the past hour was replaced with a peaceful stillness. Her eyes fluttered open as he gently sat on the bed next to her, and reached out to tenderly caress her cheek, nestling his fingers into her hair.

She turned her face into his hand and kissed his palm, and he rewarded her gesture with a soft kiss on her forehead.

"I find it difficult to believe that women are the weaker sex," he remarked only half in jest as he pulled back to gaze at her with loving admiration.

Margaret smiled at his observation. "We learn to endure much," she offered gently.

He took her hand and she happily twined her fingers with his. "You were incredible," he praised.

"You are now a father," she announced with joy in an endeavor to deflect attention from herself.

"And you a mother," he countered with a warm smile. "Are you happy?" he asked, his blue eyes piercing her for her honest answer.

"I am tired, but very content," she replied with an effusive smile. "She is so beautiful, is she not?" she asked of their new daughter.

"She is," he agreed. "Very beautiful," he uttered in a reverent whisper as he bent to kiss his wife's forehead again.

"You are happy," she pronounced with tentative certainty, her eyes hopeful as she sought the answer in his eyes.

"I am the happiest husband and father in Milton," he declared with absolute surety and felt her squeeze his hand tightly in response. "I should let you rest," he decided, although he made no move to leave.

"Will you stay with me a little longer?" she gently pleaded, enjoying his loving attentions.

"As you desire," he replied with a broad smile. He stood up, spontaneously deciding to join her in the bed. He hadn't realized until that moment how weary he felt now that the battle with tension and terror was over. He took off his stockings and shoes and climbed into the bed next to her, taking her hand in his again and bringing it to his lips. They both fell soundly asleep.

The rest of the day passed as a blur, and after a night spent alone in his bed, Mr. Thornton felt less than energetic as he rose to dress for work the following morning. When he sat in his office chair later holding his quill, he found that he had lost his purpose. He had no desire or interest to work.

Higgins passed the open door and stopped to retrace his steps at the sight of the Master. "Am I to offer you congratulations?" he asked with a cheery grin as he stood in the doorway.

The Master's face illuminated at his friend's words. "I am the father of a daughter," he announced with pride.

"Aye! Congratulations, Thornton!" he said as he stepped forward to shake his friend's hand. "She'll steal your heart, and you'll not get it back," he warned with a knowing smile.

Mr. Thornton let out a breathy laugh and nodded his head.

"How's Margaret?" Higgins asked more seriously.

"She's doing well. She's resting," the new father answered.

Higgins studied his friend's stooped posture and slightly tousled hair. "Looks like you could use a little rest yourself. Why don't you go back to your wife and child? The mill can manage a day or two without you," he encouraged the Master with fond respect.

Mr. Thornton gazed at his employee with some surprise. He had never even considered taking a day off, so ingrained was his daily habit. "I believe I will," he answered, giving his friend a grateful smile.

Higgins turned to leave.

"Higgins," the Master called out to stay him a moment more. "Tell the men there will be cake and ale to celebrate. The lunch hour can be extended today," he happily pronounced with a beaming face.

Nicholas gave an approving nod with a twitch of a smile.

Mr. Thornton was already out the door and crossing the mill yard when a hearty cheer erupted from the workers at Higgins' announcement. The Master's friend could not suppress the grin that pulled at his face. He felt a fatherly pride to share in the Thorntons' happiness for their recent blessings and good fortune. No other master in town would receive such good wishes from his workers. But then, no other mill owner reached the stature and decency of the Master at Marlborough Mills.

In the days that followed, Mr. Thornton felt his home life was turned upside down. Retiring early, his wife slept in her room while Dixon dozed on a cot nearby. Dixon brought the baby to the mistress for feedings and took the babe away to the nursery for the latter part of each night to give the new mother peaceful rest.

Although he knew the arrangement was meant to be convenient for the nursing mother as well as to give him undisturbed sleep, Mr. Thornton missed the comfort of his wife's presence at night. Restless and lonely, he slept fitfully, and woke often to the sound his daughter's cries, lying awake afterward as he tried to imagine the scene that lay just beyond the wall of his room.

One evening, Mr. Thornton woke to the cries of his child and lay with his eyes open as the babe continued to cry between a few short lulls of silence. When he could take no more, he threw back his covers and pulled on his trousers to see if he could be of assistance.

Dixon looked surprised as the disheveled Master suddenly entered the room without announcement. Margaret looked pleadingly at her husband. Holding the wailing infant in her arms, she appeared on the verge of tears. "She will not stop crying. We have tried everything," she quavered in desperation.

Mr. Thornton reached forth to take the babe, and his wife willingly handed her bundle to him. He walked slowly about the room, softly crooning his own crafted lullaby to the child as he rocked her in his arms. In moments, the babe was asleep, and he returned the tiny bundle to his wife.

Both women stared at him in astonishment.

"Should she not know her own father's voice?" he queried with a smile.

Margaret handed the baby to Dixon, who carefully carried the infant to the nursery for the remainder of the evening.

Reluctant to leave, Mr. Thornton remained standing in the middle of the room. "Will you join me in the other room? I have been rather lonely of late," he humbly confessed with a look of longing.

"I've missed you, too," she answered with a warming smile as she stepped forward to wrap her arms about him.

Mr. Thornton woke the next morning feeling much refreshed. He knew the reason why. A delicate hand loosely clutched at his arm and long auburn tresses nestled against his shoulder. He carefully turned onto his side to watch his wife as she slept. Unable to resist the urge to touch her, he gently brushed her cheek with the back of his fingers before stretching forward to place a light kiss on her forehead.

Margaret gently stirred, and her eyes fluttered open. She stared at her husband for a moment before sitting up with a start. "The baby! Dixon will be bringing her..." she began, flustered at the thought of Dixon's confusion at her absence.

"She will find you. It's quite all right," her husband soothed, sitting up and gently stroking her arm. No sooner had he spoken than a knock was heard at the dressing room door and Margaret beckoned Dixon to enter.

The stout maid gave a disgruntled sigh and wary glance at the Master, whom she was sure had persuaded Margaret to abandon her own bed.

She reluctantly handed her mistress the wakeful babe, discomfited at the thought that Margaret would be exposing herself to her husband's curious gaze by remaining in his bed. She shook her head in helpless resignation as she left the room. There was no use arguing the point with such a strong-willed girl.

"Thank you for helping last night," Margaret said as she prepared to nurse their child. "I'm sorry to have disturbed you. Perhaps I should move to the nursery."

"No, I prefer you to be closer. In fact, I rather hoped you could return to this bed - with me," he confided haltingly, the hopefulness in his voice warming her heart.

"But you need your sleep," she countered, wanting to know if he was certain of his choice.

"To tell the truth, I have not slept well these last few days. I am awake at our daughter's every cry, regardless of the wall between us. I see no reason why you should remain apart. Perhaps I could be of assistance," he suggested.

"If you wish it," she replied with a searching gaze.

"I do," he answered with conviction as a warm smile spread over his face.

On the first morning of spring, faint sunshine spilled into the grand bedchamber. Mr. Thornton awoke with a feeling of calm contentment. His wife lay facing him with their babe snuggled between them. He gently stroked his daughter's tiny head and traced his fingers along her small arm. Then, he reached to lay his arm over his wife's waist as she slept. He could not help but smile. His world was awash in the glow of love, permeating everything he did with a deep-settled purpose. Not so very long ago, he could not have imagined that such happiness could be possible for one such as he. Gazing with wonder at the beautiful features of his wife's sleeping face, he thanked the heavens for the thousandth time for having sent the girl from the Hampshire countryside to Milton.

Chapter Twenty-three

Pale light streamed through the far windows of the Master's grand bedchamber early one morning in May. Mr. Thornton awoke to the faint chatter of birds perched upon the rooftop. He rolled toward his wife and studied her face in its serene repose before leaning over to place feathered kisses on her nose, eyelids, and cheek. "It was one year ago this day that we were married," he told her quietly, his deep voice quavering with reverence at the remembrance of that glorious day.

"You remembered," she answered sleepily, stretching her arms and limbs as a contented smile spread over her face. She finally opened her eyes to see her husband gazing tenderly at her.

"I could hardly forget. I am reminded of my great blessing every morning when I wake to see you here beside me," he uttered, drawing her closer to the warmth of his body.

"And I know mine every evening when you come home to me," she responded, looking straight into his eyes. She basked in the bliss of his closeness, and longed to feel the press of his weight upon her.

"Margaret," he murmured in delight at her answer and brought his lips to hers as reward. She melded to him instantly, igniting the passion that flowed through their veins.

A slow groan rose from his throat as she slid her hand slowly up his back and delved her fingers into his hair to clasp him closer. He moved to capture her beneath him, but just then a small cry was heard from beyond their bed.

Mr. Thornton reluctantly lifted his head to break contact from the intoxicating kisses that had consumed them. He rolled back to release her from his possession with a small sigh as Margaret climbed out of bed and picked up her daughter from the nearby crib.

His ardor ebbed, transformed into sweet pleasure to see his wife lift his infant daughter from her crib. He smiled as he watched Margaret kiss the babe's plump, pink cheeks. Sophie had stopped crying now that her mother held her in her arms.

Mr. Thornton remained in bed a moment longer before he swept aside the covers to begin his morning routine. His wife's eyes followed him across the room as he doffed his nightshirt to make his ablutions.

"I thought we could take the carriage for a picnic lunch today," he suggested, raking his hand through his slightly dampened hair and wiping his face dry. "I could come home at noon to fetch you," he offered as he walked to the wardrobe to retrieve a shirt.

"That would be lovely; it looks to be very fair weather today," Margaret answered cheerfully. The babe suckled quietly as the young mother sat against the pillows of the bed.

"Good. I have a few matters to finish at the mill this morning, but I intend to take my leisure with you for the remainder of the day," he explained, his lips turning up in a crooked smile.

"Then I will hold you to your promise," she replied with a playful gleam in her eye.

Their afternoon excursion was pleasant. The sloping, grassy fields beyond Milton provided them a picturesque view of the city. As the carriage rolled on towards home, Margaret looked out over the spring greenery with fondness until a gentle squeeze on her clasped hand brought her attention to the man sitting next to her. She gave him a warm smile and he leaned toward her for a kiss.

Their lips brushed gently and tenderly at first, but as Mr. Thornton reached out to cup her face and hold her to him, his kisses swiftly became more passionate. They had only recently renewed their more intimate relations as man and wife, but the time they had for such loving was not as regular as Mr. Thornton wished. His wife was often exhausted at day's end, and mornings were fraught with the fear of waking the baby. At present, only Sunday afternoons could be relied upon to provide the perfect opportunity, when the baby took a long nap in the nursery.

Alone in the privacy of their coach, her kisses kindled his desire until it became a consuming fire. He dropped his hands to restlessly follow the curves of her silhouette.

Margaret gently pushed at his chest and broke free from his kiss. Her luminous eyes pleaded for him to understand. "We will soon be travelling the city streets," she cautioned, feeling her heart twist at the flicker of disappointment in his eyes.

He nodded his compliance and pressed her head to his shoulder in tender solicitude to her gentler sensibilities. She nestled happily against him, her hand joined with his on his thigh as the carriage rattled on.

Mr. Thornton's expression was placid as he vaguely took in the passing scenery. He chastised himself for his sullen mood, but could not repress the frustration that lingered as his thwarted desires slowly subsided. He leaned to place a kiss on his wife's head; her hair smelled of the fresh spring air. His heart lightened to recall the reason for their small excursion. They had been married a year ago this day. For that singular occasion, he would be eternally grateful. Reminded of the great love that existed between them, he could not help but smile as he squeezed the small hand in his with affection and held her closer to him.

No sooner had they arrived then Margaret swept upstairs at the sound of the baby's cries, leaving Mr. Thornton to keep his mother company in the drawing room.

The new mother returned sometime later with Sophie in her arms. The babe was well-sated and alert, her blue eyes focused on her mother. "I could not find Dixon," Margaret offered as an explanation for bringing the child downstairs.

"It is Tuesday, I'm certain she's gone to fetch the pressing," Mrs. Thornton answered. "Give the babe to me. I will enjoy entertaining her for awhile," she insisted, holding out her arms eagerly to take the child.

Margaret handed the infant to her doting grandmother, who smiled in satisfaction at having secured her precious grandchild in her arms.

"Why don't you two go rest? I will take care of Sophie," she suggested, already caught up in adoration of the babe. Her eyes twinkled in delight at the baby's open gaze. "Go on," she shooed the couple with a quick toss of her head.

Mr. Thornton rose from his chair, eager to be alone with his wife. He followed Margaret quietly up the stairs and into their room, securing the door behind them.

She turned to face him, but before she could speak, he closed the distance between them and encircled her in his arms. Her breath stilled as she recognized his purpose; his blue eyes blazed with the intensity of his need. She offered no resistance as he brought his lips to hers. His hungering kisses melted her and she felt the molten heat of her own desire rise up to answer his. Running her hands along the front of his waistcoat, she trembled to feel the firmness of his form before locking her arms around his neck in absolute surrender.

That evening at bedtime, Dixon finished fastening the hooks at the back of Margaret's wedding dress as the young wife stood in front of the long mirror. The stout woman gave a small smile at the girl's romantic notion. The dress did not quite fit around the bust, but that was to be expected. Dixon shook her head. It was hard to believe her young charge was already a mother. But she was happy, the faithful servant reminded herself, her heart warming at the thought of Margaret's contentment in the life she had chosen.

A faint knock sounded on the connecting door. "Margaret?" the Master's voice sounded, patiently requesting admittance.

"Thank you, Dixon. That will be all," Margaret quietly dismissed her maid before answering her husband's call in more resonant tones. "Come in," she beckoned with faint anxiety, swiftly arranging her skirts to their full advantage.

He took one step inside before he stilled to see her, the poignant memory of their wedding day touching him to the core.

Drawn like a magnet, he was at her side in an instant to place a lingering kiss on the lips that continually enticed him with their supple softness. "You are as beautiful as ever," he uttered reverently, as his gaze swept over her features, his face close to hers. She was, he mused, even more beautiful, for he now knew every nuanced expression of her face and every contour of her body. She had reached scarcely beyond girlhood when they had married, but now she stood before him as a well-loved woman who had borne a child.

"It does not fit perfectly, but I so wished to try it on," she confessed, pleased by his favorable reaction. She gloried in the remembrance of the day that held such special significance to her. "What do you have?" she asked curiously about the package he held firmly with one arm.

"Happy anniversary," he answered with a warm smile, holding out the wrapped gift to her.

She looked inquiringly into his eyes, giving him a sweet smile as she lifted the large box from his hands. Her husband watched perplexed as she turned to set the package down on the bed and crossed to retrieve something from within her wardrobe. She returned to him, placing in his hands a rolled canvas.

Mr. Thornton untied the ribbon that bound it, and unrolled the paper to view a painting of a brook that bent past a peaceful forest with lush, green grasses in the foreground. "This is where we stayed... in Helstone," he stammered as he studied the picture in wonder at its likeness to the spot he remembered with such fondness.

"It was one of the paintings I did while I waited Sophie's arrival. I wanted to surprise you," she explained, glowing with pleasure at his response.

"It is very good. I knew at once the spot - with the large rock and the way the brook turns just there," he pointed out as he commended her work. "I will have it framed and put in my study," he remarked, looking to her with great appreciation.

"I did not know if it would suit..." she began modestly.

"It will suit very well," he finished with decision. "I will cherish this as a reminder of those wondrous first days," he told her, bending to give her an affectionate kiss of thanks. "Now, you must open your present," he directed, a warm smile spreading over his face in anticipation of her approval.

Margaret carefully tore at the paper to reveal a handsome rosewood box with brass inlay. She took in her breath at the sight. "Oh, John, it's beautiful," she enthused.

"Open it," he gently encouraged, eager for her to see more.

She lifted the lid to find various jars with silver-plated lids nestled in small compartments lined with green velvet. "It's a travelling case!" she mused aloud as she inspected the designs engraved on the silver tops.

"There's a drawer below for your jewelry," he mentioned eagerly, willing her to open it.

She pulled out a small velvet-lined drawer to find a small scroll tied with ribbon. She looked at him quizzically and he nodded for her to open it. Untying the ribbon, she unfurled the parchment to read her husband's missive.

Happy anniversary, my darling wife,

Words could never describe what this year has meant to me. You alone can fathom it - for when I look into your eyes I know my heart has found its home.

Will you come to Helstone with me once more? I have made arrangements for us to stay at the cottage for a fortnight this summer. I am eager to return to the place where heaven and earth seem to meet. The memories of those days I will treasure in my heart forever.

Your own,

John

Margaret's eyes flew to her husband's glowing face. "Truly? Are we to go back again?" she asked in excitement as she threw herself into his embrace, her arms resting upon his chest.

"Did I not say we should?" he answered, thrilled at her elation as he encircled her waist tighter.

"When do we go?" she asked eagerly, her shining eyes looking up to him.

"The Thompsons proposed early July, so we have a month to wait. I thought we could bring mother to see the countryside and to help care for Sophie. I'm sure you will have plenty of time to arrange everything as it should be," he remarked.

"I will count the days," she proclaimed in earnest.

Mr. Thornton threw his head back to laugh at her bright enthusiasm. "I will be counting them as well, but for now I wish to enjoy the moment at hand," he responded as his voice lowered softly.

Margaret raised her face to his in answering accord. Their lips met and moved in gentle fervency, until a spark turned into flame.

❧

When the day of their departure arrived, the hustle and noise of the station amplified the couple's excitement to begin their holiday away. To ordinary passersby, Hannah Thornton's countenance did not betray anxiety; but her shifting eyes and pursed lips were duly noted by her son, who recognized her uneasiness at being taken away from every familiar pattern of life for a fortnight.

The elder woman's restlessness vanished as soon as Sophie was placed in her arms. Margaret was well aware of the comforting joy the baby gave her mother-in-law. The young mother could not be more pleased that such a precious bond had formed between the generations, and remembered with a twinge of amusement how dour and unfeeling she had assumed Mrs. Thornton to be upon their first encounters.

Mr. Thornton could not contain the easy smile that played upon his face. Already he felt the weight of his business responsibilities lifted from his shoulders for a time, and he was eager to revisit the beautiful countryside where he had spent the most glorious week of his life.

When they had travelled several hours and Milton lay far behind them, Mr. Thornton found himself alone in the compartment with his bride. Sophie lay sleeping at their feet in her small cradle, and the regular sway and clacking of the train had cajoled his mother into a restful nap. Her hands still gently grasped her embroidery.

The Master surveyed the compartment – they were as good as alone. A broad smile lightened his face as he slid his arm around his wife's shoulders. Margaret turned from the window to give him a warm smile and nestled closer within her husband's comfortable embrace.

"We have perhaps an hour, maybe a bit more, until we reach London," he stated softly.

"Yes, I know. I was just thinking about the last time I travelled to London - with Aunt Shaw," she replied with a slight waver in her voice at the bittersweet memory of the day she had left Milton without him.

A shudder of emotion passed through Mr. Thornton as he vividly recalled how intense his pain had been to part with her so soon after discovering that she was willing to accept his proposal of marriage. "I thought my heart would be torn in half to watch you leave me that day. I still could scarcely believe you should care for me," he answered in a low voice.

"But I did care for you!" she responded, turning her face up to his so that he saw that her eyes shone with eager compassion. "Although I had not quite admitted how much so, even to my own heart, until I discovered that you still had feelings for me!" she confessed, dipping her gaze and raising it again to his. "When I found that note in the book you gave to me....I had not dared to dream that you should still love me after all I had done."

Mr. Thornton cradled her face in his hands. "I could not stop loving you. When you came to say your good-bye to me, I felt as if my world was coming to an end. I was certain you should never return to a place that I thought you despised. When you told me that you had grown fond of Milton, my hopes soared to think you might hold me in some regard after all. I could not let you leave without knowing whether I had a chance of gaining your affection. I prayed you would find the note before long, but I had not dreamed you would send your answer so quickly!" he professed, his eyes searing hers with tender passion at the reminiscence of that day's events.

She returned his gaze with a measure of wonder at his retelling; her throat was choked with emotion. "Once I realized what your note implied, I could not let you believe anything but the truth for one moment longer - that I loved you, John. Finally, I could see it clearly. I loved you, John Thornton, for longer than you would have believed," she revealed, her luminous eyes sparking with the love she felt for him.

No words were needed to answer her this time. Mr. Thornton captured her lips with his and the couple kissed gently and fervently for as long as privacy allowed.

In London, the Thornton family had arranged to stay at Harley Street for a night to visit Margaret's family before they headed to Helstone the following day. It was a pattern that would become standard practice in the years to come.

Aunt Shaw was pleased to see her niece looking radiantly happy and everyone was glad to meet little Sophie. Edith and Maxwell were delighted to show their new addition to the family. Baby Emmeline had been born the previous month. Edith was certain that someday Sophie and Emmeline would be as good friends as Margaret and Edith had been.

Sholto took little notice of the babies and quickly became a fast friend again with Mr. Thornton during the short time he visited with the family in the parlor.

Hannah Thornton endeavored to be as sociable as possible, and took a liking to Maxwell's good-humored honesty in all things. She appraised the house silently as the others talked, noting the blithe grandeur in which

Margaret had lived for so many years. Although she was not inclined to be overly impressed with Mrs. Shaw's residence, Hannah appreciated that Margaret had never contrived to make her home in Marlborough Mills a stunning replica of such London finery.

When it was time to leave late the following morning, Edith lamented that the visit had been too short; she insisted that the Thorntons must come to visit before too long. Margaret had enjoyed her visit very much and smiled at her cousin's protestations; however, was eager to continue their journey to Helstone.

The carriage ride from the Southampton station was refreshingly scenic, even if the roads were at times less than ideal to their comfort. The sweet scent of gorse permeated the air for miles and the copses and rolling hills seemed alive with the rich color of nature's hues. As the coach grew nearer to the cottage, Margaret smiled at her husband and he took her hand in his with a glint of understanding at her excitement. They both felt the consummate joy of returning to the place where they had spent such blissful days.

When they finally arrived, Margaret descended rapidly from the carriage, unable to wait a moment longer, and breathed in the fragrant scent of lavender which grew in profusion along the front pathway. Mr. Thornton aided his mother, who felt the peacefulness of the beautiful setting in front of her as soon as she had alighted from the coach.

Margaret walked through the house with Sophie in her arms to see that all was just the same as she recalled before climbing the stairs to her room.

Mr. Thornton entered their bedroom a moment later to happily survey the room that he remembered with particular fondness. He closed his arms around his wife's waist from behind, pulling her and his daughter into his embrace. Finding a spot on her neck with his lips he brushed light kisses from her shoulder to her ear. "Pity we are not alone," he whispered huskily, sending a shiver of promised delight down Margaret's spine.

"We should make sure your mother is well settled," she answered calmly, though her heart beat faster at his continuing ministrations upon her neck.

He broke from her reluctantly to offer assistance to his mother.

After they had settled their belongings into their bedchambers, Mrs. Thornton declined their polite offer to rest, declaring that the journey had not been long and that she would much rather enjoy the fresh air. The party soon moved outdoors, and John and Margaret gave Mrs. Thornton a short tour of the property around the cottage.

It was not long before Mr. Thornton brought out a chair for his mother, and she was comfortably situated under a great oak tree with a wakeful Sophie upon her knee. A cradle and sewing basket stood ready for her use on either side. Margaret watched her daughter look up into the branches as her mother-in-law lifted the child to her face for a kiss.

Mr. Thornton squeezed his wife's hand. "Shall we go for a walk?" he asked gently, convinced his mother was well settled with the baby.

Margaret glanced at the sun's position in the sky and took note of the warm air. "I should change out of my travelling clothes into something cooler," she replied. "Perhaps you would like to leave your coat," she suggested as she tugged his hand and headed toward the cottage.

She dropped his hand to climb the stairs ahead of him. After ascending a few steps, she cast a mischievous glance over her shoulder and dashed up the stairs.

Not to be left behind, her husband bounded after her with a devilish grin growing upon his face at her playfulness. He swiftly followed her into their room and secured the door behind him. To his delight, she threw herself into his arms and pressed her body to his, banishing all pretense of her purpose in returning to the cozy room which held such intimate memories.

They emerged from the cottage later in more comfortable attire. Margaret wore a pale blue skirt and white blouse, her cheeks aglow. Mrs. Thornton was somewhat taken aback to see her son casually dressed in his shirtsleeves, but was pleased to see him looking so completely content. The couple explained their intent to take a walk and promised to return within the hour.

The day was warm, and the beauty and calm of the verdure surrounding them was peacefully inviting. They strolled happily hand-in-hand to the bank of the stream, their favorite location. The water sparkled in the hot sunshine and the grasses swayed upon the banks. The forest offered shade for the wildflowers growing on the opposite bank.

"It is just as I recall," Mr. Thornton said as his eyes drank in the sight. He pulled Margaret into his arms, relinquishing the scenic view for one altogether more enchanting. "It has been a year since I brought you home to be my bride. Has your life been as you hoped - with me?" he inquired, his pure blue eyes questing hers.

She wrapped her arms around his neck and smiled warmly. "I never doubted that I would be happy as long as you loved me. I have only wished to bring you happiness in return," she replied hopefully as her soulful eyes searched his.

He gave her a fervent kiss in reply before releasing her gently from his binding hold. "When I kissed you in the brook on our wedding day, I knew that my days would never be dull or empty again. You have filled my life with love and every joy a man could desire. I could not imagine my existence without you," he declared ardently.

"And I could have married no one but you," she returned with an adoring gaze that took his breath away.

He bent to bestow his affection and she received his kiss with trembling tenderness. Above them, white clouds billowed and passed unhurriedly. Beyond these, a pale blue sky expanded infinitely heavenward.

Epilogue

Milton - 1858

Sophie Thornton watched eagerly out the window for any sign of a carriage at the gates. Leaning on tiptoes, she pressed her face against the glass to gain a wider view. "He's here, Mama!" she called out excitedly, her dark ringlets bobbing as she bounded with glee toward her mother.

The sight of her daughter's sparkling blue eyes warmed Margaret's heart. How much those bright eyes reminded her of John! She beamed back at her daughter as the smaller girl in her lap sprang forward to run to the window.

"I don't see him!" the little one pouted as she peered out the window, her henna curls glinting with a golden hue in the sunlight.

"Come, Lydia, he will be here soon enough," Margaret called her youngest daughter, who would be three years old come summer's end. Lydia and Sophie each took an outstretched hand and stood next to their mother in the drawing room as they waited for their father to appear at the doorway.

"Papa!" the littlest one exclaimed as Mr. Thornton's dark-clad form entered the room. She bolted to him, hands outstretched, as he quickly fell to one knee to catch her. Sophie darted to her father's side in rapid order with an excited greeting of her own and he duly swept her into his embrace with a wide swing of his arm. He hugged them both tight against him and told them that he'd missed them.

Grinning at his warm reception, Mr. Thornton looked up at his wife who stood watching the unfolding scene with a glowing face. He gathered Lydia up in one arm and guided Sophie forward as he approached Margaret. "And how is my biggest girl?" he asked, the silken tones of his voice meant only for her. Their eyes spoke of the loneliness they had suffered apart and sparkled with glad relief to be in one another's presence once more.

"I'm tolerably well, but you have been sorely missed," she confided with a playful smile that could not refrain from drawing up at the corners as he snaked his arm around her waist and pulled her against him with little Lydia still in his grasp.

"Have I?" he answered in a whisper before soundly kissing her lips, savoring the taste of her after five days' absence. His days in London had been busy enough, but at night, when the quietness had been amplified by her absence, his bed had seemed empty and he had ached to feel her arms around him.

She did not answer him, but her lingering kiss and the loving look she gave him told him all he needed to know.

"Where is mother?" he asked.

"I am here, with your son," his mother answered as she approached the gathered family. A dark-haired lad lay his head lazily on his grandmother's shoulder, his plump arms wrapped loosely around her neck. Having just awoken from his nap, the little one appeared uninterested in his surroundings, his eyes half closed in a sleepy stupor.

His father leaned down to meet his tired gaze, a warming smile growing on his lips at the sight of the boy who had grown so much in just one year. "Hello, Johnny. Papa's home," he said gently, encouraging the boy to wake up fully and notice him.

"Papa," Johnny responded, his blue eyes alert now in recognition. He lifted his head and extended his arms toward his father.

Mr. Thornton received him in one arm, Lydia still secured to his side with the other.

"How were you received in Parliament?" Hannah Thornton inquired with great interest.

"Very well, I suppose," he answered forthrightly, as if considering for the first time the success of his trip. "I was introduced to a great number of Members and was asked to several subsequent meetings to answer all their questions." He had gone to speak to Parliament on behalf of the cotton industry as a guest of Mr. Wilkinson. It was a duty he was pleased to perform in order to convey the issues of his business as he understood them.

His wife and mother smiled in knowing pride at his obvious accomplishments, but the children were anxious to commandeer their father's attention to things of far more importance.

"Papa, Mr. Bell sent me a new doll for my birthday! Will you come see her?" Sophie asked eagerly, bouncing on her tiptoes as she spoke.

Lydia squirmed down out of her father's hold to join her sister. "He gave me a new doll, too!" the smaller girl added with equal excitement.

"Your birthday?" Mr. Thornton inquired suspiciously. "I thought he already sent you a present for your birthday some time ago. It seems to me that Mr. Bell is spoiling the both of you. He gave you enough presents at Christmas to last you the year," he teased them with a twinkle in his eye.

"Come now, you can show your father your gifts, but then we must let him relax. It was a long journey from London," Margaret told them as she shepherded them towards the stairs.

"Did you see Sholto and Emmeline?" Sophie demanded.

"I did. They are eager for you to visit when we go on our holiday this summer," he replied as they all climbed the stairs.

After Mr. Thornton had made the obligatory visit to the girls' room, Margaret left the children in Hannah's care for a moment as she led her husband down the hall. He stopped her when she would have continued past their room. "Where are you going?" he asked, his voice sultry as his hand clasped her arm.

"To pour you a bath; you have traveled a long way..." she began, looking questioningly at him.

He pulled her into his arms in the middle of the hall. "Will you not first welcome me properly?" he murmured as a suggestive smile spread over his face. His breath caught in his throat as she raised her soulful eyes to meet his, and he wondered yet again at the power she held to entrance him. She was so beautiful!

Margaret raised a hand to caress his face, running her palm over his cheek and brushing her fingers into the hair at his temple. She brought her other hand up to slide along his jaw and neck. He had only been gone a few days, yet she felt as if he had been lost to her for years. She did not take -- she would never take -- his love for granted. He was the embodiment of each manly strength, and all that was right and good in this world. He was so gloriously handsome! Did he not know it? She doubted that he did – she doubted that he knew he had the power to render her breathless when she received such looks from his piercing blue eyes.

Gazing into those eyes and gently stroking his face, she saw the boy who was eager to learn and do, who held within him a gentle heart and an aching need to be loved. She reached up and grasped the nape of his neck to pull his lips toward hers. She would love him, and love him fiercely, all the days of her life.

Mr. Thornton returned the ardor of her kiss. When they stopped to catch their breath, he swept her into the bedroom and closed the door.

That evening, Margaret entered their shared bedroom as usual only to find that her husband was not there. She walked straight through the room without hesitating, knowing where she would find him. Gathering her dressing robe around her, she moved swiftly down the hallway to the girls' room.

She stopped in the doorway and received a quick glance from her husband, but he did not interrupt the story that held both of their daughters' rapt attention. Margaret smiled as she realized that he was concocting another episode in the continuing saga of an adventuresome little mouse that supposedly lived in the floorboards of the girls' room. This time, the mouse had traveled to London in their father's pocket. Margaret covered her mouth to suppress the laughter that bubbled up through her at the sight of Lydia's spell-bound and trusting face.

When Mr. Thornton finished, both parents gave the girls a kiss goodnight and tucked them into bed.

Once inside their room, Margaret sat at her dressing table and brushed her hair as her husband prepared for bed. It was a great comfort to have him home again, she thought. Her nightly routine had seemed void of purpose while he had been gone, and the bedroom had been terribly empty.

She was proud, however, that Milton's own Member of Parliament had asked John to speak to the House of Commons concerning the booming cotton industry and the multitude of issues surrounding it. "What did Mr. Wilkinson think of your success?" she asked curiously. They had discussed much about his London trip at dinner with his mother, but had not touched upon certain aspects.

"He said that I had made quite an impression. I believe I explained our issues well. These men have much to deliberate on many fronts, so I try to make my points clear and reasonable without being too complicated," he answered humbly as he took off his waistcoat and hung it in the wardrobe. He turned to face his wife as he began to undo his shirt. "He was rather adamant that I should consider joining him. There is a seat opening up next year. A Mr. Dalton of Lancashire will be retiring his position," he cautiously revealed to her.

Margaret stilled her brush and turned to look at him. "In Parliament?" she questioned, somewhat aghast at the casualness of his tone at such a commendation.

"Yes," he answered simply, looking to her for her reaction.

Margaret endeavored to quell the thrill of contemplating her husband in such an honorable position and the mixed emotions that followed to think of leaving Milton. She did not wish to appear so excitable, if he was not truly interested in pursuing the possibility. She got up from her seat and crossed the room, taking off her dressing gown and turning the covers down to climb into bed. At last she spoke. "What do you think of his recommendation?" she calmly inquired.

Mr. Thornton let out a sigh and finished putting on his nightshirt as he spoke. "I've had time to consider it on the train ride home, but honestly, I'm not quite sure what to think. It is an honor, to be certain, and I feel on one hand that I might be able to forward some progress in Parliament..." he began.

Margaret studied his face from her seated position in the bed. "But?" she prodded him, noting his reluctance to continue.

He lifted the covers to join her as he answered, "But I'm unsure I would feel well placed in such an environment. There is no determinable daily progress in such a job. I fear that every day would be consumed in endless talk and discussion, with favors and politicking as the members try to push for some advantage for their people. I'm not certain I could keep myself convinced of my practical use in such a place," he equivocated.

His wife was quiet a moment as she reflected on the truth of his doubts. "I know it would be a very different type of work from what you have done, but I know you could help forward improvements, not only for the sake of Milton but for the whole country," she responded with gentle encouragement.

He smiled at her confidence in him but then knit his brow as he contemplated his reluctance. "I don't feel quite comfortable leaving Milton at this time. Events in America are unsettling and I am beginning to doubt the wisdom or morality of continuing to depend on their cotton," he confessed, staring blindly at the burgundy coverlet, deep in thought.

Margaret contemplated his remark as she moved to lie down, facing him. "I suppose it would be best to be where you can do the most good," she rationalized.

He looked at her in thoughtful agreement and lay his head down on the pillow next to hers.

"I'm sure you will do the right thing...whatever you decide," she finished with an affectionate smile.

He could only grin at her faith in him. "You trust my judgment?" he queried with a slight arch of his eyebrows.

"Of course," she replied with a tinge of teasing reproach for his doubtfulness.

"And you would not be disappointed if I declined to pursue such a prestigious position - and the opportunity to live in London for a time?" he asked tentatively.

She leaned forward to plant a kiss on his lips. "It does not matter to me if you are bestowed some worldly title, although I'm quite sure you would deserve it. I know the man I married," she affirmed, studying him with adoration. "As for London - I do not mind where we live, as long as you are with me," she answered with conviction as she glided her hands along his arm to rest on his shoulders.

He reached behind her waist to draw her closer. "I missed you," he told her once again, reveling in the simple pleasure of being in his own bed again - with her.

"I have a confession to make," Margaret revealed with a sheepish smile as she lay face to face with him.

Mr. Thornton crinkled his brow quizzically at her statement, a partial smile gathering at the corners of his mouth.

"I brought the girls to bed with me last night so that I would not be lonely," she admitted shyly before bringing her gaze to his.

He laughed at her transgression in having altered the children's bedtime routine.

"Shall I fetch them once more?" he teased, moving to raise himself from his prone position.

"No!" she declared as she quickly gripped his nightshirt to restrain him and pull him back down. "I wish to have you all to myself," she said with a seductive smile as she wound her arms around his neck and wriggled to bring her body into contact with his. "You have been gone for far too many nights, Mr. Thornton," she chastised him mockingly before reaching her lips to his.

As he returned her kiss, he felt the blissful assurance of her love envelop him. It mattered not what the future would bring, he thought, as long as he could hold her in his arms at the close of every day.

Milton - 1862

"Come, girls, it's nearly noon." Margaret Thornton encouraged her daughters to hasten their steps as they made their way down the dirty streets towards the other side of town.

"Cousin Ophelia and cousin Emmeline would never go to such places, Mother," Sophie remarked somewhat disdainfully as she endeavored to keep pace with her mother, holding her untied bonnet and stepping carefully around the garbage strewn in their path. Lydia hopped over the untidy mess and hurried to follow.

"Then they will not gain the satisfaction that you may attain in following the Lord's injunction to love your brother as yourself," her mother responded adamantly. Fanny's and Edith's daughters had not been taught to look beyond their own realm of pleasant security and luxury, Margaret thought to herself with exasperation. She was resolute, however, in her determination that her own offspring would not look down their noses at those in need.

Sophie let out a small sigh. She was weary of this daily task, but knew her mother was right.

When they reached the drafty brick warehouse, they slipped past the snaking line of bedraggled men, women, and children and entered the large kitchen that had been assembled there.

Margaret and the girls quickly took up their allotted tasks, serving thick stew into bowls and portioning out the bread to the constant stream of tired and wan faces that passed by the long table near the warm stoves that churned out loaves of steaming bread.

It had been nearly a year now since war had erupted between the states in America and almost as long since the last of the American cotton had reached England's shores. Those unprepared for the upheaval had had to close their mills, throwing hundreds of the struggling poor out of work. Churches and charities as well as the city leaders rallied to allay the plight of the unemployed. Margaret knew many of the people who passed her by and she greeted them kindly and asked about their families. The soup kitchen was keeping many fed, but Margaret knew more should be done. She had pleaded with local authorities to set up a system whereby to distribute provisions: clothes and clogs, coal and food staples were desperately needed. All hope that the conflict in America would be brief had long faded.

As Sophie ladled mutton stew into bowls, her attention was drawn to a pale girl about her own age who leaned against her mother, endeavoring to share a dilapidated shawl. When the girl reached the table to take her portion, Sophie met her solemn gaze and gave her a meek smile. In the next instant, the mill owner's daughter tugged at the cashmere shawl around her shoulders and wordlessly handed it to the girl. Somewhat startled and confused, the girl hesitated at the gesture until Sophie implored her to take it with a friendly nod.

The shivering girl gave a meek nod in thanks, accompanied by a faint twitch of a smile.

A chill enveloped her shoulders, but Sophie Thornton barely took notice. Instead, an indescribable warmth welled up from within her and her whole body radiated a deeply felt peace.

⌘

Mr. Thornton concluded his consultation with the foreman at Hamper's former mill amidst the shouting and noise of men hoisting heavy looms onto carts to be hauled away. With a grim face he surveyed the emptying mill. Hamper had been a fool, staking his business on the vain hope that the growing turmoil in the States would not interfere with trade.

Well before war had erupted, Mr. Thornton had endeavored to persuade his colleagues to be cautious in relying solely on American cotton. Watson, Slickson, and others had eventually been convinced of his arguments. Slickson had partially converted to Surat cotton from India, altering half of his machines to process the lower grade cotton. Carefully regarding his brother-in-law's wisdom and sound business sense, Watson had switched his mill to spin and weave the same fine, Egyptian cotton as that made at Marlborough Mills. Watson's new wealth, however, had emboldened his ambitions and he had opened a woolen mill.

Hamper had not heeded the warning, except to horde a supply of cotton in his warehouse. When the Union's blockade prevented him from replenishing his store, he had been forced to close his mill. Mr. Thornton had stepped forward to buy it at a very good price, but the machinery had been old, and he had been obliged to consider diversifying his own enterprise. He had finally decided that he would begin weaving silk, and had ordered Jacquard looms that were to arrive within a fortnight. There would be much to tend to in the following weeks and months.

The weary Master took out his pocket watch to see that it was nearly time for dinner and quickly turned on his heels to head home. Although his schedule was increasingly daunting, he counted his time with his family dear and rarely missed spending at least a portion of his evening in the comfort of his own home.

As the tall manufacturer strode toward Marlborough Mills, he brooded over the mounting challenges that beleaguered the city. Some mills had been forced to reduce production, offering short time work for employees at lowered wages. Applications for relief to the Poor Law Unions were increasing, and local relief committees were attempting to find ways to aid those in need. Mr. Thornton had personally hired as many men as possible, even offering work related to the maintenance of his mill and his house, but still felt the need to do more.

Mr. Thornton's scowl grew deeper as he considered the bales of raw cotton hoarded uselessly in local warehouses by greedy speculators whose only thought was for self-aggrandizement as they waited for the price of cotton to escalate to even more exorbitant figures. His fists clenched at the thought of what he would like to say to such callous individuals, who only exacerbated the suffering and struggles of their fellow man.

His mind was still mired in the quagmire of distress as he bounded up the stairs of his home. The buoyant exclamations from the children at his entrance into the drawing room at once began to lift the heavy weight of his thoughts. A light embrace and chaste kiss from his wife elicited a smile from his lips and filled his heart with an effusion of warm affection. He greeted his mother fondly, noting that she was teaching Lydia some intricacy of embroidery.

Before he took a step further into the room, a small boy with wisps of copper curls toddled up to his father with a spinning top hoisted eagerly in his chubby hands. Johnny closely followed him.

"Papa do it!" the smaller boy demanded with an eager expectancy of gaining his father's immediate compliance.

Mr. Thornton crouched to his youngest son's level, giving him a broad smile. "You want me to spin the top, Richard?" he asked the boy gently as he studied his stout lips and the curve of his nose that so resembled his mother's.

The little lad nodded and his father took the top and proceeded to set it spinning vigorously on the hardwood floor. The last vestiges of Mr. Thornton's pressing cares melted into oblivion at the sight of the innocent glee and wonderment in his son's wide eyes.

The summer found the Thornton family once more in their beloved Helstone. One afternoon, a welcome breeze lifted a few silver strands of Hannah Thornton's hair as she enjoyed the outdoors with the family. The grass around her gently swayed as she sat on a blanket, shielded from the relentless sun by a canopy devised by her son. Summers spent in Helstone were therapeutic to her soul. She had not known how hardened she had become in her daily habits and thoughts until she had allowed her mind to flow freely under the open sky and breathtaking verdure of the country. Examining the hidden byways of her memories, and letting gratitude and hope for the future take hold, she found herself returning to a gentler nature that she had thought was lost to her long ago.

The corners of her mouth turned upward as she watched Margaret and her daughters collect wildflowers on the edge of the sun-dappled forest. The brook flowing in front of them sparkled in the light and gurgled effortlessly over the smooth pile of rocks her grandsons had made near the bank.

Having gathered their fill, the girls gingerly crossed the stream one by one over protruding stones. Sophie and Lydia, nine and seven years of age respectively, raced up the bank toward their grandmother and plopped themselves on the blanket beside her as their mother calmly followed.

Hannah happily helped them make garlands of the flowers, a craft that Margaret had demonstrated years before to her oldest daughter and her mother-in-law. Lydia stood proudly when she finished her long circle of flowers and promptly adorned her grandmother's neck with her handiwork. Hannah gave her granddaughter a loving hug of thanks and smiled as both girls ran to join their father and younger brothers by the stream.

Mr. Thornton was occupied in helping his older son find salamanders. Johnny held two such creatures captive in a tin cup and helped his father overturn the stones underwater to discover more. Little Richard had lost interest in their enterprise, instead entertaining himself by scooping up water in his own tin cup and pouring it out again in an endless game.

Crouched at the brook's edge with his sons on either side, Mr. Thornton turned his head briefly in the direction of his littlest son to ensure he had not wandered far. Suddenly aware of his father's presence beside him, the tot stood abruptly and poured a cupful of water over his papa's unsuspecting head.

Mr. Thornton yelped his surprise and stood up to shake off the water from his dripping hair as his mother and wife laughed from afar at the comedic scene. Scooping the little boy up in his arms, he mirthfully admonished him for the dousing and tickled him in retaliation. Richard screamed his delight.

In the next moment, Mr. Thornton was assailed from behind as Lydia used her brother's dropped cup to fling water on her father's back. The grown man set down his son and raced to the brook to seek his revenge, scooping water into his cupped hands as his daughter squealed for mercy and dashed to higher ground. Pandemonium ensued as the chase soon involved all the children and everyone took their turn in the volley of attacks and reprisals.

When Margaret swooped down to protect her youngest child from the fray, she was splashed by one of her brood. She cried out her surprise to be caught up in the onslaught, and playfully pouted in protest at her dampened blouse.

Her husband laughed at her misfortune and rushed forward to swing her around by the waist and plant a firm kiss on her petulant lips.

Hannah stood surveying the merriment of the bedraggled entourage with unbridled amusement. These were the memories that would be emblazoned in the hearts of these children, if not upon their minds. And it would be these sunny days, she knew, that her son and his wife would call to memory when darker days closed in around them.

The next afternoon, as the family played croquet on the lawn behind the house, a lanky man with white hair appeared on the veranda to greet them.

"Mr. Bell!" the children exclaimed excitedly, dropping their mallets to climb the stairs to the open terrace where the smiling old gentleman stood. "Have you brought us anything?" Johnny asked eagerly as the children surrounded him.

"And what makes you think I remembered to bring you something?" Mr. Bell retorted with a knowing smirk.

"John, you know very well it is not polite to ask such a thing. Have you greeted Mr. Bell properly?" Margaret chided her offspring as she reached the group gathered on the terrace, her husband and mother-in-law close behind.

"We are very glad to see you, Mr. Bell. We don't mind if you have not brought us anything this time," Lydia said in apology for her brother's impropriety.

The old man threw his head back with a laugh. "Of course not," he allowed sarcastically. "But it so happens that I do believe there is something in my bag for you," he added with a mysterious twinkle in his eye. Rummaging through the contents of his portmanteau, he pulled out four small bags filled with colorful candies and treats.

The children gasped with gleeful anticipation and thanked him kindly as he handed each one their small parcel.

"You are certain to spoil them, Mr. Bell," Margaret mockingly imputed.

"I consider it my sworn duty," he rejoined with a satisfied smile as he gave his goddaughter a kiss on the cheek before greeting Mr. Thornton and his mother in turn.

Mr. Bell was happy to be welcomed as part of the family at Christmas and whenever else he chose to visit. He was fond of the estate that Thornton had built just beyond Margaret's childhood village some years ago. Helstone Manor was a handsome brick and stone mansion set in the midst of the rolling fields of the New Forest with a few ancient trees prominently lending a stately grace and natural beauty to the property.

Thornton had measured up to and indeed surpassed all of Mr. Bell's expectations. The man had prospered in all he had set his hand to, and had found a fountain of wealth by investing in steel manufacturing - an investment Mr. Bell had gainfully imitated. Shrewd and decisive in his business dealings, Thornton had also proven to be wisely prescient not only in his investments, but in his caution for the adverse course of events that would wrack his industry.

Mr. Bell knew that Margaret had helped to nurture Thornton's philanthropic vision. Her husband's efforts to alleviate the divide between masters and workers had propelled him to a seat in the Milton Central Committee, which had been set up to offer relief to the un-employed engendered by the cotton famine. Mr. Bell had had no qualms in giving generously to the fund, knowing that Thornton had a steady hand on the helm.

The Oxford scholar drew a deep breath and gazed at the distant heathland. He was glad to see the Thorntons escape the city for part of the year. If only Hale had lived to see his daughter so happily situated! He would have been pleased and proud to see the life she had created with his favorite pupil!

Margaret invited her godfather to sit down when a servant brought lemonade and biscuits to the veranda, and everyone settled themselves to take refreshments and enjoy the gathered company.

After tending to her long tresses that evening, Margaret laid her brush upon the dressing table and crossed the spacious bedroom to join her husband, who stood in darkness on the stone balcony overlooking the wide expanse of fields behind their home. An indigo sky was lit brilliantly by endless stars, and the crickets' song permeated the cool night air.

The smell of honeysuckle and roses and the entrancing rhythm of the crickets' chirping filled his senses. Mr. Thornton stared transfixed at the glory of the open sky and the distant land beyond which beckoned his mind to wonder at the vastness of creation.

"It is difficult to imagine that there is war and suffering in the world when everything here is so peaceful," he stated quietly, his eyes focused on the grandeur of the night scene. "There is no tumult or striving... it is as if discord was merely a dream of existence, and all is meant to be in perfect harmony...... Will it ever be so among men?" he wondered aloud, finally bringing his gaze to the woman standing next to him.

Margaret moved closer to wrap her arms lovingly around his waist and rested her cheek against his chest as she considered his words. He lifted his arms to enfold her in a gentle embrace.

She knew her husband felt strongly the weight of his responsibility in Milton during these difficult times. "I don't know... I suppose there is always hope that we may bring about a higher peace in this world. We can only do what we can to set things right within our sphere of influence," she answered his musings thoughtfully.

"You are doing your best, John. With all that you have been given, you are doing a great work," she continued, looking up at him beseechingly. She was proud of the leading role he had taken in trying to prevent the local economy from crumbling and in diligently endeavoring to find a solution for every adverse situation that arose. She desired that his time in the country allowed him to release his concerns for a time, so that he might become carefree and buoyant again. "Is it not beneficial to fill our hearts with all that is good, to replenish our souls for the work ahead of us?" she asked hopefully, her eyes searching his in the dim starlight.

He answered by holding her face between his hands and brushing her cheeks gently with his thumbs in tender adoration. He placed a kiss on her lips and her forehead before gathering her to him with a contented sigh. Holding each other in a comforting embrace, they both looked out serenely over the tranquil night.

1872

The gentle sway and constant drone of the train settled Margaret into a contemplative mood. She enjoyed the long ride from London to Milton, a journey they had made many times in the years since John had been made a member of the House of Commons.

She looked across to study her husband, who was staring out of the window, deep in thought. Although the years had not been without trial, he bore no egregious signs of aging other than graying hair at his temples and a more distinguished countenance. She thought him the most admirable man in all of England, and herself the most fortunate of women to be his wife. He did not yearn for grandeur or especial prestige, but had earned such from his steadfast labor to improve the lives of others by passing rightful laws in Parliament. She was proud of his integrity and firm resolve to carry out the purpose he had dutifully chosen in answering the call to serve in government.

A fierce pride swelled within Margaret's breast to recall the great honor that had been bestowed on him recently when the Queen had knighted him for saving Milton from devastation during the hard years of the cotton famine. With foresight and ingenuity he had prevented many factories from shutting down. With persuading fervor and his own generosity, he had worked to ensure that no one in Milton was left without the basic necessities of life. Margaret smiled to think of his grand title: Sir John Thornton. It suited him well, although he was too humble to wear it with any sense of self-importance.

Lady Thornton, she thought to herself, trying out the sound of her own new title in her mind. Her heart warmed to think of the commendation that she received as part of his life. It had pleased her immensely that her London relatives had finally come to recognize her husband's worth and admire the stature he had attained.

Margaret's gaze rested on her daughter, Sophie, who sat quietly next to her father reading a book. She had grown into a young lady during their time in London, being about the age that Margaret herself had been when her family had made the momentous move to Milton. Sophie was a striking beauty with her raven black hair and father's eyes. She had caught the eye of many men, and a certain ambitious young lawyer had become a significant suitor.

Even Lydia, who sat next to her, had blossomed during the years they had rented a pleasant home near Harley Street. Lydia had excelled in academics and, although not as fond of dancing as her sister, had learned to play the piano quite well. She was more bookish and quiet than her sister, but bore herself with a mature grace that matched her intellect.

The girls had enjoyed a close friendship with Edith's children, Sholto and Emmeline. Margaret's boys, Johnny and Richard, had taken to Henry's sons, who were closer in age to the Thornton boys and nearly as boisterous.

Margaret turned her head to study her sons, who were playing cards with their grandmother across the aisle. Both boys had shown an aptitude for their studies and were generally well behaved. They had thrived on their outings with their father, and had been especially excited when their city adventures with him had taken them on the London Underground.

It was when they took their holiday in Helstone every summer that the boys could run and disport themselves as all young children should. Margaret's fondest memories of her children included watching them spend carefree days of spirited play in the fields and forests of the bucolic village of her childhood.

As Margaret gazed fondly across the way, it was Mr. Thornton's turn to study his wife of almost twenty years with admiration. Her beauty had not diminished in any way. The delicate grace with which she bore herself belied the strength and determination that lay beneath. She had bolstered him in the days when he had doubted his usefulness, weary of endless deliberations and frustrated with overly cautious thinkers. She had never swayed in her faith in his ability to promulgate progress, and had often lent her sage opinion in matters of great weight.

He knew she was not fond of the glittering social life that many women aspired to, but she had nevertheless shone as a gem at the various formal engagements they had been obliged to attend. Captivating in her elegance and compelling in her conversation, Mr. Thornton recognized that she was a great asset in gaining the admiration and respect of his most reluctant opponents. Carefully veiling her own convictions as simple truths, she had often convinced the curmudgeons of progress of the errors of their rigid hold upon the status quo.

During their years in London, their children had flourished and she had remained cheerful and ambitious in all her doings. She had enriched his days more than he could have ever imagined, and he knew that he would remain under the spell of her charms forever, and was glad to offer her a life of activity and purpose.

It filled his heart with special joy to know that she was eager to return to Milton, just as he was. She had often spoken of her excitement to him in recent weeks. They were both anxious to become involved once again in the daily pace of life in Milton, where they could feel the energy of the future taking form and bring their hopes of an advanced humanity to life.

Margaret turned her head to catch her husband's fond gaze. She smiled at him knowingly and he returned her smile in perfect accord.

On Sunday afternoon, the Thornton family left the grand townhouse in Milton's wealthiest district that was to be their new home and walked the streets of town to pay a visit to their closest friends, the Higgins.

When they arrived at the familiar gates of Marlborough Mills, Margaret felt a wistful pang of affection for the place where they had spent so many happy years. No matter how many times they visited, she would always feel the same about the home they had first shared.

Nicholas greeted them in the drawing room, which was respectably furnished with pieces collected slowly since the time Nicholas had become the Master of the mill in John's absence. "Thornton!" he called out warmly as he took the former Master's hand. "Sir John, if you'll forgive my muddled mind," he amended in haste.

"There's no need for formalities between friends, Higgins," Mr. Thornton assured with a broad smile.

Margaret gave Mary a hug and shook the hand of her husband, Robert Campbell, who had long worked at the mill and was still teased for taking away the best cook the dining hall had ever had. The couple had two children, Bessie and Jacob, who were friends with the Thornton's older children, having grown up together in earlier years. All but two of the Boucher children had moved out of their house to homes of their own.

As the adults enjoyed an animated conversation with old friends, Margaret was happy to note how well the children got along in the ante room, where Lydia had begun to play a piece on the piano.

Higgins told them of the continued success of the school that Margaret had started so long ago. The new Master was proud to announce that Marlborough Mills refused to employ any child under the age of sixteen. Instead, a small dividend was paid to those workers whose children attended the school. With time, this dividend had expanded substantially in size and scope. The mill also paid workers for short absences due to illness, and the workers had agreed to put in a portion of their wages to create a fund for health expenses, which the mill subsidized.

Mr. Thornton was pleased to hear of the progress in his own mill, which was becoming a studied example of the forward policies he had championed during his years in London. He was eager to become involved again in managing the mills he owned, and looked forward to continuing the social experiments that had so far been implemented. Having heard of Tom Boucher's interest in the sciences, Mr. Thornton mentioned that he would be especially interested to encourage and support any student's interest in that field of study, having a particular fondness for the promise of new inventions and discoveries of every kind.

Margaret explained her hope that they might extend the school to teach adults at night, and incorporate a library where books might be available to all. Perhaps now, Margaret mentioned hopefully, they might have the opportunity to go to Spain and visit Fred again. They had not done so for many years. Her husband smiled at her fondly in answer to her yearning.

Amongst all the excited talk of their plans and accomplishments, Mr. Thornton recalled his admiration for Higgins' initiative in calling a meeting of mill workers during the hard days of the cotton famine, to bolster morale. The workers had all decided to send a letter to His Excellency Abraham Lincoln proclaiming their support of the President's work to eradicate slavery. Higgins nodded his head in acknowledgement. It had been one of his proudest moments to receive a letter from President Lincoln in return. He retained a copy of that letter, which was prominently placed in a gilded frame.

At dinner in the Thornton home the following evening, conversation turned to social events and Margaret asked her younger daughter if she would miss London.

"I will miss Sholto and Emmeline, but I must admit I am glad there are not as many balls here. I suppose that Sophie will miss London terribly - perhaps especially a certain Stanton Langford," Lydia quipped with a suppressed smirk as she shot a mischievous glance at her sister.

Sophie colored slightly as her parents' eyes fell upon her. She was growing quite fond of Mr. Langford, who had been paying calls at their London home rather regularly before their recent departure. As an aspiring politician, Stanton adulated her father. However, the young lawyer trembled in his shoes in speaking to the man as a suitor to his eldest daughter.

"I suppose I will miss all the dances a little," Sophie hesitated uncomfortably. "But there's something...oh, I don't know...something special about being back home in Milton," Sophie concluded thoughtfully, to the surprise of her family.

Margaret looked to her husband across the long table. He returned her gaze, and they smiled in shared understanding.

Helstone Manor – 1929

"Is this the box you meant, grandmother?" a young lady of sixteen inquired as she entered the finely furnished drawing room. Born the year the *Titanic* sank, Arabella Sheppard was Sophie Thornton Langford's youngest granddaughter.

"Yes, Bella," replied the aged woman as the girl drew closer and settled on the green velvet sofa near the family matriarch. Sitting across from them was Lydia Bancroft, who had recently come to live with her sister in the family's country home after the passing of her husband the previous winter. Lydia had married one of the teachers at the Academy of Science and Industry in Milton that her father had helped found.

Arabella set the pretty papered box between them. The faint sound of voices and laughter rose from the long open windows toward the back of the great house, where her family and relatives were playing lawn games. She could smell the wild yellow roses that seemed to flourish everywhere on the estate. She preferred to stay inside today, feeling a romantic penchant to look at all the old family photos and memorabilia with her grandmother and Great Aunt Lydia. "What's inside it?" she asked her grandmother.

"Take a peek and see," Sophie answered with a kind smile.

Arabella opened the lid. As she gazed into the box, her grandmother noted yet again the girl's wavy chestnut hair and large, expressive eyes. She held a close likeness to her great grandmother, Margaret Thornton. Perhaps that was why she held a special interest in her ancestor's past.

"Letters," the girl announced with great interest as she pulled out a batch of envelopes tied with ribbon.

"Those are the letters that your great grandfather wrote to his lady love. My mother neatly put away all her letters from father for safekeeping," Sophie explained. Her thoughts flew to her own sweetheart for a moment, recalling the letters that had passed between her and the young lawyer who had won her heart. Stanton Langford had worked for Parliament for many years, eventually becoming a Member of the House of Commons in his later years. Sophie had been a spirited supporter of women's suffrage, with her husband's proud approval.

Arabella raised her eyes to study the great family portrait that hung above the marble fireplace. Sir John Thornton was a legend in her family, as he was in Milton. She stared at the handsome man in the painting who sat next to his wife, with their children surrounding them. To the left of the couple was her grandmother and Aunt Lydia, who appeared nearly the same age as herself.

The young girl gazed at the young faces of her great uncles, John and Richard. They were old men now, and had retired from their years of work in the north. Great Uncle John had taken over the small empire his father had built in Milton, running several mills, whereas Great Uncle Richard had become a scholar who had returned from Oxford to teach at the Academy.

Her eyes returned to her great grandparents. Arabella was entranced to think of the imposing patriarch of her family as a lover. The corners of her mouth turned upward as she noted the clasped hands of the couple resting on the edge of Margaret Thornton's lap. She was quite convinced that it was that loving grasp that made a subtle smile play on both of their faces. They had been in love all their years together and had lived a long and full life - so the young girl had always heard.

Snapping out of her reverie, Bella returned her attention to the box and looked to discover what other treasures remained within. She pulled out a small pile of flat letters and gingerly picked up the one on the top, which was creased and worn on the edges. From the salutation, it appeared to be a letter from Margaret to John.

"What of this one, grandmama?" Arabella asked curiously.

Her grandmother took it gently to examine it closer.

"Was not this the first letter father received from mother?" Great Aunt Lydia posed to her sister. The sisters had gone through the contents of the box together long ago with their mother, and more recently on their own. They remembered much of what their mother had told them.

"Yes, it is," Sophie confirmed, noting the tattered edges of the letter. "Mother was in London during their engagement of several weeks. This was the first letter father ever received from her, and he kept it with him for many days, perhaps weeks - folded in his pocket or some such thing," she elaborated, much to Bella's amusement.

She could imagine the pair as young lovers, for she had often stopped in the middle of the grand staircase to stare at the daguerreotypes of her great grandfather and grandmother taken on their honeymoon.

Arabella looked down into the box once more to see one last item - a folded sheet of paper. She unfolded it to read the simple message. "If you have had a change of heart, give me but a sign. My heart remains forever yours. John Thornton," Arabella read aloud before looking to her grandmother with a furrowed brow of intrigue.

Sophie's eyes sparkled mysteriously. "Those were undoubtedly the most important words my father ever composed," she revealed, smiling at her granddaughter's expression of incredulity.

"Has your mother never told you of the great devotion with which our father pursued his wife's hand - how she almost slipped father's grasp when she left for London?" the aged matriarch asked with some surprise.

The young girl shook her head, eager to be enlightened.

Sophie gave her sister a knowing smile before turning to her granddaughter. Her face lightened with a soft glow of reverence. "Well then, my dear, let me tell you of a timeless love story...."

Made in the USA
Coppell, TX
11 August 2023

20220903R00223